THE CRITICS LOVE JOHN GRISHAM

BY JOHN GRISHAM

A Time to Kill	*The Broker*
The Firm	*The Innocent Man*
The Pelican Brief	*Playing for Pizza*
The Client	*The Appeal*
The Chamber	*The Associate*
The Rainmaker	*Ford County*
The Runaway Jury	*The Confession*
The Partner	*The Litigators*
The Street Lawyer	*Calico Joe*
The Testament	*The Racketeer*
The Brethren	*Sycamore Row*
A Painted House	*Gray Mountain*
Skipping Christmas	*Rogue Lawyer*
The Summons	*The Whistler*
The King of Torts	*Camino Island*
Bleachers	*The Rooster Bar*
The Last Juror	*The Reckoning*

The Theodore Boone Books

Kid Lawyer
The Abduction
The Accused
The Activist
The Fugitive
The Scandal
The Accomplice

JOHN GRISHAM

———— ◆ ————

THE RECKONING

A NOVEL

DELL BOOKS • NEW YORK

The Reckoning is a work of fiction. Names, characters, businesses,
organizations, places, events, and incidents are the product of
the author's imagination or are used fictitiously. Any resemblance
to actual persons, living or dead, or locales is entirely coincidental.

2019 Dell Mass Market Edition

Published in the United States by Dell, an imprint of Random House,
a division of Penguin Random House LLC, New York.

DELL and the HOUSE colophon are registered trademarks of
Penguin Random House LLC.

Originally published in hardcover in the United States by Doubleday,
an imprint of Random House, a division of
Penguin Random House LLC, in 2018.

ISBN 978-0-525-62093-8
International edition ISBN 978-1-9848-1995-6
Ebook ISBN 978-0-385-54416-0

Cover photograph: Steve Robinson

Printed in the United States of America

randomhousebooks.com

2 4 6 8 9 7 5 3 1

Dell mass market edition: June 2019

THE RECKONING

PART ONE

THE KILLING

CHAPTER 1

On a cold morning in early October of 1946, Pete Banning awoke before sunrise and had no thoughts of going back to sleep. For a long time he lay in the center of his bed, stared at the dark ceiling, and asked himself for the thousandth time if he had the courage. Finally, as the first trace of dawn peeked through a window, he accepted the solemn reality that it was time for the killing. The need for it had become so overwhelming that he could not continue with his daily routines. He could not remain the man he was until the deed was done. Its planning was simple, yet difficult to imagine. Its aftershocks would rattle on for decades and change the lives of those he loved and many of those he didn't. Its notoriety would create a legend, though he certainly wanted no fame. Indeed, as was his nature, he wished to avoid the attention, but that would not be possible. He had no choice. The truth had slowly been revealed, and once he had the full grasp of it, the killing became as inevitable as the sunrise.

He dressed slowly, as always, his war-wounded legs stiff and painful from the night, and made his way through the dark house to the kitchen, where he turned on a dim light and brewed his coffee. As it percolated, he stood ramrod straight beside the breakfast table, clasped his hands behind his head, and gently bent both knees. He grimaced as pain radiated from his hips to his ankles, but he held the squat for ten seconds. He relaxed, did it again and again, each time sinking lower. There were metal rods in his left leg and shrapnel in his right.

Pete poured coffee, added milk and sugar, and walked outside onto the back porch, where he stood at the steps and looked across his land. The sun was breaking in the east and a yellowish light cast itself across the sea of white. The fields were thick and heavy with cotton that looked like fallen snow, and on any other day Pete would manage a smile at what would certainly be a bumper crop. But there would be no smiles on this day; only tears, and lots of them. To avoid the killing, though, would be an act of cowardice, a notion unknown to his being. He sipped his coffee and admired his land and was comforted by its security. Below the blanket of white was a layer of rich black topsoil that had been owned by Bannings for over a hundred years. Those in power would take him away and would probably execute him, but his land would endure forever and support his family.

Mack, his bluetick hound, awoke from his slumber and joined him on the porch. Pete spoke to him and rubbed his head.

The cotton was bursting in the bolls and straining to

be picked, and before long teams of field hands would load into wagons for the ride to the far acres. As a boy, Pete rode in the wagon with the Negroes and pulled a cotton sack twelve hours a day. The Bannings were farmers and landowners, but they were workers, not gentrified planters with decadent lives made possible by the sweat of others.

He sipped his coffee and watched the fallen snow grow whiter as the sky brightened. In the distance, beyond the cattle barn and the chicken coop, he heard the voices of the Negroes as they were gathering at the tractor shed for another long day. They were men and women he had known his entire life, dirt-poor field hands whose ancestors had toiled the same land for a century. What would happen to them after the killing? Nothing, really. They had survived with little and knew nothing else. Tomorrow, they would gather in stunned silence at the same time in the same place, and whisper over the fire, then head to the fields, worried, no doubt, but also eager to pursue their labors and collect their wages. The harvest would go on, undisturbed and abundant.

He finished his coffee, placed the cup on a porch rail, and lit a cigarette. He thought of his children. Joel was a senior at Vanderbilt and Stella was in her second year at Hollins, and he was thankful they were away. He could almost feel their fear and shame at their father being in jail, but he was confident they would survive, like the field hands. They were intelligent and well-adjusted, and they would always have the land. They would finish their education, marry well, and prosper.

As he smoked he picked up his coffee cup, returned

to the kitchen, and stepped to the phone to call his sister, Florry. It was a Wednesday, the day they met for breakfast, and he confirmed that he would be there before long. He poured out the dregs, lit another cigarette, and took his barn jacket off a hook by the door. He and Mack walked across the backyard to a trail that led past the garden where Nineva and Amos grew an abundance of vegetables to feed the Bannings and their dependents. He passed the cattle barn and heard Amos talking to the cows as he prepared to milk them. Pete said good morning, and they discussed a certain fat hog that had been selected for a gutting come Saturday.

He walked on, with no limp, though his legs ached. At the tractor shed, the Negroes were gathered around a fire pit as they bantered and sipped coffee from tin cups. When they saw him they grew silent. Several offered "Mornin', Mista Banning," and he spoke to them. The men wore old, dirty overalls; the women, long dresses and straw hats. No one wore shoes. The children and teenagers sat near a wagon, huddled under a blanket, sleepy-eyed and solemn-faced, dreading another long day picking cotton.

There was a school for Negroes on the Banning land, one made possible by the generosity of a rich Jew from Chicago, and Pete's father had put up enough in matching funds to see it built. The Bannings insisted that all the colored children on their land study at least through the eighth grade. But in October, when nothing mattered but the picking, the school was closed and the students were in the fields.

Pete spoke quietly with Buford, his white foreman. They discussed the weather, the tonnage picked the day before, the price of cotton on the Memphis exchange. There were never enough pickers during peak season, and Buford was expecting a truckload of white workers from Tupelo. He had expected them the day before but they did not show. There was a rumor that a farmer two miles away was offering a nickel more per pound, but such talk was always rampant during the harvest. Picking crews worked hard one day, disappeared the next, and then came back as prices fluctuated. The Negroes, though, did not have the advantage of shopping around, and the Bannings were known to pay everyone the same.

The two John Deere tractors sputtered to life, and the field hands loaded into the wagons. Pete watched them rock and sway as they disappeared deep into the fallen snow.

He lit another cigarette and walked with Mack past the shed and along a dirt road. Florry lived a mile away on her section of land, and these days Pete always went there on foot. The exercise was painful, but the doctors had told him that long walks would eventually fortify his legs and the pain might one day subside. He doubted that, and had accepted the reality that his legs would burn and ache for the rest of his life, a life he was lucky to have. He had once been presumed dead, and had indeed come very close to the end, so every day was a gift.

Until now. Today would be the last day of his life as he knew it, and he had accepted this. He had no choice.

Florry lived in a pink cottage she had built after their mother died and left them the land. She was a poet with no interest in farming but had a keen interest in the income it generated. Her section, 640 acres, was just as fertile as Pete's, and she leased it to him for half the profits. It was a handshake arrangement, one as ironclad as any thick contract, and grounded on implicit trust.

When he arrived, she was in the backyard, walking through her aviary of chicken wire and netting, scattering feed as she chatted to her assortment of parrots, parakeets, and toucans. Beside the bird haven was a hutch where she kept a dozen chickens. Her two golden retrievers sat on the grass, watching the feeding with no interest in the exotic birds. Her house was filled with cats, creatures neither Pete nor the dogs cared for.

He pointed to a spot on the front porch and told Mack to rest there, then went inside. Marietta was busy in the kitchen and the house smelled of fried bacon and corn cakes. He said good morning to her and took a seat at the breakfast table. She poured him coffee and he began reading the Tupelo morning paper. From the old phonograph in the living room, a soprano wailed in operatic misery. He often wondered how many other folks in Ford County listened to opera.

When Florry was finished with her birds, she came in the rear door, said good morning to her brother, and sat across from him. There were no hugs, no affection. To those who knew them, the Bannings were thought to be cold and distant, devoid of warmth and rarely emotional. This was true but not intentional; they had simply been raised that way.

Florry was forty-eight and had survived a brief and bad marriage as a young woman. She was one of the few divorced women in the county and thus looked down upon, as if somehow damaged and perhaps immoral. Not that she cared; she didn't. She had a few friends and seldom left her property. Behind her back she was often referred to as the Bird Lady, and not affectionately.

Marietta served them thick omelets with tomatoes and spinach, corn cakes bathed with butter, bacon, and strawberry jam. Except for the coffee, sugar, and salt, everything on the table came from their soil.

Florry said, "I received a letter from Stella yesterday. She seems to be doing fine, though struggling with calculus. She prefers literature and history. She is so much like me."

Pete's children were expected to write at least one letter a week to their aunt, who wrote to them at least twice a week. Pete wasn't much for letters and had told them not to bother. However, writing to their aunt was a strict requirement.

"Haven't heard from Joel," she said.

"I'm sure he's busy," Pete said as he flipped a page of the newspaper. "Is he still seeing that girl?"

"I suppose. He's much too young for romance, Pete, you should say something to him."

"He won't listen." Pete took a bite of his omelet. "I just want him to hurry up and graduate. I'm tired of paying tuition."

"I suppose the picking is going well," she said. She had hardly touched her food.

"Could be better, and the price dropped again yesterday. There's too much cotton this year."

"The price goes up and down, doesn't it? When the price is high there's not enough cotton and when it's low there's too much of it. Damned if you do, damned if you don't."

"I suppose." He had toyed with the idea of warning his sister of what was to come, but she would react badly, beg him not to do it, become hysterical, and they would fight, something they had not done in years. The killing would change her life dramatically, and on the one hand he pitied her and felt an obligation to explain. But on the other, he knew that it could not be explained, and attempting to do so would serve no useful purpose.

The thought that this could be their last meal together was difficult to comprehend, but then most things that morning were being done for the last time.

They were obliged to discuss the weather and this went on for a few minutes. According to the almanac, the next two weeks would be cool and dry, perfect for picking. Pete offered the same concerns about the lack of field hands, and she reminded him that this complaint was common every season. Indeed, last week over omelets he had lamented the shortage of temporary workers.

Pete was not one to linger over food, especially on this awful day. He had been starved during the war and knew how little the body needed to survive. A thin frame kept weight off his legs. He chewed a bite of bacon, sipped his coffee, turned another page, and listened as Florry went on about a cousin who had just died at ninety, too soon in her opinion. Death was on his mind and he wondered what the Tupelo paper would say about him in the days to come. There would be stories, and perhaps a lot of them, but he had no desire to attract attention. It was inevitable, though, and he feared the sensational.

"You're not eating much," she said. "And you're looking a bit thin."

"Not much of an appetite," he replied.

"How much are you smoking?"

"As much as I want."

He was forty-three, and, at least in her opinion, looked older. His thick dark hair was graying above his ears, and long wrinkles were forming across his forehead. The dashing young soldier who'd gone off to war was aging too fast. His memories and burdens were heavy, but he kept them to himself. The horrors he had survived would never be discussed, not by him anyway.

Once a month he forced himself to ask about her writing, her poetry. A few pieces had been published in obscure literary magazines in the last decade, but not much. In spite of her lack of success, she loved nothing more than to bore her brother, his children, and her small circle of friends with the latest developments in her career. She could prattle on forever about her "projects," or about certain editors who loved her poetry but just couldn't seem to find room for it, or fan letters she had received from around the world. Her following was not that wide, and Pete suspected the lone letter from some lost soul in New Zealand three years earlier was still the only one that arrived with a foreign stamp.

He didn't read poetry, and after being forced to read his sister's he had sworn off the stuff forever. He preferred fiction, especially from southern writers, and especially William Faulkner, a man he'd met before the war at a cocktail party in Oxford.

This morning was not the time to discuss it. He was facing an ugly chore, a monstrous deed, one that could not be avoided or postponed any longer.

He shoved his plate away, his food half-eaten, and finished his coffee. "Always a pleasure," he said with a smile as he stood. He thanked Marietta, put on his barn coat, and left the cottage. Mack was waiting on the front steps. From the porch Florry called good-bye to him as he walked away and waved without turning around.

Back on the dirt road he lengthened his stride and shook off the stiffness caused by half an hour of sitting. The sun was up and burning off the dew, and all around the thick bolls sagged on the stems and begged to be picked. He walked on, a lonely man whose days were numbered.

Nineva was in the kitchen, at the gas stove stewing the last tomatoes for canning. He said good morning, poured fresh coffee, and took it to his study, where he sat at his desk and arranged his papers. All bills were paid. All accounts were current and in order. The bank statements were reconciled and showed sufficient cash on hand. He wrote a one-page letter to his wife, addressed and stamped the envelope. He placed a checkbook and some files in a briefcase and left it beside his desk. From a bottom drawer he withdrew his Colt .45 revolver, checked to make sure all six chambers were loaded, and stuck it in the pocket of his barn jacket.

At eight o'clock, he told Nineva he was going to town and asked if she needed anything. She did not, and he left the front porch with Mack behind him. He opened the door to his new 1946 Ford pickup, and Mack jumped onto the passenger's side of the bench seat. Mack rarely missed a ride to town and today would be no different, at least for the dog.

The Banning home, a splendid Colonial Revival built by Pete's parents before the crash in 1929, sat on Highway 18, south of Clanton. The county road had been paved the year before with postwar federal money. The locals believed that Pete had used his clout to secure the funding, but it wasn't true.

Clanton was four miles away, and Pete drove slowly, as always. There was no traffic, except for an occasional mule-drawn trailer laden with cotton and headed for the gin. A few of the county's larger farmers, like Pete, owned tractors, but most of the hauling was still done by mules, as were the plowing and planting. All picking was by hand. The John Deere and International Harvester corporations were trying to perfect mechanized pickers that would supposedly one day eliminate the need for so much manual labor, but Pete had his doubts. Not that it mattered. Nothing mattered but the task at hand.

Cotton blown from the trailers littered the shoulders of the highway. Two sleepy-eyed colored boys loitered by a field road and waved as they admired his truck, one of two new Fords in the county. Pete did not acknowledge them. He lit a cigarette and said something to Mack as they entered the town.

Near the courthouse square he parked in front of the post office and watched the foot traffic come and go. He wished to avoid people he knew, or those who might know him, because after the killing any witnesses were apt to offer such banal observations as "I saw him and he seemed perfectly normal," while the next one might say, "Bumped into him at the post office and he had a deranged look about him." After a tragedy, those with even the slightest connections to it often exaggerate their involvement and importance.

He eased from his truck, walked to the letter box, and mailed the envelope to his wife. Driving away, he circled the courthouse, with its wide, shaded lawn and gazebos, and had a vague image of what a spectacle his trial might be. Would they haul him in with handcuffs? Would the jury show sympathy? Would his lawyers work some magic and save him? Too many questions with no answers. He passed the Tea Shoppe, where the lawyers and bankers held forth each morning over scalding coffee and buttermilk biscuits, and wondered what they would say about the killing. He avoided the coffee shop because he was a farmer and had no time for the idle chitchat.

Let them talk. He expected little sympathy from them or from anyone else in the county for that matter. He cared nothing for sympathy, sought no understanding, had no plans to explain his actions. At the moment, he was a soldier with orders and a mission to carry out.

He parked on a quiet street a block behind the Methodist church. He got out, stretched his legs for a moment, zipped up his barn jacket, told Mack that he would return shortly, and began walking toward the church his grandfather had helped build seventy years earlier. It was a short walk, and along the way he saw no one. Later, no one would claim to have seen him.

The Reverend Dexter Bell had been preaching at the Clanton Methodist Church since three months before Pearl Harbor. It was the third church of his ministry, and he would have been rotated onward like all Methodist preachers but for the war. Shortages in the ranks had caused a shifting of duties, an upsetting of schedules. Normally, in the Methodist denomination, a minister lasted only two years in one church, sometimes three, before being reassigned. Reverend Bell had been in Clanton for five years and knew it was only a matter of time before he was called to move on. Unfortunately, the call did not arrive in time.

He was sitting at his desk in his office, in an annex behind the handsome sanctuary, alone as usual on Wednesday morning. The church secretary worked only three afternoons each week. The reverend had finished his morning prayers, had his study Bible open on his desk, along with two reference books, and was contemplating his next sermon when someone knocked on his door. Before he could answer, the door swung open, and Pete Banning walked in, frowning and filled with purpose.

Surprised at the intrusion, Bell said, "Well, good morning, Pete." He was about to stand when Pete whipped out a pistol with a long barrel and said, "You know why I'm here."

Bell froze and gawked in horror at the weapon and barely managed to say, "Pete, what are you doing?"

"I've killed a lot of men, Preacher, all brave soldiers on the field. You're the first coward."

"Pete, no, no!" Dexter said, raising his hands and falling back into his chair, eyes wide and mouth open. "If it's about Liza, I can explain. No, Pete!"

Pete took a step closer, aimed down at Dexter, and squeezed the trigger. He had been trained as a marksman with all firearms, and had used them in battle to kill more men than he cared to remember, and he had spent his life in the woods hunting animals large and small. The first shot went through Dexter's heart, as did the second. The third entered his skull just above the nose.

Within the walls of a small office, the shots boomed like cannon fire, but only two people heard them. Dexter's wife, Jackie, was alone in the parsonage on the other side of the church, cleaning the kitchen when she heard the noise. She later described it as the muffled sounds of someone clapping hands three times, and, at the moment, had no idea it was gunfire. She couldn't possibly have known her husband had just been murdered.

Hop Purdue had been cleaning the church for twenty years. He was in the annex when he heard the shots that seemed to shake the building. He was standing in the hallway outside the pastor's study when the door opened and Pete walked out, still holding the pistol. He raised it, aimed it at Hop's face, and seemed ready to fire. Hop fell to his knees and pleaded, "Please, Mista Banning. I ain't done nothin'. I got kids, Mista Banning."

Pete lowered the gun and said, "You're a good man, Hop. Go tell the sheriff."

CHAPTER 2

Standing in the side door, Hop watched Pete walk away, calmly putting the pistol in his jacket pocket as he went. When he was out of sight, Hop shuffled—his right leg was two inches shorter than his left—back to the study, eased through the open door, and studied the preacher. His eyes were closed and his head was slumped to one side, with blood dripping down his nose. Behind his head there was a mess of blood and matter splattered on the back of his chair. His white shirt was turning red around his chest, and his chest was not moving. Hop stood there for a few seconds, maybe a minute, maybe longer, to make sure there was no movement. He realized there was nothing he could do to help him. The pungent odor of gunpowder hung heavy in the room and Hop thought he might vomit.

Because he was the nearest Negro he figured he would get blamed for something. Stricken with fear and afraid to move, he touched nothing and managed to slowly back out of the room. He closed the door and began sobbing. Preacher Bell was a gentle man who had treated him with respect and shown concern for his family. A fine man, a family man, a loving man who was adored by his church. Whatever he had done to offend Mr. Pete Banning was certainly not worth his life.

It occurred to Hop that someone else might have heard the gunshots. What if Mrs. Bell came running and saw her husband bloodied and dead at his desk? Hop waited and waited and tried to compose himself. He knew he didn't have the courage to go find her and break the news. Let the white folks do that. There was no one else in the church, and as the minutes passed he began to realize that the situation was in his hands. But not for long. If someone saw him running from the church he would undoubtedly become the first suspect. So he left the annex as calmly as possible and hurried down the same street Mr. Banning had taken. He picked up his pace, bypassed the square, and before long saw the jail.

Deputy Roy Lester was getting out of a patrol car. "Mornin', Hop," he said, then noticed his red eyes and the tears on his cheeks.

"Preacher Bell's been shot," Hop blurted. "He's dead."

With Hop in the front seat and still wiping tears, Lester sped through the quiet streets of Clanton and minutes later slid to a dusty stop in the gravel parking lot outside the annex. In front of them the door flew open and Jackie Bell ran through it, screaming. Her hands were red with blood, her cotton dress was stained as well, and she had touched and streaked her face. She was howling, screaming, saying nothing they could understand, just shrieking in horror, her face contorted in shock. Lester grabbed her, tried to restrain her, but she tore away and yelled, "He's dead! He's dead! Somebody killed my husband." Lester grabbed her again, tried to console her and keep her from returning to the study. Hop watched and had no idea what to do. He was still worried that he might get blamed and wanted to limit his involvement.

Mrs. Vanlandingham from across the street heard the commotion and came running, still holding a dish towel. She arrived just as the sheriff, Nix Gridley, wheeled into the parking lot and slid in the gravel. Nix scrambled out of his car, and when Jackie saw him she screamed, "He's dead, Nix! Dexter's dead! Somebody shot him! Oh my God! Help me!"

Nix, Lester, and Mrs. Vanlandingham walked her across the street and onto the porch, where she fell into a wicker rocker. Mrs. Vanlandingham tried to wipe her face and hands but Jackie shoved her away. She buried her face in her hands, sobbing painfully while groaning, almost retching.

Nix said to Lester, "Stay with her." He crossed the street where Deputy Red Arnett was waiting. They entered the annex and slowly crept into the study, where they found Preacher Bell's body on the floor beside his chair. Nix carefully touched his right wrist and after a few seconds said, "There's no pulse."

"No surprise there," Arnett said. "Don't reckon we need an ambulance."

"I'd say no. Call the funeral home."

Hop stepped into the study and said, "Mista Pete Banning shot him. Heard him do it. Saw the gun."

Nix stood, frowned at Hop, and said, "Pete Banning?"

"Yes, suh. I was out there in the hall. He pointed the gun at me, then told me to go find you."

"What else did he say?"

"Said I was a good man. That's all. Then he left."

Nix folded his arms across his chest and looked at Red, who shook his head in disbelief and mumbled, "Pete Banning?"

Both looked at Hop as if they didn't believe him. Hop said, "That's right. Seen him myself, with a long-barreled revolver. Aimed it right here," he said, pointing to a spot in the center of his forehead. "Thought I was dead too."

Nix pushed his hat back and rubbed his cheeks. He looked at the floor and noticed the pool of blood spreading and moving silently away from the body. He looked at Dexter's closed eyes and asked himself for the first time, and the first of many, what could have possibly provoked this?

Red said, "Well, I guess this crime is solved."

"I suppose it is," Nix said. "But let's take some pictures and look for slugs."

"What about the family?" Red asked.

"Same thought here. Let's get Mrs. Bell back in the parsonage and get some ladies to sit with her. I'll go to the school and talk to the principal. They have three kids, right?"

"I think so."

"That's right," Hop said. "Two girls and a boy."

Nix looked at Hop and said, "Not a word out of you, Hop, okay? I mean it, not a word. Don't tell a soul what happened here. If you talk, I swear I'll throw you in jail."

"No, suh, Mista Sheriff, I ain't sayin' nothin'."

They left the study, closed the door, and walked outside. Across the street more neighbors were gathering around the Vanlandingham porch. Most were housewives standing on the lawn, wide-eyed with their hands over their mouths in disbelief.

Ford County had not seen a white murder in over ten years. In 1936, a couple of sharecroppers went to war over a strip of worthless farmland. The one with the better aim prevailed, claimed self-defense at trial, and walked home. Two years later, a black boy was lynched near the settlement of Box Hill, where he allegedly said something fresh to a white woman. In 1938, though, lynching was not considered murder or a crime of any sort anywhere in the South, especially Mississippi. However, a wrong word to a white woman could be punishable by death.

At that moment, neither Nix Gridley nor Red Arnett nor Roy Lester nor anyone else under the age of seventy in Clanton could remember the murder of such a prominent citizen. And, the fact that the prime suspect was even more prominent stopped the entire town cold in its tracks. In the courthouse, the clerks and lawyers and judges forgot their business, repeated what they had just heard, and shook their heads. In the shops and offices around the square the secretaries and owners and customers passed along the stunning news and looked at each other in shock. In the schools, the teachers quit teaching, left their students, and huddled in the hallways. On the shaded streets around the square, neighbors stood near mailboxes and worked hard to think of different ways to say, "This can't be true."

But it was. A crowd gathered in the Vanlandingham yard and gazed desperately across the street at the gravel lot, where three patrol cars—the county's entire fleet— along with the hearse from Magargel's Funeral Home were parked. Jackie Bell had been escorted back to the parsonage, where she was sitting with a doctor friend and some ladies from the church. Soon the streets were crowded with cars and trucks driven by the curious. Some inched along, their drivers gawking. Others parked haphazardly as close to the church as possible.

The presence of the hearse was a magnet, and the people moved onto the parking lot, where Roy Lester told them to stand back. The rear door of the hearse was partially open, which meant, of course, that a body would soon be brought to it and loaded for the short drive to the funeral home. As with any tragedy—crime or accident—what the curious really wanted was to see a body. Stunned and shocked as they were, they inched forward in muted silence and realized they were the lucky ones. They were witnesses to a dramatic piece of an un-imaginable story, and for the rest of their lives they could talk of being there when Preacher Bell was taken away in a hearse.

Sheriff Gridley walked through the annex door, glanced at the crowd, and removed his hat. Behind him, the stretcher appeared, with old man Magargel holding one end and his son the other. The corpse was covered with a black drape and only Dexter's brown shoes were visible. All the men instantly removed their hats and caps and all the women bowed their heads, but they did not close their eyes. Some were sobbing quietly. When the body was properly loaded and the rear door was closed, old man Magargel got behind the wheel and drove away. Never one to miss the opportunity for some extra drama, he poked through the side streets until he entered the square, then did two slow laps around the courthouse so the town could have a look.

An hour later, Sheriff Gridley called with instructions to transport the body to Jackson for an autopsy.

Nineva could not remember the last time Mr. Pete had asked her to sit with him on the front porch. She had better things to do. Amos was in the barn churning butter and needed her help. After that, she had a mess of peas and beans to can. There was some dirty laundry to wash. But if the boss said sit there in that rocker and let's visit for a spell, then she could not argue. She sipped iced tea while he smoked cigarettes, more than usual, she would recall later when she told Amos. He seemed preoccupied with the traffic out on the highway, a quarter of a mile down the drive. A few cars and trucks inched along, passing trailers filled with cotton and headed to the gin in town.

When the sheriff's car made its turn, Pete said, "There he comes."

"Who?" she asked.

"Sheriff Gridley."

"What he want?"

"He's coming to arrest me, Nineva. For murder. I just shot and killed Dexter Bell, the Methodist preacher."

"Git outta here! You done what?"

"You heard me." He stood and walked a few steps to where she was sitting. He leaned down and pointed a finger at her face. "And you will never say a word to anyone, Nineva. You hear me?"

Her eyes were as big as eggs and her mouth was wide open, but she could not speak. He pulled a small envelope out of his coat pocket and handed it to her. "Get in the house now, and as soon as I leave take this to Florry."

He took her hand, helped her to her feet, and opened the screen door. When she was inside she let loose with a painful howl that startled him. He closed the front door and turned to watch the sheriff approach. Gridley was in no hurry. He stopped and parked by Pete's truck, got out of his patrol car with Red and Roy for support, and walked toward the porch before stopping at the steps. He stared at Pete, who seemed unconcerned.

"Better come with us, Pete," Nix said.

Pete pointed to his truck and said, "The pistol is on the front seat."

Nix looked at Red and said, "Get it."

Pete slowly stepped down and walked to the sheriff's car. Roy opened a rear door, and as Pete was bending over he heard Nineva wail in the backyard. He looked up and saw her scampering toward the barn, holding the letter.

"Let's go," Nix said as he opened his door and situated himself behind the wheel. Red sat next to him and held the gun. In the rear seat, Roy and Pete were side by side, their shoulders almost touching. No one said a word, indeed no one seemed to breathe as they left the farm and turned onto the highway. The lawmen were going through the motions with a sense of disbelief, shocked like everyone else. A popular preacher murdered in cold blood by the town's favorite son, a legendary war hero. There had to be a damned good reason for it, and it was only a matter of time before the truth spilled out. But, at that moment, the clock had stopped and events were not real.

Halfway to town, Nix glanced in his mirror and said, "I'm not going to ask why you did it, Pete. Just want to confirm it was you, that's all."

Pete took a deep breath and looked at the cotton fields they were passing and said, "I have nothing to say."

The Ford County jail had been built in a prior century and was barely fit for human habitation. Originally a small warehouse, it had been converted to this and to that and finally bought by the county and divided in two by a brick wall. In the front half, six cells were configured to hold the white prisoners, and in the back eight cells were squeezed in for the blacks. The jail was rarely filled to capacity, at least up front. Attached to it was a small office wing the county had later built for the sheriff and the Clanton police department. The jail was only two blocks off the square and from its front door one could see the top of the courthouse. During criminal trials, which were rare, the accused was often walked from the jail with a deputy or two as escorts.

A crowd had gathered in front of the jail to get a glimpse of the killer. It was still inconceivable that Pete Banning did what he did, and there was also a general disbelief that he would be thrown in jail. Surely, for someone as prominent as Mr. Banning, there would be another set of rules. However, if Nix indeed had the guts to arrest him, there were enough curious folks who wanted to see it for themselves.

"I guess word's out," Nix mumbled as he turned in to the small gravel lot by the jail. "Not a word by anybody," he instructed. The car stopped and all four doors opened. Nix grabbed Banning by the elbow and ushered him to the front door, with Red and Roy following. The crowd, gawking, was still and silent until a reporter with *The Ford County Times* stepped forward with a camera and snapped a photo, with a flash that startled even Pete. Just as he was entering the door, someone yelled, "You'll die in hell, Banning!"

"That's right, that's right," someone else added.

The suspect didn't flinch and seemed oblivious to the crowd. Soon he was inside and out of sight.

Waiting inside, in a cramped room where all suspects and criminals were signed in and processed, was Mr. John Wilbanks, a prominent lawyer in town and longtime friend of the Bannings.

"And to what do we owe this pleasure?" Nix said to Mr. Wilbanks, obviously not pleased to see him.

"Mr. Banning is my client and I'm here to represent him," Wilbanks replied. He stepped forward and shook hands with Pete without a word.

Nix said, "We'll do our business first, then you can do yours."

Wilbanks said, "I've already called Judge Oswalt and we've discussed bail."

"Wonderful. When you've discussed it to the point of him granting bail, I'm sure he'll give me a call. Until then, Mr. Wilbanks, this man is a suspect in a murder and

I'll deal with him accordingly. Now, would you please leave?"

"I would like to speak with my client."

"He's not going anywhere. Come back in an hour."

"No interrogation, you understand?"

Banning said, "I have nothing to say."

Florry read the note on her front porch as Nineva and Amos watched. They were still panting from their sprint from the main house and horrified at what was happening.

When she finished she lowered it, looked at them, and asked, "And he's gone?"

"The law took him, Miss Florry," Nineva said. "He knew they were comin' to get him."

"Did he say anything?"

"He said he done kilt the preacher," Nineva replied, wiping her cheeks.

The note instructed Florry to call Joel at Vanderbilt and Stella at Hollins and explain to them that their father had been arrested for the murder of the Reverend Dexter Bell. They were to speak to no one about this, especially reporters, and they were to stay away at college until further notice. He was sorry for this tragic turn of events but hopeful that one day they would understand. He asked Florry to visit him the following day at the jail to discuss matters.

She felt faint but could show no weakness in front of the help. She folded the note, stuck it in a pocket, and dismissed them. Nineva and Amos backed away, more frightened and confused than before, and slowly walked across her front yard to the trail. She watched them until they were out of sight, then sat in a wicker rocker with one of her cats and fought her emotions.

He had certainly seemed preoccupied at breakfast, only a few hours earlier, but then he had not been right since the war. Why hadn't he warned her? How could he do something so unbelievably evil? What would happen to him, his children, his wife? To her, his only sibling? And the land?

Florry was far from a devout Methodist, but she had been raised in the church and attended occasionally. She had learned to keep her distance from the ministers because they were gone by the time they'd settled in, but Bell was one of the better ones.

She thought of his pretty wife and children, and finally broke down. Marietta eased through the screen door and stood beside her as she sobbed.

CHAPTER 3

The town descended upon the Methodist church. As the crowd grew, a deacon told Hop to unlock the sanctuary. The stricken mourners filed in and filled the pews and whispered the latest, whatever that happened to be. They prayed and wept and wiped their faces and shook their heads in disbelief. The faithful members, those who knew Dexter well and loved him dearly, clung together in small groups and moaned in their suffering. For the less committed, those who attended monthly but not weekly, the church was a magnet that drew them as close as possible to the tragedy. Even some of the truly backslidden arrived to share in the suffering. At that awful moment, everyone was a Methodist and welcomed in Reverend Bell's church.

The murder of their preacher was emotionally and physically overwhelming. The fact that he had been killed by one of their own was, initially, too astonishing to believe. Joshua Banning, Pete's grandfather, had helped build the church. His father had been a deacon his entire adult life. Most of those present had sat in those same pews and offered countless prayers for Pete during the war. They had been devastated when the news arrived from the War Department that he was presumed dead. They had held candlelight vigils at his second coming. They had rejoiced in tears when he and Liza made their grand reentry the week after the Japanese surrendered. Every Sunday morning during the war, Reverend Bell had called out the names of soldiers from Ford County and offered a special prayer. First on his list was Pete Banning, the town's hero and the source of immense local pride. Now the rumor that he had murdered their preacher was simply too incredible to absorb.

But as the news sank in, the whispering intensified, in some circles anyway, and the great question of "Why?" was asked a thousand times. Only a few of the bravest dared to suggest that Pete's wife had something to do with it.

What the mourners really wanted was to get their hands on Jackie and the children, to touch them and have a good cry, as if that would soften their shock. But Jackie, according to the gossip, was next door in the parsonage, secluded in her bedroom with her three children, and seeing no one. The house was packed with her closest friends and the crowd spilled out onto the porches and across the front yard, where grim-faced men smoked and grumbled. When friends stepped outside for fresh air, others stepped inside to take their places. Still others moved next door to the sanctuary.

The stricken and the curious continued to come, and the streets around the church were lined with cars and trucks. Folks drifted toward the church in small groups, moving slowly as if they weren't sure what they would do when they got there but were needed nonetheless.

When the pews were packed, Hop opened the door to the balcony. He hid in the shadows below the belfry and avoided everyone. Sheriff Gridley had threatened him and he was saying nothing. He did marvel, though, at the way the white folks managed to keep their composure, most of them anyway. The slaying of a popular black preacher would provoke an outpouring far more chaotic.

A deacon suggested to Miss Emma Faye Riddle that some music might be appropriate. She had played the organ for decades, but wasn't sure if the occasion was right. She soon agreed, though, and when she hit the first notes of "The Old Rugged Cross," the weeping intensified.

Outside, under the trees, a man approached a group of smokers and announced, "They got Pete Banning in jail. Got his gun too." This was met with acceptance, commented on, then passed along until the news entered the sanctuary, where it spread from pew to pew.

Pete Banning, arrested for the murder of their preacher.

When it became obvious that the suspect indeed had nothing to say, Sheriff Gridley led him through a door and into a narrow hallway with little light. Iron bars lined both sides. There were three cells on the right, three on the left, each about the size of a walk-in closet. There were no windows and the jail felt like a damp, dark dungeon, a place where men were forgotten and time went unnoticed. And, evidently, a place where everyone smoked. Gridley stuck a large key into a door, pulled it open, and nodded for the suspect to step inside. A cheap cot was at the far wall, and there was nothing else in the way of furnishings.

Gridley said, "Not much room, I'm afraid, Pete, but then it is a jail, after all."

Pete stepped inside, glanced around, and said, "I've seen worse." He stepped to the cot and sat on it.

"Bathroom's down the hall," Gridley said. "If you need to use it, just yell."

Pete was staring at the floor. He shrugged, said nothing. Gridley slammed the door and returned to his office. Pete stretched out and consumed the full length of his cot. He was two inches over six feet; the cot was not quite that long. The cell was musty and cold and he picked up a folded blanket, one that was practically threadbare and would be of little use at night. He didn't care. Captivity was nothing new, and he had survived conditions that now, four years later, were still hard to imagine.

When John Wilbanks returned less than an hour later, he and the sheriff argued briefly over where, exactly, the attorney-client conference would take place. There was no designated room for such important meetings. The lawyers usually walked into the cell block and huddled with their clients with a row of bars between them, and with every other prisoner straining to eavesdrop. Occasionally, a lawyer would catch his client outside in the rec yard and give advice through chain link. Most often, though, the lawyers did not bother to visit their clients at the jail. They waited until they were hauled into court and chatted with them there.

But John Wilbanks considered himself to be superior to every other lawyer in Ford County, if not the entire state, and his new criminal client was certainly a cut above the rest of Gridley's prisoners. Their status warranted a proper place to meet, and the sheriff's office would work just fine. Gridley finally acquiesced—few people won arguments with John Wilbanks, who, by the way, had always supported the sheriff at election time— and after some mumbling and cussing and a few benign rules left to fetch Pete. He brought him in with no handcuffs and said they could chat for half an hour.

When they were alone, Wilbanks began with "Okay, Pete, let's talk about the crime. If you did it, tell me you did it. If you didn't do it, then tell me who did."

"I have nothing to say," Pete said and lit a cigarette.

"That's not good enough."

"I have nothing to say."

"Interesting. Do you plan to cooperate with your defense lawyer?"

A shrug, a puff, nothing more.

Wilbanks offered a professional smile and said, "Okay, here's the scenario. In a day or two they'll take you over to the courtroom for an initial appearance before Judge Oswalt. I assume you'll plead not guilty, then they'll bring you back here. In a month or so, the grand jury will meet and indict you for murder, first degree. I would guess that by February or March, Oswalt will be ready for a trial, which I'm ready to handle, if that's what you want."

"John, you've always been my lawyer."

"Good. Then you have to cooperate."

"Cooperate?"

"Yes, Pete, cooperate. On the surface, this appears to be cold-blooded murder. Give me something to work with, Pete. Surely you had a motive."

"It's between me and Dexter Bell."

"No, it's now between you and the State of Mississippi, which, like all states, takes a dim view of cold-blooded murder."

"I have nothing to say."

"That's not a defense, Pete."

"Maybe I don't have a defense, not one that folks would understand."

"Well, the folks on the jury need to understand something. My first thought, indeed my only one at this moment, is a plea of insanity."

Pete shook his head and said, "Hell no. I'm as sane as you are."

"But I'm not facing the electric chair, Pete."

Pete blew a cloud of smoke and said, "I'm not doing that."

"Great, then give me a motive, a reason. Give me something, Pete."

"I have nothing to say."

Joel Banning was walking down the steps outside Benson Hall when someone called his name. Another student, a freshman he knew of but had not met, handed him an envelope and said, "Dean Mulrooney needs to see you at once, in his office. It's urgent."

"Thanks," Joel said, taking the envelope and watching the freshman walk away. Inside, a handwritten note on official Vanderbilt stationery instructed Joel to please come without delay to the dean's office in Kirkland Hall, the administration building.

Joel had a literature class in fifteen minutes and the professor frowned on absences. If he sprinted, he could run by the dean's office, tend to whatever matter was at hand, then arrive late for class and hope the professor was in a good mood. He hustled across the quad to Kirkland Hall and bounded up the stairs to the third floor, where the dean's secretary explained that he was to wait until precisely 11:00 a.m., when his aunt Florry would call from home. The secretary claimed to know nothing. She had spoken to Florry Banning, who was calling on her rural party line and thus without privacy. Florry planned to drive into Clanton and use the private line at a friend's home.

As he waited, he assumed someone had died and he could not help but think of those relatives and friends he preferred to lose before the others. The Banning family was small: just his parents, Pete and Liza, his sister, Stella, and his aunt Florry. The grandparents were dead. Florry had no children; thus, he and Stella had no first cousins on the Banning side. His mother's people were from Memphis but had scattered after the war.

He paced around the office, ignoring the looks from the secretary, and decided it was probably his mother. She had been sent away months earlier and the family was reeling. He and Stella had not seen her and their letters went unanswered. Their father refused to discuss his wife's treatment, and, well, there were a lot of unknowns.

Would her condition improve? Would she come home? Would the family ever be a real family again? Joel and Stella had questions, but their father preferred to talk about other matters when he chose to talk at all. Likewise, Aunt Florry was of little help.

She called at 11:00 a.m. on the dot. The secretary handed Joel the phone and stepped around a corner, though probably within earshot, he figured. Joel said hello, then listened for what seemed an eternity. Florry began by explaining that she was in town at the home of Miss Mildred Highlander, a woman Joel had known his entire life, and she, Florry, was there because the call needed to be private and there was no privacy on their rural party line, as he well knew. And, really, nothing was private in town right now because his father had driven to the Methodist church just hours earlier and shot and killed the Reverend Dexter Bell, and was now in jail, and, well, as anyone could understand, the entire town was buzzing and everything had come to a complete stop. Don't ask why and don't say anything that might get overheard, wherever you are, Joel, but it's just awful and God help us.

Joel leaned on the secretary's desk for support as he felt faint. He closed his eyes, took a deep breath, and listened. Florry said she had just talked to Stella at Hollins and she did not take it well. They had her in the president's office with a nurse. She explained that Pete had given her specific instructions, in writing no less, that they—Joel and Stella—were to stay at school and away from home and Clanton until further notice. They should make plans to spend Thanksgiving holidays with friends as far away from Ford County as possible. And, if they were contacted by reporters, investigators, police, or anybody else, they were to say absolutely nothing. Not a word to anyone about their father or the family. Not a word, period. She wrapped things up by saying that she loved him dearly, would write a long letter immediately, and that she wished she could be there with him at this horrible moment.

Joel put the phone down without a word and left the building. He drifted across the campus until he saw an empty bench partially hidden by shrubbery. He sat there and fought back tears, determined to find the stoicism taught by his father. Poor Stella, he thought. She was as fiery and emotional as their mother, and he knew she was a mess at the moment.

Frightened, bewildered, and confused, Joel watched the leaves fall and scatter in the breeze. He felt the urge to go home, immediately, to catch a train and be in Clanton before dark, and once there he would get to the bottom of things. The thought passed, though, and he wondered if he would ever go back. Reverend Bell was a gifted and popular minister, and at the moment there was probably great hostility toward the Bannings. Besides, his father had given him and Stella strict instructions to stay away. Joel, at the age of twenty, could not remember a single instance when he had disobeyed his father. With age, he had learned to respectfully disagree with him, but he would never disobey him. His father was a proud soldier, a strict disciplinarian who said little and valued authority.

There was simply no way his father could commit murder.

CHAPTER 4

The courthouse, and the shops and offices lining the neat square around it, closed at five each weekday. Usually by that time all doors were locked, all lights were off, the sidewalks were empty, and everyone was gone. However, on this day the townsfolk lingered a bit later in case more facts and/or gossip emerged about the killing. They had talked of nothing else since nine that morning. They had shocked each other with the first reports, then spread along later developments. They had stood in solemn respect as old man Magargel paraded his hearse around the square to provide a glimpse of the corpse outlined under a black cape. Some had ventured to the Methodist church and held vigil while offering prayers, then returned to their places around the square with near-breathless descriptions of what was happening on the front line. Baptists, Presbyterians, and Pentecostals were at a disadvantage since they could claim no real connection to either the victim or his killer. The Methodists, though, were in the spotlight, with each one eager to describe relationships that seemed to grow stronger as the day progressed. On this unforgettable day, the Clanton Methodist Church had never known so many congregants.

For most people in Clanton, among the white folks anyway, there was a sense of betrayal. Dexter Bell was popular and highly regarded. Pete Banning was a near-mythical figure. To have one kill the other was such a senseless loss it touched almost everyone. Motive was so incomprehensible that no solid rumor emerged to address it.

Not that there was a shortage of rumors; there certainly was not. Banning would be in court tomorrow. He was refusing to say anything. He would plead insanity. John Wilbanks had never lost a trial and was not about to lose this one. Judge Oswalt was a close friend of Banning's, or maybe he was a close friend of Dexter Bell's. The trial would be moved to Tupelo. He had not been right since the war. Jackie Bell was heavily sedated. Her kids were a mess. Pete would put up his land as security for bail and go home tomorrow.

To avoid seeing anyone, Florry parked on a side street and hurried to the law office. John Wilbanks was working late and waiting for her in the reception room on the first floor.

In 1946, there were a dozen lawyers in Ford County and half of them worked for the firm of Wilbanks & Wilbanks. All six were related. For over a hundred years, the Wilbanks family had been prominent in law, politics, banking, real estate, and farming. John and his brother Russell studied law up north and ran the firm, which seemed to run most other commercial matters in the county. Another brother was the chairman of the largest bank in the county, along with owning several businesses. A cousin farmed two thousand acres. Another cousin handled real estate and was also a state representative with ambitions. It was rumored that the family met in secret the first week of January of each year to tally up the various profits and divide the money. There seemed to be plenty to go around.

Florry had known John Wilbanks since high school, though she was three years older. His firm had always taken care of the Bannings' legal matters, none of which had ever seemed that complicated until now. There had been the sticky problem of shipping Liza off to the asylum, but John had discreetly pulled the right strings and away she went. Florry's ancient divorce had likewise been swept under the rug by John and his brother, with hardly a record of it in the county books.

He greeted her with a solemn hug and she followed him upstairs to his large office, the finest in town, with a terrace that overlooked the courthouse square. The walls were covered with grim portraits of his dead ancestors. Death was everywhere. He waved at a rich leather sofa and she took a seat.

"I met with him," John began as he struck a match and lit a short black cigar. "He didn't say much. In fact he's refusing to say anything."

"What in God's name, John?" she asked as her eyes watered.

"Hell if I know. You didn't see it coming?"

"Of course not. You know Pete. He doesn't talk, especially about private matters. He'll chat a bit about his kids, go on like all farmers about the weather and the price of seed and all that drivel. But you get nothing personal. And something as awful as this, well, no, he would never say a word."

John sucked on his cigar and blasted a cloud of blue smoke at the ceiling. "So you have no idea what's behind this?"

She dabbed her cheeks with a handkerchief and said, "I'm too overwhelmed to make any sense of it, John. I'm having trouble breathing right now, forget thinking clearly. Maybe tomorrow, maybe the next day, but not now. Everything is a blur."

"And Joel and Stella?"

"I've spoken with both of them. Poor children, away at school, enjoying the college life, nothing really to worry about, and they get the news that their father has just murdered their minister, a man they admired. And they can't come home because Pete gave strict instructions, in writing no less, that they stay away until he changes his mind." She sobbed for a minute as John worked his cigar, then she clenched her jaws, dabbed some more, and said, "I'm sorry."

"Oh, go ahead, Florry, cry all you want. I wish I could. Get it out of your system because it's only natural. This is no time to be brave. Emotion is welcome here. This is a perfectly awful day that will haunt us for years to come."

"What is coming, John?"

"Well, nothing good, I can promise you that. I spoke with Judge Oswalt this afternoon and he will not even consider the notion of bail. Out of the question, which I completely understand. It is murder, after all. I met with Pete this afternoon, but he's not cooperative. So, on the one hand he will not plead guilty, and on the other he won't provide any cooperation for a defense. This could change, of course, but you and I both know him and he doesn't change his mind once it's made up."

"What kind of defense?"

"Our options appear to be rather limited. Self-defense, irresistible impulse, an alibi perhaps. Nothing fits here, Florry." He pulled again on the cigar and exhaled another cloud. "And there's more. I received a tip this afternoon and walked over to the land records office. Three weeks ago, Pete signed a deed transferring ownership of his land to Joel and Stella. There was no good reason for doing this, and he certainly didn't want me to know about it. He used a lawyer from Tupelo, one with few contacts in Clanton."

"And the point is? I'm sorry, John, help me here."

"The point is Pete was planning this for some time, and to protect his land from possible claims to be made by the family of Dexter Bell, he gave it to his children, took his name off the title."

"Will that work?"

"I doubt it, but that's another issue for another day. Your land is, of course, in your name and will not be affected by any of this."

"Thanks, John, but I haven't even thought about that."

"Assuming he goes to trial, and I can't imagine why he will not, the land transaction will be entered into evidence against him to prove premeditation. It was all carefully planned, Florry. Pete had been thinking about this for a long time."

Florry held the handkerchief to her mouth and stared at the floor as minutes passed. The office was perfectly still and quiet; all sounds from the street below were gone. John stood and stubbed his cigar into a heavy crystal ashtray, then walked to his desk and lit another one. He went to the windows of a French door and gazed at the courthouse across the street. It was almost dusk and the shadows were falling on the lawn.

Without turning around, he asked, "How long was Pete in the hospital after he escaped?"

"Months and months. I don't know, maybe a year. He had extensive wounds and weighed 130 pounds. It took time."

"How about mentally? Were there problems?"

"Well, typically, he's never talked about them if they in fact existed. But how can you not be a bit off in the head after going through what he endured?"

"Was he diagnosed?"

"I have no idea. He is not the same person after the war, but how could he be? I'm sure a lot of those boys are scarred."

"How is he different?"

She stuck her handkerchief in her purse, as if to say the tears were over for now. "Liza said there were nightmares at first, a lot of sleepless nights. He's moodier now, prone to long stretches of silence, which he seems to enjoy. But then, you're talking about a man who's never said a lot. I do remember thinking that he was quite happy and relaxed when he got home. He was still convalescing and gaining weight, and he smiled a lot, just happy to be alive and happy the war was over. That didn't last, though. I could tell things were tense between him and Liza. Nineva said they were not getting along. It was really strange because it seemed as though the stronger he got, the more he got himself together, the quicker she unraveled."

"What were they fighting about?"

"I don't know. Nineva sees and hears everything, so they were careful. She told Marietta that they often sent her out of the house so they could discuss things. Liza was spiraling. I remember seeing her once, not long before she went away, and she looked thin, frail, and sort of beleaguered. It's no secret that she and I have never been close, so she never confided in me. I guess he didn't either."

John puffed his cigar and returned to his seat near Florry. He stared at her with a pleasant smile, one old friend to another, and said, "The only possible connection between Reverend Bell, your brother, and a senseless murder is Liza Banning. Do you agree?"

"I'm in no position to agree to anything."

"Come on, Florry, help me out here. I'm the only person who might be able to save Pete's life, and that looks pretty doubtful right now. How much time did Dexter Bell spend with Liza when we thought Pete was dead?"

"Good God, John, I don't know. Those first days and weeks were just awful. Liza was a wreck. The kids were traumatized. The house was a beehive as everybody in the county stopped by with a ham or a pork shank and a spare shoulder to cry on, along with a dozen questions.

Sure, Dexter was there, and I remember his wife too. They were close to Pete and Liza."

"But nothing unusual?"

"Unusual? Are you suggesting something went on between Liza and Dexter Bell? That's outrageous, John."

"Yes it is, and so is this murder, the defense of which I'm now in charge of, if there is to be a defense. There's a reason Pete killed him. If he won't explain things, then it's up to me to find a motive."

Florry raised her hands and said, "I'm done. It's been a stressful day, John, and I can't go on. Maybe another time." She got to her feet and headed for the door, which he quickly opened for her. He held her arm down the stairs. They hugged at the front door and promised to talk soon.

His first meal as an inmate was a bowl of soup beans with a wedge of stale corn bread. Both were cold, and as Pete sat on the edge of his cot and held the bowl he pondered the question of how difficult it might be to keep the beans warm long enough to serve them to the prisoners. Surely that could be done, though he would suggest it to no one. He would not complain, for he had learned the hard way that complaining often made matters worse.

Across the dark passageway another prisoner sat on his cot and dined under the dim glow of a bare bulb at the end of a cord. His name was Leon Colliver, a member of a family known for making good moonshine, a flask of which he had hidden under his cot. Twice throughout the afternoon Colliver had offered a swig to Pete, who declined. According to Colliver, he would be shipped out to the state penitentiary at Parchman, where he was scheduled to spend a few years. It would be his second visit there and he was looking forward to it. Any place was better than this dungeon. At Parchman, the inmates spent most of their time outdoors.

Colliver wanted to chat and was curious as to why Pete was in jail. As the day wore on, the gossip spread, even to the other four white inmates, and by dusk everyone knew Pete had killed the Methodist preacher. Colliver had plenty of time to talk and wanted some details. He got nothing. What Colliver didn't know was that Pete Banning had been shot, beaten, starved, tortured, locked in barbed wire, ship hulls, boxcars, and POW camps, and one of many survival lessons he'd picked up during his ordeal was to never say much to a person you don't know. Colliver got nothing.

After dinner, Nix Gridley appeared in the cell block and stopped at Pete's cell. Pete stood and took three steps to the bars. In a voice that was almost a whisper, Gridley said, "Look, Pete, we got some nosy reporters pesterin' us, hangin' around the jail, wantin' to talk to you, me, anybody who'll engage them. Just want to make sure you have no interest."

"I have no interest," Pete said.

"They're comin' from all over—Tupelo, Jackson, Memphis."

"I have no interest."

"That's what I figured. You doin' all right back here?"

"Doin' fine. I've seen worse."

"I know. Look, Pete, just so you'll know, I stopped this afternoon and had a word with Jackie Bell, at the parsonage. She's holdin' up okay, I guess. Kids are a mess, though."

Pete glared at him without a trace of sympathy, though he thought about saying something smart like "Please give her my regards." Or, "Aw shucks, tell her I'm sorry." But he only frowned at the sheriff as if he were an idiot. Why tell me this?

When it was obvious Pete would not respond, Gridley backed away and said, "If you need anything, let me know."

"Thanks."

CHAPTER 5

At 4:00 a.m., Florry finally abandoned all efforts at sleep and went to the kitchen to make coffee. Marietta, who lived in the basement, heard noises and soon appeared in her nightshirt. Florry said she couldn't sleep, didn't need anything, and sent her back to her room. After two cups with sugar, and another round of tears, Florry bit her lip and decided the dreadful nightmare might inspire creativity. For an hour she fiddled with a poem but tossed it at dawn. She turned to nonfiction and began a diary dedicated to the tragedy in real time. She skipped a bath and breakfast and by 7:00 a.m. was in Clanton, at the home of Mildred Highlander, a widow who lived alone and was, as far as Florry knew, the only person in town who understood her poetry. Over hot tea and cheese biscuits, they talked of nothing but the nightmare.

Mildred took both the Tupelo and the Memphis morning papers and, expecting the worst, they were not disappointed. It was the lead story on the front page of the Tupelo paper with the headline "War Hero Arrested For Murder." Memphis, with obviously less interest in what happened down in Mississippi, ran the story on the front page, metro section, under the headline "Popular Preacher Shot Dead At Church." The facts varied little from one article to the other. Not a word from the suspect's lawyer or any of the authorities. General shock around town.

The local paper, *The Ford County Times,* was a weekly that hit the stands early each Wednesday morning, so it missed the excitement by one day and would have to wait until the following week. Its photographer, though, had nailed Pete Banning as he walked into the jail, and the same photo was used by both the Memphis and the Tupelo papers. Pete, with three good-ole-boy cops in mismatching uniforms and hats, being led into the jail with a look of complete indifference.

Since it seemed as though Clanton was suffering from a case of collective lockjaw, the reporters dwelled on Pete's colorful record as a war hero. Relying heavily on their archives, both newspapers detailed his career and his exploits as a legendary soldier in the South Pacific. Both used smaller photos of Pete when he returned to Clanton the year before. Tupelo even used a photo of Pete and Liza during a ceremony on the courthouse lawn.

Vic Dixon lived across the street from Mildred, and was one of the few people in Clanton who subscribed to the Jackson morning paper, the largest in the state but one with a slim following in the northern counties. After he read it that morning with his coffee, he walked over and offered it to Mildred, who had requested it. While in her den, he spoke to Florry and passed along his condolences, or sympathies, or whatever the hell one is supposed to offer to the sister of a man who is charged with murder and appears guilty of it. Mildred shooed him away, but only after squeezing a promise that Vic would save his dailies.

Florry wanted everything for her file, or scrapbook, or nonfiction account of the nightmare. She wanted to save, record, and preserve it all. For what purpose she was not quite certain, but a long, sad, and also truly unique story was unfolding, and she had no intentions of missing any of it. When Joel and Stella finally returned home, she wanted to be able to answer as many questions as possible.

She was disappointed, though, when she realized that Jackson, which was farther away from Clanton than Tupelo or Memphis, had even fewer details, and fewer photos. It ran the rather lame headline "Prominent Farmer Arrested in Clanton." Nevertheless, Florry clipped a subscription coupon and planned to mail it with a check.

Using Mildred's private line, she called Joel and Stella and tried to assure them that things at home were not as catastrophic as they might seem. She failed miserably, and when she finally rang off both her niece and her nephew were in tears. Their father was in jail, damn it, and charged with an awful murder. And they wanted to come home.

At nine, Florry braced herself and drove to the jail in her 1939 Lincoln. It had less than twenty thousand miles on the odometer and rarely left the county, primarily because its owner had no driver's license. She had flunked the test twice, been stopped by the police on several occasions, without penalties, and continued to drive because of a handshake agreement with Nix Gridley that she would drive only to town and back, and never at night.

She walked into the jail, into the sheriff's office, said hello to Nix and Red, and announced that she was there to see her brother. In a heavy straw bag, she had packed three novels by William Faulkner, three pounds of Standard Coffee, mail-ordered from the distributor in Baltimore, one coffee mug, ten packs of cigarettes, matches, a toothbrush and toothpaste, two bars of soap, two bottles of aspirin, two bottles of painkillers, and a box of chocolates. Every item had been requested by her brother.

After some awkward conversation, Nix finally asked her what was in the bag. Without offering it, she explained there were a few harmless items for her brother, stuff he had requested.

Both cops made a mental note to write this down and pass it along to the prosecutor. The prisoner planned his crime so carefully he made a list of items to be brought to the jail by his sister. Clear evidence of premeditated murder. An honest but potentially damaging mistake by Florry.

"When did he request these items?" Nix asked nonchalantly, as if it meant nothing.

Florry, eager to cooperate, said, "Oh, he left a note with Nineva, told her to bring it to me after he was arrested."

"I see," Nix said. "Tell me, Florry, how much did you know about his plans?"

"I knew nothing. I swear. Absolutely nothing. I'm as shocked as you, even more so because he's my brother and I can't imagine him doing anything like this." Nix glanced at Red with a look that conveyed doubt, in something. Doubt that she knew nothing beforehand. Doubt that she knew nothing about motive. Doubt that she was telling everything. The look exchanged between the two cops startled Florry, and she realized she shouldn't be talking. "Could I please see my brother?" she practically demanded.

"Sure," Nix said. He looked again at Red and said, "Go fetch the prisoner." When Red stepped out, Nix took the bag and examined its contents. This irritated Florry, who said, "What are you looking for, Nix, guns and knives?"

"What's he supposed to do with this coffee?" Nix asked.

"Drink it."

"We have our own, Florry."

"I'm sure you do, but Pete is particular about his coffee. Goes back to the war, when he couldn't get any. It has to be Standard Coffee from New Orleans. That's the least you can do."

"If we serve him Standard, then we have to serve the same to the rest of the prisoners, at least to the white ones. No preferential treatment here, Florry, you understand? Folks already suspect Pete'll get a special deal."

"I can accept that. I'll haul in all the Standard Coffee you want."

Nix held up the coffee mug. It was ceramic, off-white in color, with light brown stains, obviously well used. Before he could say anything, Florry added, "That's his favorite mug. They gave it to him at the military hospital after his surgeries while he was convalescing. Surely, Nix, you will not deny a war hero the simple favor of drinking coffee from his favorite mug."

"I suppose not," Nix mumbled as he began placing the items back in the bag.

"He's not your typical prisoner, Nix, remember that. You've got him locked up back there with God knows who, probably a bunch of thieves and bootleggers, but you must remember that he is Pete Banning."

"He's locked up because he murdered the Methodist preacher, Florry. And as of right now he's the only murderer back there. He will not be given special treatment."

The door opened and Pete walked in with Red behind him. He looked stone-faced at his sister and stood erect in the middle of the room, looking down at Nix.

"I suppose you want to use my office again," Nix said.

"Thanks, Nix, that's mighty nice of you," Pete said. Nix grudgingly stood, picked up his hat, and left the room with Red. His gun and holster hung from a rack in a corner, in plain sight.

Pete moved a chair, took a seat, and looked at his sister, whose first words were "You idiot. How could you be so stupid and selfish and shortsighted and absolutely idiotic? How could you do this to your family? Forget me, forget the farm and the people who depend on you. Forget your friends. How in the world could you do this to your children? They are devastated, Pete, frightened beyond belief and absolutely distraught. How could you?"

"I had no choice."

"Oh, really? Care to explain things, Pete?"

"No, I will not explain, and lower your voice. Don't assume they're not listening."

"I don't care if they're listening."

His eyes glazed as he pointed a finger at her and said, "Settle down, Florry. I'm in no mood for your theatrics and I will not be abused. I did what I did for a reason and perhaps one day you will understand. For now, though, I have nothing to say about the matter and since you don't understand I suggest you watch your words."

Her eyes instantly watered and her lip quivered. She dropped her chin to her chest and mumbled, "So you can't even talk to me?"

"To no one, not even you."

She stared at the floor for a long time as his words sank in. The day before they'd had their usual fine Wednesday breakfast with no hint of what was to come. Pete was like that now: aloof, distant, often in another world.

Florry looked at him and said, "I'm going to ask you why."

"And I have nothing to say."

"What did Dexter Bell do to deserve this?"

"I have nothing to say."

"Is Liza involved in this?"

Pete hesitated for a second and Florry knew she had touched a nerve. He said, "I have nothing to say," and went about the deliberate business of removing a cigarette from a pack, tapping it on his wristwatch for some unfathomable reason, as always, then lighting it with a match.

"Do you feel any remorse or sympathy for his family?" she asked.

"I try not to think about them. Yes, I'm sorry it had to happen, but this was not something I wanted to do.

They, along with the rest of us, will simply learn to live with what has happened."

"Just like that? It's over. He's dead. Too bad. Just deal with it as life goes on. I'd like to see you trot this little theory out in front of his three beautiful children right now."

"Feel free to leave." She made no movement except for the gentle dabbing of her cheeks with a tissue. Pete blew some smoke that settled into a fog not far above their heads. They could hear voices in the distance, laughter coming from the sheriff and his deputies as they went about their business.

Finally, Florry asked, "What are the conditions like back there?"

"It's a jail. I've seen worse."

"Are they feeding you?"

"The food's okay. I've seen worse."

"Joel and Stella want to come home and see you. They are terrified, Pete, absolutely frightened stiff, and, understandably, quite confused."

"I've made it very clear they are not to come home until I say. Period. Please remind them of this. I know what's best."

"I doubt that. What's best is for their father to be at home going about his business and trying to keep a fractured family together, not sitting in jail charged with a senseless murder."

Ignoring this, he said, "I worry about them, but they are strong and smart and they'll survive."

"I'm not so sure about that. It's easy for you to assume they're as strong as you, given what you went through, but that may not be the case, Pete. You can't just assume that your children will survive this unscarred."

"I'll not be lectured. You are welcome to come visit, and I appreciate it, but not if you feel the need to deliver a sermon with each visit. Let's keep things on the light side, Florry, okay? My days are numbered. Don't make them worse."

CHAPTER 6

The Honorable Rafe Oswalt had been the circuit court judge for Ford, Tyler, Milburn, Polk, and Van Buren Counties for the past seventeen years. Because he lived next door in Smithfield, the seat of Polk County, he had never met either the defendant or the deceased. Like everyone else, though, he was intrigued by the facts and eager to assume jurisdiction over the matter. During his unremarkable career on the bench, he had presided over a dozen or so rather routine murders—drunken brawls, knife fights in black honky-tonks, domestic conflicts—all crimes of rage or passion that usually ended in short trials followed by long prison sentences. Not a single murder had involved the death of such a prominent person.

Judge Oswalt had read the newspaper reports and heard some of the gossip. He had spoken twice on the phone with John Wilbanks, a lawyer he greatly admired. He had also spoken on the phone with the district attorney, Miles Truitt, a lawyer he admired less. On Friday morning, the bailiff cracked the door to the judge's chambers behind the courtroom and reported that a crowd was waiting.

Indeed it was. Friday just happened to be a scheduled docket day for routine appearances for criminal matters and motion hearings in civil suits. No jury trials were planned in Ford County for months, and normally such a dull lineup on a Friday would attract almost no spectators. Suddenly, though, there was curiosity, and admission was free. The curiosity wasn't limited to the few courthouse regulars who whittled carvings and dipped snuff under the old oaks on the lawn while waiting for some action inside. The curiosity consumed Ford County, and by 9:00 a.m. the courtroom was filled with dozens of people wanting to get a glimpse of Pete Banning. There were reporters from several newspapers, one from as far away as Atlanta. There were a lot of Methodists, now committed anti-Banning folks who bunched together on one side behind the prosecutor's table. Across the aisle were assorted friends of Pete and Dexter Bell, along with the courthouse regulars, as well as a lot of townsfolk who managed to sneak away from their jobs for the moment. Above them, in the balcony, sat a few Negroes, isolated by their color. Unlike most buildings in town, the courthouse allowed them to come and go through the front door, but once inside they were banished to the balcony. They too wanted a look at the defendant.

No members of the Bell or Banning family were present. The Bells were in mourning and preparing for a funeral the following day. The Bannings were staying as far away as possible.

Because they were officers of the court, the town's lawyers were allowed to come and go beyond the bar and around the bench. All twelve were present, all wearing their best dark suits and feigning important legal business while the crowd looked on. The clerks, normally a languid if not lethargic group, were shuffling their useless paperwork with vigor.

Nix Gridley had two full-time deputies—Roy Lester and Red Arnett—and three part-timers, along with two volunteers. On this fine day the entire force of eight was present, all in proper, well-starched, and almost matching uniforms and presenting an impressive show of muscle. Nix himself seemed to be everywhere—laughing with the lawyers, flirting with the clerks, chatting with a few of the spectators. He was a year away from reelection and couldn't pass up the opportunity to appear important in front of so many voters.

And so the show went on as the crowd grew and the clock ticked past nine. Judge Oswalt finally emerged from behind the bench in his flowing black robe and assumed his throne. Acting as if he hadn't noticed the spectators, he looked at Nix and said, "Mr. Sheriff, bring in the prisoners."

Nix was already at the door by the jury box. He opened it, disappeared for a moment, then reappeared with Pete Banning in handcuffs and wearing bulky gray overalls with the word "Jail" across the front. Behind Pete was Chuck Manley, an alleged car thief with the misfortune of being arrested a few days before Pete shot the preacher. Under normal circumstances, Chuck would have been hauled in from the jail, frog-marched in front of the judge, appointed a lawyer, and sent back to jail with hardly a soul knowing anything about it. Fate intervened, though, and Manley's alleged crime would now be known to many.

Pete moved as if on parade, ramrod straight with an air of confidence and a nonchalant look. Nix led him to a chair in front of the empty jury box, and Manley sat beside him. Their handcuffs were not removed. The lawyers found their seats and for a moment all was quiet as His Honor studiously reviewed a few sheets of paper. Finally, he said, "The matter of *State versus Chuck Manley*."

A lawyer named Nance jumped to his feet and motioned for his client to join him in front of the bench. Manley stepped over and looked up at the judge, who asked, "You are Chuck Manley?"

"Yes, sir."

"And Mr. Nance here is your lawyer?"

"I guess. My momma hired him."

"Do you want him to be your lawyer?"

"I guess. I'm not guilty, though; this is just a misunderstanding."

Nance grabbed his elbow and told him to shut up.

"You were arrested last Monday and charged with stealing Mr. Earl Caldwell's 1938 Buick out of his driveway over in Karraway. How do you plead?"

Manley said, "Not guilty, sir. I can explain."

"Not today, son. Maybe later. Your bond is hereby set at $100. Can you pay this?"

"I doubt it."

Nance, eager to say something in front of such a crowd, bellowed, "Your Honor, I suggest that this young man be released on his own recognizance. He has no criminal record, has a job, and will show up in court whenever he is supposed to."

"That true, son, you have a job?"

"Yes, sir. I drive a truck for Mr. J. P. Leatherwood."

"Is he in the courtroom?"

"Oh, I doubt it. He's very busy."

Nance jumped in with "Your Honor, I've spoken with Mr. Leatherwood and he is willing to sign a guarantee that my client will appear in court when directed. If you'd like to talk to Mr. Leatherwood, I can arrange this."

"Very well. Take him back to jail and I'll call his boss this afternoon."

Manley was escorted out of the courtroom less than five minutes after entering it. His Honor signed his name a few times and reviewed some papers as everyone waited. Finally he said, "In the matter of *State versus Pete Banning*."

John Wilbanks was on his feet and striding to the bench. Pete stood, grimaced slightly, then walked to a spot next to his lawyer. Judge Oswalt asked, "You are Pete Banning?"

He nodded. "I am."

"And you are represented by the Honorable John Wilbanks?"

Another nod. "I am."

"And you have been arrested and charged for the first-degree murder of the Reverend Dexter Bell. Do you understand this?

"And do you understand that first-degree murder is based on premeditation and can possibly carry the death penalty, whereas second-degree murder is punishable by a long prison sentence?"

"I understand this."

"And how do you wish to plead?"

"Not guilty."

"The court will accept your plea and enter it on the docket. Anything else, Mr. Wilbanks?"

The lawyer replied, "Well, yes, Your Honor, I respectfully request the court to consider setting a reasonable bond for my client. Now, I realize the gravity of this charge and do not take it lightly. But a bond is permissible in this case. A bond is nothing but a guarantee that the defendant will not flee, but rather will appear in court when he's supposed to. Mr. Banning owns an entire section of land, 640 acres, free and clear, with no debts whatsoever, and he is willing to post the deed to his property as security for his bond. His sister owns the adjacent section and will do the same. I might add, Your Honor, that this land has been in the Banning family for over one hundred years and neither my client nor his sister will do anything to jeopardize it."

Judge Oswalt interrupted with "This is first-degree murder, Mr. Wilbanks."

"I understand, Your Honor, but my client is innocent until proven guilty. How does it benefit the State or anyone else to keep him in jail when he can post a secure bond and remain free until trial? He's not going anywhere."

"I've never heard of a bond for a charge this serious."

"Nor have I, but the Mississippi Code does not prohibit it. If the court would like, I will be happy to submit a brief on this point."

During the back-and-forth, Pete stood at attention,

stiff and unmoving as a sentry. He stared straight ahead, as if hearing nothing but absorbing it all.

Judge Oswalt thought for a moment and said, "Very well. I'll read your brief, but it will have to be quite persuasive to change my mind. Meanwhile, the prisoner will remain in the custody of the sheriff's office."

Nix gently took Pete by the elbow and led him from the courtroom, with John Wilbanks in pursuit. Waiting outside next to the sheriff's car were two photographers, and they quickly snapped the same shots they had taken when the defendant was entering the courthouse. A reporter yelled a question in Pete's direction. He ignored it as he ducked into the rear seat. Within minutes, he was back in his cell, handcuffs and shoes off, reading *Go Down, Moses* and smoking a cigarette.

The burying of Dexter Bell became a glorious affair. It began on Thursday, the day after the killing, when old man Magargel opened the doors of his funeral home at 6:00 p.m. and the mob descended. Half an hour earlier, Jackie Bell and her three children were allowed to privately view the body. As was the custom, at that time and in that part of the world, the casket was open. Dexter lay still and quiet on a bed of shiny cloth, his black suit visible from the waist up. Jackie fainted as her children screamed and bawled and fell all over themselves. Mr. Magargel and his son were the only others in the room and they tried to render assistance, which was impossible.

There was no good reason for an open casket. No law or verse of sacred scripture commanded such a ritual. It was simply what folks did to create as much drama as possible. More emotion equaled more love for the deceased. Jackie had sat through dozens of funerals conducted by her husband, and the caskets were always open.

The Magargels had little experience with gunshot wounds to the face. Most of their clients were old folks whose frail bodies were easy to prepare. But not long into the embalming of Reverend Bell they realized they needed help and called a more experienced colleague from Memphis. A large chunk of the back of the skull had been blown off during the exit of bullet number three, but that was not of any significance. No one would ever see that part of the deceased. With the entry, though, right above the nose, there was a sizable divot that required hours of skillful rebuilding and molding with all manner of restructuring putty, glue, and coloring. The end product was okay, but far from great. Dexter continued to frown, as though he would forever be staring in horror at the gun.

After half an hour of private viewing, a perfectly miserable time in which even the experienced and cold-blooded Magargels were pushed to the brink of tears, Jackie and her children were arranged in seats near the casket and the doors were opened and the crowd rushed in. What followed were three hours of unrestrained agony, grieving, and suffering.

After a break, it continued the following afternoon when Dexter was rolled down the aisle of his church and parked under his pulpit. Jackie, who'd seen enough, asked that the casket not be opened. Old man Magargel frowned at this, though he complied and said nothing. He hated to miss such a rich opportunity to see folks racked with grief. For three more hours, Jackie and her children stood gamely by the casket and greeted many of the same people they'd greeted the evening before. Hundreds showed up, including every able-bodied Methodist in the county and many from other churches, and friends of the family, with a lot of children far too young for such mourning but drawn to the wake out of friendship with the Bells. Also paying respects were many outright strangers who simply didn't want to miss the opportunity to wedge themselves into the story. The pews were filled with people who waited patiently to proceed past the casket and say something banal to the family, and as they waited they prayed, and whispered softly, passing along the latest news. The sanctuary suffered under the weight of inconsolable loss, which was made even worse by the pipe organ. Miss Emma Faye Riddle churned away, playing one sorrowful dirge after another.

Hop watched from a corner of the balcony, vexed again at the strange ways of white folks.

After two days of these preliminaries, the weary gathered for the last time at the church on Saturday afternoon for the funeral. A preacher friend of Dexter's led the ceremony, which was complete with a full choir, two solos, a lengthy homily, more of Miss Emma Faye and her organ, scripture readings, three eulogies, tears by the bucket loads, and, yes, an open casket. Though he tried valiantly, the preacher failed to make sense of the death. He relied heavily on the theme of "God works in mysterious ways" but that found little traction. He finally surrendered and the choir rose to its feet.

After two grueling hours, there was nothing left to say, and they loaded Dexter into the hearse and paraded across town to the public cemetery, where he was finally laid to rest amid a sea of flowers and a tide of raw emotion. Long after they were dismissed by the preacher, Jackie and the children sat in their folding chairs under the canopy and stared at the casket and the pile of black dirt beside it.

Mrs. Gloria Grange was a devout Methodist who missed none of the ceremonies, and after the interment she stopped by the home of Mildred Highlander, for tea. Mildred was a Presbyterian and unacquainted with Reverend Bell; thus she didn't attend the wake or funeral. But she certainly wanted all the details, and Gloria unloaded.

Late Saturday afternoon, Florry hustled to town, also for tea with Mildred. She was eager to hear the details of the suffering caused by her brother, and Mildred was just as eager to pass them along.

CHAPTER 7

For the first time in his young life, Joel Banning disobeyed his father. He left Nashville Saturday morning and took the train to Memphis, a four-hour ride that allowed plenty of time to consider his act of disobedience, and by the time he arrived in Memphis he had convinced himself that it was justified. Indeed, he could even articulate his reasons: He needed to check on Florry to see how she was holding up; he needed to meet with Buford the overseer and make sure the harvest was going well; perhaps he would meet with John Wilbanks and discuss his father's defense, or maybe not. Their little family was disintegrating on all fronts and someone had to step forward and try to save it. Besides, his father was in jail, and if Joel eased in and out the way he planned, his quick visit would not be discovered, his act of disobedience undetected.

The train from Memphis to Clanton stopped six times, and it was after dark when he stepped onto the platform and pulled his hat low over his eyes. A few people got off and no one seemed to recognize him. There were two cabs in town and both were idling outside the station, their drivers leaning on the same fender chewing tobacco and smoking hand-rolled cigarettes.

"Is that telephone box still outside the drugstore?" Joel asked the nearest driver.

"It is."

"Can you take me there?"

"Hop in."

The square was packed with late Saturday shoppers. Even during the picking season, the farmers and their field hands cleaned up after lunch and headed to town. The stores were filled, the sidewalks packed, the Atrium was showing Bing Crosby in *Blue Skies,* and a long line waited around the corner. Live bluegrass was entertaining a throng on the courthouse lawn. Joel preferred to avoid the crowds and asked his driver to stop on a side street. The phone box in front of Gainwright's Pharmacy was occupied. Joel stood beside it, fidgeting for the benefit of the young lady using the phone, and tried his best to avoid eye contact with the packs of people passing by. When he was finally inside he punched in a nickel and called Aunt Florry. After a few rings she answered.

Assuming, as always, that someone was listening on their rural party line, he said quickly, "Florry, it's me. I'll be there in twenty minutes."

"What? Who?"

"Your favorite nephew. Bye."

As the only nephew, he was confident she got the message. Showing up unannounced would give her too much of a shock. Plus, he was starving and figured a little advance notice might get some hot food on the table. Back in the cab, he asked the driver to ease by the Methodist church. As they left the bustling square, they passed Cal's Game Room, a pool hall known for its bootleg beer and craps in the back. As a young teenager in Clanton, Joel had been strictly warned by his father to stay away from Cal's, in much the same way that all proper young men had been cautioned. It was a rowdy place on weekends, with a rough crowd, and there were usually fights and such. Because it was off-limits, Joel had always been tempted to sneak in during his high school days. His friends would brag about hanging out at Cal's, and there were even stories of girls upstairs. Now, though, with three years of college behind him, and in the big city at that, Joel scoffed at the notion of being tempted by such a low-end dive. He knew the fine bars of Nashville and all the pleasures they offered. He could not imagine ever returning to live in Clanton, a town where the beer and liquor were illegal, as were most things.

The lights were on in the sanctuary of the Methodist church, and as they passed it the driver said, "You from around here?"

"Not really," Joel said.

"So you haven't heard the big news this week, about the preacher?"

"Yeah, I read about it. A strange story."

"Shot him right there," the driver said, pointing to the annex behind the sanctuary. "Buried him this afternoon. Got the guy in jail but he won't say anything."

Joel did not respond, did not wish to pursue this conversation that he had not initiated. He gazed at the church as they eased past it, and he remembered with great fondness those Sunday mornings when he and Stella would be dressed in their finest, bow ties and bonnets, and walked into the sanctuary holding hands with their parents, who were also turned out in their Sunday best. Joel knew at a young age that his father's suits and his mother's dresses were a bit nicer than the average Methodist's, and their cars and trucks were always newer, and they talked of finishing college and not just high school. He realized a lot as a child, but because he was a Banning he was also taught humility and the virtue of saying as little as possible.

He had been baptized in that church when he was ten years old; Stella at nine. The family had faithfully attended the weekly services, the fall and spring revivals, the cookouts, potluck suppers, funerals, weddings, and an endless schedule of social events because for them, and for many in their town, the church was the center of society. Joel remembered all of the pastors who had come and gone. Pastor Wardall had buried his grandfather Jacob Banning. Ron Cooper had baptized Joel, and his son had been Joel's best friend in the fourth grade. And on and on. The pastors came and went until Dexter Bell arrived before the war.

Evidently, he stayed too long.

Joel said, "Head out Highway 18. I'll show you where to stop."

The cabbie replied, "To where? Always like to know where I'm goin'."

"Out by the Banning place."

"You a Banning?"

There was nothing worse than a nosy cabdriver. Joel ignored him and glanced through the rear window at the church as it disappeared around the corner. He had liked Dexter Bell, though by his early teens he was beginning to question his harsh sermons. It was Pastor Bell who had sat with the family on that horrible evening when they had been informed that Lieutenant Pete Banning was missing and presumed dead in the Philippines. During those dark days, Pastor Bell took charge of the mourning—directing the church ladies and their endless parade of food, organizing prayer vigils at the church, shooing folks away from the house when privacy was needed, and counseling the family, almost daily, it seemed. Joel and Stella even whispered complaints when they grew tired of the counseling. What they wanted was to spend time alone with their mother, but the reverend was always around. Often he brought his wife, Jackie; other times he did not. As Joel grew older, he found Jackie Bell cold and aloof, and Stella didn't like her either.

Joel closed his eyes and shook his head again. It wasn't really true, was it? His father had murdered Dexter Bell and was now locked up?

The cotton began at the edge of town, and under a full moon it was plain to see which fields had been picked. Though he had no plans to farm like his ancestors, Joel checked the market on the Memphis Cotton Exchange every day in *The Nashville Tennessean*. It was pretty damned important. The land would one day belong to him, and to Stella, and the annual harvest would be crucial.

"Gonna be a nice crop this year," the cabbie said.

"That's what I hear. About another mile and I'll get out."

Moments later, Joel said, "Up there at Pace Road, that'll be fine."

"In the middle of nowhere?"

"That's right." The cab slowed, turned onto a gravel road, and stopped. "That'll be a dollar," the driver said. Joel handed him four quarters, thanked him for the lift, and got out with his small duffel. After the cab turned around and was headed back to town, he walked the quarter mile to the driveway leading to his home.

The house was dark and unlocked, and as he eased through it he figured Mack, the bluetick hound, was either at Nineva's or at Florry's. Otherwise, he would have been barking when Joel approached on the gravel drive. In earlier times and not that long ago, the house would have been alive with the voices of his parents, and music on the radio, and perhaps friends over for dinner on a Saturday night. But tonight it was a tomb, dark and still and smelling of stale tobacco.

Now they were both locked away: his mother in a state asylum, his father in the county jail.

He left through the rear door, swung wide to avoid the small home of Nineva and Amos, and picked up the trail by the barns and tractor shed. This was his land and he knew every inch of it. A hundred yards away, a light shone in the window of Buford's cottage. He had been their overseer, or foreman as he preferred to be called, since before the war, and his importance to the family had just been greatly elevated.

All lights were on in Florry's cottage and she was waiting near the door. She hugged him at first, then scolded him for coming, then hugged him again. Marietta had made a pot of venison stew two days earlier and it was warming on the stove. A thick, meaty aroma filled the house.

"You're finally gaining some weight," Florry said as they sat at the dining table. She was pouring coffee from a ceramic pot.

"Let's not talk about our weight," Joel said.

"Agreed." Florry was gaining too, though not on purpose.

"It's so good to see you, Joel."

"It's good to be home, even under these circumstances."

"Why did you come?"

"Because I live here, Aunt Florry. Because my father is in jail and my poor mother has been sent away, so what the hell is happening to us?"

"Watch your language, college boy."

"Please. I'm twenty years old and I'm a senior. I'll cuss, smoke, and drink anytime I wish."

"Lawd have mercy," Marietta said as she walked by.

"That's enough, Marietta," Florry snapped. "I'll take care of the stew. You're done for the night. See you late tomorrow morning."

Marietta yanked off her apron, tossed it on the counter, pulled on her coat, and went to the basement.

They took deep breaths, sipped their coffee, and let a moment pass. Calmly, Joel asked, "Why did he do it?"

Florry shook her head. "No one knows but him, and he refuses to explain things. I've seen him once, the day after, and he's in another world."

"There has to be a reason, Aunt Florry. He would never do something so random, so awful, without a reason."

"Oh, I agree, but he's not going to talk about it, Joel. I've seen the look on his face, seen it many times, and I know what it means. It's a secret he'll take to his grave."

"He owes us an explanation."

"Well, we're not going to get one, I can promise you that."

"Do you have any bourbon?"

"You're too young for bourbon, Joel."

"I'm twenty," he said, standing. "I'll graduate from Vanderbilt next spring, then go to law school." He was walking to the sofa where he'd left his duffel. "And I'm going to law school because I have no plans to become another farmer, regardless of what he wants." He reached into his duffel and retrieved a flask. "I have no plans to live here, Aunt Florry, and I think you've known that for a long time." He returned to the table, unscrewed the top of the flask, and took a swig. "Jack Daniel's. Would you like some?"

"No."

Another swig. "And even if I were considering a return to Ford County, I would say that that possibility has been pretty much shot to hell now that my father has become the most famous murderer in local history. Can't really blame me, can you?"

"I suppose not. You haven't mentioned law school before."

"I've been thinking about it all year."

"That's wonderful. Where will you go?"

"I'm not sure. Not Vanderbilt. I like Nashville but I need a change. Maybe Tulane or Texas. I was considering Ole Miss but now I have this strong desire to get far away from this here."

"Are you hungry?"

"Starving."

Florry went to the kitchen and filled a large bowl with stew from the pot on the stove. She served it to him with leftover corn bread and a glass of water. Before she sat down, she reached deep into the cupboard and retrieved a bottle of gin. She mixed two ounces with a splash of tonic water, and sat across from him.

He smiled and said, "Stella and I found your gin once. Did you know that?"

"No! Did you drink it?"

"We tried to. I was about sixteen and we knew you kept it hidden in the cupboard. I poured a little in a glass and took a sip. Almost puked. It burned to my toes and tasted like hair tonic. How do you drink that stuff?"

"With practice. What was Stella's reaction?"

"The same. I don't think she's touched alcohol since."

"I'll bet she has. You seem to have developed a taste."

"I'm a college boy, Aunt Florry. It's part of my education." He took a large spoonful of stew and then another. After four or five, he put down his spoon and paused to allow his food to settle. He helped it with a sip of sour mash, then smiled at his aunt and said, "I want to talk about my mother, Aunt Florry. There are secrets back there and you know a lot that you haven't told us."

Florry shook her head and looked away.

He went on, "I know she broke down when they told us he was dead, or presumed dead. Hell, didn't we all, Aunt Florry? I couldn't leave the house for a week. Remember that?"

"How could I forget? It was awful."

"We were like ghosts, just sleepwalking through the

days and dreading the nights. But we somehow found a little strength to go on, and I think Mom did okay, don't you? Didn't Mom sort of get tough and put on a brave face?"

"She did. We all did. But it wasn't easy."

"No, it wasn't. It was a living hell, but we survived. I was at Vanderbilt when she called that night with the news that he wasn't dead after all, that he'd been found and rescued. They said he was badly wounded, but that didn't seem important. He was alive! I hurried home and we celebrated, and I remember Mom being quite happy. Am I right, Aunt Florry?"

"Yes, that's the way I remember it. We were elated, almost euphoric, and that lasted for a few days. Just the fact that he was alive was a miracle. Then we began reading stories about how badly the POWs were treated over there, and we worried about his injuries, and so on."

"Sure, now back to my mother. We were thrilled when he was released, and when he came home a hero my mother was the proudest woman in the world. They could not have been happier, hell, we were all ecstatic, and that was only a year ago, Aunt Florry. So what happened?"

"Don't assume I know what happened because I don't. For the first few weeks all was well. Pete was still recovering and getting stronger by the day. They were happy; things seemed to be fine. Then they weren't. I was not aware of their troubles until long after they had started. Nineva told Marietta that they were fighting, that Liza was acting crazy, prone to long bouts of foul moods and time alone in her room. They stopped sleeping together and your father moved into your bedroom.

I wasn't supposed to know this so I couldn't really ask. And you know it's a waste of time to ask your father anything about his private matters. I've never been close to Liza and she would never confide in me. So, I was in the dark, and, frankly, that's not always a bad place to be."

A long pull on the whiskey and Joel said, "Then she was sent away."

"Then she was sent away."

"Why, Aunt Florry? Why was my mother committed to the state mental hospital?"

Florry sloshed her gin around her glass and studied it at length. Then she took a sip, grimaced as if it was awful, and set down the glass. "Your father decided she needed help, and there's no one around here. The professionals are at Whitfield, and that's where he sent her."

"Just like that? She got shipped off?"

"No, there were proceedings. But let's be honest, Joel, your father knows the right people and he's got the Wilbanks boys in his back pocket. They talked to a judge; he signed the order. And your mother acquiesced. She did not object to the commitment order, not that she had a choice. If Pete insisted, which I'm sure he did, she could not fight him."

"What's her diagnosis?"

"I have no idea. Being a woman, I guess. Keep in mind, Joel, that it's a man's world, and if a husband with connections feels as though his wife is suffering through the change and depressed and her moods are swinging right and left, well, he can send her off for a spell."

"I find it hard to believe that my father would have my mother committed to a mental institution because of the change. She seems kind of young for that. There's a lot more to it, Aunt Florry."

"I'm sure there is, but I was not privy to their discussions and conflicts."

Joel returned to his stew and gulped a few bites, followed with more of his whiskey.

In a futile effort to change the subject, Florry asked, "Are you still seeing that girl?"

"Which girl?"

"Well, I guess that's enough of an answer. Any girl in your life these days?"

"Not really. I'm too young and I have law school in front of me. You said on the phone that you've spoken with John Wilbanks. I assume he's taken charge of the defense."

"He has, or what there is of it. Your father is not co-operating. Wilbanks wants to use an insanity defense, says it's the only way to save his life, but your father will have none of it. Says he's got more sense than Wilbanks or the next lawyer, which I won't argue."

"More proof that he's crazy. He has no choice but to plead insanity, there's no other defense. I did the research myself at the law school yesterday."

"Then you can help Wilbanks. He needs it."

"I've written him a letter and I thought about seeing him tomorrow."

"That's a bad idea, Joel. I doubt he works on Sundays, and you cannot be seen around town. Your father would be upset if he knew you were here. My advice to you is to leave town as quietly as you sneaked in, and not to return until Pete says so."

"I'd like to talk to Buford and check on the crops."

"You can't do a thing to help the crops. You're not a farmer, remember. Besides, Buford has things under control. He reports to me; I plan to run by the jail and report to Pete. We're in the midst of a good harvest so don't try to screw things up. Besides, Buford would tell your father that you're here. Bad idea."

Joel managed a laugh, his first, and swigged his whiskey. He shoved his bowl away, which prompted her to say, "Half a bowl. You should eat more, Joel. You're finally filling out but you have a ways to go. You're still too thin."

"Not much of an appetite these days, Aunt Florry, for some reason. Mind if I smoke?"

She nodded and said, "On the porch." Joel stepped outside with a cigarette while she cleared the table, then she refreshed her drink, laid another log on the fire in the den, and fell into her favorite armchair to wait for him. When he returned, he grabbed his flask, joined her in the den, and sat on the worn leather sofa.

She cleared her throat and said, "There's something you should know, since we were discussing the cotton. I suppose it's no real secret since there is a public record of it in the courthouse. About a month ago, your father hired a lawyer in Tupelo to write a deed transferring ownership of his farm to you and Stella jointly. My land, of course, belongs to me and was not involved. John Wilbanks told me this last Wednesday in his office. Of course, you and Stella would one day inherit the land anyway."

Joel thought for a moment, obviously surprised and confused. "And why did he do this?"

"Why does Pete do anything? Because he can. It wasn't very smart, according to Wilbanks. He was moving his assets to protect them from the family of a man he was planning to murder. Plain and simple. In doing so, though, he handed a gift to the prosecution. The DA can prove at trial that the murder was premeditated. Pete planned everything."

"Is the land protected?"

"Wilbanks doesn't think so, but we didn't go into it. It was the day after and we were still stunned. Still are, I guess."

"Aren't we all? Wilbanks thinks Bell's family will come after the land?"

"He implied that but didn't say it outright. It might be fodder for your research, now that you've found the law library."

"This family needs a full-time lawyer." He took a drink and finished his flask. Florry watched him carefully and loved every ounce of his being. He favored her side, the Bannings, tall with dark eyes and thick hair, while Stella was the image of Liza, both in looks and in temperament. He was grieving, and Florry ached with his pain. His happy, privileged life was taking a dramatic turn for the worse, and he could do nothing to correct its course.

Quietly, he asked, "Has anyone talked about Mom getting out? Is it even a possibility? Dad sent her away, and now that his influence is rather limited, is there a chance she can come home?"

"I don't know, Joel, but I've heard nothing about that. Before this, your father would drive to Whitfield once a month to see her. He never said much, but on a couple of occasions he mentioned his visits, said she was not getting any better."

"How is one supposed to improve in an insane asylum?"

"You're asking the wrong person."

"And why can't I visit her?"

"Because your father said no."

"I can't see my father and I can't visit my mother. Is it okay to admit that I miss my parents, Florry?"

"Of course you do, dear. I'm so sorry."

They watched the fire for a long time and nothing was said. It hissed and crackled and began dying for the night. One of the cats jumped up onto the leather sofa and looked at Joel as if he were trespassing. Finally, Joel said softly, "I don't know what to do, Florry. Nothing makes sense right now."

For the first time his words were not clear, his tongue thick.

She took a sip and said, "Well, coming home tonight is not the answer. The train for Memphis leaves at nine thirty in the morning, and you'll be on it. There's nothing to do here but worry."

"I suppose I can worry at college."

"I suppose you can."

CHAPTER 8

The Ford County grand jury convened on the third Monday of each month to listen to evidence of the latest crimes among the locals. On the docket for October 21 was the usual laundry list: a domestic dispute that devolved into a severe beating; Chuck Manley and his alleged stolen car; a Negro who fired a pistol at another, and though he missed, the bullet shattered the window of a rural white church, which added gravity to the incident and elevated it to a felony; a con man from Tupelo who had blanketed the county with bad checks; a white man and a black woman who were caught in the act of enthusiastically violating the state's antimiscegenation laws; and so on. The list totaled ten crimes, all felonies, and that was about average for a peaceful community. Last on the list was the matter of Pete Banning and his murder charge.

Miles Truitt had been the district attorney since his election seven years earlier. As the chief prosecutor, he handled the grand jury, which was little more than a rubber stamp for whatever he wanted. Truitt selected the eighteen people who served, picked which crimes needed to be pursued, called witnesses who gave evidence that favored only the prosecution, leaned heavily on the jury when the evidence seemed a bit shaky, and secured the indictments that were then served upon the defendants. After that, Truitt controlled the criminal trial docket and decided which cases would be tried first and last. Almost none actually went to trial. Instead they were settled with a deal, a plea bargain in which the defendant confessed to being guilty in return for as light a sentence as possible.

After seven years of routine prosecutions, Miles Truitt had been lulled into the mundane rut of putting away bootleggers, wife beaters, and car thieves. His jurisdiction covered the five counties of the Twenty-Second District, and the year before he had tried only four cases to verdicts. All other indictees had pled out. His job had lost its luster, primarily because there simply was not enough exciting crime in his corner of northern Mississippi.

But Pete Banning had broken the monotony, and in spectacular fashion. Every prosecutor dreams of the sensational murder trial, with a prominent (white) defendant, a well-known victim, a crowded courtroom, lots of press, and, of course, an outcome favorable to the prosecutor and all the fine citizens who voted for him. Truitt's dream was coming true, and he tried to control his eagerness to get on with the prosecution of Pete Banning.

The grand jury assembled in the courthouse in the same room used by trial juries. It was a cramped space hardly wide and long enough for a trial jury of twelve, with chairs wedged around a long narrow table. Of the eighteen, only sixteen were present, all white men. Mr. Jock Fedison from Karraway had called in sick, though it was widely believed he was really too busy in his cotton fields to be bothered with trifling judicial matters. Mr. Wade Burrell had not bothered to call at all and had been neither seen nor heard from in weeks. He was not a farmer but was rumored to be having trouble with his wife. She said flatly that the bum had gone off drunk and wasn't coming back.

Sixteen was a sufficient quorum, and Truitt called them to order. Sheriff Gridley was brought in as the first witness and sworn to tell the truth. Truitt began with Chuck Manley's case and Gridley laid out the facts. The vote was sixteen to zero in favor of an indictment for grand larceny, with no discussion. The bad-check artist was next, and the sheriff presented copies of the checks and affidavits from some of the aggrieved merchants. Sixteen to zero again, and the same for the pulpwood cutter who broke his wife's nose, among other injuries.

Justice was sailing right along until Truitt called up the miscegenation case. The two lovers had been caught in the act in the back of a pickup truck parked in an area known for such activities. Deputy Roy Lester had received an anonymous tip by phone that the two were planning such a rendezvous, and he got there first. The identity of the tipster was unknown. Lester hid in the darkness and was pleased to learn that the tip was accurate. The white man, who later admitted to having a wife and a kid, drove his truck to a spot very near Lester's hiding place, and commenced to partially undress while the black girl, aged eighteen and single, did likewise. The area being deserted at that moment, they decided to get down to business in the back of the truck.

Testifying before the grand jury, Lester claimed he watched calmly from behind some trees. In truth, though, he found the encounter quite erotic and was anything but calm. The grand jurors hung on every word, and Lester was discreet, even understated, with his descriptions. As the white man was reaching his climax, Lester jumped from his hiding place, brandished his weapon, and yelled, "Stop right there!" Which was probably the wrong command because who could really stop at that critical juncture? As they hurriedly dressed, Lester waited with the handcuffs. He walked them to his patrol car hidden down a dirt trail, and hauled them to jail. Along the way, the white man began crying and begging for mercy. His wife would certainly divorce him and he loved her so.

When he finished his testimony, the room was silent, as if the grand jurors were lost in their own imaginations and wanted more of the narrative. Finally, Mr. Phil Hobard, a science teacher at Clanton High and a transplanted Yankee from Ohio, asked, "If he's twenty-six years old and she's eighteen, then why is having relations against the law?"

Truitt was quick to take control of the discussion. "Because sex between a Caucasian and a Negro is against the law, and it's against the law because the state legislature made it illegal many years ago."

Mr. Hobard was not satisfied. He ignored the frowns from his colleagues and pressed on. "Is adultery against the law?"

A few of the men dropped their stares and glanced at

some papers on the table. Two even squirmed, but the zealots looked even fiercer as if to say, "If it's not it certainly should be."

Truitt replied, "No, it is not. At one time it was, but the authorities found it rather difficult to enforce."

Hobard said, "So, let me get this straight. In Mississippi today it's not against the law to have sex with a woman who's not your wife so long as she is of the same race. A different race, though, and you can be arrested and prosecuted, right?"

"That's what the code says," Truitt answered.

Hobard, who was evidently the only one on the grand jury with the courage to dig deeper, asked, "Don't we have better things to do than to prosecute two consenting adults who were evidently having a lot of fun, in bed, or in the back of a truck, or wherever?"

Truitt replied, "I didn't write the law, Mr. Hobard. And if you want to change it, then take up the matter with your state senator."

"Our state senator is an idiot."

"Well, perhaps, but that's outside the scope of our jurisdiction. Are we ready to vote on this indictment?" Truitt asked.

"No," Hobard said sharply. "You're trying to speed things along. Fine, but before we vote I'd like to ask my colleagues on this grand jury how many of them have ever had sex with a black woman. If you have, then there's no way you can vote to convict these two people."

An unseen vacuum sucked all the air out of the room. Several of the grand jurors turned pale. Several turned red with anger. One zealot blurted, "Never!" Others spoke:

"Come on, this is ridiculous."

"You're nuts. Come on, let's vote!"

"It's a crime and we have no choice."

Nix Gridley stood in a corner, looked at their faces, and managed to conceal a smile. Dunn Ludlow was a regular at the colored whorehouse in Lowtown. Milt Muncie had kept the same black mistress for at least as long as Nix had been sheriff. Neville Wray came from an old family of plantation owners who had been mixing and mingling for generations. Now, though, all fifteen were posturing in various awkward stages of piousness.

The state's antimiscegenation law was similar to others throughout the South and had little to do with sex between white men and black women; such relations were hardly frowned on. The purpose of the law was to protect the sanctity of white women and keep the Negroes away from them. But, as history had proven many times, if two people want to have sex they do not spend time thinking about code sections. The law prevented nothing, but was used occasionally as punishment after the fact.

Truitt waited until all comments ceased, then said, "We need to move along. Can we have a vote here. All in favor of these two being indicted, raise your hands." Fifteen hands went up, all but Hobard's.

An indictment did not require a unanimous vote. Two-thirds would suffice, and Truitt had never lost one. The grand jury soon dispatched with the other cases, and Truitt said, "And now we come to the matter of Mr. Pete Banning. First-degree murder. I'm sure you all know as much as I do. Sheriff Gridley."

Nix stepped over some boots and shoes and managed

to return to the seat at the end of the table. Half the men were smoking and Nix told Roy Lester to crack a window. Truitt lit a cigarette and blew smoke at the ceiling.

Nix began with the crime scene and passed around two photos of Dexter Bell lying dead in his office. He described the scene, recounted the testimony of Hop Purdue, and told the story of driving out to arrest Pete, who told him where to find the gun. Nix produced the gun and three slugs, and said there was no doubt they did the damage. The state police had sent a report. Since his arrest, Pete Banning had refused to discuss the case. He was represented by Mr. John Wilbanks. If indicted, it appeared as though there would be a trial in the near future.

"Thank you, Sheriff," Truitt said. "Any questions?"

A hand shot up and Milt Muncie asked loudly, "Do we have to vote on this? I mean, I know Pete Banning and I knew Dexter Bell, and I really don't want to get involved here."

"Neither do I," said Tyus Sutton. "I grew up with Pete Banning and I don't feel right sittin' in judgment."

"That's right," said Paul Carlin. "I'm not touchin' this case, and if you try to force me, then I'll just resign. We can resign from this grand jury, can't we? I'd rather resign than deal with it."

"No, you can't resign," Truitt said sharply as his rubber stamp unraveled.

"How about we abstain?" asked Joe Fisher. "It makes sense that we have the right to abstain in a case where we are personally acquainted with those involved, right? Show me where in the law it says we can't abstain when we want to."

All eyes were on Truitt, who, in matters of grand jury

procedure, usually made up the rules as he went along, as did all DAs around the state. He could not remember any reference to abstentions in these situations, though, truthfully, he had not looked at the code sections in years. He had become so accustomed to the rubber-stamp approach that he'd neglected the procedural intricacies.

As he stalled and tried to think of a response, his thoughts were not on the grand jury but on the trial jury. If the men of Ford County were so split, and so eager to avoid the case, how could he possibly convince twelve of them to return a verdict of guilty? The biggest case of his career was melting before his eyes.

He cleared his throat and said, "May I remind you that you took an oath to properly and without bias listen to the evidence and decide if in all probability the alleged crime was committed? You are not here to pass judgment on Mr. Banning's guilt or innocence; that's not your job. Your duty is to decide whether he should be charged with murder. The trial court will determine his fate. Now, Sheriff Gridley, do you have any doubt that Pete Banning murdered Dexter Bell?"

"None whatsoever."

"And that, gentlemen, is all that is sufficient for an indictment. Any further discussion?"

"I ain't votin'," Tyus Sutton said defiantly. "Pete had a reason for doin' what he did and I ain't passin' judgment."

"You're not passing judgment," Truitt snapped. "And if he had a reason and has a legal defense it will all come out at trial. Anybody else?" Truitt was angry and glared at his jurors as if ready for a brawl. He knew the law and they didn't.

Tyus Sutton was not easily intimidated. He stood and

pointed a finger across the table at Truitt. "I'm at a point in my life where I will not be yelled at. I'm leavin', and if you want to tattle to the judge and get me in trouble, I'll remember that the next time you run for office. And I know where to find a lawyer." He stomped to the door, opened it, walked through it, and slammed it behind him.

Down to fifteen. Two-thirds were required for an indictment, and at least three of those remaining didn't want to vote. Truitt was suddenly sweating and breathing heavily, and he was racking his brain as he strategized on the fly. He could dismiss them and present the Banning case next month. He could dismiss them and ask the judge for a new panel. He could press for a vote, hope for the best, and if he failed to get ten he could always present the case again in November. Or could he? Did double jeopardy apply to grand jury cases? He didn't think so, but what if he made the wrong move? He had never been in such a position.

He decided to press on as if he'd been in this situation many times. "Any more discussion?"

There were some anxious glances around the table but no one seemed eager to join Tyus Sutton. "Very well," Truitt continued. "All those in favor of indicting Pete Banning for the first-degree murder of the Reverend Dexter Bell raise your hands."

With no enthusiasm, five hands slowly went up. Five more eventually joined them. All others remained under the table.

"You can't abstain," Truitt snapped at Milt Muncie.

"And you can't make me vote," Muncie shot back angrily, ready to either throw a punch or take one.

Truitt looked around the room, counted quickly, and

announced, "I count ten. That's two-thirds, enough for an indictment. Thank you, Sheriff. We are dismissed."

As the days passed, Pete busied himself by improving conditions at the jail. The coffee was his first target and by the end of his third day the entire jail—prisoners, guards, and cops—were drinking Standard Coffee from New Orleans. Florry delivered it in five-pound bags, and during her second visit asked Nix what the colored prisoners were drinking. He replied that they were not served coffee, and this angered her. During the ensuing tirade, she threatened to withhold all coffee until it was offered to everyone.

At home, she snapped Marietta and Nineva into high gear and they began cooking and baking with a vengeance. Almost daily, Florry arrived at the jail with cakes, pies, cookies, brownies, and pots of beef stew, venison stew, collard greens, red beans and rice, and peas and corn bread. The quality of the jailhouse cuisine rose dramatically, for all inmates, with most of them eating far better than on the outside. When Amos gutted a fatted hog, the entire jail gorged on smoked spare ribs. Nix and his boys feasted as well, and saved a few bucks on lunch. He had never experienced the incarceration of a wealthy landowner who had plenty of acreage for growing food and the staff to prepare it.

After the first week, Pete convinced Nix to appoint him a jail trusty, which meant his cell was not locked during the day and he could roam as he pleased as long as he did not leave the building. Nix was somewhat sensitive to the potential rumors that Pete was getting special treatment, and at first didn't like the idea of using him as a trusty. But, every respectable jail had at least one trusty, and at the moment Nix had none. The last one, Homer Galax, served the county faithfully for six years and had three to go on his aggravated assault conviction when he ran off with a widow who was rumored to have some money. They had not been seen since, and Nix had neither the time, the interest, nor the energy to look for them.

Another rule, one that was evidently nonbinding as well, was that a trusty had to first be convicted of his crime and sentenced to serve his time in the county jail rather than the state pen. Nix brushed this aside as well, and Pete became the trusty. As such, he served the much improved meals to the other four white prisoners, and to the six or seven black ones on the back side of the jail. Since all prisoners soon knew where the food was originating, Pete was a popular trusty. He organized work details to clean up the jail, and he paid for a plumber to modernize the equipment in both restrooms. For a few bucks, he devised a venting system to clear the smoke-clogged air, and everyone, even the smokers, breathed easier. He and a black prisoner overhauled the furnace and the cells were almost toasty at night. He slept hard, napped frequently, exercised on the hour, and encouraged his new pals to do likewise. When he was bored he read novels, almost as fast as Florry could deliver them. There were no shelves in his tiny cell so she hauled them back to his study, where his library numbered in the thousands. He also read stacks of newspapers and magazines that she brought him.

Pete offered his reading materials to the others, but

there was little interest. He suspected they were either fully or partially illiterate. To pass the time, he played poker with Leon Colliver, the moonshiner across the hall. Leon was not particularly bright, but he was sharp as hell at cards and Pete, who had mastered all card games in the army, had his hands full. Cribbage was his favorite, and Florry brought his cribbage board. Leon had never heard of the game, but absorbed it with no effort and within an hour was up a nickel. They played for a penny a game. IOUs were acceptable and no one really expected to collect any money.

Late in the afternoon, after all chores were done and the jail was spiffier than ever, Pete would unlock Leon's cell and they would move their rickety chairs into the hallway, completely blocking it. The cribbage board was placed on a small square of plywood Pete kept in his cell. It was balanced on a wooden barrel that once held nails. The games began. Leon managed to keep a flask full of corn whiskey, distilled, of course, by his family, and at first Pete showed no interest. However, as the days dragged on and he began to accept the reality that he would be either executed or sent to prison forever, he said what the hell. In the heat of a tense cribbage game, Leon would glance around, up and down the hall, remove the flask from his front pants pocket, unscrew the top, take a swig, and hand it over. Pete would look around, take a drink, and hand it back. They weren't selfish; there simply wasn't enough to go around. And besides, every jail had a snitch, and Sheriff Gridley would frown on the drinking.

The two were hunched over the game board, talking

of nothing but the score, when the door opened and Nix entered the narrow hallway. He was holding some papers.

"Evenin', fellas," he said. They nodded politely. He handed the papers to Pete and said, "The grand jury met today and here's your indictment. First degree."

Pete sat straight and took the papers. "No real surprise, I guess."

"It was pretty cut-and-dried. Trial's set for January 6."

"They can't do it any sooner?"

"You'll have to talk to your lawyer about that." Nix turned around and left.

CHAPTER 9

A month after the death of her husband, Jackie Bell moved with her three children to her parents' home in Rome, Georgia. She took the few meager pieces of furniture that didn't belong to the parsonage. She took a flood of beautiful memories of the past five years in Clanton. She took the painful farewells of a congregation that had nurtured her and her family. And, she took her husband. In the chaos after his murder, she'd agreed to have him interred in Clanton because it was simpler. However, they were not from Mississippi, had no relatives there and no real roots, and she wanted to go home. Why leave him behind? Part of her day was a trip to the cemetery to lay flowers and have a good cry, a ritual she planned to continue forever, and she couldn't do that from Georgia. Dexter was from Rome too, so she had him reburied in a small cemetery behind a Methodist church.

They had married when he was in seminary in Atlanta. Their nomadic journey began upon graduation, when he was assigned the position of associate pastor of a church in Florida. From there they zigzagged across the South, having three children with no two born in the same place, and finally got assigned to Clanton a few months before Pearl Harbor.

Jackie loved Clanton until the day Dexter died, but not long after the funeral she realized she couldn't stay. The most immediate reason was that the church wanted the parsonage. A new minister would be assigned and his family would need a place to live. The church hierarchy generously offered to provide housing for a year at no cost, but she declined. Another reason, indeed the most significant one, was that the children were suffering. They adored their father and could not accept his absence. And in such a small town, they would be forever stigmatized as the kids whose father was gunned down under mysterious circumstances. To protect them, Jackie moved to a place they knew only as the home of their grandparents.

Once in Rome, and once the children returned to the ritual of school, she realized how temporary the arrangements were. Her parents' home was modest and certainly not large enough for three children. She collected $10,000 in life insurance and began looking for a place to rent. Much to the concern of her parents, she began skipping church. They were devout Methodists who never missed a Sunday. Indeed, few people in their part of the world missed church and those who did were talked about. Jackie was not in the mood to do much explaining, but she made it clear to her parents that she was struggling with her faith and needed time to reexamine her beliefs. Privately, she was asking the obvious question: Her husband, a devout servant and follower of Christ, was reading his Bible and preparing his sermon, at church, when he was murdered. Why couldn't God protect him, of all people? Upon deeper reflection, this often led to the more troubling question, one she never asked aloud: Is there really a God? The mere consideration of this as a passing thought frightened her, but she could not deny its existence.

Before long, she was being talked about, according to her mother, but she didn't care. Her suffering was at a level far above anything a few local gossips could inflict. Her kids were struggling in a new school. Day-to-day living was a challenge.

Two weeks after moving in with her parents, she moved out and into a rental home on the other side of town. It was owned by a lawyer named Errol McLeish, a thirty-nine-year-old bachelor she had known years earlier at Rome High School. McLeish and Dexter had been in the same class, though in different circles. Like everyone in the small town, McLeish knew the story behind Dexter's demise and wanted to help his young widow.

After weeks of barely eating enough to sustain herself, Jackie had finally lost the pounds she'd gained six years earlier with her last pregnancy. It was not a weight loss scheme she would recommend to anyone, and it was so far the only bright spot in an otherwise hideous nightmare, but she had to admit, as she looked at herself in the mirror, that she was skinnier than she had been in years. Now at thirty-eight, she weighed same as on her wedding day, and she admired her newly uncovered hip bones. Her eyes were puffy and red from all that weeping, and she vowed to finally stop it.

McLeish stopped by twice a week to check on things, and Jackie began using a bit of makeup and wearing tighter dresses when he was around. She felt guilty at first, with Dexter still warm in the ground, but she wasn't even flirting yet. She had no plans to pursue a romance for the remainder of her life, she told herself, but then educated bachelors were probably scarce in Rome. She was, after all, now single, and what was wrong with looking nice?

For his part, McLeish thought her cute but with serious baggage. The widowhood was one thing, and something that could be dealt with over time, but he wanted no part of a ready-made family. As an only child who had spent little time around children, he found the idea overwhelming. He led her along, though, quietly taking advantage of her pain and loneliness, and the noticing advanced to flirting.

His real interest was in her possible lawsuit. McLeish owned several properties, all heavily mortgaged, and he had debts from other deals, and after lawyering for ten years he realized it was not going to be that profitable. As soon as Jackie moved back to Rome, McLeish began setting his traps. He traveled to Clanton and snooped around the courthouse long enough to learn about the Bannings. He spent hours digging through the land records, and when confronted with the inevitable inquiry, he claimed to be a leasing agent for a "big oil and gas company." As he expected, this rippled through the courthouse and around the square and through the law offices and before long Clanton was seized by its first and only oil rush.

Lawyers and their assistants pored over dusty old plat books while keeping a sharp ear for gossip and a close eye on this stranger. McLeish, though, soon vanished as quietly as he had arrived, leaving the town to wonder when the oil boom was coming. He was back in Georgia, where he checked on the widow Bell with a polite regularity, never appearing eager or interested but always thoughtful, almost deferential, as though he understood her tangled world and wanted no part of it.

In 1946, Hollins had an enrollment of 375 students, all female. The college was a hundred years old and had a sterling reputation, especially among upper-class southern ladies. Stella Banning chose it because many of her mother's well-to-do friends in Memphis went there. Liza did not, primarily because her family couldn't afford it.

The girls wrapped themselves around Stella like a tight cocoon and shielded her from intrusions and negativity. They found it hard to believe that someone as pretty and sweet as Stella could be in the midst of such a tragic family drama, but it certainly wasn't her fault. No one at Hollins had ever been to Clanton. A few knew her father was a war hero, but to most girls that mattered little. No one had met her parents, though her brother, Joel, had made quite a splash during a recent visit for alumni weekend.

In the days and weeks after the killing, Stella was never alone. Her two roommates stayed with her during the nights when she often awoke with nightmares and bursts of emotion. During the days, she was surrounded by friends who kept her busy. Her professors understood

her fragility and she was allowed to miss class and postpone homework and papers. Counselors checked on her
daily. The president monitored her situation and was
briefed by a provost twice a week. It was soon known
that she would not be going home for the Thanksgiving
holiday. Her father had ordered her to stay away. This
prompted a flood of invitations, some from friends and
professors, some from girls she hardly knew.

Stella was touched almost to tears and thanked them
all, then left Roanoke on the train with Ginger Reed,
perhaps her best friend, and headed to Alexandria, Virginia, for a week of partying in D.C. She had been once
before, with Ginger, and she was enthralled by the big
city. Though she had not told her parents, nor Joel, she
planned to graduate as soon as possible and follow the
bright lights. New York was her first choice, D.C. her
second. New Orleans was a distant third. Long before the
killing, she knew she would never again live in Ford
County. After the killing, she wanted to stay as far away
from the place as possible.

Though her dreams had been interrupted, she was
still determined to become a writer. She adored the short
fiction of Eudora Welty and the bizarre and colorful
characters of Carson McCullers. Both were strong southern women writing in authentic voices about families,
conflicts, soil, and the tortured history of the South, and
they were successfully publishing in a time when men
dominated American fiction. Stella read them all, men
and women, and she was convinced there was room for
her. She might start with stories about her own family,
she often thought to herself, now more than before, but
knew that would not happen.

She would land a job with a magazine in New York, and live in a cheap apartment in Brooklyn with friends, and she would begin her first novel as soon as she settled in and inspiration hit. She was reasonably certain that her parents and her aunt Florry would support her if necessary. Being a Banning, she had been raised with the unspoken belief that the land would always remain in the family and provide support.

Enjoy life in New York, work for a magazine, start a novel, and do it all with the knowledge that there was money back home. The dream was exciting and it was real, until the murder. Now home was far away and nothing was certain.

Ginger's family lived in Old Town, in an eighteenth-century mansion on Duke Street. Her parents and younger sister had been briefed on the details of the Banning family nightmare and it was never mentioned. Stella was treated to a week of cocktail parties, long dinners, walks along the Potomac, and a string of clubs frequented by students where they smoked cigarettes, drank too much, listened to swing bands, and danced through the night.

On Thanksgiving Day, she called Aunt Florry, and for ten minutes they talked as if there was nothing out of order. Joel was the guest of a fraternity brother's family in Kentucky, and Florry reported that he was hunting non-stop and enjoying the break. They would be together for Christmas, she promised.

Later in the afternoon, Florry loaded up a small tub containing two roasted turkeys, with potatoes, carrots, beets, and turnips, along with a pan of dressing, giblet gravy, yeast rolls, and two pecan pies. She drove the feast to the jail, where she supervised the carving of the turkeys by her brother. The meal was for all prisoners, and for Mr. Tick Poley, the ancient part-time jailhouse guard who worked nights and most holidays so Nix and his men could take the day off. Florry and Pete dined alone in Nix's office, with his unlocked gun case in plain view. An unsecured door opened to the gravel lot. Tick was content to eat by himself in the jail's lobby as he guarded the front door.

Pete took a few bites, then lit a cigarette. In spite of his sister's efforts, he was still eating little and looked thin, and because he never went outside his skin was pale. As usual, she had commented on this. As usual, he ignored her. He did manage to perk up when she replayed the calls from Stella and Joel. In Florry's version, they were doing quite well and enjoying the season. Pete smiled as he smoked, his eyes drifting to the ceiling and beyond.

CHAPTER 10

By Thanksgiving, the cotton had been picked for the third and final time and Pete was pleased with the harvest. He watched the markets and reviewed the books each week when Buford came to the jail. He signed checks, paid bills, reviewed deposits and accounts, and directed the selling of his cotton through the Memphis exchange. He ordered the reopening of the colored school on his property, and approved pay raises for the teachers and the installation of new stoves for winter heat. Buford was itching to buy the latest model John Deere tractor. Many of the larger farmers now owned them, but Pete said not now, maybe later. Facing such an uncertain future, he was reluctant to spend a lot of money.

The price of cotton was also being watched closely by Errol McLeish. Georgia produced almost as much cotton as Mississippi, so he was no stranger to its economics. As the spot price on the Memphis Cotton Exchange rose, so did his commitment to the welfare of Jackie Bell.

. . . .

After weeks of discussion and research, John Wilbanks and his brother Russell finally decided the trial of Pete Banning should not take place in Clanton. They would seek a change of venue and try to have it moved somewhere far away.

Initially, they had been encouraged by the courthouse rumors that Miles Truitt came close to a mutiny with his grand jury. Evidently, their client had some friends and admirers who were sympathetic, and the vote to indict barely passed. Only rumors, of course, and since grand jury proceedings were not recorded in any fashion, and supposedly confidential, they could not be sure about what really happened. With time, though, they grew skeptical about the impartiality of a trial jury. They and their employees talked to countless friends around the county in an effort to judge public sentiment. They consulted a few of the other lawyers in town, and two retired judges, and a handful of former deputies, and a couple of old sheriffs. Since the jury would consist of white men only, and virtually all would claim membership in a church, they chatted with preachers they knew, men from all denominations. Their wives talked to other wives, at other churches, and at garden clubs and bridge clubs, and almost anywhere the conversation could be initiated without being awkward.

It became clear, at least to John Wilbanks, that sentiment was running strongly against his client. Time and again, he and his staff and his friends heard folks say something to the effect of "Whatever conflict those two had, it could have been settled without bloodshed." And the fact that Pete Banning was saying nothing to defend himself made it even easier to convict him. He would always be a legendary war hero, but no one had the right to kill without a good reason.

Under John's guidance, his firm conducted thorough research of every venue change case in American law, and he wrote a masterful fifty-page brief supporting his request. The endeavor took hours and hours, and eventually led to a heated discussion between John and Russell regarding the pressing matter of their fees. Since Pete's arrest, John had been reluctant to broach the matter. Now, though, it was inevitable.

Also eating up the clock was the not insignificant matter of mounting a defense. Pete had not minced words when John mentioned a claim of insanity, but there was nothing else to argue before the jury. Obviously, a perfectly normal human who shoots another three times at point-blank range cannot be in possession of his full mental faculties, but to build such a case required the defense to inform the court with a notice and a brief. John wrote one, along with supporting case law, and was prepared to file it at the same time he filed the motion for a change of venue.

Before doing so, however, he needed his client's approval. He haggled with Nix Gridley until he got his way, and late one afternoon a week before Christmas, Nix and Roy Lester left the jail with Pete Banning and drove him to the square. If he enjoyed his first breath of fresh air, he did not show it. He did not take in the festive decorations on the storefronts, did not seem at all interested in what the town was doing, did not even seem appreciative that he was being allowed to meet his lawyer in his office, as opposed to the jail. He sat low in the rear seat wearing a hat and bound by handcuffs, and stared at his feet during the brief ride. Nix parked behind the Wilbanks Building, and no one saw Pete enter with a cop at each elbow. Inside, the handcuffs were removed and he followed John Wilbanks to his office upstairs. Wilbanks's secretary served Nix and Roy black coffee with a pastry in the downstairs foyer.

Russell sat in one chair, John the other, with Pete on a leather sofa across a coffee table. They attempted small talk, but it was awkward. How do you chat about the weather and the holidays with a man who's sitting in jail accused of murder?

"How are things at the jail?" John asked.

"Fine," Pete said, stone-faced. "I've seen worse."

"I hear you're pretty much running things over there."

A slight grin, nothing more. "Nix made me a trusty, so I'm not always confined."

Russell smiled and said, "I hear the prisoners are getting fat, thanks to Florry."

"The food has improved," Pete said as he reached for a cigarette.

John and Russell exchanged glances. Russell got busy lighting his own cigarette, leaving John alone with the unpleasant business. He cleared his throat and said, "Yes, well, look, Pete, we've never had a conversation about attorneys' fees. Our firm is putting in a lot of hours. The trial is three weeks away and between now and then we'll work on little else. We need to get paid, Pete."

Pete shrugged and asked, "Have you ever sent me a bill that didn't get paid?"

"No, but then you've never been charged with murder."

"How much are you talking about?"

"We need $5,000, Pete, and that's on the low side."

He filled his lungs, exhaled a cloud, looked at the ceiling. "I'd hate to see the high side. Why is it so expensive?"

Russell decided to enter the ring. "Hours, Pete, hours and hours. Time is all we have to sell, and we're not making money here. Your family's been with this firm forever, we're old friends, and we are here to protect you. But we have office expenses and bills to pay too."

Pete flicked his ashes into a tray and took a quick puff. He wasn't angry or surprised. His expressions conveyed nothing. Finally, he said, "Okay, I'll see what I can do."

Well, what you can do is write us a damned check, John wanted to say, but let it go. The issue had been addressed and Pete would not forget it. They would discuss it later.

Russell reached for some papers and said, "We have some stuff for you to read, Pete. They're preliminary motions for your trial, and before we file them you need to read them and sign off."

Pete took the papers, and after glancing at them said, "There's a lot of stuff here. Why don't you just summarize, preferably in layman's terms?"

John smiled and nodded and took the lead. "Sure, Pete. The first motion is a request to the court to change the venue of the trial, move it somewhere else, as far away as possible. We've come to believe that public sentiment is fairly strong against you, and we know it will be difficult to find sympathetic jurors."

"Where do you want the trial?"

"The judge has complete discretion in that matter, according to the case law. Knowing Judge Oswalt, he'll want to retain control over the trial without having to travel too far. So, if he grants our motion, which, by the way, Pete, is a long shot on a good day, he'll probably keep it somewhere in this judicial district. We'll argue to the contrary, but, frankly, any place will be better than here."

"And why do you believe that?"

"Because Dexter Bell was a popular preacher with a large congregation, and there are eight other Methodist churches in this county. In numbers, it's the second-largest denomination behind the Baptists, which present another problem. Baptists and Methodists are first cousins, Pete, and they often stick together on tough issues. Politics, whiskey, school boards. You can always count on those two clans to march to the same drum."

"I know that. But I'm a Methodist too."

"Right, and you have some supporters, old friends and such. But most people view you as a cold-blooded murderer. I'm not sure you realize that. The people in this county think of Pete Banning as a war hero who, for reasons known only to himself, walked into the church and murdered an unarmed preacher."

Russell added for emphasis, "Pete, you don't have a dog's chance in hell."

Pete shrugged as if that was okay with him. He did what he had to do; damn the consequences. He took a long drag as smoke swirled around the room. "What makes you think things will be different in another county?"

John asked, "Do you know the preachers at the Methodist churches in Polk, Tyler, or Milburn Counties? Of course not. Those counties are right next door yet we know very few folks who live there. They will know neither you nor Dexter Bell personally."

Russell said, "We're trying to avoid the personal relationships, Pete. I'm sure a lot of those folks have read the newspapers, but they've never met you or Dexter Bell. Without the personal knowledge, we stand a better chance of getting by the raw feelings and planting doubt."

"Doubt? Tell me about this doubt," Pete said, gently surprised.

"We'll get to that in a minute," John said. "Do you agree that we need to ask for a change of venue?"

"No. If I have to do it, I want my trial to be right here."

"Oh, you have to, Pete. The only way to avoid a trial is to plead guilty."

"Are you asking me to plead guilty?"

"No."

"Good, because I'm not, and I will not ask for a change of venue. This is my home, always has been, same for my ancestors, and if the people of Ford County want to convict me, then it'll happen across the street in the courthouse."

John and Russell looked at each other in frustration. Pete laid the papers on the coffee table without having read the first word. He lit another cigarette, casually crossed his legs as if he had all the time in the world, and looked at John as if to say, "What's next?"

John took his copy of the brief and dropped it loudly

on the coffee table. "Well, there goes a month of fine legal research and writing."

Pete replied, "And I guess I'm supposed to pay for that. If you'd asked me up front I could've saved you all that work. No wonder your fees are so high."

John seethed as Russell fumed and Pete puffed away. After a pause, Pete continued, "Look, boys, I don't mind paying legal fees, especially since I'm in a jam like this, but $5,000? I mean, I farm almost a thousand acres that require backbreaking work for eight months by thirty field hands, and if I'm lucky and the weather cooperates and the spot price stays high and the fertilizer works and the boll weevils stay away and enough labor shows up to pick, then every three or four years I get a decent crop and maybe I'll clear, after all bills, $20,000. Half goes to Florry. That leaves me with ten and you want half of that."

"Your numbers are low," John said without hesitation. His family raised more cotton than the Bannings. "Our cousin had a very good crop and so did you."

Russell said, "If you object to our fees, Pete, you can always hire someone else. There are other lawyers in town. We're just doing our best to protect you."

"Come on, boys," Pete said. "You've always taken care of me and my family. I have no gripe with what you want, but it may take some time to round up the money."

Both John and Russell strongly suspected that Pete could write the check with ease, but he was, after all, a farmer, and as a breed they enjoyed squeezing a nickel. And the lawyers were sympathetic too, because in all likelihood he would never farm again and would either die soon in the electric chair or much later in some awful prison hospital. His future was worse than bleak, and they couldn't blame him for trying to save all the money possible.

A secretary tapped on the door and entered with an elegant coffee service. She filled three porcelain cups and offered cream and sugar. Pete deliberately mixed his blend, took a sip, and stubbed out a cigarette.

When she was gone, John said, "Okay, moving right along. We have another motion we need to discuss. Our only possible defense is one based on temporary insanity. If you're found not guilty, and that's highly unlikely, it will be because we can convince the jury that you were not thinking rationally when you pulled the trigger."

"I've already told you that I don't want that."

"And I heard you, Pete, but it's not just about what you want. It's more of what's available to us at trial. Insanity is all we have. Period. Take away insanity, and all we can do is sit in the courtroom and listen like spectators while the prosecutor strings you up. Is that what you want?"

Pete shrugged as if he didn't care and said, "Do what you gotta do, but I will not pretend to be insane."

Russell said, "We've found a psychiatrist in Memphis who's willing to examine you and testify on your behalf at trial. He's well-known and is effective in these situations."

"Well, he must be a first-class kook if he'll say I'm crazy," Pete said with a smile, as if somewhat humorous. Neither lawyer returned the smile. John sipped his coffee while Russell lit another cigarette. The air was not only thick with smoke but heavy with tension. The lawyers were doing their best but their client didn't seem to appreciate either their work or his own predicament.

John cleared his throat again and shifted his weight. "So, to recap where we are, Pete, we have no defense, no excuses, no explanation for what happened, and no chance of moving the trial to a less hostile environment. And you're okay with all this?"

Pete shrugged and said nothing.

John began pinching his forehead as if in pain. A full moment passed without a sound. Finally, Russell said, "There is one other matter, Pete, something you should be aware of. We've done some digging into Dexter Bell's background and found a matter of interest. Eight years ago, when he was pastoring a church in a small town in Louisiana, there was a problem. The church had a young secretary, twenty years old and newly married, and there appears to have been some type of relationship between the girl and her pastor. Lots of rumors and not many facts, but Bell was soon reassigned. The secretary and her husband moved to Texas."

John added, "Obviously, we haven't dug that deep, and it may be impossible to prove anything of value. It appears as though the matter was kept under tight wraps."

"Can that come into court here?" Pete asked.

"Not without some additional evidence. Do you want us to pursue it?"

"No, not on my behalf. It's not to be mentioned in my trial."

"May I ask why not, Pete?" John asked with a frown. "You're giving us absolutely nothing to work with here." Russell rolled his eyes again and seemed ready to leave the room.

"I said no," Pete repeated. "And don't bring it up again."

Proof that Dexter Bell was a philanderer would likely be excluded at trial, but it would certainly help explain the motive for his murder. If he had a wandering eye, and if it caught the attention of Liza Banning when she was mourning the loss of her husband, then the great mystery would be solved. But it was now apparent that Pete had no interest in solving it. He would take his secrets to his grave.

John said, "Well, Pete, it's going to be a very short trial. We have no defense, no witnesses to call, nothing to argue in front of the jury. We should be in and out in a day or so."

"If that long," Russell said.

"So be it," Pete said.

CHAPTER 11

Three days before Christmas, Joel stepped onto a train at Union Station in downtown Nashville, and waiting for him in a dining car was his lovely and fashionable sister. Stella was now nineteen, only eighteen months younger than her brother, but during the past semester she had grown from a late-blooming teenager into a beautiful young woman. She seemed taller, and her skinny figure had developed some pleasant curves, which he couldn't help but notice. She looked older, fuller, and wiser, and when she lit a cigarette she reminded Joel of an actress straight from the big screen.

"When did you start smoking?" he asked. The train was rolling out of the city and heading south. They were at a dining table with cups of coffee in front of them. Waiters hustled about taking lunch orders.

"I've been sneaking since I was sixteen," she said. "Same as you. At college, most girls come out into the open when they turn twenty, though it's still frowned upon. I was going to quit, and then Pete got trigger-happy. Now I'm smoking more than ever to settle my nerves."

"You should quit."

"What about you?"

"I need to quit too. It's great to see you, sis. Let's not begin our little trip talking about Pete."

"Begin? I've been on this train for six hours. We left Roanoke at five this morning."

They ordered lunch and iced tea and talked for an hour about college life: courses, favorite professors, friends, plans for the future, and the challenge of going about their days as if things were normal while having both parents locked away. When they caught themselves dwelling on family, they immediately changed the subject and talked about the upcoming year. Joel had been accepted to law school at Vanderbilt but wanted a change of scenery. He had also been accepted at Ole Miss, but that was only an hour from Clanton and, given the circumstances, seemed far too close to home.

Stella was halfway through her sophomore year and eager to move on. She loved Hollins but longed for the anonymity of a big city. At college, everyone knew her and now knew about her father. She wanted strangers in her life, people who didn't know or care where she was from. On the romantic front, there wasn't much activity. Over the Thanksgiving break she'd met a boy in D.C. and they had gone dancing twice and to the movies once. He was a student at Georgetown, had a nice family and all, appeared to be well groomed and mannered, and he was writing her letters, but there was really no spark. She'd string him along for another month or so, then break his heart. Joel reported even more tepid progress. A few dates here and there but none worth talking about. He claimed he really wasn't in the market, what with three years of law school on the horizon. He had always vowed to remain single until his thirtieth birthday.

Try as they might, they could not stay off the most obvious subject. Joel told her for the first time that their father had transferred his land to them as joint owners three weeks before the killing. Pete might have thought he was clever but it was a really stupid move. The prosecution would use the deed as evidence that he was carefully planning his crime and taking steps to protect his property. Joel was spending time in the law school library, and the more he researched the bleaker the future looked. According to a friend whose father was a lawyer, there was an excellent chance that Jackie Bell would sue Pete Banning in a wrongful death action. This had driven Joel to spend hours researching lawsuits. He was also digging into the unpleasant subject of fraudulent transfers. The deed from their father to them could be attacked by lawyers working for the Bells. The law was uniform throughout the country that a person facing civil damages could not hide or move property around to dodge valid claims.

However, Joel had faith in the Wilbanks firm, not only for its legal muscle, but also for its political finesse. He could tell Stella was alarmed by the thought of losing their land. She had already been consumed with the horror of losing her father. She had no idea what would happen to her mother. And now this—the possibility of losing everything. At one point her eyes watered and she fought back tears. Joel managed to soothe things somewhat by explaining that any potential lawsuit could always be settled on favorable terms. Besides, they had far more urgent matters. Their father would be put on trial in two weeks. And, pursuant to his commands, his children would not be allowed anywhere near the courthouse.

When they finished lunch, they moved to a private cabin and closed the door. They were in Mississippi now, stopping at towns like Corinth and Ripley. Stella nodded off and slept for an hour.

They were going home because their father had finally summoned them. By letter, he had outlined the parameters of their Christmas visit: home on December 22, no more than three nights in the house, stay away from downtown, don't even think about going to church, limit contact with friends, do not discuss family business with anyone, spend time with Florry, and he would arrange some private time with them, but not much.

Florry had written too, as always, and promised some plans of her own, with a big surprise in the works. She was waiting at the station in Clanton when they arrived at dusk. In the spirit of the season, she was garbed in a bright green dress that flowed around her much like a tent designed to conceal her girth. It fell in ripples to her ankles and shimmered in the dim platform lights. On her head was a red fedora that only a circus clown would contemplate, and around her neck was an assemblage of gaudy trinkets that rattled when she moved. When she saw Stella she bellowed and burst forward, practically tackling her with a bear hug. Joel glanced around during the assault, and by the time Florry grabbed him her eyes were moist. Stella was crying. The three embraced as other passengers hurried by.

The kids were home. The family was sinking. They clutched each other for support. What in God's name had Pete done to them?

Joel carried the luggage as the women walked arm in arm, both talking excitedly at the same time. They crawled into the rear seat of Florry's 1939 Lincoln, still talking, with Florry breaking long enough to tell Joel he was driving. And that was fine with him. He'd ridden with his aunt enough to know the dangers. He punched the gas and they sped away from Clanton, exceeding every posted limit.

As they roared down Highway 18, with no traffic in sight, Florry informed them that they would be staying with her in the pink cottage and not in their home. The pink cottage was covered with Christmas decorations, warmed by a roaring fire, and smelled of Marietta's cooking. Their home was practically deserted, cold and dark and without spirit and not a sign of the season anywhere, and besides Nineva was depressed and did nothing but mope around the house talking to herself and crying, at least according to Marietta.

When Joel turned in to their drive, the talking stopped as they approached the only home he and Stella had ever known. It was indeed dark, lifeless, as if the people who had lived there were all dead and the place had been abandoned. He stopped the car with its lights shining in the front windows. He turned off the ignition and for a moment nothing was said.

"Let's not go in," Florry mumbled.

Joel said, "One year ago, we were all there, all together for Christmas. Dad was home from the war. Mom was happy and beautiful and buzzing around the house, so excited to have her family together. Remember the dinner we had on Christmas Eve?"

Stella said softly, "Yes, the house was packed with guests, including Dexter and Jackie Bell."

"What the hell has happened to us?"

Because there was no answer, no one tried to offer one. Pete's truck was parked next to the house and next to it was the family sedan, a Pontiac bought before the war. The vehicles were where they were supposed to be, as if those who owned them were inside the house and tucking in for the night, as if all was well around the Banning home.

Florry said, "Okay, enough of this. We'll not spend our time wallowing in misery. Start the car and let's go. Marietta has a pot of chili on the stove and she's baking a caramel fudge pie."

Joel backed away from the house and followed a gravel road that swung wide around the barns and sheds of the Banning compound. They passed the small white house where Nineva and Amos had lived for decades. A light was on, and Mack, Pete's dog, watched them from the front porch.

"How's Nineva?" Stella asked.

"Cranky as always," Florry said. Her feuds with Pete's housekeeper had been settled years earlier when both women decided to simply ignore each other. "Actually, she's worried, same as everybody else. No one knows what's in the future."

"Who's not worried?" Stella mumbled aloud.

They were moving slowly along a dark stretch of road with endless fields around them. Joel suddenly stopped and turned off the ignition and the lights. Without turning around, he said, "Okay, Aunt Florry, here we are in the middle of nowhere with no one to eavesdrop on our conversation. Just the three of us, alone and together for the first time. You always know more than anyone else, so let's have it. Why did Pete kill Dexter Bell? There must be a good reason and you know it."

She didn't respond for a long time, and the longer she waited the more Stella and Joel anticipated her words. Finally, she would reveal the great mystery and make sense of the insanity. Instead, she said, "As God is my witness, I don't know. I just don't know, and I'm not sure we'll ever understand it. Your father is perfectly capable of taking his secrets to his grave."

"Was Dad angry with Dexter, any kind of disagreement or feud over a church matter?"

"Not to my knowledge."

"Did they have business dealings of any kind? I know it's a ridiculous question but stick with me, okay? I'm trying to eliminate possible conflicts."

Florry said, "Dexter was a preacher. I'm not aware of any business dealings."

"So that brings us to the obvious, doesn't it? Our mother was the only connection between Dad and Dexter Bell. I remember those first days when we thought he was dead. The house was crawling with people, so many people that I had to get out and go for long walks around the farm. And I remember Dexter came over a lot to sit with Mom. They would pray and read the Bible and sometimes I sat with them. It was horrible and we were all in shock, but I remember Dexter as being calm and reassuring. Don't you, Stella?"

"Oh, yes, he was wonderful. He was there all the

time. His wife came with him occasionally, but she was never that comforting. After the initial shock of it all, the crowds thinned out and we sort of got back into our routines."

Florry said, "The country was at war. Men were dying everywhere. We managed to move on, still hopeful, still praying a lot, but we got about our business. Goodness, we had to keep living."

"The question is how long did Dexter hang around, Florry?" Joel asked. "That's what I want to know."

"I have no idea, Joel, and I'm not sure I appreciate your tone. It's accusatory and I've done nothing wrong, nor am I hiding anything."

"We just want answers," he said.

"And maybe there are none. Life is full of mysteries and we're not guaranteed the answers. I was never suspicious of anything between Dexter Bell and your mother. In fact, the mere suggestion is shocking to me. I've never heard a peep from Marietta or Nineva or anyone for that matter, not the slightest hint that things were going on." There was a long pause as Florry caught her breath.

Stella said, "Please start the car, Joel, I'm getting cold."

He made no move toward the ignition.

Florry said, "At the same time, I have always kept my distance from Liza, and certainly from Nineva. I can't imagine Pete living in the same house with both of those women, but then that was never any of my business."

To which Joel wanted to reply something along the lines that the house was actually quite pleasant, before the war anyway, back when life was normal. And Stella thought, though she would never say, that it had always seemed to be Aunt Florry who caused trouble in the family. But then, too, it had been before the war, back when both of her parents were more or less in one piece.

Joel pinched the bridge of his nose and said, "I'm not accusing my mother of anything, you understand? I certainly have no proof, but the circumstances demand these questions."

Stella said, "You sound like such a lawyer."

Florry snapped, "Good heavens, Joel, it's thirty degrees outside and I'm freezing. Let's go."

At noon on Christmas Eve, as Nineva was buzzing around their kitchen preparing at least five dishes at once and Joel and Stella were trying their best to pester her and make her laugh, the phone rang. Joel grabbed it first and said hello to Nix Gridley. The call was expected. When he hung up he informed Stella that their father would be home in about an hour. Then he left to fetch Aunt Florry.

Ten weeks in jail would weather any man, but Pete Banning seemed to be aging faster than most. His hair was grayer and the wrinkles were spreading at the corners of his eyes. In spite of Florry's takeover of the jailhouse kitchen, he somehow managed to look even thinner. Of course, for some prisoners ten weeks meant time closer to freedom. For men like Pete, though, there would be no freedom; thus no hope, no reason to keep the spirit alive. One way or another, he would die as a captive, away from home. For Pete Banning, death had certain advantages. One was physical; he would live the rest of his life in pain, at times severe pain, and that was not a pleasant prospect. One was mental; he would always carry images of indescribable human suffering, and at times these burdens drove him to the brink of madness. Almost every hour, a battle raged as he tried gamely to purge them from his mind. Only rarely was he successful.

As Pete looked at the future, he figured this was to be his last Christmas. He convinced Nix of that and finagled a quick visit to the farm. He had not seen his children in months and might not see them for a long time. Nix was sympathetic to a point, but he was also unable to erase the thoughts of the Bell children never seeing their father again. As the weeks dragged on and the trial approached, Nix was even more convinced that sentiments in the county were running strongly against Pete Banning. The hard-won admiration he had enjoyed only the year before had vanished in a matter of seconds. His trial wouldn't take long either.

At any rate, Nix agreed to a brief visit—one hour max. No other prisoner was allowed such leniency and Pete was to tell no one inside the jail where he was going. Dressed in street clothes, he rode in the front seat with Nix, as usual saying nothing and staring at the empty fields. When they stopped behind his truck, Nix at first insisted on waiting in his car, but Pete would have none of it. The weather was frigid and there was hot coffee inside.

For half an hour Pete sat at the kitchen table, with Joel on one side and Stella and Florry on the other. Nineva stood by the stove, drying dishes and all but taking part in the conversation. Pete was relaxed, delighted to see his children, and asked a hundred questions about school and their plans.

Sheriff Gridley sat alone in the living room, sipping

coffee and flipping through a farmer's magazine with one eye on the clock. It was, after all, Christmas Eve, and he had some shopping to do.

Pete and the children moved from the kitchen to his small office, where he closed the door for privacy. He and Stella sat side by side on a small sofa and Joel pulled a wooden chair close. As he began to talk about his trial, Stella was already fighting tears. He had no defense to offer and expected to be convicted with little effort. The unknown was whether the jury would recommend death or life in prison. Either was okay with him. He had accepted his fate and would face his punishment.

Stella cried harder, but Joel had questions. However, Pete cautioned them that the one question they could never ask was why he did it. He had good reasons, but they were between him and Dexter Bell. More than once he apologized for the shame, embarrassment, and hardship he was causing them, for the irrevocable damage to their good name. He asked for their forgiveness, but they were not ready for that. Until he could make some sense out of what was happening, they could not contemplate mercy. He was their father. Who were they to forgive him? And why forgive when the sinner had yet to come clean with his motives? It was confusing and terribly emotional, and finally even Pete shed a tear or two.

When an hour had passed, Nix knocked on the door and ended the little reunion. Pete followed him to the patrol car for the ride back to jail.

For the sake of her children, Jackie Bell took them to church for the Christmas Eve service. They sat with their grandparents, who smiled with pride at the lovely family, minus the father. Jackie sat at the far end of the pew, and two rows behind her sat Errol McLeish, a rather wayward Methodist himself and occasional attendee of the church. She had mentioned that she was taking the kids to the service, and Errol just happened to drop by too. He was not stalking her at all, just keeping tabs from a distance. She was terribly wounded, and rightfully so, and he was smart enough to respect her mourning. It would pass eventually.

After church, Jackie and the kids went to her parents' home for a long Christmas dinner, then stories by the fire. Each child unwrapped a gift and Jackie took pictures with her Kodak. It was late when they returned to their little duplex. She put them to bed and killed an hour by the tree, sipping hot cocoa, listening to carols on the phonograph, and wrestling with her emotions. Dexter should be there, quietly assembling toys as they shared a special moment. How could she be a widow at the age of thirty-eight? And, more urgently, how was she supposed to provide for those three precious children sleeping just down the hallway?

For at least the past ten years, she had often doubted if the marriage would last. Dexter loved ladies and had an eye that was always roving. He used his good looks and charisma, as well as his pastoral duties, to manipulate the younger women of his churches. He had never been caught outright, and certainly had never confessed, but he had left a trail of suspicions. Clanton was his fourth church assignment, second as senior pastor, and Jackie had been watching closer than ever. Because she had no hard evidence, she had yet to confront him, but that day would come. Or would it? Would she ever have the courage to blow up the family and drag it through a terrible divorce? She had always known that she would be blamed. Would it be easier to suffer in silence to protect the children, and to protect his career? In her most private moments, she had grieved over these conflicts.

And now they were moot. She was single, without the stigma of a divorce. Her children were scarred, but the country was emerging from a war in which half a million American men were killed. Families everywhere were scarred, wounded, trying to cope, and picking up the pieces.

It appeared as though Dexter finally messed with the wrong woman, though Jackie had not suspected Liza Banning. She was certainly pretty enough, and vulnerable. Jackie had been watching and had seen nothing out of line, but with a husband prone to cheat every pretty woman was a potential target.

Jackie wiped a tear as she ached for her husband. She would always love him, and her deep love made the suspicions even more painful. She hated it, and hated him for it, and at times she hated herself for not being strong enough to walk out. But those days were gone, weren't they? Never again would she watch Dexter drive away to visit the sick and wonder where he was really going. Never again would she be suspicious as he counseled behind a locked office door. Never again would she notice the round backside of a young lady in church and wonder if Dexter was admiring it too.

The tears turned to sobs and she couldn't stop. Was she crying out of grief, loss, anger, or relief? She didn't know and couldn't make sense of it. The album finished and she walked to the kitchen for something else to drink. On the counter was a tall, layered cake with red icing, a Christmas concoction Errol McLeish had dropped off for the kids. She cut a slice, poured a glass of milk, and returned to the den.

He was such a thoughtful man.

CHAPTER 12

After a large Christmas brunch of bacon, omelets, and buttermilk biscuits, they said good-bye to Marietta in the pink cottage, and to all the birds, cats, and dogs, and they loaded themselves and their luggage into the car for a road trip. Joel was the chauffeur again, evidently a permanent position because there was no offer of help from either of the two ladies in the rear seat. Both talked nonstop, cackling away and amusing their driver. WHBQ out of Memphis ran nothing but Christmas carols, but to hear them Joel was forced to crank up the radio. The girls complained about the volume. He complained about their constant racket. Everyone laughed and the road trip was off to a great start. Leaving Ford County behind was a relief.

Three hours later, they arrived at the imposing gate of the Mississippi State Hospital at Whitfield, and the mood in the car changed dramatically. Liza had been sent there seven months earlier and there had been almost no news about her treatment. They had written letters but received no replies. They knew that Pete had spoken to her doctors, but, of course, he had passed along nothing from their conversations. Florry, Joel, and Stella were assuming Liza knew about the murder of Dexter Bell, but they wouldn't know for sure until they met with her doctors. It was entirely possible they were keeping such dreadful news away from her as protection. Again, Pete had told them nothing.

A uniformed guard had some paperwork, then some directions, and the gate eventually swung open. Whitfield was the state's only psychiatric hospital, and it was an expansive collection of buildings spread over thousands of acres. It was called a campus, looked more like a grand old estate, and was surrounded by fields, woods, and forests. Over three thousand patients lived there, along with five hundred employees. It was segregated, with separate facilities for whites and blacks. Joel drove past a post office, a tuberculosis hospital, a bakery, a lake, a golf course, and the wing where they sent the alcoholics. With a lot of help from the backseat, he eventually found the building where his mother was housed and parked nearby.

For a moment, they sat in the idle car and stared at the imposing structure. Stella asked, "Do we have any clue as to her diagnosis? Is it depression, or schizophrenia, or a nervous breakdown? Is she suicidal? Does she hear voices? Or did Pete just want her out of the house?"

Florry was shaking her head. "I don't really know. She spiraled quickly and Pete told me to stay away from the house. We've had these conversations."

Trouble began just inside the front door when a surly

clerk demanded to know if they had made an appointment. Yes, Florry explained, she had called two days earlier and spoken with a Mrs. Fortenberry, an administrator in building 41, where they were now standing. The clerk said Mrs. Fortenberry had the day off because it was, after all, Christmas Day. Florry replied that she knew exactly what day it was, and the two young people with her were the children of Liza Banning and they wanted to see their mother on Christmas.

The clerk disappeared for a long time. When she returned, she brought with her a gentleman who introduced himself as Dr. Hilsabeck. At his reluctant invitation, they followed him down the hall to a small office with only two chairs for visitors. Joel stood by the door. In spite of his white lab coat, Hilsabeck didn't look like a doctor, not that they'd had much experience with psychiatrists. He had a slick head, squeaky voice, and shifty eyes, and he did not inspire confidence. Once situated, he arranged a file in the center of his desk and began with "I'm afraid there is a problem." He spoke with an obnoxious northern accent, clearly condescending. And the name Hilsabeck was certainly not from anywhere in the South.

"What kind of problem?" Florry demanded. She had already determined that she didn't like building 41 and the people who ran it.

Hilsabeck lifted his eyebrows but not his eyes, as if he preferred to avoid direct contact. "I cannot discuss this patient with you. Her guardian, Mr. Pete Banning, has instructed me and the other doctors to engage in no consultations with anyone but him."

"She's my mother!" Joel said angrily. "And I want to know how she's doing."

Hilsabeck did not react to the anger, but simply lifted a sheet of paper as if it were the Gospel. "This is the court order from Ford County, signed by the judge up there." He looked at the order when he spoke, again preferring to avoid eye contact. "The commitment order, and it names Pete Banning as the guardian, Liza Banning as his ward, and it quite clearly states that in all matters regarding her treatment we, her doctors, are to have discussions with no one but him. All visits from family and friends must first be approved by Pete Banning. Indeed, Mr. Banning phoned yesterday afternoon. I spoke with him for a few minutes, and he reminded me that he had approved no visits with his ward. I'm sorry, but there's nothing I can do."

The three looked at each other in disbelief. They had met with Pete for an hour the day before in the Banning home. Joel and Stella had asked about their mother, got no response from their father, and had not mentioned this visit.

Joel glared at Florry and asked, "Did you tell him we were coming?"

"I did not. Did you?"

"No. We had talked about it and decided to keep it quiet."

Hilsabeck closed the file and said, "I'm really sorry. It's out of my control."

Stella buried her face in her hands and began weeping. Florry patted her knee and snarled at Hilsabeck, "They haven't seen their mother in seven months. They're worried sick about her."

"I'm very sorry."

Joel asked, "Can you at least tell us how she's doing? Are you decent enough for that?"

Hilsabeck stood with his file and replied, "I will not be insulted. Ms. Banning is doing better. That's all I can say right now. Now, if you'll excuse me." He stepped around his desk, stepped over Joel's feet, and squeezed through the door.

Stella wiped her cheeks with the back of a hand and took a deep breath. Florry watched her and held her hand. Under his breath, Joel hissed, "That son of a bitch."

"Which one?" Florry asked.

"Your brother. He knew we were coming down here."

"Why would he do this?" Stella asked.

When no one replied they let the question hang in the air for a long time. Why? Because he was hiding something? Maybe Liza was not mentally unbalanced and got herself shipped off because her husband was angry with her? That was not unheard of. Florry had a childhood friend who was put away while suffering through a bad case of menopause.

Or perhaps Liza was really sick. She had suffered a severe breakdown with the news that Pete was missing and presumed dead and perhaps she had never fully recovered. But why would he shield her from her own children?

Or was Pete the crazy one? Perhaps he was scarred from the war and finally cracked up when he killed Dexter Bell. And it was futile to try and understand his actions.

A slight knock on the door startled them. They

stepped out of the office and were met by two unarmed security guards in uniform. One smiled and sort of waved down the hall. They were followed out of the building and the guards watched them drive away.

As they passed the lake, Joel noticed a small park with benches and a gazebo. He turned and drove in that direction. Without a word, he stopped the car, got out and closed the door, lit a cigarette, and walked to a picnic table under a leafless oak. He gazed at the still waters and at the row of buildings on the other side. Stella was soon at his side, asking for a cigarette. They leaned on the table, smoking, saying nothing. Florry arrived a moment later, and the three braved the cold and thought about their next move.

Joel said, "We should go back to Clanton, go to the jail, have a showdown with him, and demand that he allow us to see Mom."

"And you think that'll work?" Florry replied.

"Maybe, maybe not. I don't know."

"Don't be ridiculous," Stella said. "He's always one step ahead of us. Somehow he knew we were coming. And here we are—staring at a lake instead of visiting with Mom. I'm not going back to Clanton right now."

"Neither am I," said Florry. "We have reservations in the French Quarter, and that's where I'm going. It's my car."

"But you have no license," Joel said.

"That's never stopped me before. I've actually driven to New Orleans on one occasion. Down and back without a hitch."

Stella said, "Come on, we deserve some fun."

. . .

Five hours later, Joel turned off Canal Street and onto Royal. The French Quarter was alive with the season and its narrow sidewalks were packed with locals and tourists hustling to dinner and clubs. Buildings and streetlamps were adorned with festive lighting. At the corner of Iberville, Joel stopped in front of the majestic Hotel Monteleone, the grandest hotel in the Quarter. A bellhop took their bags as a valet disappeared with Florry's car. They strolled into the elegant lobby and entered another world.

Three years earlier, during the depths of the war, when the family was certain Pete was dead but still praying for a miracle, Florry had convinced Liza to allow her to take the kids on a New Year's trip. In fact, Liza had been invited, but she declined, saying she was simply not in the mood to celebrate. Florry had expected her to say no and was relieved when she did. So, they boarded the train without her, rode six hours from Clanton to New Orleans, and spent three memorable days roaming the Quarter, a place Florry adored and knew well. Their base was the Hotel Monteleone. In its popular bar one night, when she was drinking gin and Joel was sipping bourbon and Stella was eating chocolates, Florry had told them of her great dream of living in the French Quarter, far away from Ford County, in another world where writers and poets and playwrights worked and lived and threw dinner parties. She longed for her dream to come true, but the next morning she apologized for drinking too much and talking so foolishly.

On this Christmas night, the manager was summoned when she arrived with her niece and nephew. There were warm greetings all around, then a glass of champagne. A nine o'clock dinner reservation was confirmed, and they hustled to their rooms to freshen up.

Over cocktails, Florry laid down the ground rules for their stay, which amounted to nothing more than the promise not to discuss either of their parents for the next four days. Joel and Stella readily agreed. Florry had checked with the concierge to find out what was happening in the city, and there was much to explore: a new jazz club on Dauphine, a Broadway production at the Moondance, and several promising new restaurants. In addition to wandering the Quarter and admiring French antiques on Royal, and watching the street acts in Jackson Square, and having chicory coffee and beignets at any one of a dozen cozy sidewalk cafés, and loafing along the levee with the river traffic, and shopping at Maison Blanche, there was, as always, something new in town.

Of course there would be a long dinner at the town house on Chartres Street where Miss Twyla would be waiting. She was a dear old friend from Florry's Memphis years. She was also a poet who wrote a lot and published little, like Florry. Twyla, though, had the benefit of marrying well. When her husband died young she became a rich widow, one who preferred the company of women over men. She left Memphis about the same time Florry built the pink cottage and went home.

For dinner, they were seated at a choice table in the elegant dining room and surrounded by a well-dressed crowd in the holiday spirit. Waiters in white jackets brought platters of raw oysters and poured ice-cold Sancerre. As the wine relaxed them, they poked fun at the other diners and laughed a lot. Florry informed them she had extended their reservations for an entire week. If they were up to it, they could ring in the New Year at a rowdy dance in the hotel's grand ballroom.

Ford County was far away.

CHAPTER 13

At 5:00 a.m. on Monday, January 6, 1947, Ernie Dowdle left his shotgun house in Lowtown and began walking toward the railroad tracks owned by Illinois Central. The temperature was around thirty degrees, seasonal according to the almanac Ernie kept in his kitchen. The weather, especially in the dead of winter, was an important part of his job.

The wind picked up from the northwest, and by the time he arrived at the courthouse twenty minutes later his fingers and feet were cold. As he often did, he stopped and admired the old, stately building, the largest structure in the county, and allowed himself a bit of pride. It was his job to make it warm, something he'd been doing for the past fifteen years, and he, Ernie Dowdle, was very good at it.

This would be no ordinary day. The biggest trial he could remember was about to begin, and that courtroom up there on the second floor would soon be filled. He

unlocked the service door on the north side of the building, closed and locked it behind him, turned on a light,
and took the stairs to the basement. In the boiler room
he went through his wintertime ritual of checking the
four burners, only one of which he'd left on through the
weekend. It kept the temperature throughout the building at roughly forty degrees, enough to protect the pipes.
Next, he checked the dials on the two four-hundred-
gallon tanks of heating oil. He had topped them off the
previous Friday in anticipation of the trial. He removed a
plate and looked inside the exhaust flue. When he was
satisfied that the system was in order, he turned on the
other three burners and waited for the temperature to
rise in the steam boiler situated above them.

As he waited he assembled a table from three soft-
drink cases and took a seat with an eye on the dials and
gauges and began to eat a cold biscuit his wife had baked
the night before. His table was often used for breakfast
and lunch, and when things were slow he and Penrod,
the janitor, would pull out a checkerboard and play a
game or two. He poured black coffee from an old ther-
mos, and as he sipped it he thought about Mr. Pete Banning. He had never met the man, but a cousin lived on
the Banning farm and worked the fields. In years past,
decades even, Ernie's people had been farmworkers and
most were buried out near the Banning land. Ernie considered himself lucky to have escaped the life of a field
hand. He'd made it all the way to town, and to a much
better job that had nothing to do with picking cotton.

Ernie, like most black folks in Ford County, was fascinated by the murder of Dexter Bell. After it happened,
it had been widely believed that a man as prominent as

Pete Banning would never be put on trial. If he'd shot a black man, for any reason whatsoever, he probably would not have been arrested. If a black man murdered another black man, justice would be arbitrarily sought, and by white men only. Issues such as motive, standing, drunkenness, and criminal past were important, but the overriding factor was usually whom the defendant worked for. The right boss could get you a few months in the county jail. No boss could get you strapped to the electric chair.

Now that it was apparent that Mr. Banning would indeed face a jury of his peers, no one, at least in Lowtown, believed he would be convicted and punished. He had money and money could buy slick lawyers. Money could bribe the jurors. Money could influence the judge. White people knew how to use money to get whatever they wanted.

What made the case so compelling to Ernie was the fact that no colored folks were involved. No blame could be placed on any of them. There were no black scapegoats. A serious crime with a white victim always led to the roundup of the usual black suspects, but not in this case. It was just a good old-fashioned brawl among the white folks, and Ernie planned to watch as much of the trial as possible. Like everyone else he wanted to know why Banning did it. He was certain it involved a woman.

He finished his biscuit and studied the gauges. The steam was boiling now and ready to go. When the temperature rose to 175 degrees, he slowly pulled levers and released the steam. It ran through a maze of pipes that led to radiators in every room of the courthouse. He adjusted settings on the burners while keeping an eye on the dials. Satisfied, he climbed the service stairs to the second floor and stepped through the door beside the jury box. The courtroom was dark and cold. He turned on one light—the rest would wait until exactly 7:00 a.m. He walked through the bar and along the benches and to a wall where a black cast-iron radiator was rattling and coming to life. The steam from below was pumping through it and emanating the first wave of warm air that broke the chill. Ernie smiled, quietly proud that the system he maintained so well was working.

It was 6:30 now, and given the size of the courtroom, with its thirty-foot ceilings and balcony, and old leaky windows that were still frosty, Ernie figured it would take over an hour for his six radiators to raise the temperature to around seventy degrees. The front doors of the courthouse opened at 8:00, but Ernie suspected the regulars, the clerks and employees and probably even some of the lawyers, would begin drifting in through the side doors before then, all eager to watch the opening of the trial.

Judge Rafe Oswalt arrived at a quarter to eight and found Penrod sweeping the floor of his chambers behind the courtroom. They exchanged pleasantries, but Penrod knew the judge was in no mood for small talk. A moment later, Ernie Dowdle stopped by to say hello and ask His Honor about the temperature. It was perfect, as always.

John Wilbanks and his brother Russell arrived for the defense. They claimed their table, the one away from the jury box, and began covering it with thick law books and files and other lawyerly effects. They wore fine dark suits and silk ties and looked the part of wealthy, successful lawyers, which was the look everyone in town expected of them. Miles Truitt arrived for the State, along with his assistant district attorney, Maylon Post, a rookie fresh from Ole Miss law school. Truitt and John Wilbanks shook hands and began a friendly chat as they watched the crowd file in.

Nix Gridley arrived with his two men, Roy Lester and Red Arnett, all three in clean, pressed, and matching uniforms, and with a thick layer of shiny black polish on their boots. For the occasion, Nix had deputized two volunteers and given them guns and uniforms and strict instructions to keep order in the courtroom. Nix moved around the courtroom chatting with the clerks, laughing with the lawyers, and nodding at those he recognized in the jury pool.

The spectators were shown to the left, or south, side of the courtroom, and the pews there were filling fast not long after the doors opened. Among the curious were some reporters, and they were given front-row seats.

To the right, the bailiff, Walter Willy, herded those who had been summoned. Seventy registered voters had been selected by Judge Oswalt and the circuit court clerk, and they had been mailed letters two weeks before. Fourteen had been disqualified for various reasons. Those left in the pool looked nervously around the courtroom, uncertain as to whether they should feel honored to be chosen or terrified of serving in such a notorious case. Though their letters gave no indication of who was on trial, the entire county knew it was Pete Banning. Of the fifty-six, only one had ever served on a trial jury before.

Full-blown trials were rare in rural Mississippi. Everyone in the pool was white; only three were women.

Above them, the balcony was filling with Negroes, and Negroes only. Signs in the hallways of the courthouse kept matters segregated—restrooms, water fountains, entrances to offices, and the courtroom. Penrod, a man with status, was sweeping the balcony floor and explaining to others how the court system worked. This was his turf. He'd watched trials before and was quite informed. Ernie moved up and down the staircase, stopping by the balcony to flirt with some ladies. Hop from the Methodist church was the man of the hour in the balcony because he would be called to testify. He was the State's most important witness, and he made sure his people knew it. They wished him well.

At exactly nine o'clock, Walter Willy, who'd been the volunteer bailiff for longer than anyone could remember, marched to his position in front of the bench, stood at attention, or at least his version of it, and commenced to howl: "All rise for the court!" His high-pitched squeal startled those who'd never heard it before, and everyone scrambled to their feet as Judge Oswalt emerged from the door behind his bench.

Walter Willy tilted his head back, and with his eyes on the ceiling continued yodeling, "Hear ye, hear ye, the circuit court of the Twenty-Second Judicial District of the great State of Mississippi is hereby called to order. The Honorable Rafe Oswalt presiding. Let all who have business before this court come forward. God bless America and God bless Mississippi."

Such language was not required and could not be found in any code section, rule of procedure, court order, or local ordinance. When he had somehow assumed the job years earlier, and no one could recall exactly how he had become the court's permanent bailiff, Walter Willy had spent a lot of time perfecting his call to order, and now it was an accepted part of the opening of court. Judge Oswalt really didn't care; however, the lawyers despised it. Regardless of the importance of the hearing or the trial, Walter was there to give his earsplitting call to rise.

Another part of his act was his homemade uniform. The matching shirt and pants were olive khaki, nothing remotely similar to what the real deputies were wearing, and his mother had sewn his name above the pocket in bold yellow letters. She had also added some random patches with no significance on his sleeves. He wore a bright gold badge he'd found at a flea market in Memphis, and a thick black ammo belt with a row of shiny cartridges that gave the impression that Walter might just shoot first and ask questions later. He could not, however, because he had no weapon. Nix Gridley flatly refused to deputize him and wanted no part of Walter Willy and his routine.

Judge Oswalt tolerated it with a wink because it was harmless and added a bit of color to the otherwise drab courtroom and dull proceedings.

He settled himself at his bench, said, "Please be seated," and arranged his flowing black robe around himself. He looked at the crowd. Both the gallery and the balcony were full. In his seventeen years on the bench, he had never seen so many in this courtroom. He cleared his throat and said, "Well, good morning and welcome.

There's only one case on the docket this week. Mr. Sheriff, would you bring in the defendant?"

Nix was waiting at a side door. He nodded, opened the door, and seconds later appeared with Pete Banning, who walked in slowly, with no handcuffs, tall and erect, his face showing no concern but with his eyes on the floor. He seemed not to notice the crowd watching his every move. Pete hated neckties and wore a dark jacket over a white shirt. John Wilbanks had thought it important to wear a suit to show proper respect for the proceedings. Pete had asked how many men on the jury would be wearing suits, and when his lawyer said probably none, the issue was settled. The truth was Pete didn't care what he wore, what the jurors wore, what anyone wore.

Without as much as a glance at the audience, he took his seat at the defense table, crossed his arms, and looked at Judge Oswalt.

Florry was three rows back at the end of a pew. Beside her was Mildred Highlander, her best friend in town, and the only one who'd volunteered to sit through the trial with her. She and Pete had argued over her attendance. He was dead set against it. She was determined to watch. She wanted to know what was happening for her own benefit, but also to report to Joel and Stella. Too, she figured that Pete would have almost no one else there pulling for him. And she was correct. Everywhere she turned she got harsh looks from angry Methodists.

Judge Oswalt said, "In the matter of the *State of Mississippi versus Pete Banning,* what says the State?"

Miles Truitt rose with a purpose and replied, "Your Honor, the State of Mississippi is ready for trial."

"And what says the defense?"

John Wilbanks stood and said, "As is the defense." When both sat down, Judge Oswalt looked at the prospective jurors and said, "Now, we summoned seventy of you folks here as prospective jurors. One has passed away, three have not been found, and ten have been sent home, disqualified. So we now have a panel of fifty-six. I have been informed by the bailiff that all fifty-six are present, are above the age of eighteen, under the age of sixty-five, and have no health problems that would prevent jury duty. You have been arranged in numerical order and will be addressed as such."

It would serve no purpose to explain that the ten who had been disqualified were basically illiterate and had been unable to complete a rudimentary questionnaire.

Judge Oswalt shuffled some papers, found the indictment, and read it aloud. The facts as alleged constituted first-degree murder under Mississippi law, punishable by either life in prison or death in the electric chair. He introduced the four lawyers and asked them to stand. He introduced the defendant, but when asked to stand, Pete refused. He didn't budge and seemed not to hear. Judge Oswalt was irritated but decided to ignore the slight.

It was not a wise thing to do, and John Wilbanks planned to give his client an earful during the first recess. What could Pete possibly hope to gain by being disrespectful?

Moving right along, the judge launched into a windy narrative in which he described both the alleged murder victim and the alleged murderer. At the time of his death, Dexter Bell had been the minister of the Clanton Methodist Church for five years, and as such was active in the community. He was well-known, as was the defendant. Pete Banning was born in Ford County to a prominent family, and so on.

When the buildup was finally finished, Judge Oswalt asked the prospective jurors if anyone was related by blood or marriage to either Dexter Bell or Pete Banning. No one moved. Next he asked if anyone considered himself a personal friend of Pete Banning's. Two men stood. Both said they were longtime friends and they could not pass judgment on Pete, regardless of what the evidence proved. Both were excused and left the courtroom. Next he asked how many were friends with a member of the immediate Banning family and he named Liza, Florry, Joel, and Stella. Six people stood. One young man said he finished high school with Joel. One said his sister and Stella were friends and he knew her well. Another knew Florry from years back. Judge Oswalt quizzed them individually and at length and asked if they could remain fair and impartial. All six assured him they could and they remained in the pool. Three said they were friends with the Bells but claimed they could remain impartial. John Wilbanks doubted this and planned to challenge them later in the day.

With the war so recent and its memories still so vivid, Judge Oswalt knew he had no choice but to confront it head-on. Giving almost no background, he described Pete Banning as a highly decorated army officer who had been a prisoner of war. He asked how many veterans of war were in the pool. Seven men stood, and he called them by name and questioned them. To a man, each said he was able to set aside any bias or favoritism and follow the law and the orders of the court.

Eleven men from Ford County had been killed in the war, and Judge Oswalt and the circuit clerk had tried diligently to exclude those families from the pool.

Moving to the other side of the matter, Judge Oswalt asked if any were members of Dexter Bell's church. Three men and one woman stood, and they were excused outright. Down to fifty. And how many were members of other Methodist churches scattered around the county? Five more stood. Three said they had met Dexter Bell; two had not. Judge Oswalt kept them all on the panel.

He had granted each side five peremptory challenges to be used later in the day. If John Wilbanks didn't like the looks or body language of a certain Methodist, he could dismiss him for no reason. If Miles Truitt suspected an acquaintance of the Banning family might be sandbagging, he could invoke a challenge and the person was gone. The four lawyers sat perched on the edges of their chairs and watched every twitch, smile, and frown from the jury pool.

Judge Oswalt preferred to take control of the selection of his juries. Other judges gave the lawyers more leeway, but they usually talked too much and tried to curry favor. After an hour of skillful questioning, Oswalt had trimmed the panel to forty-five and he yielded the floor to Miles Truitt, who stood and offered a big smile and tried to seem relaxed. He began by repeating and emphasizing something the judge had already covered: If the State proved every element of its charge of first-degree murder, the jury would then be asked to impose the death penalty. Can you really do that? Can you really sentence Pete Banning to the electric chair? If you follow the law, then you have no choice. It will not be easy, but sometimes following the law takes a lot of courage. Do you have that courage?

Truitt paced along the bar and was quite effective at forcing each juror to consider the gravity of the task at hand. Some probably had doubts, but at that moment no one admitted to any. Truitt was concerned about the veterans and suspected they would be more sympathetic than they were willing to admit. He called on one, asked him to stand, thanked him for his service, and quizzed him for a few minutes. When he seemed to be satisfied, he moved on to the next veteran.

The selection process crept along, and at 10:30, the judge needed a break and a cigarette. Half of the courtroom lit up too as folks stood and stretched and quietly exchanged opinions. Some left for the restrooms; others went back to work. Everyone tried to ignore the jurors, pursuant to instructions from the bench.

At 11:00 a.m., John Wilbanks stood and looked at the prospective jurors. So much of what he wanted to say had been taken away from him by his own client. His plan had been to sow the seed of insanity early in the jury selection process, and then follow it with testimony that would be shocking, sad, credible, and convincing. But Pete would have none of it. Pete had done nothing to help save his own skin, and John could not decide if his client carried some type of perverse death wish, or simply was so arrogant as to believe no jury would convict him. Either way, the defense was hopeless.

John had already seen enough and knew which jurors

he wanted. He would try to avoid all Methodists and aim for the veterans. But he was a lawyer, and no lawyer onstage with a captive audience can resist saying a few words. He smiled and seemed warm and thoroughly honored to be there doing what he was doing, defending a fine man who had defended our country. He lobbed a few questions at the panel as a whole, then he zeroed in on a couple of Methodists, but for the most part his comments were designed not to uncover some hidden bias, but rather to convey warmth, trust, and likability.

When he finished, Judge Oswalt recessed court until 2:00 p.m. and asked everyone to leave the courtroom. It took a few minutes for the crowd to file out, and while they waited the judge informed the clerks and other curious insiders that it would be a good time to go find lunch. When the courtroom was practically empty, he said, "Mr. Wilbanks, I believe you have a matter that you would like to present, on the record."

John Wilbanks stood and said, "Yes, Your Honor, but I prefer we do it in chambers."

"We'll do it here. It's rather crowded back there. Besides, if we're on the record it's really not a confidential matter, is it?"

"I suppose not."

Judge Oswalt nodded at the court reporter and said, "We're now on the record. Please proceed, Mr. Wilbanks."

"Thank you, Your Honor. This is really not a motion or a petition to the court, because the defense is not asking for any type of relief. However, I am compelled to state the following for the record so there will never be any doubt about my defense of my client. I had planned to pursue two strategies aimed at securing a fair trial for my client. First, I planned to ask the court for a change of venue. I was convinced then, as I certainly am now, that my client cannot receive a fair trial in this county. I've lived here my entire life, as has my father and his father, and I know this county. As we have already seen this morning, the facts of this case are well known to the friends and neighbors of Pete Banning and Dexter Bell. It will be impossible to find twelve people who are open-minded and impartial. After watching and studying the pool this morning, I am convinced that many are not exactly forthcoming with their true feelings. It is simply unfair to hold this trial in this courtroom. However, when I discussed a change of venue with my client, he strongly opposed such a move, and he still does. I would like for him to be on the record."

Judge Oswalt looked at Pete and asked, "Mr. Banning, is this true? Are you opposed to a motion to change venue?"

Pete stood and said, "Yes, it's true. I want my trial right here."

"So, you have chosen to ignore the advice of your lawyer, correct?"

"I'm not ignoring my lawyer. I'm just not agreeing with him."

"Very well. You may sit. Continue, Mr. Wilbanks."

John rolled his eyes in frustration and cleared his throat. "Second, and even more important, at least in my opinion, is the issue of a proper defense. I had planned to notify the court that the defense would invoke a plea of insanity, but my client would have none of it. I had planned to present extensive testimony of the inhumane and, frankly, indescribable conditions that he suffered and survived during the war. I had located two psychiatric experts and was prepared to use them to evaluate my client and testify at this trial. However, once again my client refused to cooperate and instructed me not to pursue such a course."

Judge Oswalt asked Pete, "Is this true, Mr. Banning?"

Without standing, Pete said, "I'm not crazy, Judge, and for me to try and act crazy would be dishonest."

The judge nodded. The court reporter scribbled away. The words were being recorded for history. For the defense the words were damning enough, but it was his last utterance that would not be forgotten. Almost as an afterthought, Pete, who weighed every word in every situation, said, "I knew what I was doing."

John Wilbanks looked at the judge and shrugged, as if in surrender.

CHAPTER 14

Juror number one was a mystery. James Lindsey, age fifty-three, married; occupation—none; address—a rural road out from the remote settlement of Box Hill, almost to Tyler County. His questionnaire said he was a Baptist. He had volunteered nothing during the morning session, and no one seemed to know anything about him. Neither John Wilbanks nor Miles Truitt wanted to waste a challenge, so James Lindsey became the first juror selected for the trial.

Judge Oswalt called the name of juror number two, a Mr. Delbert Mooney, one of the sprawling Mooney clan from the town of Karraway, the only other incorporated municipality in Ford County. Delbert was twenty-seven years old, had spent two years in the army fighting in Europe, and had been injured twice. John Wilbanks wanted him desperately. Miles Truitt did not, and he exercised his first peremptory challenge.

They were still in the courtroom but they were alone,

just Judge Oswalt and the lawyers. The defendant had been taken back to jail for lunch, and until further orders. The bailiff, court reporter, clerks, and deputies had been banished. The final selection of the trial jurors was a confidential matter involving only the judge and the lawyers, and it was not on the record. They nibbled on sandwiches and sipped iced tea, but they were too preoccupied to enjoy lunch.

The judge called the name of juror number three, one of two women left. Some rules were written, others simply assumed. For serious crimes, the juries always comprised twelve white men. There was no discussion as to why or how this came to be; it was simply understood. John Wilbanks said, "We should remove her 'for cause,' don't you think, Miles?" Miles was quick to agree. A "for cause" challenge meant the prospect was obviously unsuited for jury duty, and rather than embarrass him or her in open court with a public dismissal, the ploy of a "for cause" strike was reserved for private discussions. And, most important, it did not count as a peremptory challenge. The judge simply ruled that the person would not serve, and this discretion was never debated.

There was no urgency in their work. With very few prosecution witnesses and perhaps none for the defense, the trial, once under way, would not last long. So they worked their way through the remaining names, accepting some, culling others, arguing professionally at times, but always making steady progress. At 3:00 p.m. Judge Oswalt needed another smoke, and he decided to send word to the crowd waiting in the hallways and sitting on the stairs and loitering outdoors in the cold that the trial would begin at nine sharp the following morning. Those in the jury pool would remain nearby. At 4:30, the doors were opened. A few spectators drifted in with the jurors, and a few Negroes returned to the balcony. After the defendant was brought in and placed at the defense table, Judge Oswalt said that a jury had been selected. He called twelve names, and they made their way to the jury box and took their seats.

Twelve white men. Four Baptists; two Methodists; two Pentecostals; one Presbyterian; one Church of Christ. And two who claimed no church membership and were likely headed straight to hell.

They raised their right hands and swore to uphold their duties; then they were sent home with strict instructions to avoid talking about the case. Judge Oswalt adjourned court and disappeared. When the courtroom was empty, John Wilbanks asked Sheriff Gridley if he could have a few minutes alone with his client. It was far easier to chat at the defense table than at the jail, and Nix agreed.

As Penrod swept the floor around the spectators' benches, and as Ernie Dowdle fiddled with his radiators, the defense team huddled with their client. Russell said, "I don't like your demeanor in court, Pete."

John quickly added, "You seem arrogant and aloof and the jury will pick up on this. Plus, you were disrespectful to Judge Oswalt. This cannot happen again."

Russell said, "When the trial starts tomorrow, those jurors will spend half their time looking at you."

"Why?" Pete asked.

"Because they're curious. Because their job is to judge you. They've never done this before and they're in awe of these surroundings. They will absorb everything, and it's important that you look somewhat sympathetic."

"Not sure I can do that," Pete said.

"Well, try, okay?" John said. "Take some notes and flip through some papers. Look like you're interested in your own case."

"Who picked that jury?" Pete asked.

"Us. The lawyers and the judge."

"I'm not so sure about it. Looks to me like they've already made up their minds. I didn't see too many friendly faces."

"Well, show them one, okay, Pete?" John looked away in frustration. "Remember, those folks get to decide how you spend the rest of your life."

"That's already been decided."

Ernie's radiators were humming along at 9:30 Tuesday morning when Miles Truitt rose to address the jury in his opening statement. The courtroom was warm and once again packed, and Ernie and Penrod crouched in a corner of the packed balcony and watched with great anticipation.

Everyone grew still and quiet. Truitt wore a dark brown wool suit with a vest. A gold chain dropped from a vest pocket. It was a new suit, one bought for this moment, the biggest trial of his career. He stood before the jury and offered a warm smile, then thanked them for their service to the State of Mississippi, his client. They had been carefully chosen to hear the evidence, to evaluate the witnesses, to weigh the law, and finally to decide guilt or innocence. It was a heavy responsibility, and he thanked them again.

First-degree murder was the most serious crime on the books in Mississippi. Truitt read its definition straight from the code: "The intentional, deliberate, and premeditated killing of another human being without the authority of law by any means or in any manner." He read it a second time, slowly and loudly, each word echoing around the courtroom. And the punishment: "Upon conviction of first-degree murder, the jury shall decide to impose death by the electric chair, or life without parole."

Truitt turned, pointed at the defendant, and said, "Gentlemen of the jury, the Reverend Dexter Bell was murdered in the first degree by Pete Banning, who now deserves to die." It was a pronouncement that was certainly expected, but dramatic nonetheless.

Truitt talked about Dexter: his childhood in Georgia, his call to the ministry, his marriage to Jackie, his early churches, his children, his powerful sermons, his compassion for all, his leadership in the community, his popularity in Clanton. There were no blemishes on Dexter, no missteps along the way. A fine young minister dedicated to his calling and his faith, gunned down at church by an army sharpshooter. Such a waste. A loving father taken away in an instant and leaving three beautiful children behind.

The State of Mississippi would prove its case beyond a reasonable doubt, and when the witnesses were finished he, Miles Truitt, would return to this very spot and ask for justice. Justice for Dexter Bell and his family. Justice for the town of Clanton. Justice for humanity.

John Wilbanks watched the performance with admiration. True, Miles Truitt had the facts on his side and that was always a major advantage. But Truitt was subtle in his approach, understating some facts instead of taking a sledgehammer to them. The murder was so monstrous on its face that it didn't need affected drama. As Wilbanks watched the faces of the jurors, he confirmed what he had known for a long time. There would be no sympathy for his client. And with no proof of their own, the defense was dead, as was the defendant.

The courtroom was silent as Miles Truitt sat down. Judge Oswalt looked at John Wilbanks, nodded, and said, "And for the defense."

Wilbanks stood and fiddled with the knot of his fine silk tie as he approached the jury box. He had nothing to say, and he wasn't about to blast away with some preposterous claim of mistaken identity or conjure up a bogus alibi. So he smiled and said, "Gentlemen of the jury, the rules of procedure in trials like this allow the defense to waive its opening statement until later when the prosecution is finished. The defense chooses to exercise this option." He turned and nodded to the bench.

Judge Oswalt shrugged and said, "Fine with me. Mr. Truitt, please call your first witness."

Truitt stood and bellowed, "The State of Mississippi calls Mrs. Jackie Bell to the stand."

From the second row behind the prosecution's table, Jackie stood and moved to the end of the pew. She was sitting with Errol McLeish, who had driven her from Rome, Georgia, on Sunday afternoon. Her parents were keeping her children. Her father had insisted on accompanying her to the trial, but she dissuaded him. Errol had volunteered and was eager to make the trip. She was staying with a friend from church, and Errol had a room at the Bedford Hotel on the Clanton square.

All eyes were on Jackie, and she was prepared for the attention. Her thin figure was wrapped tight in a slim-fitting black belted suit. She wore black suede pumps, a small black velvet half hat, and a simple string of pearls. The emphasis on black worked perfectly and she emanated grief and suffering, sort of. She was very much the widow, but a young and attractive one at that.

All twelve men watched every step as she made her approach, as did the lawyers, the judge, and virtually everyone else. Pete, though, was not impressed and kept his eyes on the floor. The court reporter swore her to tell the truth, and Jackie situated herself in the witness chair and looked at the crowd. She carefully crossed her legs and the crowd watched every move.

From behind a podium, Miles Truitt smiled at her and asked her name and address. He had coached her well and she looked sincerely at the faces of the jurors as she spoke. Other essentials followed: She was thirty-eight years old, had three children, had lived in Clanton for five years but moved to Georgia after the death of her husband. "I became a widow," she said sadly.

"Now, on the morning of October 9 of last year, at approximately nine o'clock, where were you?"

"At home. We lived in the parsonage beside the Methodist church."

"Where was your husband?"

"Dexter was in his office at the church, at his desk, working on his sermon."

"Tell the jury what happened."

"Well, I was in the kitchen, putting away dishes, and

I heard some sounds I'd never heard before. Three of them, in rapid succession, as if someone on the front porch had clapped his hands loudly three times. I thought little of it, at first, but then I became curious. Then something told me to check on Dexter. I went to the phone and called his office. When he didn't answer, I left the parsonage, walked around the front of the church and into the annex where his office was." Her voice broke as her eyes watered. She touched her lips with the back of her hand and looked at Miles. She was holding a tissue she had taken to the stand.

He asked, "And did you find your husband?"

She swallowed hard, seemed to grit her teeth, and continued, "Dexter was at his desk, still in his chair. He'd been shot and was bleeding; there was blood everywhere." Her voice broke again, so she paused, took a deep breath, wiped her eyes, and was ready to move on.

The only sound in the courtroom was the quiet hum and rattle of Ernie Dowdle's radiators. No one moved or whispered. They stared at Jackie and waited patiently as she gamely pulled herself together and told her horrible story. There was no hurry. The town had been waiting for three months to hear the details of what happened that morning.

"Did you speak to him?" Miles asked.

"I'm not sure. I remember screaming and running around his desk to his chair and grabbing him and pulling him, and, well, I'm not sure of everything. It was just so awful." She closed her eyes and lowered her head and wept. Her tears created others, and many of the women who knew her and Dexter were wiping their eyes too.

Her testimony was unnecessary. The defense offered

to stipulate that Dexter Bell was in fact dead and that his death was caused by three bullets fired from a .45-caliber Colt pistol. Sympathy was irrelevant to the facts, and any evidence deemed irrelevant was by law inadmissible. However, Judge Oswalt, along with every other judge in the state, and the entire country as well, always allowed the prosecution to trot out a surviving relative or two to ostensibly prove death. The real purpose, though, was to stir up the jurors.

Jackie gritted her teeth again and plowed forward, or at least tried to. Dexter was lying on the floor, she was talking to him, but he was not responsive. She remembered running from his office covered in blood and screaming, and that's when the deputy showed up with Hop and, well, after that, she just didn't remember things that clearly.

Another pause as Jackie broke down, and after a painful gap seemed unable to continue. Judge Oswalt looked at Miles and said, "Mr. Truitt, I think we've heard enough from this witness."

"Yes, Your Honor."

"Any cross-examination, Mr. Wilbanks?"

"Of course not, Your Honor," John Wilbanks said with great sympathy.

"Thank you, Mrs. Bell, you are excused," the judge said.

Walter Willy jumped to his feet, took her hand, and led her past the jurors and the lawyers, through the bar, and back to her pew. Judge Oswalt needed a smoke and called for a recess. The jurors were led out first, by Walter, and when they were gone the crowd relaxed and everyone wanted to talk. Many of the church folks lined up for a hug with Jackie, all eager to get their hands on her. Errol McLeish inched away from the mob and watched her from a distance. Other than Jackie, he didn't know a soul in the courtroom and no one knew him.

Hop wobbled to the witness stand and swore to tell the truth. His real name was Chester Purdue, which he gave, and then explained that he'd been called Hop since childhood, for obvious reasons. Hop was beyond nervous. He was terrified, and glanced repeatedly at the balcony for support from his people. From that vantage point, testifying looked so much easier. Down here, though, with everybody staring at him, all those white people—the lawyers and judge and jurors and clerks, not to mention the crowd—well, he was instantly rattled and had trouble talking. Mr. Miles Truitt had worked with him for hours down the hall in his office. They had walked through his testimony several times, with Mr. Truitt repeatedly telling him to just relax and tell his story. He was relaxed, yesterday and the day before in Mr. Truitt's office, but now this was the big show, with everybody watching and nobody smiling.

"Just look at me, nobody else," Mr. Truitt had said over and over.

So Hop stared at the DA and told his story. It was a Wednesday morning and he was cleaning the stained-glass windows of the sanctuary, a job he did once a month and it took the better part of three days. He left the sanctuary and walked into the annex headed to a storage room where he kept his supplies. He passed the door to Reverend Bell's office. It was closed and Hop knew better than to disturb the preacher in the morning. Hop did not hear voices. He did not see anyone enter the annex. As far as he knew, there were only two people in the church—him and the preacher. He was reaching for a bottle of cleaner when he heard three loud noises. All three the same and they practically shook the building. He was startled and ran into the hallway, where he heard a door open. Mr. Pete Banning stepped out of the preacher's office holding a gun.

"How long have you known Pete Banning?" Truitt asked.

"A long time. He's a member of the church."

"Would you point to the man who was holding the gun?"

"If you say so." Hop pointed at the defendant. He described how Mista Banning pointed the gun at his head, how he fell to his knees pleading, and how Mista Banning said he was a good man. Now go tell the sheriff.

Hop watched him walk away, then slipped into the office, though he didn't really want to. Reverend Bell was in his chair, bleeding in the head and chest, eyes closed. Hop wasn't sure how long he stood there; he was too terrified to think straight. Finally, he backed away without touching a thing and ran to get the sheriff.

No lawyer could score points by impeaching Hop or casting doubts about his veracity. There was nothing to impeach. What reason did Hop have to cut corners with the truth? He saw what he saw and he had embellished not a word. John Wilbanks stood and quietly said that he did not wish to cross-examine the witness. Indeed, he had nothing to throw at any of the State's witnesses.

As he sat and listened, and seethed, John asked himself, and not for the first time, why he had been so quick to rush to Pete's defense. The man was guilty and had no desire to appear otherwise. Why couldn't some other lawyer sit benignly at the defense table and captain this sinking ship? From the perspective of an accomplished trial lawyer, it was unsettling, almost embarrassing.

The next witness for the State was a man everybody knew. Slim Fargason had been the elected chancery clerk for decades, and one of his duties was the recording and preservation of all of the county's land records. In short order, he looked at a certified copy of a deed and explained to the jury that on September 16 of the previous year Mr. Pete Banning had transferred by quitclaim deed a section of land, 640 acres, to his two children, Joel and Stella Banning. The land had been owned by Pete since 1932 when his mother died and bequeathed it to him by her last will and testament.

On cross-examination, John Wilbanks fleshed out the chain of title and made much of the fact that the land had been owned by the Banning family for well over a hundred years. Wasn't it common knowledge in Ford County that the Bannings kept their land? Slim confessed that he couldn't attest to what was common knowledge, could only speak for himself, but, yes, he figured the land would eventually be owned by the next generation.

When the questions were over, Slim hustled off the stand and returned to his office.

Deputy Roy Lester was called to testify. Following Mississippi law, he removed his service revolver, holster, and belt before stepping into the witness stand. As Truitt lobbed questions, Lester picked up Hop's narrative and described the scene when they arrived. First, they tried to subdue Mrs. Bell, who was hysterical, and rightly so. He was with her when Sheriff Gridley arrived on the scene, and he walked her across the street to Mrs. Vanlandingham's porch. He later went to the church and helped with the investigation.

John Wilbanks had nothing on cross.

Miles Truitt had the facts on his side, which was usually the case with prosecutors, and for that reason he was deliberate and plodding. Creativity was not necessary. He would slowly piece together the narrative and walk the jurors step by step through the crime and its aftermath. His next witness was Sheriff Nix Gridley, who unlatched his weaponry and took the stand.

Nix laid out the crime scene, and through a series of enlarged color photos the jurors finally saw the dead body, and all the blood. The photos were gruesome, inflammatory, and prejudicial, but trial judges in Mississippi always allowed them. The truth was that murders were messy, and the triers of fact had the right to see the damage wrought by the defendant. Fortunately, the photos were not large enough to be seen from the gallery or the balcony. Jackie Bell was spared the sight of her dead husband, but she was still troubled to learn that such evidence existed. No one had told her Dexter had been photographed as his blood crept across the floor. What would happen to the photographs after the trial?

As they were passed around the jury box, several of the jurors glared at Pete, who was flipping through a thick law book. He rarely looked up, never looked around, and most of the time seemed detached from his own trial.

Nix told of his conversation with Hop, who identified the murderer. He, Roy Lester, and Red Arnett drove out to arrest Pete Banning, who was waiting on the porch. He told them the gun was in his truck and they took it. He said nothing as they drove to the jail, where John Wilbanks was waiting. Mr. Wilbanks insisted that there was to be no interrogation without him present, so Nix never got the chance to talk to the defendant, who, to this day, has never said a word as to why he killed the preacher.

"So you have no idea as to motive?" Truitt asked.

John Wilbanks was itching to do something lawyerly. He jumped to his feet and said, "Objection. Calls for speculation. This witness is in no position to give his 'idea' or opinion as to motive."

"Sustained."

Unfazed, Truitt walked to a small table in front of the bench, reached into a cardboard box, removed a pistol, and handed it to Nix. "Is this the gun you removed from Pete Banning's pickup truck?"

Nix held it with both hands and nodded. Yes.

"Would you describe it for the jury?"

"Sure. It's made by Colt for the army, a .45-caliber, a single-action revolver, with six rounds in the cylinder. Five-and-a-half-inch barrel. A very nice gun. I'd say a legend in the business."

"Do you know where the defendant purchased this gun?"

"I do not. Again, I've never talked to the defendant about the shooting."

"Do you know how many rounds were fired by the defendant at the deceased?"

"There were three. Hop said he heard three rounds,

and, as you've heard, Mrs. Bell testified that she heard three sounds. According to the autopsy, the deceased was hit twice in the chest and once in the face."

"Were you able to recover any of the slugs?"

"Yes, two of them. One passed through the head and lodged in the foam padding of the chair in which the deceased was sitting. Another passed through the torso and lodged lower in the chair. The third was removed by the pathologist during the autopsy."

Jackie Bell burst into tears and began sobbing. Errol McLeish stood and helped her to her feet. She left the courtroom with her hands over her face as everyone watched and waited. When the door closed behind her, Miles Truitt looked at Judge Oswalt, who nodded as if to say, "Get on with it."

Truitt walked to the table, took a small package from the box, and handed it to the witness. "Can you describe these?"

"Sure. These are the three slugs that killed the preacher."

"And how do you know this?"

"Well, I sent the gun and the slugs to the crime lab. They ran the ballistics tests and sent me a report." Truitt stepped to his table, picked up some papers, and sort of waved them at Judge Oswalt. "Your Honor, I have their two reports. The first is from the ballistics expert; the second is from the doctor who performed the autopsy. I move that these be admitted into evidence."

"Any objections, Mr. Wilbanks?"

"Yes, Your Honor, the same objections I raised last week. I prefer to have these two experts here in the courtroom so I can cross-examine them. I cannot cross-examine written reports. There is no good reason why these two men were not subpoenaed here to testify. This is unfair to the defense."

"Overruled. The reports are admitted into evidence. Proceed, Mr. Truitt."

"Now, Sheriff Gridley, the jury will be able to review both reports, but can you summarize what the ballistics expert said?"

"Sure. The three spent cartridges were still in the chamber, so the analysis was easy. The expert examined them, along with the three slugs, and he test fired the weapon. In his opinion, there is no doubt that the Colt revolver we took from the defendant's truck fired the three fatal shots. No doubt."

"And can you summarize the findings of the doctor who performed the autopsy?"

"No surprise there. The three bullets fired from Pete Banning's revolver entered the body of the deceased and caused his death. It's all right here in the report."

"Thank you, Sheriff. I tender the witness."

John Wilbanks stood and glared at Gridley as if he might throw a rock at him. He stepped to the podium and pondered his first question. For weeks now, every living soul in Ford County had known that Pete Banning shot and killed Dexter Bell. If Wilbanks dared to suggest otherwise, he risked losing whatever credibility he had. He also risked outright ridicule, something his pride couldn't tolerate. He decided to poke and prod a bit, perhaps raise a little suspicion, but above all maintain his elevated status.

"Sheriff, who is your ballistics expert?"

"A man named Doug Cranwell, works down in Jackson."

"And you think he's a qualified expert in his field?"

"Seems to be. He's used by a lot of folks in law enforcement."

"Well, forgive me for asking, but I can't quiz him on his qualifications, because he's not here. Why is he not here to testify live before this jury?"

"I guess you'll have to ask Mr. Truitt. I'm not in charge of trials." Nix smiled at the jurors and enjoyed his moment of levity.

"I see. And which doctor did you use for the autopsy?"

"Dr. Fred Briley, also down in Jackson. He's used by a lot of sheriffs."

"And why is he not here to testify before this jury?"

"I think he charges too much money."

"I see. Is this a low-budget investigation? A crime that's not too important?"

"It comes out of Mr. Truitt's budget, not mine. So you'll have to ask him."

"Don't you think it's odd, Sheriff, that neither of these experts would show up here and subject himself to a rigorous cross-examination by the defense?"

Truitt stood and said, "Objection, Your Honor. This witness does not control the prosecution of this case."

"Sustained."

Nix, who was enjoying his brief visit to the witness stand, kept talking. "It's really an open-and-shut case and I guess Mr. Truitt didn't see the need for a lot of experts."

"That's enough, Sheriff," Oswalt growled.

Wilbanks bristled and asked, "So, how many murders have you investigated, Sheriff?"

"Not many. I run a tight ship around here. We don't see a lot of crime."

"How many murders?"

When it became apparent an answer was required, Gridley shifted weight, thought for a second, and asked, "Black or white?"

Wilbanks glanced away in frustration and asked, "Do you investigate them differently?"

"No, I guess not. I've seen three or four stabbings in Lowtown, and that Dulaney boy got hanged out from Box Hill. Other than that, on our side of town, we found Jesse Green floating in the river but could never tell if he'd been murdered. Body was decomposed too much. So I guess just one other murder before now."

"And how long have you been the sheriff?"

"Goin' on eight years."

"Thank you, Sheriff," Wilbanks said and returned to his table.

Judge Oswalt was shaking from a lack of nicotine. He rapped his gavel and said, "We'll adjourn for lunch and reconvene at 2:00 p.m."

CHAPTER 15

After cigarettes and sandwiches, the judge met privately with the lawyers. Truitt said he had no other witnesses and felt as though he had proven his case sufficiently. Oswalt agreed. Wilbanks couldn't deny it either and complimented the DA on how well his evidence had been presented. As for the defense, there was still doubt as to whether Pete Banning would take the stand. One day he wanted to testify and plead his case to the jury. The next day he would barely speak to his own lawyer. Wilbanks confided that he now believed Pete was mentally unbalanced, but there would be no insanity plea. Pete was still staunchly opposed to it, and the filing deadline had long since passed.

"Who's your first witness?" Judge Oswalt asked.

"Major Rusconi, U.S. Army."

"And the gist of his testimony?"

"I want to establish that my client, while on active duty and fighting the Japanese in the Philippines, was taken captive and presumed dead. This was the message sent to his family in May of 1942."

"I don't see the relevance to this crime, John," Truitt said.

"And I'm not surprised to hear that. I will attempt to lay the foundation for my client's testimony, in the event he takes the stand."

"I'm not so sure either, John," Judge Oswalt said skeptically. "You'll prove he was dead or missing or both, and this was what the family believed, and therefore the minister, in the course of doing his duties, somehow stepped out of line, thus giving the defendant an excuse. Is this what you're thinking?"

Truitt was shaking his head in disapproval.

Wilbanks said, "Judge, I don't have anything else, maybe other than the defendant himself. You must allow me to mount a defense, shaky as it sounds."

"Put him on. Miles, make your objection. I'll let him go for a few minutes and see where he takes us, but I am skeptical."

"Thanks, Judge," Wilbanks said.

When the jurors were seated after a leisurely lunch break, Judge Oswalt informed them that the State had rested and the defense was waiving its right to make an opening statement. Major Anthony Rusconi was called to the stand, and he marched right in, garbed in full military regalia. He was from New Orleans, with that thick, unmistakable accent and easy smile. He was a career officer who had served in the Pacific.

After a few preliminaries, Miles Truitt rose and politely said, "Your Honor, with all due respect to the witness, his testimony is and will continue to be of no relevance to the facts and issues involved in this case. Therefore, I would like to enter a continuing objection to his testimony."

"So noted. Continue, Mr. Wilbanks."

Before the war, Rusconi was stationed in Manila and worked in the headquarters of General Douglas MacArthur, the commander of the U.S. forces in the Philippines. The day after Pearl Harbor, the Japanese bombed the American air bases in the Philippines and the war was on.

At that time, Lieutenant Pete Banning was an officer in the Twenty-Sixth Cavalry and stationed at Fort Stotsenburg near Clark Field, sixty miles north of Manila.

The Japanese quickly destroyed the American air and naval forces and invaded with fifty thousand battlehardened and well-supplied troops. The Americans and their allies, the Filipino Scouts and the regular Philippine Army, mounted a heroic defense, but as the Japanese reinforced and tightened their noose around the islands, food, medicine, fuel, and ammunition disappeared. With no air support for protection and no navy to provide supplies and possible escape, the Americans were forced to retreat to the Bataan Peninsula, a forbidding and jungle-infested stretch of terrain jutting into the South China Sea.

Rusconi was quite the storyteller and seemed to enjoy the opportunity to talk about the war. Miles Truitt shook his head and tried to make eye contact with Judge Oswalt, who avoided him. The jurors were spellbound. The spectators were riveted and virtually motionless.

The siege lasted four months, and when the Americans were forced to surrender to a vastly superior force, it was the biggest defeat in the history of the U.S. Army. But the men had no choice. They were starving, sick, emaciated, and dying so fast burials were not possible. Malaria, dengue fever, dysentery, scurvy, and beriberi were rampant, along with tropical diseases the American doctors had never heard of. And things were about to get worse.

Rusconi himself surrendered in Manila in February of 1942. General MacArthur left in March and set up his command in Australia. Rusconi and his staff were thrown in a prison camp near Manila, but were allowed to maintain many of the records the Japanese did not deem important. They were reasonably well treated but always hungry. Things were to be far different on Bataan.

According to the scant records Rusconi was able to keep and piece together, Lieutenant Banning surrendered with his unit on April 10, 1942, on the southern tip of the Bataan Peninsula. He was one of approximately seventy thousand prisoners of war who were forced to march for days with no food and water. Thousands collapsed and died in the blistering sun and their bodies were simply tossed in roadside ditches.

Among the captured were hundreds of officers, and, as awful as the conditions were, some semblance of command was attempted. Word spread through the march that the names of those who died were to be remembered and later recorded so the families could be notified. Under the dire circumstances, it was a task that proved to be difficult. Rusconi digressed and explained to the jury that as of today, January 7, 1947, the U.S. Army was still in the grim business of finding and attempting to identify dead soldiers in the Philippines.

Miles Truitt stood, raised both hands, and said, "Your Honor, please, this is a murder trial. This story is tragic and compelling, but it has nothing to do with our business here."

Judge Oswalt was obviously struggling. The testimony was clearly irrelevant. He looked at John Wilbanks and said, "Where are you going, Counselor?"

Wilbanks managed to give the impression that he knew exactly what he was doing. He said, "Please, Your Honor, bear with me for a little longer. I think I can tie things together."

The judge looked skeptical but said to Rusconi, "Continue."

Several days into the march, Lieutenant Banning was injured and left behind. No effort was made to assist him because, as the captives had quickly learned, such an effort drew a quick bayonet from a Japanese guard. Later, during a break, some of the men from his unit listened as the Japanese soldiers finished off the stragglers. There was no doubt Lieutenant Banning had been shot by the Japanese guards.

Pete was listening because it was impossible not to, but he sat stone-faced and stared at the floor as if he heard nothing. Not once did he react or look at the witness.

Rusconi testified that at least ten thousand U.S. and Philippine soldiers died during the march. They died from starvation, dehydration, exhaustion, sunstroke, and executions by bullets, beatings, bayonetings, and beheadings. Those who survived were packed into wretched death camps where survival was even more challenging than it had been on the death march. The officers attempted to organize various ways to record the names of the dead, and during the late spring and early summer of 1942 lists of casualties began to filter into Rusconi's office in Manila. On May 19 the family of Pete Banning was officially notified that he had been captured, was missing, and was presumed dead. From that point, there was no word from the captain until the liberation of the Philippines, when he emerged from the jungle with a gang of commandos. For over two years, he had led his men in a brazen, heroic, and near-suicidal campaign of terror against the Japanese army. For his bravery and leadership, he was awarded the Purple Heart, the Silver Star, the Bronze Star, and the Distinguished Service Cross for heroism in combat.

At that moment, it was impossible to stare at Pete Banning and think of him as the man who murdered Dexter Bell. Judge Oswalt realized this and decided to intervene. "Let's take a recess," he said, reaching for a cigarette.

In his chambers, he flung off his robe and lit a Camel. He looked at John Wilbanks and said, "That's enough of that. This is a trial, not a medal ceremony. I want to know right now if your client will take the stand and I want to know how you plan to make this relevant."

Truitt was angry and said, "The damage is done, Judge. It's not relevant and it should not have been presented to the jury."

"Will he testify?" the judge demanded.

"I'm afraid not," Wilbanks said quietly in defeat. "He just told me that he does not wish to say anything."

"Do you have any more witnesses?"

Wilbanks hesitated and said, "Yes, one of the American soldiers who served with Pete."

"One of the commandos in the jungle?"

"Yes, but it's not important. My client just informed me that he will object to any more testimony about the war."

Oswalt took a long pull from his Camel and walked to a window. "Are there any more witnesses from either side?"

"The prosecution has rested, Your Honor," Truitt said.

"I have nothing else, Judge," Wilbanks said.

Oswalt turned around and stood behind his desk. "All right. I'll send the jury home. We'll work on the jury instructions in here; then you guys get some rest. You'll do your closing statements in the morning; then I'll give the case to the jury."

Clay Wampler was a cowboy from Colorado who joined the army in 1940. He was sent to the Philippines later that year as part of the Thirty-First Infantry. He surrendered on Bataan, survived the death march, and met Pete Banning in a POW camp. His life was saved when a Japanese guard sold him enough quinine to break his malaria. While being transported to a labor camp in Japan, he and Pete escaped. They decided that since they were dead men anyway, they would take their chances in the jungle, where they spent the first three days and nights lost in the bush. When they were too weak to walk and were discussing ways to commit suicide, they killed an injured Japanese soldier they caught napping in the woods. In his backpack they found food and water, and after gorging themselves they hid the body and barely escaped his patrol. Armed with a pistol, a knife, a rifle, and a bayonet, they eventually found American and Filipino guerrillas. They lived in the mountainous jungles and became quite adept at picking off enemy soldiers. Their exploits could fill a thick book.

Clay contacted John Wilbanks and offered to help in any way. He traveled to Clanton and was prepared to take the stand and say whatever was necessary to save his friend. When the lawyer informed him he would not be allowed to testify, he went to the jail on Tuesday afternoon to visit Pete.

Sheriff Gridley left the jail at five o'clock and, as was the custom now, turned his office over to his trusty and Tick Poley. Florry served her brother and Clay a fine dinner, and listened for hours as they swapped stories she had never heard before. It was the only time Pete talked about the war. As one tale led to another, Florry listened in disbelief at the descriptions of the suffering they had endured. Survival seemed like a miracle.

Clay was bewildered by the prospect of his friend being put to death by the State of Mississippi. When Pete assured him it was likely, he vowed to round up the old gang and lay siege to Clanton. The chubby deputies he had seen around the courthouse would be no match for their buddies, hardened commandos who had killed thousands in ways too awful to talk about.

"We often had to kill quietly," Clay explained gravely to Florry. "A gunshot draws attention."

She nodded as if she understood completely.

Long after dinner, Tick Poley finally knocked on the

door and said the party was over. Pete and Clay embraced and said good-bye. Clay promised to return with the gang to rescue their captain. Pete replied that those days were over.

He went to his cell, turned off his light, and fell asleep.

CHAPTER 16

A light snow was falling when Miles Truitt rose to deliver his closing argument to the jury. Few things excited the locals like a snowfall, and though the forecast was for only an inch or two, the town was buzzing as if it might get socked in for a month. Miles thought it might hurt his case. The jurors would not waste time with their deliberations but want to hurry home to prepare. John Wilbanks worried that the weather might not benefit Pete. It could distract the jurors. He was praying for one or two to hold out for a life sentence and not death, and any potential dissenters might throw in the towel, side with the majority, and get home before the roads became treacherous. An outright conviction was a certainty, but a split verdict on the sentence meant life and not death. He and Russell had been debating the pros and cons of snow throughout the early morning, with nothing set-tled. Russell was convinced it would not be a factor. The trial had been brief. The jurors were thoroughly engaged. Their decision was far too important to be affected.

The things lawyers argue about.

Miles walked to the jury box, smiled at the jurors, thanked them for their service, as if they had a choice, and said, "I ask you to ignore the testimony of the last witness, Major Rusconi, from New Orleans. Nothing he said was relevant to this case, to this charge of murder. I'm not asking you to forget the service and sacrifice of the defendant. It was extraordinary, even legendary, but that's where it ends. This country just won the greatest world war in history, and we have many reasons to be proud. Four hundred thousand Americans died, and today across this great land families are still picking up the pieces. Over five million men and women served, most of them bravely, even heroically. But, being a war hero does not give anyone the right to come home and commit such a senseless and horrible murder. What if all of our war heroes decided to take the law into their own hands and start firing away?"

Miles was pacing slowly and speaking without notes. He had rehearsed for hours, prepared for weeks, and knew this would be his finest hour.

"Instead, I ask you to think about Jackie Bell and her children. Three wonderful kids who will live the rest of their lives without their father. A fine man of God, a fine pastor, a great father and husband. A man cut down at the age of thirty-nine in cold blood, and for no apparent reason. A man with no defense, no warning, no reason to question why his friend suddenly showed up with a gun. No way to escape, no time to defend himself, no means to avoid a sudden and tragic end. A preacher who either was reading the Bible or had just finished when the defendant suddenly appeared without warning and took his life. I suppose we'll never know the cause of the conflict between Dexter Bell and Pete Banning, but I'll ask the question we've all asked each other since last October: Why in God's holy name could it not have been settled without bloodshed?"

Miles turned and glared at the defendant. He held his arms open wide and asked, "Why?"

Pete stared straight ahead, unflinching.

"But bloodshed is what we have, and it is now your duty to deal with it. There can be no doubt about the facts. The defense could not bring itself to suggest someone else did the killing. The defense did not claim that Pete Banning was mentally unstable. The defense did its best but there is no defense. Pete Banning shot and killed Dexter Bell. He acted alone and with premeditation. He planned it and he knew exactly what he was doing. When you retire to deliberate in a few moments, you'll take with you a copy of the deed he signed just three weeks before the murder. It was an attempt to transfer his biggest asset to his children, to protect his land. In legal terms, it is known as a fraudulent conveyance. A fraud, in preparation for a murder. We'll never know how long the defendant planned the killing, and it doesn't really matter. What matters is that it was carefully thought out, it was premeditated."

Miles paused, stepped to his table, and took a sip of water. He was an actor in the middle of a fine performance, and the jurors, as well as the others in the courtroom, were spellbound.

He continued, "Guilt in this case is simple, as is the

punishment. You and you alone have the power to sentence the defendant to death in the electric chair, or life without parole in Parchman prison. The reason we have the death penalty in this state is that some people deserve it. This man is guilty of first-degree murder, and under our laws he has no right to live. Our laws are not written to protect the interests of the wealthy, the privileged, or those who served this country in the war. If I am found guilty of first-degree murder, I deserve to die. Same for you. Same for him. Read the law carefully when you get back to the jury room. It's simple and straightforward and nowhere can you find an exception for war heroes. If at any time back there you find yourself tempted to show him mercy, then I ask you to take a moment and think about Dexter Bell and his family. Then I ask you to show Mr. Pete Banning the same mercy he showed Dexter Bell. God bless him. You took an oath to do your duty, and in this case your duty demands a verdict of guilty and a sentence of death. Thank you."

Judge Oswalt had set no time limits on the final summations. Truitt could have gone on uninterrupted for an hour or two, but he wisely did not. The facts were simple, the trial had been short, and his arguments were clear and to the point.

John Wilbanks would be even briefer. He began with the startling question of "How do we benefit by executing Pete Banning? Think about that for a moment." He paused and began pacing, slowly, back and forth before the jurors. "If you execute Pete Banning, do you make our community safer? The answer is no. He was born here forty-three years ago and has lived an exemplary life. Husband, father, farmer, neighbor, employer, church member, West Point graduate. He served this country with more courage than we can ever imagine. If you execute Pete Banning, do you bring back Dexter Bell? The answer is obvious. All of us have tremendous sympathy for the Bell family and their great suffering. All they want is their father and husband back, but that is not within your power. If you execute Pete Banning, do you expect to live the rest of your lives with a feeling of accomplishing something, of doing what the State of Mississippi asked you to do? I doubt it. The answer, gentlemen, is that there is no benefit in taking this man's life."

Wilbanks paused and gazed around the courtroom. He cleared his throat, and refocused on the jurors, meeting them eye to eye. "The obvious question here is, if killing is wrong, and we can all agree that it is, why is the State allowed to kill? The people who make our laws down in Jackson are no smarter than you. Their sense of good and evil, of basic morality, is no greater than yours. I know some of those people and I can assure you they are not as decent and God-fearing as you. They are not as wise as you. If you look at some of the laws they pass you'll realize that they are often wrong. But somewhere along the way, somewhere in the lawmaking process, someone with a little sense decided to give you, the jurors, a choice. They realized that every case is different, that every defendant is different, and there may come a moment, in a trial, when the jurors say to themselves that the killing must stop. That's why you have the choice between life and death. It's in the law that you have been given."

Another dramatic pause as Wilbanks looked from face to face. "We can't bring back Dexter Bell and deliver him to his children. But Pete Banning has children too. A fine young son and beautiful daughter, both away at college, both with their lives in front of them. Please don't take away their father. They've done nothing wrong. They don't deserve to be punished. Granted, Pete Banning will not have much of a life inside prison walls, but he will be there. His children can visit him on occasion. They can certainly write letters, send him photographs on their wedding days, and allow him the joy of seeing the faces of his grandchildren. Though absent, Pete will be a presence in their lives, as they will be in his. Pete Banning is a great man, certainly greater than me, greater than most of us in this courtroom. I've known him for practically his entire life. My father was close to his father. He is one of us. He was bred here of the same black dirt, raised here with the same beliefs and convictions and traditions, same as you and me. How do we benefit by sending him to his grave? If we the people execute one of our own, there will be a bloody stain on Ford County that will never wash away. Never, never, never."

His voice cracked slightly as he struggled to keep his composure. He swallowed hard, clenched his jaws, pleaded with his eyes. "I beg you, gentlemen of this jury, a jury of his peers, to spare the life of Pete Banning."

When John Wilbanks sat down next to Pete, he put an arm around his shoulder for a quick, tight hug. Pete did not respond but continued staring straight ahead, as if he had heard nothing.

Judge Oswalt gave the jury its final instructions, and everyone stood as its members filed out. "We are in recess," he said. "Court is adjourned." He tapped his gavel and disappeared behind the bench. It was almost eleven and the snow had stopped.

In complete silence, half the crowd filed out of the courtroom. The great question was how long it would take, but since no one could predict, little was said. Those who stayed behind congregated in small groups and whispered and smoked and shook their heads as the old clock above the bench ticked slowly.

Jackie Bell had heard enough. She and Errol left after a few minutes and walked to his car. He brushed snow off his windshield and they left Clanton. She had been away from her children for four days.

Florry, too, had seen enough of the trial. Avoiding the stares of the Methodists, she and Mildred Highlander gathered their coats and walked out. They drove to Mildred's home and brewed a pot of tea. At the kitchen table, they read the newspapers from Tupelo, Memphis, and Jackson. All three had reporters in the courtroom and photographers outside. Tupelo and Memphis ran long front-page stories, with pictures of Pete walking into the courthouse in handcuffs the day before. Jackson did the same on page 2. Florry clipped away and added them to her scrapbook. She would call Joel and Stella with the awful news when it arrived.

Pete returned to his cell and asked for a cup of coffee. Roy Lester fetched it and Pete thanked him. After a few minutes, Leon Colliver, the moonshiner across the way, said, "Hey, Pete, you wanna play?"

"Sure." Pete walked out of his cell, got the key ring hanging on a wall, and unlocked Leon's cell. They arranged their game board in the middle of the hall and began a game of cribbage. Leon pulled out his flask, took a sip, and handed it over to Pete, who took a shot.

"What are your chances?" Leon asked.

"Slim to none."

"They gonna give you the chair?"

"I'll be surprised if they don't."

No one volunteered to serve as foreman. As per instructions from the judge, their first order of business was to elect one. Hal Greenwood owned a country store out near the lake and was a big talker. Someone nominated him and he was unanimously elected. He quipped about deserving extra pay. The current rate in Ford County was a dollar a day.

Judge Oswalt had told them to take their time. The trial had been short; there was nothing else on the docket for that week, and it was obviously a serious case. He suggested they begin their deliberations by going through his written instructions and discussing the applicable code sections. This they did.

He said it was important to examine each exhibit placed into evidence. The gun and slugs received little attention—none was really needed. Hal slowly read aloud the autopsy and ballistics reports. He skimmed the quitclaim deed, hitting only the high points and passing on the legalese.

Walter Willy not only ran the courtroom but also was in charge of the jury. He stood guard outside the door, alone, and shooed away anyone who came close. By pressing an ear against the door he could hear almost everything being said inside. This he did, as always. He

heard the word "lunch" and backed away. Hal Greenwood opened the door and reported that the jurors were
hungry. Walter explained that he was a step ahead and
sandwiches had been ordered.

As they waited, Hal suggested they take an initial vote
on the issue of guilt. In no particular order, each of the
twelve said the word "guilty," though a couple were more
reluctant than the others.

John and Russell Wilbanks had lunch in the firm's
conference room. They usually walked down the street
to a café but were not in the mood for the stares and
banal observations from the people they saw almost every
day. Russell admired his brother's last appeal to the jury
and was convinced one or two would hold out for a life
sentence. John was not as confident. He was still frustrated, even moody and depressed over how he had handled the trial. If given free rein, he could have mounted
a strong insanity defense and saved Pete's life. His client,
though, seemed hell-bent on destruction. In perhaps the
biggest case of his career, he had been boxed in and rel-
egated to being little more than a bystander.

As he toyed with his lunch, he reminded himself that
nothing in a trial lawyer's life was as nerve-racking as
waiting on a jury.

One of Joel's fraternity brothers was from a small
town an hour from the Vanderbilt campus. When the
trial began Monday morning, Joel found it impossible to
think of anything else. His friend invited him to the family's estate, where they rode horses, hunted for hours
deep in the woods, and tried to talk of anything but what

was happening in Clanton. He called Stella each evening to check on her. She, too, was skipping classes and trying to avoid people.

Russell Wilbanks was correct. Three of the twelve could not bring themselves to vote in favor of death, at least not in the early deliberations. One, Wilbur Stack, was a veteran of the war who had been wounded three times in Italy. He had survived Miles Truitt's preemptory challenges simply because Miles used all five before he could exempt Stack. Another, Dale Musgrave, ran a sawmill down by the lake and admitted that his father had done business with Pete's father and had often expressed great admiration for the family. It was pointed out that perhaps this should have been mentioned during the selection process, but it was too late. The third, Vince Pendergrass, was a Pentecostal housepainter who claimed no ties to the Bannings but found it difficult to believe that he was expected to kill a man. Several of the other nine expressed the same feelings but were also determined to follow the law. None of the twelve were eager to vote for death, but all believed in the death penalty. On paper and in theory, it was quite popular throughout the country, and certainly in Mississippi. But very few people served on juries where they were asked to pull the switch. That was an altogether different matter.

The debate went on, in a dignified manner, with each man given ample opportunity to express his views. The snow was gone. The skies were clear, the roads passable. There was no urgency in getting home. At 3:00 p.m.,

Hal Greenwood opened the door and asked Walter for a pot of coffee and twelve cups.

After the coffee, and with the room fogged with cigarette smoke, decorum began to unravel as voices rose. The dividing line was clear but not entrenched. The nine never wavered, but the three showed signs of capitulation. It was pointed out repeatedly that they were dealing with a murder that was well planned and should have been avoided. If Pete Banning had only taken the stand and explained his motives, then there might be some sympathy. But he just sat there, seemingly oblivious to his own trial, and never once looked at the jurors.

The man was obviously damaged by the war. Why didn't his lawyer prove this? Could his motive have something to do with his wife and Dexter Bell? The Methodists resented this suggestion and defended the honor of the slain pastor. Hal Greenwood cautioned them that it was not their place to weigh the case outside the facts. They were bound by what they heard and saw in the courtroom.

Around four, Vince Pendergrass changed his mind and sided with the majority. It was the first conversion and a pivotal moment. The ten felt emboldened and ratcheted up the pressure on Wilbur Stack and Dale Musgrave.

Ernie Dowdle entered the hallway from the courtroom and caught Walter Willy dozing by the door to the jury room. It was almost five, past time for Ernie to go home, and he stopped by to ask Walter if he needed anything. Walter assured him he did not and told him to move along, he had matters firmly under control.

"What they doin' in there?" Ernie asked, nodding at the door.

"Deliberating," Walter said professionally. "Now please leave."

"Gonna get a verdict?"

"I can't say."

Ernie left and climbed a narrow stairway to the third floor, where the county kept a small law library and some storage rooms. Walking as softly as possible, he opened the door to a dark and narrow utility room where Penrod was sitting on a stool with an unlit corncob pipe in his mouth. A cast-iron air vent ran from the floor to the ceiling. A slit in the floor beside it carried not only the smell of cigarette smoke but the muted voices of the jurors directly below.

With hardly a sound, Penrod said, "Eleven to one."

Ernie looked surprised. An hour earlier the vote had been nine to three. He and Penrod were certain they would be fired and probably jailed if anyone learned of their eavesdropping, so they kept it to themselves. Most cases involving juries were civil in nature and too boring to fool with. The occasional criminal trial usually involved a black defendant and an all-white jury, with deliberations that were quick and predictable. Mr. Banning's trial was far more interesting. Were the white folks really going to convict and kill one of their own?

Having accomplished nothing through the afternoon, John Wilbanks decided to settle his nerves as darkness approached. He and Russell retired to an upstairs room where they kept a coffeepot and a fully stocked bar. Russell poured them Jack Daniel's over ice and they sat in old straw chairs that had been in the firm for decades. Through a window they could see the courthouse across the street, and on the second floor they could see silhouettes of the jurors as they occasionally moved around the room. They'd had the case for over six hours, which was not a long time in rural Mississippi.

John recalled the old story of a Depression-era jury that hung up for days over a trivial dispute. When the verdict was finally given, and the jurors dismissed, the truth came out. A dollar a day was pretty good money back then, and most of the jurors had little else to do.

They shared a laugh, poured another shot, and were discussing the possibilities of dinner when the light in the jury room went out. Moments later, the office phone rang. A secretary walked upstairs with the news that the jury was ready.

Judge Oswalt allowed some time to pass so the word could spread and the crowd could reconvene. At 7:00 p.m., as promised, he appeared on the bench in a black robe, told Walter Willy to dispense with his yodeling, and ordered Nix to bring in the defendant. Pete Banning walked to his chair and sat down without looking at a soul. When everyone was in place, Walter fetched the jury.

They filed in slowly, one by one, with each face downcast. One glanced at the audience; another glanced at Pete. They sat down and looked at the bench, as if hating the moment and wanting desperately to be some-where else.

Judge Oswalt said, "Gentlemen of the jury, have you reached a verdict?"

Hal Greenwood stood with a sheet of paper. "Yes, Your Honor, we have."

"Please hand it to the bailiff."

Walter Willy took the sheet of paper from Hal and, without looking at it, took it to the bench and gave it to the judge, who read it slowly and asked, "Gentlemen, do each of you agree with this verdict?"

All twelve nodded, some barely, none with enthusi-asm.

"Would the defendant please stand?"

Pete Banning slowly stood, straightened his back, braced his shoulders, raised his chin, and glared at Judge Oswalt.

"The unanimous verdict is as follows: 'We the jury find the defendant, Pete Banning, guilty of first-degree murder in the death of Dexter Bell. And we the jury order a sentence of death by electrocution."

Not only did the defendant fail to flinch; he didn't even blink. Others did, though, and throughout the crowd there were a few gasps and groans. And in the jury box Wilbur Stack was suddenly overcome with emotion and covered his face with his hands. For the rest of his life, he would regret the day he caved and voted to kill another soldier.

Florry kept it together, primarily because the verdict was no surprise. Her brother expected this outcome. She had watched the jurors through every word of the trial and knew there would be no compassion. And, frankly, why should there be? For reasons that seemed unfathomable, her brother had turned into a killer, one who wanted no sympathy. She touched a tissue to her cheeks and thought about Joel and Stella, but managed to keep her composure. She could lose it later, when she was alone.

Judge Oswalt picked up another sheet of paper and read, "Mr. Banning, by virtue of the power granted unto me by the State of Mississippi, I hereby sentence you to death by electrocution ninety days from today, April 8. You may sit down."

Pete took his seat with no expression. Judge Oswalt informed the lawyers they would have thirty days to file post-trial motions and appeals; then he thanked the jurors for their service and excused them. When they were gone, he pointed at Pete, looked at Nix, and said, "Take him back to the jail."

CHAPTER 17

At the Tea Shoppe on the square, the doors opened as usual at 6:00 a.m., and within minutes the place was full as lawyers, bankers, ministers, and businessmen—the white-collar crowd—gathered over coffee and biscuits and passed around the morning newspapers. No one ate alone. There was a round table for Democrats and another, across the room, for Republicans. The Ole Miss diehards huddled together in a clique near the front while those who favored the State College preferred a table near the kitchen. The Methodists had a spot, the Baptists another. Inter-table discussions were common, as were jokes and gags, but real arguments were rare.

The verdict attracted a full house. Everyone knew the facts and details and even the gossip but they came early anyway to make sure they had missed nothing. Perhaps Pete Banning had broken his silence and said something to his lawyer or Nix Gridley. Perhaps Jackie Bell had commented on the verdict to a reporter. Perhaps the Tupelo paper had sniffed out a lead the others had missed. And, the biggest topic to discuss: Would the State really execute Pete Banning?

A contractor asked Reed Taylor, a lawyer, about the appeals process. Reed explained that John Wilbanks had thirty days to notify the court that he would appeal, then thirty more to file his briefs and the necessary paperwork. The Attorney General in Jackson would handle the briefs for the State, and his office would have thirty more days to answer whatever John Wilbanks filed. That's ninety days. The state supreme court would then consider the case, and that would take a few months. If the court reversed the conviction, and Reed, frankly, saw no possible way that would happen, the case would be sent back to Ford County for a retrial. If the supreme court affirmed the conviction, John Wilbanks could stall things and attempt to appeal further to the U.S. Supreme Court. That would be a waste of time, but it might buy Pete a few months. If Wilbanks chose not to do this, then the execution could take place within the calendar year.

Reed went on to explain that in a death case the appeal was automatic. He had watched the entire trial and had seen no error upon which to base an appeal, but one had to be filed regardless. Furthermore, as Reed went on, the only possible mistake in the trial was allowing that soldier to testify about the war. And, of course, that was prejudicial to the prosecution. It gave John Wilbanks nothing to argue on appeal.

After Reed finished, the men went back into their huddles and the conversations were muted. Occasionally the door opened and a welcome blast of cold air penetrated the fog of cigarette smoke and bacon grease. The state senator arrived, seeking votes. He was not one of them, but instead lived in Smithfield down in Polk County. They saw little of him until reelection time and most of them quietly resented his presence in town during its moment of high drama. He made the rounds with a sappy smile, collecting handshakes and trying to remember names. He finally found a chair with the Baptists, all of whom were busy reading newspapers and sipping coffee. He had once waffled on the issue of statewide alcohol and they had no use for him.

As the early morning dragged on, it became apparent that there was nothing new in the Banning case. The trial had been quick, the verdict quicker. Evidently, after it was rendered nothing important had been said by the jurors, the lawyers, the defendant, or the victim's family. Efforts around the Tea Shoppe to create rumors fell flat, and by seven thirty the men were queuing up at the cash register.

Late Wednesday night, after the dreaded phone call from Aunt Florry, Joel returned to campus. Early Thursday, he went to the periodicals section of the main campus library where there were racks of a dozen morning editions from around the country. Tupelo and Jackson were not included but the *Memphis Press-Scimitar* was always there. He took it to a booth and hid, staring at the photo of his father as he left the courthouse in handcuffs, and reading accounts of what happened when the jury returned with its verdict. He still couldn't believe an execution date had been set so soon. He couldn't believe any of this tragedy.

His graduation was on for May 17. So, about five weeks or so after his father was to be strapped into an electric chair, he, young Joel Banning, age twenty-one, was expected to march proudly across the lawn in cap and gown with a thousand others and get his degree from a prestigious university. It seemed impossible.

Attending another class seemed impossible too. While his fraternity brothers had closed ranks and were trying their best to protect him and maintain some semblance of a normal college life, Joel felt stigmatized, ashamed, at times even embarrassed. He felt the stares in class. He could almost hear the whispers, on campus and off. He was a senior with good grades and could coast to graduation, which was exactly what he planned to do. He would meet with his professors and make promises. Quitting was not an option. Surviving was the challenge.

His application to the law school at Yale had been rejected. He was in at Vanderbilt and Ole Miss, and the difference in cost was substantial. Now that his father had been convicted of the murder, a wrongful death lawsuit could be expected. The family's finances were in for uncertain times, and Joel wasn't sure law school was feasible. Imagine, a Banning worried about money, and all because his father carried a grudge. Whatever the conflict between Pete and Reverend Bell, it wasn't worth the damage.

An hour passed and Joel skipped his first class. He left the library, wandered across campus, and bought a cup of coffee in the cafeteria. He drank it, skipped his second class, then returned to his dorm and called his sister.

Stella was drifting too. She had decided to take a leave and go hide in D.C. for the rest of the year. She loved

Hollins and would one day graduate, but at the moment every face she saw belonged to someone who knew her father was in jail for murder and now condemned to die. The shame and pity were too much. She ached for her mother's embrace. She grieved for her father, but she was also finding it easier to think ill of him.

Her favorite dean knew a Hollins graduate in D.C. and made the call. Stella would leave on the next train, live in a small guest cottage in Georgetown, babysit some kids, tutor them, be a nanny, a gofer, or whatever. And outside her host family, no one she encountered would know her name or where she was from. The move from Roanoke to Washington would put even more miles between her and Clanton.

Working for the *Memphis Press-Scimitar,* a cub reporter named Hardy Capley covered the trial from start to finish. His brother had been a POW during the war, and Hardy was intrigued by the presence of Clay Wampler, the Colorado cowboy who had served with Pete Banning in the Philippines. Clay was not allowed to testify but had made his presence known around the courtroom, especially during the recesses. He hung around Clanton for a few days after the trial and eventually left. Hardy badgered his editor until he relented and allowed the reporter to pursue the story. Hardy traveled by bus and train to Colorado and spent two days with Wampler, who spoke freely of his adventures and escapades fighting the Japanese as a guerrilla under the command of Pete Banning.

Hardy's story was ten thousand words and could have

been five times that. It was an incredible narrative that deserved to be published, but was simply too long for a newspaper. He refused to cut it, threatened to quit and take it elsewhere, and harangued his bosses at the newspaper until they agreed to publish it in a three-part series.

In remarkable detail, Hardy described the siege of Bataan; the bravery of the American and Filipino troops, their disease, starvation, and fear, their incredible courage in the face of a superior force, and their humiliation in being forced to surrender. The now infamous Bataan Death March was narrated so vividly that the editors were forced to tone it down somewhat. The savagery and cruelty of the Japanese soldiers was described with minor editing. The wanton murder and neglect of so many American POWs was heartbreaking and infuriating.

Though much of the story had already been told, both by escapees and by survivors, the story hit hard in Clanton because it involved one of their own. For over two years, Pete Banning had led a ragtag group of American and Filipino commandos as they harassed the Japanese, certain every morning that the day would be their last. Having avoided death so many times, they accepted it as a fact and fought with reckless abandon. They killed hundreds of Japanese soldiers. They destroyed bridges, railroads, airplanes, barracks, tanks, armories, and supply stations. They became so feared that a bounty of $10,000 was placed on the head of Pete Banning. Constantly pursued, the guerrillas could disappear into the jungles and attack days later twenty miles away from their last known position. In Wampler's biased opinion, Pete Banning was the greatest soldier he had ever known.

The series was widely read in Ford County and throttled most of the enthusiasm to see Pete executed. Judge Oswalt even commented to John Wilbanks that had the newspaper published the stories before the trial he would have been forced to move it a hundred miles away.

Pete Banning had steadfastly refused to talk about the war. Now someone else was doing the talking, and many in the county wanted a different ending to his story.

If the defendant was burdened by his conviction and death sentence, he showed no signs of it. Pete went about his duties as trusty as if the trial had never taken place. He kept the jail on a strict schedule, kept the two prisoner restrooms clean and orderly, barked at inmates who did not make their beds each morning or left trash on the floors of their cells, encouraged them to read books, newspapers, and magazines, and was teaching two of the inmates, one white and the other black, how to read. He maintained a steady supply of good food, primarily from his farm. When he wasn't busy puttering around the jail, he played cribbage for hours with Leon Colliver, read stacks of novels, and napped. Not once did he complain about his trial or mention his fate.

His mail increased dramatically after the trial. The letters came from almost every state and they were written by other veterans who had survived the horrors of war in the Philippines. Long letters, in which the soldiers told their stories. They supported Pete and found it appalling that such a hero was about to be executed. He wrote them back, short notes because of the volume, and before long he was spending two hours a day with his correspondence.

His letters to his children grew longer. He would soon be gone, but his written words would be theirs forever. Joel did not admit he was having second thoughts about law school. Stella certainly did not admit she was living in D.C. with her studies suspended. Her dean at Hollins forwarded Pete's letters, and in return mailed Stella's to him. She had not even told Florry where she was.

Pete was in the middle of a cribbage game one afternoon when Tick Poley interrupted and said his lawyer was there. Pete said thanks, then played on, making John Wilbanks wait twenty minutes until the game was over.

When they were alone in the sheriff's office, Wilbanks said, "We have to file your appeal by next Wednesday."

"What appeal?" Pete asked.

"Good question. It's really not an appeal, because we have nothing to appeal. However, the law says that in a death case the appeal is automatic, so I have to file something."

"That makes no sense, like a lot of the law," Pete said. He opened a pack of Pall Malls and lit one.

"Well, Pete, I didn't make the law, but rules are rules. I'm going to file a very thin brief and get it in under the wire. You want to read it?"

"What's it gonna say? What are my grounds for an appeal?"

"Not much. I'm sure I'll use the old standby: The verdict was against the overwhelming weight of the evidence."

"I thought the evidence sounded pretty good."

"Indeed it did. And since I was precluded from

mounting a defense on the grounds of insanity, which was our only possible strategy, and one that would have worked beautifully, then there really isn't much to write about."

"I'm not crazy, John."

"We've had this discussion and it's too late to cover it again."

"I don't like the idea of an appeal."

"Why am I not surprised?"

"I've been sentenced by a jury of my peers, good men from my home county, and they have more sense than those judges down in Jackson. Let's leave their verdict alone, John."

"I have to file something. It's automatic."

"Do not file an appeal on my behalf, do you understand me, John?"

"I have no choice."

"Then I'll find another lawyer."

"Oh, great, Pete. This is just beautiful. You want to fire me now that the trial is over. You want another lawyer so you can handcuff him too? You're headed for the electric chair, Pete. Who in hell would want to represent you this late in the fourth quarter?"

"Do not file an appeal for me."

John Wilbanks bolted to his feet and headed for the door. "I'll file it because it has to be filed, but I'm not wasting any more time, Pete. You haven't paid my fee for the trial."

"I'll get around to it."

"That's what you keep saying." Wilbanks opened the door, marched through, and slammed it behind him.

．　．　．

The appeal was filed, and John Wilbanks, to his knowledge, was not fired, nor was he paid. It was one of the thinnest filings ever received by the Mississippi Supreme Court in a murder case, and in response the State answered fully. Which was to say, with another thin brief. There was simply nothing wrong with the trial, and the defendant claimed no prejudicial errors. For a court often criticized for its glacier-like pace, the justices were reluctant to affirm so quickly in such a notorious case. Instead, they instructed their clerk to reshuffle the docket and set the Banning matter for oral argument for later in the spring. John Wilbanks informed the clerk that he had not requested oral argument and would not participate in one. He had nothing to argue.

April 8 came and went with no execution. By then word had filtered through the Tea Shoppe that delays were in the works and no firm date had been set, so the town was not counting the days. Instead, as spring arrived, the gossip around the town and county ventured away from Pete Banning and turned to the most important aspect of life, the planting of cotton. The fields were plowed and tilled and prepped for the seed, and the weather was watched intently. The farmers studied the skies as they marked their calendars. Plant too early, say in late March, and heavy rains could wash away the seed. Plant too late, say by the first of May, and the crop would be off to a bad start and run the risk of being flooded come October. Farming, as always, was an annual crapshoot.

Buford Provine, the Bannings' longtime foreman,

began stopping by the jail each morning for a cigarette with Pete. They usually met outdoors behind the jail, with Buford leaning against a tree while Pete stretched his legs on the other side of the eight-foot chain-link fence. He was in the "yard," a small square dirt patch sometimes used by the inmates for fresh air. It was also used for visitation and conferences with lawyers. Anything to get outside the jail.

On April 9, the day after he was supposed to die, Pete and Buford discussed the almanacs and forecasts from the weather service and made the decision to plant the seeds as soon as possible. As Buford drove away from the jail, Pete watched his truck disappear. He was pleased with their decision to plant, but he also knew that he would not be around for the harvest.

The day before he was to graduate from Vanderbilt, Joel packed his possessions into two duffel bags and left Nashville. He took the train to D.C. and found Stella in Georgetown. She was delighted to see him and claimed to be quite happy with her job, that of "practically raising three children." Her guest cottage was too small for another boarder, and besides her boss did not want anyone else living there. Joel found a room in a flophouse near Dupont Circle and got a job as a waiter in an upscale restaurant. He and Stella explored the city as much as her job would allow, and they reveled in being around large numbers of people who had no idea where they were from. In long letters home they explained to Aunt Florry and to their father that they had summer jobs in D.C. and life was okay. More about classes later.

On June 4, the Mississippi Supreme Court, without oral argument, unanimously affirmed the conviction and sentence of Pete Banning, and remanded the case back to Judge Oswalt. A week later, he set the execution thirty days away, on Thursday, July 10.

There were no more appeals.

CHAPTER 18

Prior to 1940, Mississippi executed its criminals by hanging, which at that time was the preferred method throughout the country. In some states the killings were done quietly with little fanfare, but in others they were public events. Tough politicians in Mississippi firmly believed that showing the people what could happen if they stepped too far out of line was an effective means of controlling crime, so capital punishment became a show in most instances. Local sheriffs made the decisions, and as a general rule white defendants were hanged in private while black ones were put on display.

Between 1818 and 1940, the state hanged eight hundred people, 80 percent of whom were black. Those, of course, were the judicial hangings for rapists and murderers who had been processed through the courts. During that same period of time, approximately six hundred black men were lynched by mobs operating outside the legal system and thoroughly immune from any of its repercussions.

The state prison was named after its first warden, Jim Parchman. It was a large cotton plantation covering eight thousand acres in Sunflower County, in the heart of the Delta. The people there did not want their home to be known as the "death county," and they had politicians with clout. As a result, hangings took place in the counties where the crimes were committed. There were no fixed gallows, no trained executioners, no standard procedures, no protocol. It wasn't that complicated, just secure a rope around the man's neck and watch him drop. The locals built the frames, crossbeams, and trapdoors, and the sheriffs were in charge of stringing up the condemned as the crowds looked on.

Hanging was quick and efficient, but there were problems. In 1932, a white man named Guy Fairley was hanged but something went wrong. His neck didn't break as planned, and he flailed about choking, bleeding, screaming, and taking much too long to die. His death was widely reported and prompted talk of reform. In 1937, a white man named Tray Samson dropped through the trapdoor and died instantly when his head snapped completely off and rolled toward the sheriff. A photographer was there, and though no newspaper would run the photo it made the rounds anyway.

In 1940, the state legislature addressed the problem. A compromise was reached when it was agreed that the state would stop hanging and move to the more modern method of electrocution. And since there was too much opposition to killing the defendants at Parchman, the state decided to construct a portable electric chair that could easily be moved from county to county. Impressed with their ingenuity, the legislators quickly passed this into law. Some problems arose when it was realized that no one in the country had ever used a portable electric chair. And, for a while anyway, no reputable electrical contractor wanted to touch this unique and clever idea.

Finally, a company in Memphis stepped forward and designed the first portable electric chair in history. It came with six hundred feet of high-tension cables, a switchboard, its own generator, helmet straps, and electrodes designed from specs borrowed from states with stationary electric chairs. The entire unit was carried from county to county in a large silver truck specially designed for such occasions.

The new state executioner was a sleazy character named Jimmy Thompson who had just been paroled from Parchman, where he had served time for armed robbery. In addition to being an ex-con, he was an ex-sailor, ex-marine, ex–carnival showboat, ex-hypnotist, and frequent drunkard. He got the job through political patronage—he personally knew the governor. He was paid $100 per execution, plus expenses.

Thompson loved cameras and was always available for interviews. He arrived early to each site, displayed his portable chair and its switchboard, and posed for photos with the locals. After his first execution, he told a newspaper the defendant died "with tears in his eyes for the efficient care I took to give him a good clean burning." The deceased, a black man named Willie Mae Bragg, who'd been convicted of killing his wife, was photographed being strapped in by deputies and then dying from electrocution. The executions were not open to the public, but there were always plenty of witnesses.

The chair was soon nicknamed Old Sparky, and its fame grew. In a rare moment, Mississippi was on the progressive end of something. Louisiana noticed it and built a copycat version, though no other states followed suit.

From October of 1940 to January of 1947, Old Sparky was used thirty-seven times as Jimmy Thompson toured the state with his road show. Practice did not make perfect and, though the citizens were quite proud of the killings, complaints arose. No two executions were the same. Some were quick and seemingly merciful. Others, though, were drawn out and dreadful. In 1943, an electrocution in Lee County went awry when Thompson improperly attached electrodes to the condemned man's legs. They caught on fire, burned his pants and flesh, and sent clouds of sickening smoke that gagged the witnesses in the courtroom. In 1944, the first jolt failed to kill the condemned man, so Jimmy pulled the switch again. And again. Two hours later, the poor man was still alive and in horrible pain. The sheriff tried to stop the ordeal but Thompson would have none of it. He ramped up the generator and finished him off with one last charge.

In May of 1947, Old Sparky was set up in the main courtroom of the Hinds County Courthouse in Jackson, and a black man convicted of murder was electrocuted.

And in July, Jimmy Thompson and his contraption headed to Ford County.

· · ·

Because John Wilbanks had heard the same question so often, and had so often given the same honest answer, there was little doubt that the execution was about to take place. There was nothing to stop it, save for a clemency petition Wilbanks filed with the governor without informing his client. Clemency was the sole province of the governor, and the chances of receiving it were slim. When John filed it he included a letter to the governor explaining that he was doing so only to cover all legal bases. Other than that, as John repeatedly explained, there was nothing to stop the execution. No pending appeals. No last-minute legal maneuverings. Nothing.

Clanton celebrated July 4 with its annual parade through downtown, with dozens of uniformed veterans marching and passing out candy to the children. The courthouse lawn was covered with barbecue grills and ice cream stands. A band played in a gazebo. Since it was an election year, candidates took turns at the microphone and made their promises. The celebration, though, was somewhat muted as the townsfolk talked of nothing but the execution. And, as John Wilbanks noted from the balcony of his office, the crowd was definitely smaller than usual.

On Tuesday, July 8, Jimmy Thompson arrived in his silver truck and parked it beside the courthouse. He unloaded it and encouraged all who were curious to have a look. As always, he allowed a few kids to sit in the electric chair and pose for photographs. Reporters were already gathering, and Jimmy regaled them with stories of his great experiences around the state. He walked them through the procedure, explaining in minute detail how the generator remained in the truck and the two-thousand-volt current would run approximately three hundred feet along the sidewalk and into the courthouse, up the stairs and into the courtroom, where Old Sparky was already in place near the jury box.

Joel and Stella arrived by train late on Tuesday night and were met at the station by Florry. They hustled away, ignoring everyone, and went to her pink cottage, where Marietta had dinner waiting. It was a somber evening with little conversation. What could be said? They were sleepwalking into a nightmare as reality slowly settled in.

Early Wednesday morning, Nix Gridley stopped by the courthouse and was not surprised to find a small crowd of gawkers staring at Old Sparky. Jimmy Thompson, a weasel the sheriff was already tired of, was holding forth on the amazing capabilities of his machine, and after a few minutes Nix left and walked to the jail. He rounded up Roy Lester, and, using a side door, they walked out with Pete Banning and quickly left in Gridley's patrol car. Pete sat in the rear seat, without handcuffs, and said virtually nothing as they raced south on the Natchez Trace Parkway. In the town of Kosciusko, they sat in the car as Roy bought biscuits and coffee from a diner. They ate in silence as the miles flew by.

The director of the Mississippi State Hospital at Whitfield was waiting at the front gate. Nix followed him through the grounds and to building 41, where Liza Banning had spent the last fourteen months. Two doctors were waiting. Stiff introductions were made, and Pete followed them to an office where they closed the door.

Dr. Hilsabeck did the talking. "Your wife is not doing well, Mr. Banning, sorry to say. And this will only make matters worse. She is in complete withdrawal and speaks to no one."

"I had to come," Pete said. "There was no other way."

"I understand. You will be surprised by her appearance, and don't expect much in the way of a response."

"How much does she know?"

"We've told her everything. She was showing some improvement until she was informed of the murder, several months ago. That caused a dramatic setback and her condition has only deteriorated. Two weeks ago, after I spoke with the sheriff, when it became apparent that the execution was inevitable, we tried to break it to her gently. That has caused a complete withdrawal. She eats almost nothing and hasn't spoken a word since then. Frankly, if the execution takes place, we have no idea of the impact. Obviously, we are deeply concerned."

"I'd like to see her."

"Very well."

Pete followed them down the hall and up one flight of stairs. A nurse was waiting beside an unmarked door. Hilsabeck nodded at Pete, who opened the door and stepped inside. The nurse and the doctor waited in the hall.

The room was lit by only a small dim ceiling light. There was no window. A door was opened to a tiny bathroom. On a narrow, wood-framed bed Liza Banning was propped up by pillows and awake, waiting. She wore a faded gray gown and was tucked in by sheets. Pete carefully walked to the bed and sat by her feet. She watched him closely, as if afraid, and said nothing. She was almost forty but looked much older, with graying hair, gaunt cheeks, wrinkles, pale skin, and hollow eyes. The room was dark, quiet, motionless.

Pete finally said, "Liza, I've come to say good-bye."

In a voice that was surprisingly firm she replied, "I want to see my children."

"They'll be here in a day or so, after I'm gone, I promise."

She closed her eyes and exhaled, as if relieved. Minutes passed and Pete began gently rubbing her leg through the sheets. She did not respond.

"The children will be fine, Liza, I promise. They're strong and they'll survive us."

Tears began running down her cheeks, then dripping off her chin. She did not reach to wipe them, nor did he. Minutes passed and the tears continued. She whispered, "Do you love me, Pete?"

"I do. I always have and I've never stopped."

"Can you forgive me?"

Pete looked at the floor and stared blankly for a long time. He cleared his throat and said, "I cannot lie. I've tried many times, Liza, but, no, I cannot forgive you."

"Please, Pete, please say you'll forgive me before you go."

"I'm sorry. I love you and I'll go to my grave loving you."

"Just like in the old days?"

"Just like in the old days."

"What happened to those days, Pete? Why can't we be together again with the kids?"

"We know the answer, Liza. Too much has happened. I'm sorry."

"I'm sorry too, Pete." She started sobbing and he moved closer and gently embraced her. She was frail and brittle and for a second he flashed back to the skeletons he was forced to bury on Bataan, once healthy soldiers starved to death and weighing less than a hundred pounds. He closed his eyes and pushed those thoughts away and somehow managed to remember her body back in the glory days when he couldn't keep his hands off her. He longed for those days, for the not too distant past when they lived in a state of near-constant arousal and never missed an opportunity.

He finally broke down and cried too.

The last supper was cooked by Nineva and it was Pete's favorite: fried pork chops, whipped potatoes and gravy, and boiled okra. He arrived after dark with the sheriff and Roy, who sat on the porch and rocked in wicker chairs as they waited.

Nineva served the family in the dining room, then left the house, in tears. Amos walked her home, after saying his good-byes.

Pete carried the conversation, primarily because no one else had much to say. What were they supposed to say at that awful moment? Florry couldn't eat and Joel and Stella had no appetites. Pete, though, was hungry and carved his pork chops as he described his visit to Whitfield. "I told your mom that you would see her on Friday, if that's what you want."

"That should be a pleasant little gathering," Joel said.

"We bury you Friday morning, then race off to the nut-house to see Mom."

"She needs to see you," Pete said, chewing.

"We tried once before," Stella said. She had not lifted a fork. "But you intervened. Why?"

"Well, we're not going to argue over our last meal, now are we, Stella?"

"Of course not. We're Bannings and we don't discuss anything. We're expected to keep a stiff upper lip and just plow on, as if everything will be okay, all secrets will be buried, life will eventually return to normal, and no one will ever know why you've put us in this horrible position. All anger is to be suppressed, all questions ignored. We're Bannings, the toughest of all." Her voice cracked and she wiped her face.

Pete ignored her and said, "I've met with John Wilbanks and everything is in order. Buford has the crops under control and he'll meet with Florry to make sure the farm runs smoothly. The land is in your names now and it will stay in the family. The income will be split each year and you'll get checks by Christmas."

Joel put down his fork and said, "So life just goes on, right, Dad? The State kills you tomorrow, we bury you the next day, then we leave and go back to our own little worlds as if nothing has changed."

"Everybody dies at some point, Joel. My father did not see fifty, nor did his father. Bannings don't live long."

"Now, that's comforting," Florry said.

"Male Bannings, I should say. The women folk tend to live longer."

Stella said, "Could we talk about something other than dying?"

Joel said, "Oh, sure, sis. The weather, the crops, the Cardinals? What's on your mind at this terrible hour?"

"I don't know," she said as she touched her napkin to her eyes. "I can't believe this. I can't believe we're sitting here trying to eat when this is the last time we'll ever see you."

"You have to be strong, Stella," Pete said.

"I'm tired of being strong, or pretending to be. I can't believe this is happening to our family. Why have you done this?"

There was a long gap as both women wiped their eyes. Joel took a bite of potatoes and swallowed without chewing. "So, I guess you plan to take your secrets to your grave, right, Dad? Even now, at the last hour, you can't tell us why you killed Dexter Bell, so we are destined to spend the rest of our lives wondering why. Is that where we are?"

"I've told you I'll not discuss it."

"Of course not."

"You owe us an explanation," Stella said.

"I don't owe you a damned thing," Pete snapped angrily, then took a deep breath and said, "I'm sorry. But I'll not discuss it."

"I have a question," Joel said calmly. "And since this will be my last chance to ask it, and it's something I'll be curious about for the rest of my life, I'm going to ask. You saw a lot of terrible things in the war, a lot of suffering and dying and you yourself killed a lot of men in battle. When a soldier sees that much death, does it make you callous? Does it make life and living somewhat cheaper? Do you reach a point where you think that death is not that big of a deal? I'm not being critical, Dad, I'm just curious."

Pete took a bite of a pork chop and chewed it as he considered the question. "I suppose so. I reached a point where I knew I was going to die, and when that happens in battle a soldier accepts his fate and fights even harder. I lost a lot of friends. I even buried some of them. So I stopped making friends. Then I didn't die. I survived, and because of what I went through it made life even more precious. But I realized that dying is a part of living. Everybody reaches the end. Some sooner than others. Does that answer your question?"

"Not really. I guess there are no answers."

"I thought we weren't talking about dying," Florry said.

"This is surreal," Stella said.

"Life is never cheap," Pete continued. "Every day is a gift, and don't forget that."

"What about Dexter Bell's life?" Joel asked.

"He deserved to die, Joel. You'll never understand it, and I suppose you'll learn one day that life is filled with things we can never understand. There's no guarantee that you are allowed to live with the full knowledge of everything. There are a lot of mysteries out there. Accept them and move on."

Pete wiped his mouth and shoved his plate away.

"I have a question," Stella said. "You'll be remembered for a long time around here, and not for the right reasons. In fact, your death will probably become a legend. My question is this: How do you want us to remember you?"

Pete smiled and replied, "As a good man who created

two beautiful children. Let the world say what it wants, it cannot say anything bad about the two of you. I'll die a proud man because of you and your brother."

Stella covered her face with her napkin and began sobbing. Pete slowly stood and said, "I need to be going. The sheriff has had a long day."

Joel stood with tears running down his cheeks and hugged his father, who said, "Be strong."

Stella had dissolved into a mess of tears and couldn't stand. Pete bent over, kissed her on the top of her head, and said, "Enough crying now. Be strong for your mother. She'll be back here one day."

He looked at Florry and said, "I'll see you tomorrow."

She nodded as he left the dining room. They listened as the front door closed, then all three had a good cry. Joel walked to the front porch and watched the sheriff's car disappear on the highway.

CHAPTER 19

Thursday, July 10, the date on the second death warrant signed by Judge Rafe Oswalt, Pete Banning awoke at dawn and lit a cigarette. Roy Lester brought him a cup of coffee and asked if he wanted breakfast. He did not. Roy asked if he'd slept well and he replied that he had. No, there was nothing Roy could do for him at the moment, but thanks anyway. Leon Colliver called out from across the hallway and suggested one last game of cribbage. Pete liked that idea and they arranged their game board between their cells. Pete reminded Leon that he owed him $2.35 in winnings, and Leon reminded Pete that he had not paid him for all the illegal liquor they had consumed in the past nine months. They had a laugh, shook hands, and called it even.

"Hard to believe this is really gonna happen, Pete," Leon said as he shuffled the deck.

"The law is the law. Sometimes it works for you; sometimes it doesn't."

"It just don't seem fair."

"Who said life is fair?"

After a few hands, Leon pulled out his flask and said, "You may not need this but I do."

"I'll pass," Pete said.

The door opened and Nix Gridley approached them. He appeared fidgety and tired. "Can I do anything for you, Pete?"

"I can't think of anything."

"Okay. At some point we need to walk through the schedule, just so we'll know what to expect."

"Later, Nix, if you don't mind. I'm busy right now."

"I see. Look, there's a bunch of reporters hanging around outside the jail, all wanting to know if you'll have anything to say."

"Why would I talk to them now?"

"That's what I figured. And John Wilbanks has already called. He wants to come over."

"I've had enough of John Wilbanks. There's nothing left to say. Tell him I'm busy."

Nix rolled his eyes at Leon, turned, and left.

The soldiers began arriving before noon. They came from nearby counties, easy trips of two and three hours. They came from other states, after driving all night. They came alone in pickup trucks, and they came in carloads. They came in the uniforms they once proudly wore, and they came in overalls, khakis, and suits with ties. They came unarmed with no plans to cause trouble, but one word from their hero and they would be ready to fight. They came to honor him, to be there when he died because he had been there for them. They came to say fare-well.

They parked around the courthouse and then around the square, and when there was no place to park they lined the streets of the downtown neighborhoods. They milled about, greeting each other, staring grimly at the townsfolk, people they really didn't like, because it was them, the locals, who had sentenced him to die. They roamed the halls of the courthouse and stared at the locked door of the upstairs courtroom. They filled the coffee shops and cafés and killed time, speaking gravely to each other but not to anyone from the town. They grouped around the silver truck and studied the cables that ran along the main sidewalk and into the courthouse. They shook their heads and thought of ways to stop it all, but they moved on, waiting. They glared at the police and deputies, a dozen armed and uniformed men, most sent in from nearby counties.

The governor was Fielding Wright, a lawyer from the Delta who had become a successful politician. He had stepped into the office eight months earlier, when his predecessor died, and he was currently seeking election to a full four-year term. After lunch on Thursday, he met with the Attorney General, who assured him there was nothing left in the courts that might stop the execution.

Governor Wright had received a flood of letters requesting, even demanding, clemency for Pete Banning, but others had asked for justice in the full measure of the law. He viewed his election opponents as weak and did not wish to politicize the execution, but like most people he was intrigued by the case. He left his office in the state capital in the backseat of a 1946 Cadillac, his official vehicle, with a driver and an aide. They followed two state troopers in a marked car and headed north. They stopped in Grenada, where the governor met briefly with a prominent supporter, and made another stop for the same reason in Oxford. They arrived in Clanton shortly before five and drove around the square. The governor was amazed at the crowd milling about the courthouse lawn. He had been assured by the sheriff that matters were under control and additional police were not needed.

Word had leaked that the governor was coming, and another crowd, mostly reporters, waited outside the jail. When he stepped out of his car, cameras flashed and questions were thrown at him. He smiled and ignored them and quickly went inside. Nix Gridley was waiting in his office, along with John Wilbanks and the state senator, an ally. The governor knew Wilbanks, who was supporting one of his opponents in the election. That did not matter at the moment. To the governor, this was not a political event.

Roy Lester brought in the prisoner and introductions were made. John Wilbanks asked the senator to please step outside. What was about to be discussed was none of his business. He reluctantly left. When the four men were alone, the governor went through a breezy narrative of having met Pete Banning's father years earlier at some event in Jackson. He knew the family was important to the area and had been prominent for many years.

Pete was not impressed.

The governor said, "Now, Mr. Banning, as you know

I have the power to commute your death sentence to life in prison, and that's why I'm here. I really don't see any benefit to proceeding with your execution."

Pete listened carefully, then replied, "Well, thank you, sir, for coming, but I did not request this meeting."

"Nor did anyone else. I'm here of my own volition, and I'm willing to grant clemency and stop the execution, but only on one condition. I will do so if you explain to me, and to the sheriff and to your own lawyer, why you killed that preacher."

Pete glared at John Wilbanks as if he was behind a conspiracy. Wilbanks shook his head.

Pete looked at the governor without expression and said, "I have nothing to say."

"We're dealing with life and death here, Mr. Banning. Surely you do not want to face the electric chair in a matter of hours."

"I have nothing to say."

"I'm dead serious, Mr. Banning. Tell us why, and your execution will not take place."

"I have nothing to say."

John Wilbanks dropped his head and walked to a window. Nix Gridley gave an exasperated sigh as if to say, "I told you so." The governor stared at Pete, who returned the stare without blinking.

Finally, Governor Wright said, "Very well. As you wish." He stood and left the office, walked outside, ignored the reporters again, and drove away to the home of a doctor where dinner was being prepared.

.   .   .

As dusk settled over the town, the crowd swelled around the courthouse and the streets were filled with people. Vehicles could no longer move and traffic was diverted.

Roy Lester left the jail in his patrol car and drove to the home of Mildred Highlander. Florry was waiting, and he returned to the jail with her. They managed to sneak through the rear door and avoid the reporters. She was taken to the sheriff's office, where Nix greeted her with a hug. He left her there, and a few minutes later her brother was brought in. They sat facing each other, their knees touching.

"Have you eaten?" she asked softly.

He shook his head. "No, they offered a last meal but I don't have much of an appetite."

"What did the governor want?"

"Just stopped by to say farewell, I guess. How are the kids?"

"'How are the kids?' What do you expect, Pete? They're a mess. They're devastated and who can blame them?"

"It'll be over soon."

"For you, yes, but not for us. You get to go out in a blaze of glory, but we are left to pick up the pieces and wonder why the hell this happened."

"I'm sorry, Florry. I had no choice."

She was wiping her eyes and biting her tongue. She wanted to lash out and finally unload everything, but she also wanted to hug him one last time to make sure he knew that his family loved him.

He leaned closer, took her hands, and said, "There are some things you should know."

CHAPTER 20

The prisoner made only one request. He wanted to walk from the jail to the courthouse, a short distance of only two blocks, but nevertheless a long march to the grave. It was important to him to walk proudly, head high, hands unshackled, as he bravely faced the death he had so often eluded. He wanted to show the courage that few people could ever understand. He would die a proud man with no grudges, no regrets.

At eight o'clock, he stepped from the front door of the jail in a white shirt and khaki pants. His sleeves were rolled up because the air was hot, the humidity stifling. With Roy Lester on one side and Red Arnett on the other, he followed Nix Gridley through the crowd that parted to make way. The only sounds were cameras flashing and clicking. There were no banal questions lobbed by the reporters, no shouts of encouragement, no threats of condemnation. At Wesley Avenue, they turned and headed for the square, walking down the middle of the street as the curious fell in behind. As they approached, the soldiers lining the street snapped to attention and saluted. Pete saw them, looked surprised for a second or two, then nodded grimly. He walked slowly, certainly in no hurry, but determined to get on with it.

On the square, a hush fell over the crowd as the prisoner and his guards came into view. Nix growled at some to stand back and give way and everyone complied. He turned onto Madison Street in front of the Tea Shoppe and the procession followed.

Ahead, the courthouse loomed, fully lit and waiting. It was the most important building in the county, the place where justice was preserved and dispensed, rights were protected, disputes settled peacefully and fairly. Pete Banning himself had served on a jury as a much younger man, and had been impressed with the experience. He and his fellow jurors had followed the law and delivered a just verdict. Justice had been served, and now justice awaited him.

The extra police had cordoned off the main sidewalk of the courthouse. Beside it ran the cables carrying the current. The generator in the silver truck hummed as they walked past, though Pete did not seem to notice. Following Nix, he stepped over the cables as they turned toward the building. He was surprised at the crowd, especially at the number of soldiers, but he kept his eyes straight ahead, careful not to see someone he might know.

They slowly made their way to the courthouse and stepped inside. It was empty now, the police having locked all doors and banned the curious. Nix was determined to avoid a spectacle, and he vowed to arrest anyone found inside without permission. They climbed the main stairway and stopped at the courtroom doors. A guard opened them and they entered. Cables ran down the aisle, past the bar, and to the chair.

Old Sparky sat ominously next to the jury box, facing the rows of empty benches where the spectators normally sat. But there were no spectators, only a handful of witnesses. Pete had approved none. There was no one from the family of Dexter Bell. Nix had banned all photographers, much to the dismay of Jimmy Thompson, who was eagerly waiting at the switchboard next to his beloved chair. Tables had been moved and a row of seats near the bench had been arranged for the witnesses. Miles Truitt, the prosecutor, sat next to Judge Rafe Oswalt. Next to him was Governor Wright, who had never seen an execution and had decided to stay in town for this one. He felt it was his duty to witness a capital punishment since his people were so passionately in favor of it. Beside the governor were four reporters, handpicked by Nix Gridley, and including Hardy Capley of the *Memphis Press-Scimitar*.

John Wilbanks was absent because he chose to be. Pete would have approved him as a witness, but John wanted no part of the proceedings. The case was over and he was hopeful the Banning mess was behind him. He doubted it, though, and strongly anticipated more legal fallout from the murder. At the moment, he and Russell were sitting on their office balcony watching the crowd and the courthouse and sipping bourbon.

Inside, Pete was led to a wooden chair next to Old Sparky and took a seat. Jimmy Thompson said, "Mr. Banning, this is the part of my job that I dislike."

Nix said, "Why don't you just shut up and do what you have to do?" Nix was fed up with Thompson and his theatrics.

Nothing else was said as Thompson took a set of surplus army clippers and cut Pete's hair as close to the scalp as possible. The dark brown and gray clippings fell in bunches onto his shirt and arms and Thompson deftly brushed them to the floor. He rolled up the khakis on Pete's left leg and skinned his calf. As he quickly went about his business the only sound in the courtroom was the buzzing of the clippers. None of the men watching had ever been near an execution and knew almost nothing about the procedures. Thompson, though, was a pro and went about his duties with efficiency. When he turned off the clippers he nodded at Old Sparky and said, "Please have a seat."

Pete took two steps and lowered himself into the clunky wooden throne. Thompson secured his wrists with heavy leather straps, then did the same at his waist and ankles. From a bucket, he took two wet sponges and stuck them to his calves, then secured them with a bulky strap holding an electrode. The sponges were necessary to aid the rapid flow of electricity.

Pete closed his eyes and began breathing heavily.

Thompson placed four wet sponges on Pete's head. Water dripped and ran down his face and Thompson apologized for this. Pete did not respond. The headpiece was a metal contraption, not unlike a football helmet, and when Thompson adjusted it into place, Pete grimaced, his only negative reaction so far. When the sponges were set under the headpiece, Thompson tightened it. He attached wires and fiddled with straps and seemed to be taking too much time. However, since neither Nix nor anyone else knew anything about the protocol, they waited and watched in silence. The humid courtroom grew even stickier and everyone was sweating. Because of the heat, someone had partially opened four of the tall windows on each side, and, unfortunately, someone had forgotten to close them.

Thompson felt the pressure of such a high-profile job. Most of his victims were poor black criminals, and few people cared if their executions had a flaw or two. Not a single one had ever walked away. But the execution of a prominent white man was unheard of, and Thompson was determined to pull off a clean killing, one that would not be criticized.

He picked up a black shroud and asked Pete, "Would you like a blindfold?"

"No."

"Very well." Thompson nodded at Judge Oswalt, who stood and took a few steps toward the condemned. Holding a sheet of paper, he cleared his nervous throat and said, "Mr. Banning, I am required by law to read your death warrant. 'By order of the circuit court of the Twenty-Second Judicial District for the State of Mississippi, and after having been found guilty of first-degree murder and sentenced to death by electrocution, said verdict having been affirmed by the supreme court of this state, I, Judge Rafe Oswalt, do hereby order the immediate execution of the defendant, Mr. Pete Banning.' May God have mercy on your soul." The paper was shaking as he read it without looking at Pete, and he sat down as quickly as possible.

From the darkened balcony, three colored men

watched the show in disbelief. Ernie Dowdle, who worked the courthouse basement, and Penrod, its custodian, and Hop Purdue, the church's janitor, all lay flat on their stomachs and peeked through the railing. They were too frightened to breathe because if they were seen Nix would almost certainly throw them in jail for years to come.

Thompson nodded at Nix Gridley, who stepped nearer the chair and asked, "Pete, do you have anything you want to say?"

"No."

Nix backed away and stood near the witnesses with Roy Lester and Red Arnett. The county coroner stood behind them. Jimmy Thompson stepped to his switchboard, studied it for a second, and asked Nix, "Is there any reason this execution should not go forward?"

Nix shook his head and said, "None."

Thompson turned a dial. The generator out in the silver truck whined louder as its gasoline engine increased the current. Those standing near it realized what was happening and backed away. The hot current shot through the cables and arrived in seconds at Old Sparky. A five-inch metal switch with a red plastic cover protruded from the switchboard. Jimmy took it and slammed it down. Two thousand volts of current hit Pete and every muscle in his body contracted and shot up and forward and he tore against the bindings. He screamed, a loud, mighty roar of unmitigated pain and agony that shocked the witnesses. The scream shrieked around the courtroom and continued for seconds as his body gyrated with a sickening fury. The scream escaped the courtroom through the open windows and reverberated through the night.

Later, those standing near the silver truck and its generator, on the south side of the courthouse near its front, would claim that they did not hear the scream, but those standing on the east and west ends, and especially those near the rear, heard it and would never forget it. John Wilbanks heard it as clear as thunder and said, "Oh my God." He stood and took a step closer and looked at the frightened faces of those nearest the courtroom. The scream lasted for seconds, but for many it would last forever.

The first jolt was supposed to stop his heart and render him unconscious, but there was no way to know. Pete convulsed violently for about ten seconds, though time was impossible to measure. When Thompson pulled the switch and cut the current, Pete's head slumped to his right and he was still. Then he twitched. Thompson waited for thirty seconds, as always, and lowered the switch for the second dose. Pete jerked as the current hit again, but his body resisted less and was clearly shutting down. During the second jolt, the temperature inside his body hit two hundred degrees Fahrenheit and his organs began to melt. Blood rushed from his eye sockets.

Thompson cut the current and instructed the coroner to see if Pete was dead. The coroner didn't move, but instead stood with his mouth open and stared at the ghoulish face of Pete Banning. Nix Gridley finally managed to look away and felt nauseated. Miles Truitt, who six months earlier had stood in the exact spot where Old Sparky now sat and begged the jury for the death penalty, had now witnessed his first execution and would never

be the same. Nor would the governor. For political reasons he would continue to support the death penalty
while silently wishing it would go away, at least for white
defendants.

In the balcony, Hop Purdue closed his eyes and began
crying. As the star witness, he had testified against Mista
Banning and felt responsible.

After the initial shock, the reporters recovered and
began scribbling with a fury.

"Please, sir, if you don't mind," Thompson said with
irritation as he motioned for the coroner, who was finally
able to move. Holding a stethoscope he'd borrowed from
a doctor, a fine physician who had flatly refused to get
near the execution, he stepped to the body and checked
Pete's heart. Blood and other fluids were pouring from
his eye sockets and his white cotton shirt was rapidly
changing colors. The coroner was not certain if he heard
anything or if he actually used the stethoscope correctly
because at that moment he wanted Pete dead. He had
seen enough. And, if Pete wasn't dead, then he would be
very soon. So the coroner backed away and said, "There
is no heartbeat. This man is dead."

Thompson was relieved that the execution had gone
so smoothly. Other than the excruciating scream that
seemed to rattle the windows, and perhaps the melting
eyeballs, there was nothing he had not seen before. Pete's
was his thirty-eighth execution, and the reality was that
no two were the same. Thompson thought he had seen
it all, from charred skin to bones broken as the bodies
flailed, but there was always a new wrinkle. All in all,
though, this was a good night for the State. He quickly
unlatched the headpiece, removed it, and placed the

shroud over Pete's face to hide some of the gore. He began unplugging wires and releasing bindings. As he went about his work, Miles Truitt excused himself, as did the governor. The reporters, though, remained transfixed as they tried to record every detail.

Nix pulled Roy Lester aside and said, "Look, I'm gonna finish up here and get the body to the funeral home. I promised Florry we'd let her know when it's over. She's at her place, that pink cottage, with the kids, and I want you to ride out there and deliver the news."

Roy's eyes were moist and he was obviously rattled. He managed to say, "Sure, Boss."

For over a hundred years, the Bannings had buried their dead in a family cemetery on the side of a rolling hill not far from the pink cottage. The simple tombstones were arranged neatly under the limbs of an ancient sycamore, a stately old tree that had been around as long as the Bannings. Long before Pete was born, the name Old Sycamore was given to the cemetery and became part of the family vernacular. A dead relative wasn't always dead. He or she had simply gone "home" to Old Sycamore.

At precisely 8:00 a.m. on Friday, July 11, a small crowd gathered at Old Sycamore and watched as a simple wooden casket was lowered by ropes into the grave. Four of the Bannings' field hands had dug the grave the day before, and now they managed the casket. The tombstone was already in place, complete with the name and dates: Peter Joshua Banning III Born May 2, 1903, Died July 10, 1947. Inscribed at the bottom were the words "God's Faithful Soldier."

Fifteen white people stood around the grave in their Sunday best. The burial was by invitation only, and Pete had made the list, along with detailed instructions as to starting time, scripture verses, and the construction of the casket. The guests included Nix Gridley, John Wilbanks and his wife, some other friends, and of course Florry, Stella, and Joel. Behind them were Nineva, Amos, and Marietta, the domestic help. Behind them and farther away were about forty Negroes of various ages, all Banning dependents, all dressed in the best clothing they owned. While the white folks at first tried to remain stoic and unemotional, the Negroes made no such efforts. They were crying as soon as they saw the casket being pulled from the hearse. Mista Pete was their boss and a good and decent man, and they couldn't believe he was gone.

In the 1940s, in rural Mississippi, the fate of a black family depended upon the goodness or evil of the white man who owned the land, and the Bannings had always been protective and fair. The Negroes could not grasp the logic of the white man's law. Why would they kill one of their own? It made no sense.

Nineva, who had assisted the doctor in birthing Pete forty-four years earlier, was overcome and could barely stand. Amos clutched and consoled her.

The minister was a young Presbyterian divinity student from Tupelo, the friend of a friend with almost no connections to Ford County. How Pete found him they would never know. He offered an opening prayer, and was quite eloquent. By the time he finished, Stella was once again in tears. She stood between her aunt and her brother, both with arms over her shoulders for support.

After the prayer, the minister read Psalm 23, then talked briefly about the life of Pete Banning. He did not dwell on the war but said only that Pete was decorated. He said nothing about the murder conviction and its aftermath but talked for ten minutes about grace, forgiveness, justice, and a few other concepts that he couldn't quite link with the facts at hand. When he finished, he said another prayer. Marietta stepped closer to the tombstone and sang a cappella the first two stanzas of "Amazing Grace." She had a beautiful voice and often sang along with the opera albums in the pink cottage.

When the minister said the service was over, the mourners slowly backed away to allow the gravediggers room to shovel in the dirt. The three Bannings had no desire to watch the grave filled. They spoke to a few of the friends as they headed for the car.

Nix Gridley stopped Joel and explained that many of the soldiers were still in town and wanted to stop by the grave and pay their respects. Joel discussed it with Florry and they agreed that Pete would approve.

An hour later they began arriving, and they came throughout the day. They came alone, solitary figures with lots of memories. They came in small groups and spoke to each other in whispers. They came quietly, somberly, proudly. They touched the tombstone, studied the freshly piled dirt, said their prayers or whatever they wanted to say, and they left with great sadness for a man few of them had ever met.

PART TWO

———•———

THE BONEYARD

CHAPTER 21

The Peabody hotel was built in downtown Memphis in 1869 and immediately became the center of high society. It was designed in an elaborate Italian Renaissance style with no expense spared. Its sweeping lobby featured soaring balconies and an ornate water fountain filled with live ducks. The hotel was without a doubt the most spectacular in Memphis and had no competition for hundreds of miles. It was instantly profitable as Memphians with money flocked to the Peabody for drinks and dinners, balls, galas, parties, concerts, and meetings.

Around the turn of the century, as the once wealthy cotton plantations in the Delta regions of Arkansas and Mississippi regained their footing, the Peabody became the preferred destination for big farmers looking for fun in the city. On weekends and holidays they took over the hotel, throwing lavish parties and mingling in fine style with their upper-class Memphis friends. Oftentimes they brought their wives for shopping. Other times they came alone for business and to spend romantic weekends with their mistresses.

It was said that if you parked yourself in the lobby of the Peabody hotel and stayed long enough you would see everyone who was someone from the Delta.

Pete Banning was not from the Delta and made no pretension of being so. He was from the hills of northeast Mississippi, and though his family owned land and was considered prominent, he was far from wealthy. In the social order, hill people ranked several notches below the planter class a hundred miles away. His first trip to the Peabody was at the invitation of a Memphis friend he met as a cadet at the U.S. Military Academy. The event was a debutante ball of some sort, but the real attraction, at least for Pete, was a weekend in Memphis.

He was twenty-two years old and had just graduated from the U.S. Military Academy at West Point. He was spending a few weeks on the farm near Clanton while waiting to report to Fort Riley in Kansas. He was already bored with the farm and ready for bright lights, though he was far from a hick going to town. He had been to New York City many times, for many occasions, and could hold his own in any social setting. A few Memphis snobs were not about to intimidate him.

It was 1925, and the hotel had just reopened after a complete renovation. Pete knew it by reputation but had never been there. For four years at West Point his friend had talked about the dazzling parties and scores of beautiful girls. And he was not exaggerating.

The black-tie debut was in the main ballroom on the second floor, and it was packed. For the occasion, Pete wore his formal army dress whites, solid white from collar to shoes, and he cut a fine figure as he mingled through the crowd, drink in hand. With perfect military posture, a tanned face, and an easy smile, he skipped from conversation to conversation and soon realized that a number of young ladies were taking notice. Dinner was called and he found his chair at a table filled with other friends of his host. They drank champagne, ate oysters, and talked of this and that, nothing serious, and certainly nothing to do with the military. The Great War was over. Our country was at peace. Certainly that would continue forever.

As dinner was served, Pete noticed a young lady at the next table. She was facing him, and every time he glanced over she was glancing too. In a roomful of gorgeous girls, she was undoubtedly the most beautiful one there, with perhaps the rest of the world thrown in as well. Once or twice he found it impossible to take his eyes off her. By the end of dinner, both were embarrassed by their mutual gawking.

Her name, as he soon learned, was Liza Sweeney. He followed her to the bar, introduced himself, and began chatting. Miss Sweeney was from Memphis, was only eighteen years old, and had never been tempted to do all that debutante foolishness. What she really wanted was a cigarette, but she would not smoke in front of her mother, who was trying to keep an eye on her from across the room. Pete followed her out of the ballroom—she seemed to know the hotel well—and to a patio near a pool. There they smoked three cigarettes each and downed two drinks—martinis for her, bourbons for him.

Liza had just finished high school but wasn't sure about college. She was tired of Memphis and wanted something bigger, something as big as Paris or Rome, but then she was just dreaming. Pete asked if she thought her parents would allow her to date a man four years older. She shrugged and said that for the past two years she had been dating whomever she pleased, but they were all a bunch of high school boys.

"Are you asking me for a date?" she asked with a grin.

"I am."

"When?"

"Next weekend."

"You're on, soldier boy."

Six nights later they met at the Peabody for drinks and dinner and another party. The following day, a Saturday, they took a long walk along the river, arm in arm now with a lot of touching, and strolled through downtown. That night, she invited him to dinner at her home. He met her parents and older sister. Mr. Sweeney was an actuary for an insurance company and was quite dull. His wife, though, was a beautiful woman who did most of the talking. They were an odd pair and Liza had already told Pete several times that she planned to leave home soon as possible. Her sister went to a college somewhere in Missouri.

Early in their courtship, Pete suspected that Liza was one of a thousand Memphis girls hanging around the Peabody hoping to snag a rich husband. He made it clear that he was not another wealthy Delta planter. His family owned land and grew cotton, but nothing like the big plantations. Liza at first put on some society airs, but once she realized Pete was just a commoner she quit her act. Inviting him home revealed the obvious—her family was quite modest. Pete didn't care how much money they had, or how little. He was thoroughly smitten and would chase her until he caught her, which, as he soon learned, would not be much of a challenge. Liza didn't care how big the farm was. She had found herself a soldier she adored and he was not getting away.

The following Friday, they met again at the Peabody for dinner with friends. After dinner, they sneaked away to a bar to be alone. And after drinks, they sneaked off to his room on the seventh floor. Pete had been with women before, but only those who worked the brothels of New York City. It was a West Point tradition. Liza was a virgin and ready for a change, and she embraced the lovemaking with an enthusiasm that made Pete dizzy. Around midnight he suggested that it was time for her to return home. She said she was not going anywhere, was in fact spending the night, and wouldn't mind staying in bed for most of the next day. Pete acquiesced.

"But what will you tell your parents?" he asked.

"A lie. I'll think of something. Don't worry about it. They're easy to fool and they would never expect me to do something like this."

"Whatever you say. Can we get some sleep now?"

"Yes. I know you're exhausted."

The courtship raged for a month as the two lovers forgot the world existed. Every weekend, Pete got a room at the Peabody, where he spent three nights, often with Liza sleeping over. Her friends began whispering. Her parents were getting suspicious. It was, after all, 1925, and there were strict rules that governed proper young ladies and their beaus. Liza knew the rules as well as her friends, but she also knew how much fun a girl could have if she broke a few of them. She was enjoying the martinis, the cigarettes, and especially the forbidden sex.

On a Sunday, Pete drove her to Clanton to meet his family, see the farm, and get a glimpse of where he came from. He did not plan to spend the rest of his life growing cotton. The military would be his career, and he and Liza would travel the world, or at least that was what he believed at the age of twenty-two.

He was ordered to Fort Riley in Kansas, where he would go through officer training. While he had been waiting eagerly for his orders, his first assignment, he was crushed at the thought of leaving Liza. He drove to her home in Memphis and broke the news. They knew it was coming, but being separated now seemed impossible. When he said good-bye, both were in tears. He rode the train to Fort Riley, and a week later received a letter from Liza. She got right to the point—she was pregnant.

With no hesitation, he devised a plan. Claiming urgent family matters required him to return home, he cajoled his commanding officer into lending him his car. Pete drove through the night and arrived at the Peabody in time for breakfast. He called Liza and informed her that they would now elope. She loved the idea but was not sure how she could sneak a suitcase out of the house with her mother around. Pete convinced her to forget the suitcase. There were stores in Kansas City.

Liza kissed her mom good-bye and went to work. Pete intercepted her, and they fled Memphis, racing away, giggling, laughing, and pawing at each other. They found a pay phone in Tupelo and called Mrs. Sweeney. Liza was sweet, but abrupt. Mom, sorry to surprise you like this, but Pete and I are eloping. I'm eighteen and I can do what I want. Love you and I'll call again tonight and talk to Dad. When she hung up, her mother was crying. Liza, though, was the happiest girl in the world.

Since they were in Tupelo, a town Pete knew well, they decided to get married. The better housing at Fort Riley was reserved for officers and their families, and a marriage certificate would be an asset. They went to the Lee County Courthouse, filled out an application, paid a fee, and found a justice of the peace stocking minnows in the rear of his bait shop. With his wife as the witness, and after pocketing his customary $2 fee, he pronounced them husband and wife.

Pete would call his parents later. Since the clock was now ticking on child number one, it was important to establish a wedding date as soon as possible. Pete knew the gossips in Clanton would begin looking at calendars as soon as they heard the news from his mother that her first grandchild had arrived. Liza thought the due date was about eight months away. Eight months would raise an eyebrow or two but not stir the gossip. Seven would be a stretch. Six would be downright scandalous.

They were married on June 14, 1925.

Joel was born on January 4, 1926, in an army hospital in Germany. Pete had begged for an assignment on foreign soil to get as far away from Memphis and Clanton as possible. No one there would ever see Joel's birth certificate. He and Liza waited six weeks before sending telegraphs to the grandparents back home.

From Germany, Pete was transferred back to Fort Riley in Kansas, where he trained with the Twenty-Sixth

Cavalry Regiment. He was an excellent horseman, but he was beginning to question whether mounted cavalry had a role in modern warfare. Tanks and mobile artillery were the future, but he loved the cavalry nonetheless and stayed with the Twenty-Sixth. Stella was born at Fort Riley in 1927.

On June 20, 1929, Pete's father, Jacob, died of an apparent heart attack at the age of forty-nine. Liza, with two sick toddlers, could not make the trip to Clanton for Mr. Banning's funeral. She had not been home in two years, and she preferred to stay away.

Four months after Mr. Banning's death, the stock market crashed and the country fell into the Great Depression. For career officers, the collapse of the economy was hardly felt. Their jobs, housing, health care, education, and paychecks were secure, though slightly diminished. Pete and Liza were happy with his career and their growing family, and their future was still in the army.

The cotton market also collapsed in 1929 and farmers were hit hard. They borrowed to pay expenses and debts and to plant again the following year. Pete's mother was not functioning well since the sudden death of her husband and was unable to manage the farm. His older sister, Florry, was living in Memphis and had little interest in agriculture. Pete hired a foreman for the 1930 planting but the farm lost money again. He borrowed money and hired another foreman for the following year, but the market was still depressed. The debts were piling up and the Banning land was in jeopardy.

During the Christmas holidays of 1931, Pete and Liza discussed the gloomy prospect of leaving the army and returning to Ford County. Neither wanted to, especially

Liza. She could not picture herself living in such a small backwater town as Clanton, and she could not stomach the thought of living in the same house with Pete's mother. The two women had spent little time together, but enough to realize that they needed separation. Mrs. Banning was a devout Methodist who knew the answers to everything because they were written right there in the holy scriptures. Using the divine authority of God's word, she could and would tell anyone exactly how to live his or her life. She wasn't loud or obnoxious, just overly judgmental.

Pete wanted to avoid her too. Indeed, he had entertained thoughts of selling the farm to get out of the business. This idea fell flat for three reasons. First, he didn't own the farm. His mother inherited it from his father. Second, there was no market for farmland because of the Depression. And third, his mother would have no place to live.

Pete loved the army, especially the cavalry, and wanted to serve until retirement. As a boy, he had chopped and picked cotton and spent long hours in the fields, and he wanted a different life. He wanted to see the world, perhaps fight in a war or two, earn some medals, and keep his wife happy.

So he borrowed again and hired the third foreman. The crops were beautiful, the market was strong, and then, in early September, the rains came like monsoons and washed everything away. The 1932 crop produced nothing, and the banks were calling. His mother continued to decline and could hardly take care of herself.

Pete and Liza discussed a move to Memphis or maybe Tupelo, anywhere but Clanton. A bigger city would provide more opportunities, better schools, a more vibrant social life. Pete could work the farm and commute, or could he? On Christmas Eve, they were planning their evening when a telegram arrived. It was from Florry and the news was tragic. Their mother had died the day before, possibly of pneumonia. She was only fifty.

Instead of unwrapping gifts, they hurriedly packed their bags and made the long drive to Clanton. His mother was buried at Old Sycamore, next to her husband. Pete and Liza made the decision to stay and never returned to Fort Riley. He resigned his commission but remained in the reserves.

There were rumblings of wars. The Japanese were expanding in Asia and had invaded China the year before. Hitler and the Nazis were building factories that were building tanks, airplanes, submarines, cannons, and everything else a military needed to aggressively expand. Pete's colleagues in the army were alarmed at what was happening. Some predicted an inevitable war.

As Pete turned in his uniform and went home to save the farm, he could not hide his pessimism. He had debts to pay and mouths to feed. The Depression was entrenched and had the entire nation in its grip. The country was lightly armed and vulnerable and too broke to fund a wartime military.

But if war came, he would not stay on the farm and miss it.

CHAPTER 22

After back-to-back bumper crops in 1925 and 1926, Jacob Banning decided to build a fine home. The one Pete and Florry knew as children had been built before the Civil War, and over the decades had been added to and retrofitted. It was certainly nicer than most homes in the county, but Jacob, with money in his pocket, wanted to make a statement and build something his neighbors would admire long after he was gone. He hired an architect in Memphis and approved a stately Colonial Revival design, a two-story home dominated by red brick, sweeping gables, and a wide front porch. Jacob built it on a small rise closer to the highway, but still far enough away so that the traffic could admire it without being worrisome.

Now that Jacob was dead, as was his wife, the spacious home was Liza's domain, and she wanted to fill it with children. Typically, she and Pete went about this project with great enthusiasm, but the results were disappointing.

She had one miscarriage at Fort Riley, then another when they moved to the farm. After a few months of dark mood swings and a lot of tears, she bounced back as vigorous as before, much to Pete's delight. Liza had only one sibling, as did Pete, and they agreed that small families were boring. She dreamed of having five children, Pete wanted six, three of each, so they pursued their marital duties with a fierce determination.

When he wasn't in bed with his wife, Pete was aggressively getting the farm into shape. He spent hours in the fields doing the manual work himself and setting the example for his workers. He cleared land, rebuilt a barn, repaired outbuildings, laid down fencing, bought new livestock, and usually worked from sunrise to dusk. He met with the bankers and told them bluntly that they would have to wait.

The weather cooperated in 1933, and with Pete driving his field hands into the ground the crop was abundant. The market cooperated as well, and the farm had its first breathing room in years. Pete kept the banks happy as he made payments, but he also buried some money in the backyard. The Banning land consisted of two sections, 640 acres each, and if more of it could be cleared, more cotton could be planted. For the first time in his life, Pete began to see the long-term potential of his inheritance.

He owned one section, Florry the other, and they struck a deal whereby he would cultivate her land for half the profits. In 1934, she built her pink cottage and moved from Memphis. Her arrival on the farm added some life to the place. She liked Liza and they were amiable, at first.

Not that life was dull; it was not. Liza enjoyed being a full-time mother as she tried in vain to add to her family. Pete taught her how to ride a horse, built a barn, and filled it with horses and ponies. Before long she had Joel and Stella in the saddle, and the three of them rode for hours around the farm and the neighboring countryside. Pete taught her how to shoot and they hunted birds together. He taught her how to fish and the little family spent hours on Sunday afternoons down by the river.

If Liza missed the big city, she rarely complained. At the age of thirty, she had a happy marriage with a husband she adored and was blessed with two beautiful children. She lived in a fine home surrounded by farmland that provided security. For a party girl, though, the social life was disappointing. There was no country club, no fancy hotel, no dance clubs or decent bars. Indeed, there were no bars at all because Ford County, like the entire state, was as dry as a bone. Alcohol sales were illegal in all eighty-two counties and every city. Those of a more sinful nature were forced to rely upon bootleggers, who were plentiful, or friends who hauled back booze from Memphis.

Social life was dictated by the church. In the case of the Bannings, of course, it was the Methodist church, the second largest in Clanton. Pete insisted that they attend faithfully, and Liza fell into the routine. She had been raised as a lukewarm Episcopalian, of which there were none—devout or otherwise—to be found in Clanton. At first, she was a bit turned off by the narrowness of Methodist teachings, but soon understood that things could be worse. The county was full of other, more strident strains of Christianity—Baptists, Pentecostals, and Churches of

Christ—hard-core believers even more fundamental than the Methodists. Only the Presbyterians seemed slightly less dogged. If there was a solitary Catholic in town he kept it quiet. The nearest Jew was in Memphis.

People were classified, and often judged, by their denomination. And they were certainly condemned if they didn't claim one. Liza joined the Methodist church and became an active member. What else was there to do in Clanton?

However, because she was an outsider, regardless of her husband's pedigree, it would take a long time to fit in. The locals really didn't trust you unless their ancestors had known your grandfather. She attended faithfully and grew to enjoy the worship services, especially the music. Eventually, she was asked to join a women's Bible study group that met once a month. Then she was asked to assist in the planning of a wedding. She helped out with a couple of important funerals. A traveling evangelist came to town for the spring revival, and Pete offered their guest room for the week. As it turned out, he was quite handsome, and the ladies envied Liza's closeness to the charismatic young preacher. Pete kept a close eye on the situation and was pleased when the revival was over.

But there was always another upcoming revival. The Methodists had two each year, the Baptists three, and the Pentecostals seemed to be in a constant state of frenzied renewal. At least twice a year some itinerant street preacher threw up a big top beside the feed store near the square and raged every night through his loudspeakers. It was not at all uncommon for one church to "visit" another church when a hotshot preacher was in town. Every denomination worshipped for at least two hours on Sunday morning. Others came back for more on Sunday evening. (These were the white churches; the black ones kept it going all day and into the night.) Wednesday night prayer meetings were common. Add in all the revivals, religious holiday services, vacation Bible schools in the summer, funerals, weddings, anniversaries, and baptisms, and at times Liza felt exhausted from her church work.

She insisted that they get out of town occasionally. If Florry agreed to keep the kids, they headed for the Peabody and a long weekend of partying. Occasionally, Florry went with them, along with Joel and Stella, and the whole family enjoyed the big city, especially the lights. On two occasions, and with Florry's insistence, the entire family loaded onto a train and went to New Orleans for a week's vacation.

In 1936, there was a stark contrast in electrical service in the South. Ninety percent of urban areas had power, while only 10 percent of the small towns and countryside had electricity. Downtown Clanton was wired in 1937, but the rest of the county was still dark. Shopping in Memphis and Tupelo, Liza and the other ladies from the farms were awed by the fancy electrical appliances and gadgets that were flooding the market—radios, phonographs, stoves, refrigerators, toasters, mixers, even vacuum cleaners—and they were untouchable. The country folks dreamed of electricity.

Liza wanted to spend as much time as possible in Memphis and Tupelo, but Pete resisted. He was a farmer now, and as such grew more tightfisted each year. So she settled into the quiet life and kept her complaints to herself.

Nineva and Amos came with the house and the farm. Their parents had been born into slavery and had worked the same land Pete now farmed. Nineva claimed to be "around sixty" but there was no clear record of her birth date. Amos didn't care when he was born, but to irritate his wife he often said he was born after her. Their oldest son had a birth certificate proving that he was forty-eight. It was unlikely Nineva gave birth when she was twelve. Amos said she was at least twenty. The Bannings knew she was actually "around seventy," though this subject was off-limits. She and Amos had three other children and a yard full of grandchildren, but by 1935 most had migrated north.

Nineva worked her entire life in the Banning home as the sole domestic servant. Cook, dishwasher, maid, laundress, nanny, babysitter, midwife. She helped the doctor deliver Florry in 1898 and her little brother, Pete, in 1903, and practically raised both of them. To Pete's mother, she was a friend, therapist, sounding board, confidante, and adviser.

To Pete's wife, though, she was more of a rival. The only white people Nineva trusted were Bannings, and Liza was not a Banning. She was a Sweeney, a city girl who knew nothing about the ways of country blacks and whites. Nineva had just said good-bye to her dearest friend, "Miz Banning," and she was not ready to welcome a new madam to the home.

At first, Nineva resented the beautiful young wife with a considerable personality. She was warm and pleasant and gave every indication of wanting to fit in, but all

Nineva saw was more work. She had spent the past four years taking care of Miz Banning, who asked for little, and Nineva could admit to herself that she had grown a bit lazy. Who cared if the house wasn't spotless? Miz Banning noticed virtually nothing in her declining years. Suddenly, with this new woman around, Nineva's lethargic routines were about to change. It was immediately obvious that Pete's wife loved clothes, all of which of course had to be washed, occasionally starched, and always ironed. And Joel and Stella, as precious as they were, would require meals and clean clothes, towels, bedsheets. Instead of tending to Miz Banning's birdlike appetite, Nineva suddenly faced the reality of cooking three meals each day for an entire family.

At first, Liza was uncomfortable with the presence of another woman in her home throughout the day, and a strong and established woman at that. She had not been raised with maids and servants. Her mother had been able to take care of the home, with the help of her husband and two daughters. However, it took only a few days to realize that properly maintaining such a large home was more work than she could handle. Without igniting a turf battle or hurting Nineva's feelings, Liza quickly acquiesced.

Both women were smart enough to realize that neither was leaving. They had no choice but to get along, at least superficially. The house was big enough to provide space for each. The first weeks were strained, but as they felt each other out the tension subsided. Pete was of no help. He was in the fields, where he was happy and unconcerned. Let the women work things out.

Amos, on the other hand, adored Liza from day one.

Each spring, he planted a large vegetable garden that fed the Bannings and many of their dependents, and Liza was drawn to it. As a city girl, she had grown nothing but a few daisies in a small flower bed. Amos's garden was half an acre of perfect rows of squash, corn, lettuce, beans, carrots, yams, peppers, eggplant, cucumbers, okra, strawberries, onions, and at least four varieties of tomatoes. Next to the garden was a small orchard with trees of apples, peaches, plums, and pears. Amos was also in charge of the chickens, pigs, and milk cows. Fortunately, someone else took care of the livestock.

His new assistant was more than welcome. After breakfast each morning, Liza was in the garden watering the plants, pulling weeds, picking off insects, harvesting the ripe produce, and either humming merrily along or asking him a dozen questions about gardening. She wore a wide-brimmed straw hat to ward off the sun, and chinos rolled up to her knees and gloves to her elbows. She didn't mind the dirt and mud but she somehow managed to keep it off her clothing. Amos thought she was the most beautiful woman he'd ever seen and developed a crush, though he went through his routine of appearing frustrated with her intrusions. She wanted to learn everything about vegetable gardening, and when she ran out of questions they went to the dairy barn, where he taught her to milk cows, churn butter, and make cheese.

They were often assisted by Jupe, the teenage grandson of Amos and Nineva. Jupe's mother had named him Jupiter, which he couldn't stand, so he shortened it. She was in Chicago, never to return, but Jupe preferred life on the farm and lived with his grandparents. At fifteen, he was a strapping, muscular boy who was fascinated by Liza but terribly shy around her.

At first, Amos suspected her enthusiasm was driven by a desire to get out of the house and away from Nineva, and this was partly true. But a friendship developed, much to the surprise of both. Liza wanted to know about his family and his background, his parents and grandparents and their harsh lives on the farm. Her father was from the North. Her mother was raised in Memphis. Liza had never been around Negroes and showed sympathy for their plight. Using his words carefully and always choosing less instead of more, he explained that he and Nineva and their children were the luckier ones. They had a nice little house, one built for them by Pete's father when he tore down the old family place. They had plenty of food and clothing. No one went hungry on the Banning land, but the field hands were quite poor. Their little shacks were barely livable. The children, and there were plenty of them, were always barefoot.

Liza knew that Amos was being cautious. He could not be accused of criticizing his boss. And, he was always quick to point out that there were plenty of poor whites around them who were just as desperate as the field hands.

On horseback and alone, Liza covered the Banning property, about two-thirds of which was farmland. The rest was heavily forested. She found tiny settlements of shacks tucked away in the woods, cut off from the world. The children on their porches were dirty and wide-eyed and refused to speak when she spoke to them. The mothers nodded and smiled as they herded the children back inside. In a village of sorts she found a store and a church with a cemetery behind it. Clusters of shanties lined the dusty streets.

Liza was stunned by the poverty and living conditions, and she vowed to one day find ways to make improvements. Initially, though, she kept her thoughts to herself. She did not tell Pete about her rides through the woods, though he soon knew. One of the field hands reported the sighting of an unknown white woman on a horse. Liza said of course it was her, and what was the problem? She had not been told that some places were off-limits, had she?

No, nothing was off-limits. There was nothing to hide. What were you looking for?

I was riding my horse. How many Negroes live on our land?

Pete wasn't sure, because the families were always growing. About a hundred, but not all worked for them. Some had other jobs. Some moved away; some came back. A few of the men had multiple families. Why do you want to know?

Just curious. Liza knew the project would take years, and now was not the time to start trouble. Pete still owed the banks. The country was still in a depression. There was little spare money. Even their trips to Memphis were budgeted.

In late March of 1938, as Liza and Amos were taking advantage of a warm, sunny day and planting peas and butter beans, she began to feel dizzy. She stood to catch her breath and then fainted. Amos scooped her up and ran with her to the back porch, where Nineva met them.

Nineva, who was the resident nurse, doctor, and midwife, wiped her face with a cold towel and coaxed her back to life. After a few minutes, Liza felt fine and said, "I feel like I'm pregnant."

No surprise there, Nineva thought but didn't utter a word. That afternoon, Pete drove Liza to the doctor in Clanton, and he confirmed that she was two months along. Joel and Stella were too young for such news and nothing was said around the house. Privately, Pete and Liza were thrilled. After two miscarriages, and a lot of effort, they had finally succeeded. Pete demanded that she leave the gardening to Amos and take it easy for a spell.

A month later, Liza miscarried again. It was a crushing loss and she fell into a dark depression. She closed the curtains and, for a month, rarely left her bedroom. Nineva, as always, stepped up and waited on her as often as she would allow. Pete spent as much time as possible with her, but nothing seemed to revive her spirits, not even Joel and Stella. Finally, Pete drove her to Memphis to see a specialist. They stayed two nights with her parents, but that did nothing to lighten her mood. Early one morning over coffee, he confided in Nineva that he was terribly worried. It was almost frightening to watch someone as vivacious as Liza fall into such a morbid state.

Nineva had experience with depressed white women. Miz Banning didn't smile the last four years of her life, and Nineva had held her hand every day. She began sitting with Liza for long periods of time and trying to engage her. At first Liza said almost nothing and cried a lot. So Nineva talked and talked, and told stories of her mother and grandmother and life as a slave. She brought tea and chocolate cookies, and slowly pulled back the curtains. Day after day they sat and talked, and gradually Liza began to realize that her life was not nearly as harsh as others'. She was privileged, and lucky. She was thirty years old, and healthy, with her best days in front of her. She was already a mother, and if she had no more children she would always have a beautiful family.

Nine weeks after the miscarriage, Liza awoke one morning, waited until Pete was out of the house, dressed in her chinos, found her gloves and straw hat, and announced to Nineva that she was needed in the garden. Nineva followed her there and whispered to Amos. He watched her carefully, and when the sun was up and she began to sweat, he insisted they take a break. Nineva arrived with iced tea and lemon, and the three of them sat under a shade tree and had a laugh.

Before long she and Pete were back to their old ways, and while they enjoyed themselves immensely, there was no pregnancy. Two years passed with no news. By her thirty-third birthday, in November of 1940, Liza was convinced beyond any doubt that she was barren.

CHAPTER 23

The cotton looked especially promising by late summer of 1941. The seeds were in the ground by mid-April. The stalks were waist high by July 4, chest high by Labor Day. The weather was cooperating nicely with hot days, cooler nights, and a heavy rain every other week. After a long winter of clearing land, Pete had managed to plant an additional eighty acres. His bank loans had been extinguished and he was privately vowing to never borrow against his land. As a farmer, though, he knew such vows were not binding. There was so much he could not control.

The encouraging outlook in the fields, though, was tempered by events around the world. In Europe, Germany invaded Poland two years earlier to start the war. The following year it began bombing London, and in June of 1941 Hitler attacked Russia with the largest invasion force in history. In Asia, Japan had been fighting in China for ten years. Its success there prompted it to invade the British, French, and Dutch colonies in the South Pacific. Japan's goal of the complete domination of East Asia appeared unstoppable. In August of 1941, the United States supplied Japan with 80 percent of its oil. When President Roosevelt announced a complete oil embargo, Japan's economic and military strength was imperiled.

War seemed imminent on both fronts, and the great debate was how long the U.S. could sit on the sidelines. Pete had many friends who were still active in the army, and not a single one believed the country could remain neutral.

Eight years earlier, he had left the military life behind, and with regret. Now, though, he had no misgivings about his future. He had grown accustomed to the life of a farmer. He adored his wife and children and found happiness in the flow of the seasons, the rhythm of the plantings and harvests. He was in the fields every day, often on horseback and often with Liza at his side, watching his crops and pondering ways to acquire more land. Joel was now fifteen and when he wasn't in school or doing his numerous chores on the farm, he was in the woods with Pete stalking white-tailed deer and wild turkeys. Stella was thirteen and breezing through school with perfect grades. The family had dinner together every night promptly at seven, and they talked about everything. Increasingly, the conversations were about war.

As a reservist, Pete was certain that he would soon be activated, and the thought of leaving home was painful. He scoffed at his old dreams of military glory. He was a farmer now, too old to be a soldier, at least in his opinion. He knew, though, that the army would not be concerned with his age. Almost weekly he received another letter from a West Point pal who had been activated. All of them vowed to keep in touch.

His orders came on September 15, 1941. He was to report to Fort Riley, Kansas, the home of the Twenty-Sixth Cavalry, his old regiment that was already in the Philippines. He requested a thirty-day delay to oversee the fall harvest, but it was denied.

On October 3, Liza invited a small group of friends to the house to say farewell. In spite of Pete's efforts to allay all fears, it was not a happy occasion. There were smiles and hugs and offers of good luck and so on, but the fear and tension were palpable. Pete thanked everyone for their thoughts and prayers, and reminded them that across the country scores of young men were being called into duty. The world was on the verge of another great conflict, and in trying times sacrifices were required.

The new preacher, Dexter Bell, was present, along with his wife, Jackie. They had moved to town a month earlier and had been well received. Dexter was young and enthusiastic and a real presence in the pulpit. Jackie had a beautiful voice and had wowed the church with two solos. Their three children were well mannered and polite.

Long after the guests were gone, the Bannings, with Florry, sat in the den and tried to delay the inevitable. Stella clung to her father and fought back tears. Joel, like his father, tried to appear stoic, as if all would be well. He added logs to the fire as they warmed in its glow, each subdued and frightened about the uncertainties before them. The fire eventually died and it was time for bed. Tomorrow was a Saturday and the kids would sleep in.

A few hours later, at sunrise, Pete tossed his duffel into the rear seat of his car and kissed Liza good-bye. He drove away with Jupe, who was now twenty years old and a handsome young man. Pete had known him since the day he was born, and for years Jupe had been one of Pete's favorites. He had taught the kid how to drive, got him licensed and insured, and he, Liza, and Nineva used Jupe to run errands in town. He was even allowed to drive Pete's pickup truck to Tupelo for feed and supplies.

Pete drove to Memphis and parked at the train station. He told Jupe to take care of things on the farm and watched him drive away. Two hours later, Pete boarded the train and headed for Fort Riley in Kansas. It was packed with servicemen headed to bases all over the country.

He had left the army with the rank of lieutenant, and reentered as the same. He was reassigned to his old unit, the Twenty-Sixth Cavalry Regiment, and spent a month in training at Fort Riley before being hurriedly shipped out on November 10. He was on the deck of the troop carrier when it sailed under the Golden Gate Bridge, and he wondered how long it would be before he returned. On board, he wrote two or three letters a day to Liza and his children and mailed them in port. The troop carrier stopped for supplies at Pearl Harbor, and a week later arrived in the Philippines.

Pete's timing could not have been worse. His assignment could not have been more unfortunate.

CHAPTER 24

The Philippines is a collection of seven thousand islands spread over a far-flung archipelago in the South China Sea. The terrains and landscapes change dramatically from island to island. There are mountains that top ten thousand feet, dense forests, impenetrable jungles, coastal floodplains, beaches, and miles of rocky shorelines. Many of its larger islands are crossed with swift rivers that are not navigable. In 1940, it was a country of vast mineral resources and food supplies, and thus crucial to the Japanese war effort. U.S. war planners had no doubt that the Philippines would be an early target, and they also knew that defending it would be next to impossible. It was geographically close to Japan, an ambitious enemy whose imperial army was savagely invading every neighbor in the region.

The defense of the Philippines was in the hands of Major General Douglas MacArthur, U.S. Army. In July of 1941, President Roosevelt coaxed MacArthur out of retirement and appointed him commander of all U.S. forces in the Far East. He established his headquarters in Manila, and went about the formidable task of preparing to defend the Philippines. He had lived in the country for years and knew it well, and he also knew how dire the situation really was. He had repeatedly warned Washington of the Japanese threat. His warnings were heard but not heeded. The challenge of getting his army on a war footing looked impossible, and there was little time.

Upon taking command, he immediately began demanding more troops, armaments, airplanes, ships, submarines, and supplies. Washington promised everything but delivered little. By December of 1941, as relations with the Japanese deteriorated, the U.S. Army in the Philippines numbered 22,500 men, half of whom were the well-trained Filipino Scouts, a crack unit that was comprised of Filipino-Americans and a few natives. Another 8,500 U.S. soldiers were shipped in. MacArthur mobilized the regular Philippine Army, an inexperienced, ill-equipped ragtag army of twelve infantry divisions, at least on paper. Including everyone with some semblance of a uniform, MacArthur had about 100,000 men under his command, the vast majority of whom were untrained and had never heard a shot fired in anger.

The condition of the regular Philippine Army was pathetic. The bulk of its force, the native Filipinos, were armed with World War I—vintage small arms, rifles, and machine guns. Their artillery was outdated and ineffective. Most ammunition proved defective. Many officers and enlisted men were untrained, and there were few training facilities. Few had decent uniforms. Steel helmets were in such short supply that the Filipinos used improvised headgear made from coconut shells.

MacArthur's air force numbered several hundred planes, almost all of which were leftover hand-me-downs no one else wanted. He repeatedly demanded more planes, ships, submarines, men, ammunition, and supplies, but they either did not exist or were committed elsewhere.

Pete arrived in Manila on Thanksgiving Day and caught a ride on a supply truck to Fort Stotsenburg, sixty miles north of the capital. There he joined C Troop of the Twenty-Sixth Cavalry Regiment. After presenting his orders to his commanding officers, he was assigned a bunk in the barracks and taken to the stables to select a horse.

At the time, the Twenty-Sixth had 787 enlisted men, mostly well-trained Filipino Scouts, and 55 American officers. It was the last remaining fully operational horse-mounted combat unit in the regular U.S. Army. It was well equipped, expertly drilled, and famous for its discipline. Pete spent his first days in the saddle of his newest companion, a dark chestnut thoroughbred named Clyde. Polo was popular with the Twenty-Sixth and used as part of the training. Though somewhat rusty at first, Pete quickly grew to the saddle and enjoyed the games. But tension mounted each day, and the regiment, along with the entire island force, felt the urgency. It was only a matter of time before the Japanese made their move.

In the early hours of December 8, radio operators in the Philippines heard the first reports of the attack on

Pearl Harbor. The games were over; the war was on. All American units and installations were ordered to stand ready. According to the master plan for defense of the Philippines, the air force commander, General Lewis Brereton, put his entire fleet on full alert. At 5:00 a.m., General Brereton arrived at MacArthur's headquarters in Manila to request permission to mount a B-17 bomber strike on the Japanese airfields on Formosa, two hundred miles away. MacArthur's chief of staff refused a meeting with the commander, saying he was too busy. The prewar plan was well established, well rehearsed, and called for such an attack immediately, but MacArthur had to give the final order to go. Instead, MacArthur did nothing. At 7:15, a panicked Brereton returned to the headquarters and again demanded an audience with the general. Again he was rebuffed, and told to "stand by for orders." By then, Japanese reconnaissance planes were being spotted and reports of enemy aircraft were pouring into Brereton's headquarters. At 10:00 a.m., an angry and frantic Brereton again demanded to see MacArthur. A meeting was refused, but Brereton was ordered to prepare for the attack. An hour later, Brereton ordered his bombers into the air, off the ground, to protect them from a Japanese attack. They began circling the islands, without bombs.

When MacArthur finally ordered the attack, Brereton's bombers were in the air and low on fuel. They immediately landed, along with the squadrons of fighters. At 11:30, all American aircraft were on the ground being refueled and armed. Ground crews were working frantically when the first wave of Japanese bombers arrived in perfect formations. At 11:35, they crossed the South China Sea and Clark Airfield came into view. The Japanese pilots were stunned. Below them were sixty B-17s and fighters parked in neat rows on the runways. At 11:45, the merciless bombing of Clark Field began, and within minutes the U.S. Army's air force was almost entirely destroyed. Similar attacks were made simultaneously at other airfields. For reasons that would forever remain inexplicable, the Americans had been caught flatfooted. The damage was incalculable. With no air force to protect and resupply the troops, and with no reinforcements on the way, the Battle of the Philippines was decided only hours after it began.

The Japanese were confident they could take the islands in thirty days. On December 22, a force of forty-three thousand elite troops came ashore at various landings and overwhelmed the resisting forces. During the first days of the invasion it appeared as if their confidence was well-founded. However, through sheer stubbornness and uncommon courage, the American and Filipino forces, with no hope of rescue or reinforcements, hung on for four brutal months.

Shortly after the landing invasion on December 22, C Troop was ordered north to the Luzon peninsula, where it conducted reconnaissance for the infantry and artillery and was involved in several rear-guard skirmishes. Pete's platoon leader was Lieutenant Edwin Ramsey, a horse lover who had volunteered for the Twenty-Sixth because he had heard "they had an excellent polo club." Lieutenant Banning was second-in-command.

Their days were spent in the saddle as they moved quickly through the peninsula watching the enemy's movements and gauging its strength. It was immediately evident that the Japanese forces were vastly superior in number, training, and armaments. To take the islands, they used their frontline divisions, battle-hardened veterans who had been fighting for almost a decade. And with control of the skies, the Japanese air forces were free to bomb and strafe at will. For the Americans on the ground, the most terrifying sounds were the screaming engines of Zero attack fighters as they barreled in from just above the trees with their two twenty-millimeter cannons and two seven-millimeter machine guns blasting anything that moved on the ground. Taking cover from the Zeros became a daily, often hourly, ritual. It was even more difficult for the Twenty-Sixth because the men not only had to find a ditch for themselves but had to hide their horses as well.

At dusk, they camped and fed and watered their horses. Each troop was well supported by cooks, blacksmiths, even veterinarians. After dinner, when things were quiet and the men were ready to collapse, they read the mail from home and wrote letters. Until the invasion, and the naval blockade that followed, the mail service had been fairly dependable, even remarkable given the circumstances. By late December, though, it had slowed considerably.

The week before Christmas, Pete received a carton the size of a shoe box filled with letters and cards from his family, his church, and what appeared to be most of the fine folks in Clanton. Dozens of letters and cards, and he read them all. The ones from Liza and the kids were read until practically memorized. Writing to his family, Pete described the islands, a country far different from the rolling hills of north Mississippi. He described the drudgery of life in the army. Never did he portray his situation as dangerous. Not once did he use words that could even remotely convey the notion of fear. The Japanese would soon invade, or had already invaded, and they would be repelled by the U.S. Army and its Filipino comrades.

On December 24, MacArthur put in motion the prewar plan of withdrawing his forces to the Bataan Peninsula for a last stand. Victory was not really in the cards, and MacArthur knew it. The U.S. goal was to dig in at Bataan and occupy the Japanese as long as possible, thus delaying other invasions on other fronts in the Pacific.

"Delay" was the key word. A "delaying action" became the common term.

To protect his forces as they retreated to Bataan, MacArthur established five delaying positions in Central Luzon, where the bulk of the Japanese forces were maneuvering. The Twenty-Sixth Cavalry became crucial in stalling the enemy's advance.

On January 15, 1942, Lieutenant Ed Ramsey and his platoon had finished a grueling recon assignment and were planning to rest themselves and their horses. However, C Troop received word that a major Japanese force was moving in its direction. A counterattack was planned, and Ramsey volunteered to assist in the assault.

He was ordered to take the village of Morong, a strategic point on the Batalan River in western Bataan. Morong was held by the Japanese but not heavily defended. Ramsey assembled his twenty-seven-man platoon and headed north on the main road to Morong. When they reached the Batalan River on the eastern edge of the village, they cautiously approached and realized it was deserted. The Catholic church was the only stone building in town, and it was surrounded by grass huts on stilts. Ramsey divided his men into three nine-man squads, with Lieutenant Banning leading one. As Pete and his squad approached the Catholic church, the entire platoon came under fire from a Japanese advance guard. Ramsey's men returned fire, and in doing so caught sight of the lead elements of a huge Japanese force fording the river. If those troops reached Morong, the platoon would be overwhelmed.

Without hesitation, Ramsey decided to launch a horse cavalry charge against an infantry, an attack unseen in the U.S. Army in over fifty years. He ordered his platoon into formation, raised his pistol, and yelled, "Charge!" With his men screaming and firing away, the galloping horses slammed into the Japanese front guard and sent it reeling. The terrified enemy retreated to the other side of the river and tried to regroup. With only three men wounded, Ramsey's platoon held off the Japanese until reinforcements relieved them.

It would become known as the last cavalry charge in American military history.

The Twenty-Sixth continued to harass and stall the enemy and delay its inevitable siege of Bataan. MacArthur moved the Philippine government and the bulk of his army to the peninsula, but for his command post he chose a bunker on the heavily armed island of Corregidor, protecting Manila Bay. His forces frantically established defensive positions throughout Bataan. Using barges, they ferried men and supplies from Manila in a frenzied effort to dig in. The plan was to warehouse enough food to feed forty-five thousand men for six months. Ultimately, eighty thousand troops and twenty-five thousand Philippine civilians retreated to Bataan. By mid-January, the withdrawal was complete and successful.

With the American forces confined to the peninsula, the Japanese moved swiftly to choke them with a complete air and naval blockade. Flush with confidence, the Japanese made a tactical error. They pulled back their elite divisions for action elsewhere in the Pacific, and replaced them with less capable troops. It was a mistake from which they would recover, but it ultimately added months to the siege, and the suffering.

In the first weeks of the Battle of Bataan, the Japanese incurred heavy losses as the Americans and Filipinos fought furiously to protect their last stronghold. The Allies incurred far fewer casualties, but their dead could not be replaced. The Japanese had an endless supply of men and armaments, and as the weeks wore on they bombarded their prey with heavy artillery and relentless air attacks.

Conditions on Bataan rapidly deteriorated. For weeks the Americans and Filipinos fought with little food in their stomachs. The average soldier consumed two thousand calories a day, about half the number needed for hard combat. Their hunger was acute and the supplies were dwindling. This was primarily due to another inexplicable mistake by MacArthur. In his rush to solidify his forces on Bataan, he had left most of their food behind. In one warehouse alone, millions of bushels of rice had been abandoned, enough to feed his army for years. Many of his officers had begged him to stockpile food on Bataan, but he had refused to listen. When informed that his men were hungry and complaining bitterly, he placed all units on half rations. In a letter to his men he promised reinforcements. He wrote that "thousands of troops and hundreds of planes are being dispatched. The exact time of arrival of reinforcements is unknown." But help was on the way.

It was a lie. The Pacific Fleet had been severely crippled at Pearl Harbor and had nothing left to break the Japanese blockade. The Philippines was thoroughly isolated. Washington knew it, as did MacArthur.

As the men starved, they ate anything that moved. They hunted and slaughtered carabao, the Philippine version of the water buffalo. Its tough, leathery meat had to be soaked and boiled in salt water and pounded with mallets to become somewhat chewable. It was usually served over a mush of rotten and bug-infested rice. When the carabao were decimated, the horses and mules were killed, though the soldiers of the Twenty-Sixth Cavalry refused to eat their beloved animals.

The starving soldiers hunted wild pigs, jungle lizards, even crows and exotic birds and snakes, including cobras, which were plentiful. Whatever they killed they threw into a giant pot for a common stew. By February, there was not a single mango or banana left on Bataan and the men were eating grass and leaves. The Bataan Peninsula was surrounded by the South China Sea, known for its abundance of fish. Harvesting it, though, proved impossible. Japanese fighter pilots took great pleasure in attacking and sinking even the smallest fishing boats. It was suicide to venture onto the water.

Malnutrition was rampant. By early March, the physical fitness of the troops was so impaired they were unable to mount patrols, stage ambushes, or launch attacks. Weight loss was staggering, with each man losing thirty to fifty pounds.

On March 11, MacArthur, following orders from Washington, fled Corregidor with his family and top aides. He made it safely to Australia, where he set up his command. Although he performed no acts of combat valor, as required by law, and left his troops behind, MacArthur was awarded the Medal of Honor for his gallant defense of the Philippines.

The emaciated men he left on Bataan were in no condition to fight. They suffered from swelling joints, bleeding gums, numbness in feet and hands, low blood pressure, loss of body heat, shivers, shakes, and anemia so severe many could not walk. The malnutrition soon led to dysentery with diarrhea so debilitating the men often collapsed. Bataan was a malaria-infested province in peaceful times, and the war provided countless new targets for the mosquitoes. After being bitten, the men were hit with fever, sweats, and fits of chills. By the end of March, a thousand men a day were being infected with malaria. Most of the officers suffered from it. One general reported that only half of his command could fight. The other half were "so sick, hungry, and tired they could never hold a position or launch an attack."

The men began to doubt the promises of reinforcements and rescue. Each morning, lookouts scanned the South China Sea looking for the convoys, but, of course, there were none. In late February, President Roosevelt addressed the nation in one of his famous "Fireside Chats." He told the American people that the Japanese had blockaded the Philippines and that "complete encirclement" was preventing "substantial reinforcement." And because the United States was at war in two large theaters, the country would have to concentrate the fight in "areas other than the Philippines."

The men on Bataan were listening too, on shortwave radios in their foxholes and tanks, and now they knew the truth. There would be no rescue.

At home, the Bannings had received no letters from Pete in almost two months. They knew he was on Bataan, but had no idea how grim the situation was. They, too, listened to the President, and for the first time began to grasp the extent of the danger. After the broadcast, Stella went to her room and cried herself to sleep. Liza and Joel stayed up late, talking about the war and trying in vain to find a reason to be optimistic.

Each Sunday morning when Dexter Bell began the worship hour, he called the names of the men and women from Ford County who were off at war, and the list grew longer each week. He offered a long prayer for their well-being and safe return. Most were in training and had yet to see battle. Pete Banning, though, was in a horrible place and received more prayers than the others.

Liza and the family strived to be courageous. The country was at war and families everywhere were living with fear. An eighteen-year-old kid from Clanton was killed in North Africa. Before long thousands of American families would receive the dreaded news.

CHAPTER 25

Without horses, the Twenty-Sixth Cavalry no longer existed as a fighting unit. Its men were assigned to other units and given tasks they were not accustomed to. Pete was placed with an infantry and handed a shovel with which to dig himself a foxhole, one of thousands along a thirteen-mile reserve line stretching across southern Bataan. In reality, the reserve line was the last line of defense. If the Japanese broke through, the Allies would be shoved to the tip of the peninsula and routed with their backs to the South China Sea.

In March, there was a lull in the fighting as the Japanese tightened the noose around Bataan. They regrouped and reinforced with fresh supplies. The Americans and Filipinos knew what was inevitable, and dug in even deeper.

During the days, Pete and his comrades shoveled dirt around bunkers and breastworks, though labor was difficult. The men were sick and starving. Pete estimated he

278 · JOHN GRISHAM

had lost at least forty pounds. Every ten days or so he punched another notch in his only belt to keep his pants up. So far he had managed to avoid malaria, though it was just a matter of time. He'd had two mild bouts of dysentery but had recovered quickly from both when a doctor found some paregoric. During the nights, he slept on a blanket beside his foxhole with his rifle by his side.

In the foxhole to his right was Sal Moreno, a tough Italian sergeant from Long Island. Sal was a city kid from a large, colorful family that produced a lot of good stories. He had learned to ride horses on a farm where his uncle worked. After a couple of scrapes with the law, he joined the army and found his way to the Twenty-Sixth Cavalry. A severe case of malaria almost killed him, but Pete found quinine on the black market and nursed him back to decent health.

In the foxhole to Pete's left was Ewing Kane, a Virginia blue blood who had graduated with honors from the Virginia Military Institute, as had his father and grandfather. Ewing was riding ponies when he was three years old and was the finest horseman in the Twenty-Sixth.

But their horses were gone now, and the men lamented the fact that they had been reduced to infantry status. They spent hours together talking and their favorite subject was food. Pete described with relish the dishes prepared by Nineva: battered pork chops, raised on his farm, and smoked ribs, and fried okra, fried chicken, fried green tomatoes, potatoes fried in bacon fat, fried squash, fried everything. Sal marveled at a style of cooking that involved so much grease. Ewing described the joys of smoked Virginia hams and bacon and all manner of pheasant, dove, quail, hens, and Brunswick stew. But they were amateurs compared with Sal, whose mother and grandmother prepared dishes the other two had never heard of. Baked lasagna, stuffed manicotti, spaghetti Bolognese, balsamic pork scaloppine, garlic tomato bruschetta, fried mozzarella cheese, and on and on. The list seemed endless, and at first they thought he was exaggerating. But the depth of his detail made their mouths water. They agreed to meet in New York after the war and do nothing but binge on Italian delicacies.

There were moments when they managed to laugh and dream, but morale was low. The men on Bataan blamed MacArthur, Roosevelt, and everybody else in Washington for abandoning them. They were bitter and miserable and most were unable to resist complaining. Others told them to shut up and stop the bitching. Complaints did nothing to help their rotten conditions. It was not unusual to see men weeping in their foxholes, or to see a man crack up and wander away. Pete kept his sanity by thinking of Liza and the kids, and the sumptuous meals Nineva would one day cook for him, and all those vegetables in Amos's garden. He wanted desperately to write some letters but there were no pens, no paper, no mail service. They were thoroughly blockaded with no way to correspond. He prayed for his family every day and asked God to protect them after he was gone. Death was certain, either by starvation, disease, bombs, or bullets.

While the Japanese infantry took a break, its artillery and air force never stopped pounding away. It was a lull, but there were no quiet days. Danger was never far away. To wake things up each morning, Japanese dive-bombers strafed at will, and as soon as the planes disappeared the cannons began unloading.

Late in March, 150 big guns were positioned near the American line and began a ferocious bombardment. The assault was continuous, around the clock, and the results were devastating. Many Americans and Filipinos were blown to bits in their foxholes. Bunkers thought to be bombproof disintegrated like straw shacks. Casualties were horrendous and the field hospitals were packed with the injured and dying. On April 3, after a week of nonstop artillery fire, Japanese infantry and tanks poured through the gaps. As the Americans and Filipinos fell back, their officers tried to rally them into defensive positions, only to be overrun within hours. Counterattacks were planned, attempted, and destroyed by the vastly superior Japanese forces.

By then, an American general estimated that only one soldier in ten could walk a hundred yards, raise his rifle, and shoot at the enemy. What had once been a fighting army of eighty thousand had been reduced to an effective fighting force of twenty-five hundred. Low on food, morale, ammo, and with no support from the skies or seas, the Americans and Filipinos battled on, throwing everything they had at the Japanese and inflicting horrendous casualties. But they were outnumbered and outgunned, and the inevitable soon became the reality.

As the enemy continued its relentless push, the American commander, General Ned King, huddled with his generals and colonels and discussed the unthinkable—surrender. Orders from Washington were clear: The American and Filipino forces were to fight to the last man. That might sound heroic when decided in a comfortable office in Washington, but General King now faced the awful reality. It was his decision to either surrender or have his men slaughtered. Those who were still able to fight were putting up a resistance that grew weaker each day. The Japanese were within a few miles of a large field hospital that held six thousand wounded and dying men.

At midnight on April 8, General King assembled his commanders and said, "I am sending forward a flag of truce at daybreak to ask for terms of surrender. I feel that further resistance would only uselessly waste human life. Already one of our hospitals, which is filled to capacity and directly in the line of hostile approach, is within range of enemy light artillery. We have no further means of organized resistance."

Though the decision was inevitable, it was still difficult to accept. Many of those present wept as they left to resume their duties. General King ordered the immediate destruction of anything of military value, but he spared buses, cars, and trucks to carry the sick and wounded to the prison camps.

With approximately seventy thousand soldiers under his command, General King's surrender was the largest in American history.

Pete heard the news at noon on April 9 and could not believe it. He, Sal, Ewing, and others from the Twenty-Sixth at first planned to disappear into the bush and keep fighting, but that strategy seemed almost suicidal. They hardly had the energy to mount an escape. They were ordered to destroy their weapons and ammunition, find and eat whatever they could, fill their canteens with water, and begin walking north in search of the Japanese. The men were stunned, defeated, even emotional at the reality that a once proud American army had surrendered. Their sense of shame was profound.

As they walked slowly and with a sense of fear and dread, they were joined by other dazed and emaciated Americans and Filipinos. Dozens, then hundreds of soldiers filled the road, all walking to a future that was uncertain but would certainly be unpleasant. They cleared the way for a transport truck packed with wounded Americans. On its hood sat a solitary private, holding a stick with a white flag on it. Surrender. It did not seem real.

The men were frightened. Japan's reputation as a brutal occupier was well-known. They had read stories of its war crimes in China—the rape of countless women, the execution of prisoners, the looting of entire cities. At the same time, though, they were somewhat comforted by the fact that they were American prisoners and thus protected by international law, which forbade their mistreatment. Wasn't Japan bound by the agreements of the Geneva Convention?

Pete, Sal, and Ewing stuck together as they trudged north to meet their captors. As they topped a hill, they saw a sickening sight. A row of Japanese tanks was assembled in a clearing, waiting. Behind it was a column of Japanese soldiers. In the distance, airplanes were still dropping bombs; cannons were still firing.

"Get rid of all your Jap stuff and quick," someone yelled back. The warning was repeated again and again down the line, and most of the men heard it and complied quickly. Japanese coins and souvenirs were dropped in the dirt and tossed in ditches. Pete had only three small tins of canned sardines in his pockets, along with his wristwatch, wedding band, blanket, mess kit, and a pair of sunglasses. He had twenty-one American dollars sewn inside the canvas cover of his canteen.

They were approached by Japanese soldiers waving rifles and barking in their language. Every rifle was equipped with a long bayonet. The prisoners were directed to a field, lined up in rows, and told to remain silent. One of the Japanese spoke enough English to bark commands. One by one, the prisoners were told to step forward and empty their pockets. They were frisked, though it was obvious the guards wanted little contact. Punching and slapping were okay, but nothing that required finesse around the pockets. Almost everything was stolen, or "confiscated," by the Japanese. Fountain pens, pencils, sunglasses, flashlights, cameras, mess kits, blankets, coins, razors, and blades.

Jack Wilson from Iowa was standing directly in front of Pete when a Japanese soldier began yelling at him. Jack had in his pocket a small shaving mirror, and unfortunately it had been made in Japan.

"Nippon!" the guard screamed.

Jack didn't answer in time, and the soldier rammed the butt of his rifle into his face. He fell to the ground as the soldier pounded him with the rifle butt until he was unconscious. Other guards began punching and slapping the prisoners while their officers laughed and egged them on. Pete was stunned by the sudden violence.

They would soon learn that the Japanese believed that any of the money, coins, or trinkets held by the prisoners must have been taken from their dead comrades. Thus, retaliation was called for. Several prisoners were beaten until they could not move, but the retaliation reached an unimaginable apex when a captain, not from the Twenty-Sixth, emptied his pockets. An angry little private began screaming at the captain and ordered him to step forward. The private had found some yen on the captain and was out of his mind. An officer stepped forward, a tall lanky sergeant with skin much darker than the others, and began screaming at the captain. He punched him in the gut, kicked him in the groin, and when the captain was down on all fours the "Black Jap," as he would become known, yanked out his sword, raised it above his head with both hands, and struck the captain at the back of his neck. His head sprang off his shoulders and rolled a few feet away. Blood gushed in buckets as the captain's body twitched for a few seconds, then became still.

The Black Jap smiled and admired his handiwork. He stuck his sword back in his sheath and snarled at the other prisoners. The private kept the yen and went through the captain's pockets, taking his time. The other guards lost all restraint and began beating other prisoners.

Pete gawked at the head lying in the dust and almost went berserk. He wanted to attack the nearest soldier, but to do so would be suicidal. He breathed deeply while waiting to get punched. He was lucky, at least for that moment, and was not kicked around. Down the line, another private got excited and slapped a prisoner. The Black Jap strode over, saw more yen, and pummeled the American. When he yanked out his sword, Pete looked the other way.

Two quick beheadings. The Americans had never

imagined anything like it. Pete was sickened and shocked and could not believe what was happening. His shock would wear off, though, as the murders became routine.

The prisoners stood in formation for over an hour as the tropical sun beat down on their bare heads. Pete had always hated his helmet and had left it behind. Now he wished he'd kept it. A few of the prisoners had caps, but most had nothing to shield the sun. They were soaked with sweat and many began to blister. Almost all had canteens but drinking water was forbidden. When the guards grew weary of abusing their prisoners, they retreated to the shade and took a break. The tanks eventually left. The prisoners were led back to the road and headed north.

The Bataan Death March had begun.

They walked three abreast through the heat and dust. Sal was to Pete's left, Ewing to his right. When the trail ended, they turned east on the national highway that runs across the southern tip of Bataan. Coming toward them were endless columns of Japanese infantry, trucks, tanks, and horse-drawn artillery, all preparing for the assault on Corregidor.

When the guards could not hear them, the men talked incessantly. There were about twenty from the Twenty-Sixth Cavalry. The rest had been scattered in the chaos of the surrender. Pete ordered them to organize into groups of three, to keep up with one another and help if possible. If they were caught talking, they were beaten. For sport, the guards randomly grabbed the prisoners for quick searches and more beatings. After three miles or so the men had been stripped of everything valuable. Pete received his first slap in the face by a guard who took his sardines.

The ditches beside the road were littered with fire-gutted trucks and tanks, all rendered useless by the Americans and Filipinos the day before. At one point they passed a large pile of captured rations, just waiting to be eaten. But there was no mention of food, and the men, most already suffering from malnutrition, were starving. The heat was scalding and men began to collapse. As they quickly learned, it was unwise to render assistance. The guards kept their bayonets ready and were eager to gore any prisoner who stopped to help another one. Those who fell and could not get up were kicked to the side and into the ditches and left to be dealt with later.

The Japanese bayonet was thirty inches long overall with a fifteen-inch blade. Affixed to a fifty-inch Arisaka rifle, it gave a soldier a five-and-a-half-foot spear. The privates were proud of their bayonets and eager to use them. When a prisoner stumbled and fell, or simply collapsed, he got a quick jab in the butt as encouragement. If that didn't work, he got the full blade and was left to bleed out.

Pete marched with his head down and his eyes squinted in an effort to avoid the dust and heat. He was also watching the guards, who seemed to fade away and then materialize out of nowhere. A few seemed sympathetic and unwilling to kick and slap, but most were enjoying the cruelty. Anything could set them off. They could be quiet and stern-faced one moment, then crazy with rage the next. They beat their prisoners with their fists, kicked them with their boots, pummeled them with rifle butts, and stabbed them with bayonets. They beat them for looking this way or that, for talking, for moving too slow, for not answering a question barked in Japanese, and for trying to help a comrade.

Everyone was brutalized, but the Japanese were especially cruel to the Filipinos, whom they considered an inferior race. Within the first few hours of the march, Pete witnessed the murder of ten Filipino Scouts, with all bodies kicked to the ditches and left to rot. During a break, he watched in disbelief as a column of Scouts came by. All had their hands tied behind their backs and were struggling to keep pace. The guards delighted in knocking them down and watching them roll and flounder in the dust as they tried to scramble to their feet.

Handcuffing the prisoners served no purpose. As awful as things were, Pete was thankful he wasn't a Filipino.

As they plodded along under the unrelenting sun, the men began to dehydrate. In spite of the many obvious problems, water was their principal thought. Thirst was the primary demon. Their bodies reacted by trying to conserve fluids. They stopped sweating and urinating. Their saliva turned sticky and their tongues stuck to their teeth and the roofs of their mouths. The dust and heat caused severe headaches that blurred their vision. And there was water everywhere, in fresh artesian wells along the roads, in wells near the roads and highways, in spigots on farmhouses and barns, in bubbling creeks they crossed over. Their guards saw the misery and enjoyed long drinks from their canteens and refreshing splashes on their faces. They wet bandannas and tucked them around their collars.

As the prisoners approached the charred remains of Hospital Number One, they saw many of the patients in soiled gowns and green pajamas wandering around with no idea what to do or where to go. Some were missing limbs and on crutches. Others had bloody wounds in need of care. The hospital had been bombed days before and the patients were in shock. When the Japanese commander saw them, he ordered them rounded up and added to the march. Again, assistance was forbidden, and many of the patients managed to walk only a short distance before collapsing. They were kicked aside and left to die.

When they encountered a massive traffic jam of Japanese trucks and tanks, they were led to an open field and ordered to sit in the blazing sun. This would become known as the "sun treatment," and it drove some of them to the point of breaking. As they baked, a prisoner attempted to sneak a drink of tepid water from his canteen, and this upset the guards. They yelled and punched and went from prisoner to prisoner, grabbing canteens and spilling the water on the parched soil. The guard who emptied Pete's canteen threw it back with such force it opened a small cut above his right eye.

After an hour, they resumed the march. They passed men who had been bayoneted and were begging for help as they bled to death. They passed the bodies of dead Americans. They watched in horror as two wounded Filipino soldiers were dragged from a ditch and situated in the middle of the road for tanks to run over them. The longer they marched, the more dead and dying they passed in the ditches. Pete marveled at his brain's ability to adjust to the carnage and cruelty, and he soon reached the point where he wasn't shocked anymore. The heat, hunger, and deprivation deadened his senses. But the anger boiled, and he vowed revenge. He prayed that one day soon he would find a way to kill as many Japanese soldiers as humanly possible.

He kept talking, kept encouraging the others to take another step, climb the next hill, endure another hour. Surely, at some point, they would be fed and allowed to drink water. At sundown, they were led off the road into a clearing where they were allowed to sit and lie down. There was no sign of food or water, but it was refreshing to rest for a spell. Their feet were covered with blisters and their legs were cramping. Many collapsed and fell asleep. As Pete was nodding off, a ruckus broke out as a fresh supply of guards arrived and began kicking the prisoners. They were ordered to their feet and into a column. The march resumed in the darkness, and for two hours they limped along, never at a pace fast enough to satisfy the guards.

Throughout the first day, Pete and those close to him counted three hundred prisoners in their column, but the number changed constantly. Some men collapsed and died, others were murdered, stragglers joined them, and their column often merged with others. At some point in the night, and since they had been robbed of their watches they had no idea of the hour, they were led to a clearing and told to sit. Evidently, the Japs were hungry too and it was time for dinner. After they ate, they moved through the prisoners with buckets of water and offered one small ladleful to each. The water was warm and chalky but delicious nonetheless. Each prisoner was given a ball of sticky rice. A thick steak with fried potatoes could not have been more delicious.

As they savored their food, they heard small-arms fire down the road and it soon became apparent what was happening. The "buzzard squads" were behind them, calmly finishing off those who had been unable to keep up.

The food had revived Pete's senses, if only briefly, and he was once again stunned at the wanton murder of American prisoners of war. His ordeal on the death march would last for six days, and each night he and others listened in horror at the work of the buzzard squads.

After sleeping in a rice paddy for a few hours, the men were awakened again, scolded back into formation, and forced to march. After the idleness, many found it difficult to walk, but they were encouraged by the ever present bayonets. The highway was packed with American and Filipino prisoners.

At sunrise, they were met by another massive caravan of Japanese troops and artillery. The road was too crowded for the prisoners and they were led to a field next to a small farmhouse. Behind a shed was a creek with what appeared to be clear water bubbling over the rocks. The sound of water chattering about was maddening. Their thirst was torturous and was more than some could stand. A colonel stood bravely, pointed to the creek, and asked if his men could have a drink. A guard knocked him out cold with a rifle butt.

For at least an hour, the prisoners squatted and listened to the creek as the sun rose. They watched the convoy roll past, stirring up clouds of dust. The guards drifted away and gathered by the road to enjoy a breakfast of rice cakes and mangoes. As they ate, three Filipino Scouts belly crawled to the creek and buried their faces in the cool water. A guard glanced around, saw them, and alerted the other Japanese. Without a word, they moved to within twenty feet of the creek, formed an impromptu firing line, and murdered the Filipinos.

When the traffic slowed, the prisoners were hurried back into formation and the march continued. "Soon there will be food," a guard said to Pete, who almost thanked him. As badly as his stomach ached, his thirst was far worse. By midmorning, his mouth and throat were so dry he could no longer talk. No one could, and a grim silence fell over the prisoners. They were halted near a swamp and told to squat in the sun. A guard allowed them to walk to the edge of a stagnant wallow and fill their canteens with a brown brackish liquid that had been contaminated with seawater. If not lethal it would certainly cause dysentery or worse, but the men drank it nonetheless.

At midday, they stopped near a compound and were ordered to sit in the sun. The unmistakable aroma of something cooking wafted over the prisoners, most of whom had eaten only one rice ball in the past thirty hours. Under a makeshift tent, cooks were boiling rice in cauldrons over fires. The prisoners watched as the cooks added pounds of sausage links and fresh chickens to the rice and stirred their mix with long wooden spatulas. Beyond the tent was a makeshift pen secured by barbed wire, and inside it there were about a hundred bedraggled and starving Philippine citizens, support staff who had worked for the army. More guards arrived and it became apparent that this would be a lunch site. When it was served, the Japanese ate from their mess kits and enjoyed a nice meal. One walked to the pen, held up a thick link sausage, and tossed it through the barbed wire. A mob descended upon it, squealing, scratching, clawing, fighting. The guard bent double laughing, as did his buddies. It was too much fun to pass up, so several of them walked to the barbed wire and held up chicken legs and sausages. The prisoners reached and begged and then fought viciously when the food hit the ground.

Nothing was tossed to the Americans. There was no lunch, only the putrid water and an hour in the sun. The march continued through the long afternoon with more men falling and being left behind.

Around midnight on April 12, the second day of the march, the men arrived at the town of Orani, some thirty miles from where they had started. Such a hike would have been challenging for healthy soldiers. For the survivors, it was a miracle they had made it so far. Near the center of town they were led off the highway and into a barbed-wire compound hastily built to house five hundred prisoners. There were at least a thousand already there when Pete's column arrived. There was no food or water and no latrines. Many of the men suffered from dysentery, and human waste, blood, mucus, and urine covered the ground and stuck to their boots. Maggots were everywhere. There was no room to lie down, so the men tried to sleep sitting back to back, but their cramped muscles made it impossible. The screams of the deranged did not help. Sick, dehydrated, exhausted, and starving, many of the men lost all sense of where they were and what they were doing. Many were delirious, half or fully crazed, and others were catatonic and stood about in a stupor, zombielike.

And they were dying. Many lapsed into comas and did not wake up. By sunrise, the camp was filled with dead bodies. When the Japanese officers realized this, they did not order food and water. Instead, they ordered shovels and instructed the "healthier" prisoners to start digging shallow graves along the edges of the fencing. Pete, Sal, and Ewing were still functioning and thus chosen as gravediggers.

Those who were merely delirious were stuck in a wooden shed and told to be quiet. A few of the comatose were buried alive, not that it made much difference. Death was only hours away. Instead of resting, those with shovels labored through the night as the casualties mounted and bodies were piled next to the barbed wire.

At dawn, the gates opened and guards dragged in sacks of boiled rice. The prisoners were told to sit in neat rows and hold out their cupped hands. Each received a ladleful of sticky rice, their first "meal" in days. After breakfast, they were walked in small groups to an artesian well and allowed to fill their canteens. The food and water calmed the men for a few hours, but the sun was back. By midmorning, the crazed shouting and shrieking was at full chorus. Half the prisoners were ordered out of the compound and back onto the road. The march continued.

CHAPTER 26

Anticipating the fall of Bataan, the Japanese planned to use the peninsula as a staging area to attack the nearby island of Corregidor, the last American stronghold. To do so, it was necessary to quickly clear the area of American and Filipino prisoners. The plan was to march them sixty-six miles along the Old National Road to the rail yards at San Fernando, and from there they would be taken by train to their destinations at various prisons, including Camp O'Donnell, an old Philippine fort the Japanese had converted into a POW camp. The plans called for the quick removal of about fifty thousand.

However, within hours of the surrender, the Japanese realized that they had grossly underestimated. There were seventy-six thousand American and Filipino soldiers, along with twenty-six thousand civilians. Everywhere the Japanese looked there were prisoners, all hungry and in need of food and water. How could the enemy surrender with so many soldiers? Where was their will to fight? They could not contain their contempt and hatred for their captives.

As the march dragged on, and the ranks of the prisoners continued to rise, the Japanese guards were pressured to speed it along. There was no time to eat or drink, no time to rest, no time to stop and assist those who had fallen. There was no time to bury the dead, and no time to worry about stragglers. The generals were yelling at the officers to hurry. The officers were physically abusing the privates, and they in turn released their frustrations on their prisoners. As the columns swelled and slowed, the pressure wound even tighter and the march became even more chaotic. Dead bodies littered the ditches and fields and decomposed in the blistering sun. Black clouds of flies swarmed the rotting flesh and were joined by hungry pigs and dogs. Packs of black crows waited patiently on fences, and some began following the columns, tormenting the prisoners.

Pete had lost track of the men of the Twenty-Sixth. He, Sal, and Ewing were still together, but it was impossible to keep up with anyone else. Groups of emaciated prisoners were added to one column one day and left behind at the camps the next day. Men were falling, dying, and being killed by the hundreds. He stopped thinking about anyone but himself.

On the fourth day, they entered the city of Lubao. The once busy town of thirty thousand was deserted, or at least the streets were. But from the windows upstairs, the residents were watching. When the column stopped, the windows were raised and the people began tossing bread and fruits to the prisoners. The Japanese went into a frenzy and ordered them to ignore the food. When a teenage boy darted from behind a tree and tossed a loaf of bread, a guard shot him on the spot. Prisoners who had managed to eat a bite or two were pulled from the column and beaten. One was bayoneted in the stomach and hung from a lamppost as a warning.

They marched on, somehow mustering the will to take another step, notch another mile. So many men were dying from dehydration and exhaustion that the Japanese relented somewhat and allowed them to fill their canteens, usually at a roadside ditch or a pond used by livestock.

On the fifth day, the column of prisoners ran into another long convoy of heavy trucks packed with soldiers. The stretch of road was narrower, and the guards ordered the men into single file along both shoulders. Being so close to the filthy and unshaven Americans inspired the soldiers in the trucks. For some, it was their first sighting of the hated enemy. They taunted the captives, threw rocks at them, spat on them, and cursed them. Occasionally, a truck driver would spot a prisoner a step or two out of line and ram him with the heavy bumper. If he fell under the truck, he would soon be dead. If he landed in a ditch, the buzzard squads would take care of him later. If he knocked over other prisoners, then the soldiers had a big laugh as they rode away.

Pete was choking on a face full of dust when a soldier leaning from a truck swung his rifle and made perfect contact. The stock crashed into the back of Pete's head and knocked him unconscious. He fell into a muddy ditch and landed on a tire next to a fire-gutted wagon. Sal and Ewing were ahead of him and did not see it happen.

The highway became a traffic jam and the prisoners were led to a rice paddy for another sun treatment. When Sal and Ewing couldn't find their comrade, they began whispering around. Someone told them what had happened. Their first instinct was to go find him, but their second instinct kept them in place. The mere act of standing without permission would draw a beating. Any effort to look for Pete would be suicidal. They grieved for their friend in silence, hating the Japanese even more, if that was even possible. By then, though, they had seen so many dead bodies that their senses were numb, their emotions subdued or nonexistent.

They marched until after dark, then were given the luxury of sleeping in a rice paddy. There was no make-shift compound nearby. The guards passed out filthy rice balls and gave them water, and as they tried to rest they waited to hear the unmistakable sounds of the small-arms fire from the buzzard squads. Soon enough they heard them, and they wondered which bullet had found Pete Banning.

He regained consciousness and, still stunned and groggy, had the presence of mind to simply play dead. His head ached mightily and he could feel blood oozing down his neck. The column was endless and he listened to the sounds of the miserable men as they lumbered past him. He heard the trucks roll by, with the soldiers laughing, sometimes singing. He heard the guards yell their commands and curses. After dark, he crawled through the dirt and hid under the gutted wagon. The convoys finally went away but the prisoners continued coming. Late into the night, there was finally a break. The road was empty and quiet, at least for a moment. He heard pistol fire approaching and could soon see the orange flashes as the buzzard squads finished off those who were dying or already dead. He pulled himself tighter into a ball and didn't breathe. They moved on.

Pete decided to crawl into a thicket of trees and try to escape. Escape to where? He had no idea. He was certain he would not get far, but he was a dead man anyway, so what the hell? He waited and waited. Hours passed and he fell into a deep sleep.

A bayonet interrupted his slumber. A Japanese private pressed it into his chest deep enough to wake him, but not to break skin. The sun was up and it glistened off the bayonet, which seemed ten feet long. The private smiled and motioned for him to get up. He shoved Pete back to the road, where he fell into another endless column of suffering ghosts. He was marching again. The first few steps were painful as his cramped legs tried to limber up, but he managed to keep pace. He recognized none of the other prisoners, but by then they all looked the same.

After six days, they arrived at their first destination, the city of San Fernando. They were placed in another makeshift camp with barbed wire and given nothing to eat. They were beyond starvation and convinced they were indeed on a march to death. The conditions were the worst so far. The camp had been used by hundreds of other prisoners and the ground was covered with human waste and blood. Rotting and decomposing bodies attracted maggots and flies by the millions.

San Fernando marked the end of the Bataan Death March. Seventy thousand prisoners were forcibly transferred, 60,000 Filipinos and 10,000 Americans. For Pete, the ordeal lasted six days. For many others, it took more than a week. Along the sixty-six-mile trail, an estimated 650 American and 11,000 Filipino prisoners died from disease or exhaustion, or were outright murdered. Countless Philippine civilians died. Only a fraction were buried.

And the worst was yet to come.

During his first night in the San Fernando camp, Pete managed to find a spot away from the shit and scum and rested with his back against barbed wire. The men were packed in so tight that sitting was not possible. The lucky ones who found a spot like Pete were constantly badgered to move over and make room. All semblance of discipline was long gone. A few officers tried to establish order but it was impossible. Fistfighting was out of the question because the men were too weary, so they simply cursed each other and made idle threats. The deranged ones roamed about, stepping on others while begging for food and water. Most of the men had dysentery, and with no latrines and no room to relieve themselves, they had no choice but to soil themselves where they stood.

At dawn, the gates opened and the guards spilled in. They barked orders, kicked men out of the way, and managed to organize the prisoners in rows of squatting skeletons. Three large pots of rice arrived and the guards began dishing it out into cupped hands. Those closest to the gates were fed, and when the pots were empty the guards left and locked the gates. Fewer than half the prisoners received anything, and there was precious little sharing.

Through the fence the guards promised more food and water, but the prisoners knew better. Pete was too far back to get a handful of rice. He could not remember his last bite of food. He withdrew into his shell and sat in a stupor as the morning sun arrived with all its fury. From time to time, he looked at the gaunt faces of those around him, looked in vain for Sal and Ewing or anyone he might recognize, but saw nothing familiar. He cursed himself for falling asleep under the wagon and losing his chance to escape. His head wound was bleeding but not badly. He feared infection but considered it just another affliction on a growing list of ways he might die. And what was he supposed to do about it? If he found a doctor the poor guy was probably worse off than he was.

Around midday, the gates were opened and the guards began removing prisoners one by one. They segregated them into groups of a hundred, and when there were five units, they marched them away and through the town. Pete was in the last unit.

By now, the residents were accustomed to the gaunt, filthy, and unshaven Americans being herded through their town. They hated the Japanese with as much venom as the prisoners, and they were determined to help. They tossed bread, cookies, and fruits from windows, and for some reason the guards did not intervene. Pete picked up a banana and ate it in two bites. Then he found a large broken cookie in the dirt. When it became apparent that the guards were indifferent, more food rained down upon the prisoners, who scooped up everything and ate on the march without breaking stride. From an alley, an old woman tossed a mango to Pete and he devoured it skin and all. Like before, he was amazed at how quickly his body was reenergized with the nourishment.

They stopped at the train station, where five ramshackle boxcars were waiting. They were known as "Forty and Eights," narrow freight cars twenty feet long and just large enough for either forty people or eight horses, mules, or cows. The guards were stuffing a hundred men into each one and then slamming the doors, leaving the prisoners in total darkness. Crammed shoulder to shoulder, they immediately felt suffocated and had trouble breathing. They began beating on the wooden side walls and screaming for relief. As they waited, the temperature rose dramatically and men began fainting. There was no ventilation, only a few cracks in the walls, and men fought to stick their noses into the openings.

Guards took their positions on top of the boxcars and beat the roofs with rifles while yelling, "Shut up, you assholes!"

Finally, the train jerked and rocked and began moving. As the boxcars swayed and rolled many of the men were seized with nausea and began vomiting. The food they had so eagerly devoured an hour earlier reappeared in a putrid mess, and the floor was soon covered with waste and vomit. The smell was beyond description. The air was so hot and thick with vile odors that breathing was painful.

A man fell at Pete's feet and closed his eyes. Pete's first reaction was to kick him away, but he realized he wasn't breathing. Other men were dying too, and some had no room to fall.

As the train picked up speed, the guards opened the doors to three of the boxcars and allowed ventilation. Men fought to get near the doors. One managed to jump and landed on a pile of rocks. He never moved again.

Along the three-hour ride, the train passed through several small towns. The residents lined the track and tossed food and cans of water to the open cars. The engineers were Filipino, and they slowed the train to allow the men to collect anything possible. Almost all of the food was shared.

When the train finally stopped, the men spilled out onto the platform. Those still alive were ordered to drag out the dead. The bodies were stacked like firewood near the tracks. Dozens of Filipino citizens were waiting with food and water, but they were threatened away by the guards. The men were marched a hundred yards and herded into an open field for another hour of sun treatment. The ground was almost too hot to touch.

By then the men knew they were headed to the prison camp at O'Donnell, where, surely, conditions would improve. As they began the seven-mile trek, it was obvious that many of them would not make it. Pete expected mass murder of the weaker ones, but the guards had changed strategies and now allowed the stronger prisoners to assist. But, there were few strong enough to render aid, and men began falling in the first mile. By then the locals had seen plenty of prisoners, and they hid cans of water and mangoes along the dirt trail. The guards smashed and kicked away as much as possible, but miracles happened. Pete found a can of clear water and drained it without getting caught. He would believe that he owed his life to the kindness of some unknown Filipino. When the man in front of him collapsed, Pete grabbed his skeletal remains, threw an arm over his shoulder, told him that he'd made it this far and he was not about to die, and shuffled along with him for the remaining six miles.

Their first view of O'Donnell was from the top of a hill. Spread before them was a forbidding sprawl of old buildings encircled by miles of shiny barbed wire. Guard towers stood ominously, all proudly adorned with the Japanese flag.

Pete would remember that moment well. He would soon realize that had he known the horrors that awaited him at O'Donnell, he would have bolted from the trail and run like a madman until a bullet stopped him.

CHAPTER 27

Before the war, O'Donnell had been used as a temporary base for a Philippine Army division, about twenty thousand men. With little upgrade, the Japanese had converted it into their largest POW camp. It covered six hundred acres of rice paddies and scrubland and was divided into several large, square compounds. These were sectioned off into rows of barracks and buildings, some dilapidated, some unfinished. After the fall of Bataan, some sixty thousand prisoners, including ten thousand Americans, were crammed into the dilapidated old fort. Water was scarce, as were latrines, medicines, hospital beds, stoves, and food supplies.

Pete and the other survivors limped through the eastern portal, along with hundreds of others as they were pouring into O'Donnell from all over the islands. They were greeted by guards in crisp white shirts swinging clubs that appeared to be designed solely for beating unarmed and defeated men. Eager to impress their new arrivals with their toughness, the guards began pummeling men at random while yelling orders in pidgin English no one understood. It was all so unnecessary. By then the prisoners had seen enough violence and were not impressed, and they had no fight left, no will to resist. They were pushed and shoved to a large parade ground and ordered to stand at attention in perfect rows. They baked in the sun as others arrived. They were searched again, as if they'd had the opportunity to pick up anything valuable along the way.

After an hour, there was a flurry of activity in front of a building that served as the commandant's headquarters. The great man strutted out to greet them in a goofy uniform that included baggy shorts and riding boots up to his knees. He was a runt-like, funny-looking creature with an air of great importance.

He began to roar and bellow, with a hapless Filipino interpreter trying to keep up. The commandant began by telling them that they were not honorable prisoners of war but cowardly captives. They had surrendered, an unpardonable sin. And since they were cowards they would not be treated like real soldiers. He said that he would like to kill them all but he lived by the code of a true warrior, and true warriors showed mercy. However, if they disobeyed any of his camp rules, he would gladly execute them. Then he launched into a loud, windy tirade on race and politics, with the Japanese people, of course, being the superiors because they had won the war, they had defeated America, their eternal enemy, and so on. At times the interpreter lagged far behind and was clearly making up stuff as the commandant waited for his brilliant words to be rendered in English.

In their dismal state, most of the prisoners paid little attention. As to his threats, they wondered what else the Japanese could possibly do to them, other than perhaps a quick beheading.

He roared and rambled until fatigue set in, then abruptly turned and marched away, with his bootlickers close behind. The prisoners were dismissed and divided by country. There was a camp for the Filipinos and one for the Americans.

General Ned King had been appointed by the commandant as the prisoner commander, and he met his men at a second gate. He shook their hands, welcomed them, and when they grouped around him he said, "You men remember this—you did not give up. I did. I did the surrendering. I surrendered you. You didn't surrender. I'm the one who has the responsibility for that. You let me carry it. All I ask is that you obey the orders of the Japanese so that we don't provoke the enemy any more than he already is."

The new arrivals were then turned over to their officers for orientation and a discussion of the rules. The Twenty-Sixth Cavalry had scattered and there was some confusion about who last commanded it. Pete was assigned to a group of the Thirty-First Infantry and taken to his new home. It was a ramshackle building fourteen feet wide and twenty feet long, with a partial bamboo roof that looked as though it had been torn off in a storm. The men were exposed to the sun and rain. There were no cots or mats, just two long shelves of split-bamboo poles lashed together with rattan. The men, thirty of them, slept on bamboo. Most had no blankets. When Pete asked a sergeant what happened when it rained, he was informed that the men took cover under the bamboo poles.

O'Donnell had only one artesian well with a working pump and it dispensed water through a half-inch pipe to both camps, Filipino and American. The pump worked occasionally but its gasoline engine often sputtered and died. And since there was always a shortage of gasoline, the Japanese routinely let the tank run dry to conserve.

Pete desperately wanted water, as did everyone, and eventually found his way to the water line, a long, sad assemblage of men. As he walked down the line looking for its end, he passed hundreds of men, all with the same detached and defeated eyes. No one talked as they waited and waited. The line barely moved. It took him seven hours to fill his canteen.

At dark, the men were lined up and told to sit. Dinner was served, a scoop of rice. There was no meat, bread, or fruit. After eating, the men drifted back to the barracks, which had no lighting. There was nothing to do but face the nightly adventure of sleep. Pete found it impossible to get comfortable on the bamboo poles and eventually found a pile of weeds in a corner and curled himself into a ball.

His mouth was parched and sticky and he craved water. The starvation was painful enough, but the lack of water was driving men mad. There was barely enough to drink and cook with and operate the hospital, and not a spare drop for anything else. Pete's skin was filthy and raw in places from the lack of soap and water. He had not bathed in weeks, had not shaved since before the surrender on Bataan. His clothes were rags and there was no way to clean them. His one pair of underwear had been tossed days ago. He could not remember the last time he brushed his teeth and gums and they ached from such a rotten diet. He smelled like a walking sewer, and he knew it because every other prisoner reeked.

During his first night at O'Donnell, a sharp crack of thunder awakened Pete and his bunkmates. A storm was rolling through. As the rain began, thousands of men staggered into the open and looked at the skies. They opened their mouths, spread their arms, and let the sheets of cool rainwater wash over them. It was delicious, and precious, and there was no way to collect it. The rain went on for a long time and turned the walkways into muddy ditches, but the men stood through the storm, savoring the water and happy to get a good cleansing.

At dawn, Pete hustled through the mud to the hospital. He had been told that getting there early was advisable. It was a wretched place, filled with dying, naked men, many lying on the floor in their own waste and waiting for help. A doctor looked at the gash in the back of Pete's head and thought he could help. Pete was lucky; there was no infection. With a pair of electric army shears, the doctor shaved Pete's scalp and took his whiskers while he was at it. It was refreshing and Pete felt lighter and cooler. The doctor had nothing in the way of anesthesia, so Pete gritted his teeth while six stitches were sewn to close the wound. The doctor was happy to see a patient he could treat, explaining as he worked that there was so little he could do for the others. He gave Pete some antibiotics and wished him well. Pete thanked him and hurried back to the barracks in anticipation of food.

Breakfast was rice, as were lunch and dinner. Filthy

rice, often with bugs and weevils and mold, and it didn't matter, because starving men will eat anything. The rice was steamed and stewed and boiled and stretched as thinly as possible. Traces of meat sometimes appeared, beef or water buffalo, but the portions were too small to taste. Occasionally the cooks added whatever boiled vegetables they could find, but they were tasteless. There was never fruit. As they starved between meals, the men ate leaves and grass and before long O'Donnell was picked clean of all vegetation. And when there was nothing to eat, the listless prisoners lounged in whatever shade they could find and talked about food.

They were dying of starvation. On average, they were given fifteen hundred calories a day, about half of what they required. Added to the fact that most had been starving for four months on Bataan, the diet at O'Donnell was lethal, and intentionally so.

Like water, food was plentiful in the Philippines.

The lack of it only intensified their diseases. Every man suffered from something, be it malaria, dengue fever, scurvy, beriberi, jaundice, diphtheria, pneumonia, or dysentery, or combinations of these. Half the men had dysentery when they arrived. The officers organized teams to dig latrines, but they were soon filled and overflowing. Some men were so crippled by the violent diarrhea they could not walk and soiled themselves where they lay. Some died from it. With no medicine and a pathetic diet, dysentery was soon epidemic. The entire prison reeked of a huge, open sewer.

Pete had suffered through two mild bouts of dysentery since Christmas, but he had been able to get paregoric from doctors. During his second day at O'Donnell, he was suddenly short of breath and fatigued. The warning signs arrived, and like all the prisoners he spent a few hours self-diagnosing and wondering which disease was coming. When his stomach began cramping, he suspected dysentery. Halfway through his first bout of bloody diarrhea, he knew for sure. The first few days would be the roughest.

His new pal was Clay Wampler, a cowboy from Colorado who had been a machine gunner with the Thirty-First. Clay shared a space in the barracks next to Pete and had welcomed him to his miserable new home. With Clay's assistance, Pete went to the hospital in search of paregoric, but the demand was so high there was none in the prison. Clay was a dutiful nurse and joked that he was happy to help Pete because he, Clay, would expect the same attention when he got hit with the damned disease. On the third day, Pete was somewhat relieved when he realized his current bout was not as severe as many he had witnessed. Dysentery killed many men. Others suffered the cramps and diarrhea for a week and shook it off.

That night, Pete awoke soaking wet and with violent chills. He had seen enough malaria to know the signs.

The remnants of the Twenty-Sixth Cavalry were housed in the northeast compound, as far away from Pete as possible. When it had retreated to Bataan, it was still intact and operating, with forty-one American officers and about four hundred Filipino Scouts. Early in the siege, though, cavalry proved ineffective in the treacherous jungles of the peninsula, and the horses were soon needed elsewhere as hunger became an enemy. April 9, the day of the surrender, the Twenty-Sixth had lost fourteen officers and about two hundred Scouts. At O'Donnell, thirty-six of the Americans were together, including Sal Moreno and Ewing Kane. Six of the missing were known dead, including Pete Banning. Others had evaded capture and were still at large, including Lieutenant Edwin Ramsey, the leader of the last cavalry charge at Morong. Ramsey was on his way to the mountains, where he would organize a guerrilla army.

In charge of the Twenty-Sixth was Major Robert Trumpett, a West Pointer from Maryland. He had arrived at O'Donnell two days before Pete and was busy organizing his men into a survival unit. Like everyone else, they were suffering from starvation, dehydration, exhaustion, wounds, and disease, primarily dengue fever and malaria. They had survived the death march and were quickly realizing that they would have to survive O'Donnell as well. Trumpett prepared a list of the six men killed either in action or on the march, and managed to hand it to an aide for General Ned King. The general had asked all commanders to do this so families back home could be notified.

Of the six, four had died in action, with two known to have been buried. Pete and another lieutenant had died on the march and their bodies would never be recovered.

General King asked the commandant to pass along the names of the dead and captured to an American administrative staff working under house arrest in Manila. At first the commandant refused, but later changed his mind when his superiors ordered it. The Japanese were proud of the large numbers of American casualties and wanted it known.

The hospital was a collection of flimsy bamboo huts on stilts. There were five wards, long buildings with no beds, blankets, or sheets. Patients lay shoulder to shoulder on the floor, some in agony, others in comas, still others already dead. Under manageable conditions, it could safely house two hundred patients at a time. By late spring there were over eight hundred men lined along the floors, waiting for medicines that were not going to arrive. Most of them would die.

Not long after the Bataan prisoners began flooding O'Donnell, the hospital became more of a morgue than a place to be treated. The doctors and medics, most of them also suffering from one or more maladies, had almost no medicine. Even the basics such as quinine for malaria, or paregoric for dysentery, or vitamin C for scurvy were in urgently short supply. Most of the supplies—tape, gauze, disinfectant, aspirin, and so on— were smuggled in by doctors from other hospitals. The Japanese provided virtually nothing.

The doctors were forced to hoard the medicines and give them only to the men who seemed most likely to survive. Giving drugs to a severe case was, in effect, wasting the drugs. As the supplies got thinner, the doctors devised a simple lottery system to determine the winners.

Clay dragged Pete back to the hospital and finally managed to corner a doctor. He explained that his friend had not only dysentery but malaria as well, and seemed to be fading fast. The doctor said he was sorry, but he had nothing. Clay had heard the rumor, and with so many idle men the rumor mill raged nonstop, that there was a black market for some of the more common medicines. Clay asked the doctor about this, and he claimed to know nothing. But, as they were leaving, the doctor whispered, "Behind ward four."

Behind ward four, sitting under a shade tree was a plump American with a deck of cards. On a makeshift table, he was playing some type of game that needed only one participant. The fact that he was not emaciated was clear evidence that he was gaming the system. When they had surrendered, Clay had noticed a few heavier American captives. They were generally older and worked somewhere in the army's vast administration abyss. When forced to march, many of them had fallen quickly.

This guy had not marched anywhere. Nor had he missed many meals. He was powerfully built with a thick chest, muscled arms, a squat neck. And a sneer that Clay instantly hated. He dealt some cards to himself, glanced up at Clay, and asked, "Need something?"

Clay released Pete, who managed to stand on his own, and assessed the situation. It was one he did not care for. It was one that infuriated him. Clay said, "Yeah, my friend here needs some quinine and paregoric. Somebody said you got it."

On the table, there were four small bottles of pills next to the deck of cards. The dealer glanced at the bottles and said, "Got a few pills left. A buck a pop."

Without a word, without a warning, Clay growled, "You bloodsuckin' sack of shit!" He attacked, kicking the table and sending the cards and bottles flying. The dealer jumped up, yelled "What the hell!" and threw a round-house right at Clay, who was charging. Clay ducked low, and with a right upper cut caught the dealer square in the testicles. As they popped together, he screamed and fell to the dirt. Clay kicked him viciously in the face, then dropped to his knees and pounded away as a blind rage overcame fatigue, starvation, dehydration, and whatever else Clay had at the moment. All was forgotten as he could finally, after days of wanting to fight back and kill the enemy, deliver some resistance and revenge. After a dozen or so shots to the face, he stopped and slowly stood. He said, "You low-life son of a bitch. Making a buck off men who are dying. You're lower than the damned Japs."

The dealer was not done. He managed to maneuver onto all fours, undoubtedly with more pain in his crotch than in his bloody face, then stood, although unsteadily. He glanced around and noticed that a crowd was gathering. Nothing was more enjoyable than a good fistfight, primarily because so few of the prisoners had the energy to start or finish one.

He was bleeding from the nose and the mouth and a cut above his right eye, and he should have stayed on the ground. With a limp caused by his aching balls, he stepped toward Clay and growled, "You son of a bitch."

The word "bitch" had barely escaped his mouth when a fist smacked it with such speed that the punch was barely visible. With a perfect left-right combo, Clay drew even more blood. The dealer wasn't much of a boxer and had never brawled with a cowboy, and as they sparred he had a terrible time landing a punch. Clay circled him, firing away and pretending he was punching a Jap. A hard right to the chin dropped the dealer again. He fell onto the board he'd been using as a table, and Clay, still in a rage, grabbed the board and began pounding his hapless opponent. The sound of hardwood cracking against his skull became sickening, but Clay could not stop. He had seen so much death that life was now cheap, and who in hell cared if he killed a man he considered lower than a Jap?

A guard with a bayonet on a rifle stepped next to him and stuck him gently in the back. Clay stopped his pounding, looked at the guard, and stood. He tried to catch his breath and was suddenly exhausted.

The guard smiled and said, "No stop. Fight more."

Clay looked at the battered face of the dealer. He looked at Pete, who was standing under the tree and shaking his head no. He looked at the gaunt men in the crowd who'd hurried over to watch.

He looked at the Jap and said, "No. I'm finished."

The guard raised his bayonet, poked Clay in the chest, nodded at the guy in the dirt, and said, "Kill him."

Clay ignored the bayonet and said, "No. That's what you do."

He took a step back, fully expecting the guard to lunge at him and begin something awful, but the guard only lowered his rifle and stared at Clay, who walked to the tree to retrieve Pete. The crowd slowly dispersed as the dealer came to his senses and started to move.

Pete had found a new best friend. An hour later, they were hiding from the sun behind the barracks. The odors inside their building had become so noxious that they tried to avoid it. Pete was sitting under a tree with Clay nearby. They were chatting with others, whiling away the hours, when the same guard found them. He addressed Clay, who stood and bowed and faced him in anticipation of a bad scene. Instead, the guard pulled a small bottle from his pocket, handed it to Clay, nodded at Pete, and said, "For your friend." Then he turned in a perfect about-face and marched away.

The pills were quinine, lifesavers for Pete and a few others in his barracks.

CHAPTER 28

As was her ritual, at 6:00 p.m. Nineva left supper on the stove and walked to her cottage. Liza watched her leave through a bedroom window, thankful once again that she was gone and the family was alone. In the nine years that Liza had lived in the main house, she and Nineva had learned to coexist, often side by side as they canned fruits and vegetables from the garden and talked about the children. With Pete gone, they leaned on each other daily, with each trying to appear stronger than the other. In front of the kids, they were stoic and confident that the Allies would win the war and he would be home soon. Both women shed plenty of tears, but always in private.

On Tuesday, May 19, the family was in the middle of supper, and the conversation was about the summer. Vacation began tomorrow, and Joel and Stella were eager to start the three-month holiday. He was sixteen, a rising senior, and the youngest in his class. She was fifteen and would be a sophomore. They wanted to travel some, perhaps to New Orleans or Florida, but the truth was that no definite plans could be made. They had not heard from their father in over four months, and this uncertainty dominated their lives.

From just outside the kitchen window, Mack started barking as a wave of headlights swept through the kitchen. A car had approached and was somewhere out front. Since no one was expected, the three gave each other a fearful look. Liza jumped to her feet and said, "Someone is here. I'll see who it is."

At the front door were two men in army uniforms. A moment later, they were seated in the den, facing the family on the sofa. Liza sat between Joel and Stella and held their hands. Stella was already in tears.

Captain Malone said solemnly, "I'm afraid I have some bad news, and I'm sorry. But Lieutenant Banning is now missing and presumed dead. We do not know for certain that he is dead, because his unit was unable to recover his body. But, given the circumstances, the men with him are reasonably certain that he is dead. I'm very sorry."

Stella's head fell in her mother's lap. Liza grabbed both and squeezed them close. They gasped and cried and held each other tightly as the two officers stared at the floor. The men had not volunteered for this assignment, but they had their orders and were now making such dreadful visits almost every day throughout north Mississippi.

Liza gritted her teeth and asked, "What does 'presumed dead' mean, exactly?"

Captain Malone said, "It means we did not recover the body."

"So there's a chance he's still alive?" Joel asked, wiping his cheeks.

"Yes, there is that chance, but I caution you that, under the circumstances, the men with Lieutenant Banning are reasonably certain that he was killed."

"Can you tell us what happened?" Liza asked.

"We have some details, but not many, and I'm not sure how accurate our facts are, ma'am. Lieutenant Banning was captured when the Allied forces surrendered to the Japanese on the Philippines. It was last month on April 9 and 10. The men were being marched to a POW camp when he was injured and left behind, as were many men. He was then killed by the Japanese soldiers."

At that moment it didn't really matter how he died. The shock of the moment blurred the details. The horrible truth was that Pete Banning was gone and they would never see him again. Husband, father, patriarch, friend, boss, brother, neighbor, and leading citizen. There were so many who would share their pain. They wept for a long time, and when the officers had nothing else to say, they stood, offered their condolences once more, and left the house.

Liza wanted nothing more than to go to her bedroom, lock the door, get under the covers, and cry herself to sleep. But that would be indulgent and was not an option. She had two wonderful children who now needed her more than ever, and while she wanted to collapse into a puddle of tears, she instead stiffened her spine and took the first step.

"Joel, get in the truck and drive down to Florry's.

Bring her back here. Stop along the way and inform Nineva. Tell Jupe to get on a horse and spread the word among the Negroes."

Word spread rapidly enough, and within an hour the front yard was filled with cars and trucks. Liza would have preferred to spend the first night in quiet mourning with just her kids and Florry, but things were not done that way in the rural South. Dexter and Jackie Bell arrived in the first wave and spent a few moments alone with the Bannings. He read some scripture and said a prayer. Liza explained that the family was not ready to confront a horde of well-meaning mourners, and they huddled in her bedroom while Dexter quietly asked folks to come back later. At ten o'clock, they were still arriving.

In Clanton, the gossip was of nothing else. At 8:00 a.m., Dexter opened the sanctuary of the Methodist church so those who knew Pete could stop by for a moment of prayer. In the early hours of the tragedy, much was made of the fact that he was missing and not officially dead. So there was hope, and the hope inspired his friends and neighbors to pray long and hard.

Later in the morning, Dexter and Jackie returned to the Banning home to sit with Liza and the children, who were still in no mood to greet the crowd. He quietly encouraged people to leave, and they did. They arrived in carloads and delivered cakes, pies, casseroles, food no one needed but there were traditions to follow. After a few soft words with Dexter, and once they realized they would not be allowed to hug and cry with Liza, they quietly left the house, returned to their cars, and drove away.

Liza made the decision that there would be no memorial service. There was a chance her husband was still alive, and she and her children would focus on that and ignore the bad news. Or, they would at least try to. As the days dragged on, Liza began seeing a few close friends, as did Joel and Stella. The shock gradually wore off, though the aching, numbing pain did not.

Routines developed to maintain normalcy. The family ate breakfast and supper together, often with Nineva sitting with them, a new wrinkle. Each weekday Dexter Bell arrived around ten for a short devotional—a verse or scripture, a comforting word, and a thoughtful prayer. Jackie came occasionally, but usually he was alone.

Two weeks after receiving the news, Florry took Joel and Stella to Memphis for a long weekend. Liza insisted they go in an effort to get away from the gloominess of their home, and to have a little fun. Florry had some eccentric friends in Memphis who could make anyone smile. She and the kids checked into the Peabody. Joel's room was not far from where he was conceived, though he would never know it.

While they were away, Dexter Bell arrived each day for the morning devotion. He and Liza sat in the den and talked quietly. From the kitchen, Nineva listened to every word.

Some black-market paregoric worked, and Pete's third round of dysentery improved but did not go away. His malaria lingered too. He could function with it, though at times the chills and fevers caused him to lie in the dirt and shake from head to toe. He hallucinated and thought he was back home.

He and Clay sat in the shade of the barracks and watched the parade of dead bodies being hauled to the cemetery across the road. By late April, twenty-five Americans were dying each day. By May, the number was fifty. By June, a hundred.

Death was everywhere. The living thought about dying because they saw the dead bodies, which were often piled haphazardly. They thought about dying because they too were facing death. They starved a little more each day and came closer to a collapse from which they would not recover. Diseases were running rampant and there was no way to stop them, and it was inevitable that one of a dozen would arrive any day now and bring a miserable death with it.

Pete watched men give up and die, and on several occasions he was tempted. All of them were hanging on by a thread anyway, and only those with an iron will to live managed to survive. Giving up was painless, while living meant waking up in the morning and facing another day in hell. Some were determined to cling to all hope and survive whatever the enemy threw at them, while others grew too weary from the suffering and closed their eyes.

Pete survived by thinking of his wife and kids, his farm, and his family's long and rich history in Ford County. He recalled stories he had heard as a boy about old wars and battles and feuds, all colorful tales that had been handed down from one generation to the next. He thought about Liza and those wonderful days at the Peabody when they were spending nights together, something no well-respected couple would think of doing in the 1920s. He thought of her body and her constant desire for physical pleasure. He remembered hunting and fishing with Joel in the woods on their land and bringing home deer, turkeys, rabbits, bream, and crappie that they cleaned by the barn and gave to Nineva to cook for supper. He remembered Stella as a little girl with those beautiful eyes curled up on the sofa in her pajamas listening as her father read bedtime stories. He longed for the warmth of her soft skin. He wanted to be there when his children finished college and got married.

Pete had made the decision that he would not die from disease or starvation. He was a tough farm boy, a West Point man, a cavalry officer, and he had a beautiful family back home. Perhaps luck had given him a stronger physical and mental constitution. He was tougher than most of the others, or at least he told himself so. He wanted to help the weaker ones, but there was nothing he could do. Everyone was dying, and he had to take care of himself.

As conditions worsened at O'Donnell, the men talked more and more of escape. As prisoners, they were expected to attempt it, though in their condition it seemed nearly impossible. They were too weak to run far, and there were Japs everywhere. It would be easy to get outside because of the work crews, but they were not healthy enough to survive in the jungle.

To suppress the urge to run, the Japs implemented some rules that were simple in their understanding but exceedingly brutal in their application. Initially, if you ran and got caught, you were to be struck with a bullwhip until you bled to death. To demonstrate how this rule worked, the guards rounded up several thousand

prisoners one afternoon for a show near the commandant's quarters.

Five Americans had tried to escape and been caught.
They were stripped naked and their hands were bound
together above their heads and attached to ropes looped
over a rail so that their toes barely touched the ground.
At first it looked like they might be hanged. All five were
emaciated, with their ribs jutting out. An officer with a
bullwhip strutted in front of the prisoners, and through
an interpreter explained what was about to happen,
though it was rather obvious. He was an expert with the
bullwhip, and his first stroke against the back of the first
soldier caused him to scream. The bullwhip popped with
each blow, and his back and buttocks were soon bloodied. When he appeared to be unconscious, the officer
moved a few steps to the second soldier. The mauling
lasted for half an hour, under a hot sun. When all five
were bloodied and still, the commandant stepped forward and announced a new rule: If a prisoner escaped,
then ten of his comrades would be whipped and left to
die in the sun.

Needless to say, the demonstration curtailed many escape schemes that had been in the works.

Clay found a Filipino Scout who was working as a
truck driver and had managed to establish a black market
for food within the American section of O'Donnell. His
prices were fair and he offered tins of salmon, sardines,
and tuna, along with peanut butter, fruit, and cookies.

Pete and Clay made a decision. They would take the
cash hidden in Pete's canteen cover, buy the food they

could afford, share it between themselves but include no one else, and try to survive. The scheme would take both of their efforts because it was difficult to hide and eat black market food. Everyone was ravenous and watching everyone else. They felt lousy hiding and not sharing, but they damned sure could not feed the sixty thousand starving souls at O'Donnell. Clay's first haul was a tin of salmon, four oranges, and two coconut cookies, and for $1.50 they ate like kings.

The plan was to stretch the money as far as possible, and when it was gone, they would think of something else. The extra food energized Pete and he began roaming the prison looking for his old friends from the Twenty-Sixth Cavalry.

The Japanese rarely entered the camp and had little interest in what went on there. They knew the conditions were inhumane and deteriorating, but they simply ignored the prisoners when possible. As long as they remained locked up, and worked when they were instructed, the Japanese didn't seem to care.

However, the piles of dead bodies could not be ignored. The commandant ordered that they be burned, but General King pleaded for a more respectful burial. The Japanese might believe in cremation, but the Americans did not.

With the Americans dying at a rate of a hundred per day, General King organized burying rituals. Groups of gravediggers took turns at the shovel, while other groups hauled the bodies. Most came from the morgue at the hospital, but there were decomposing bodies all over the prison.

Pete and Clay learned that those who stayed busy lived longer than those who sat around in a stupor, so they volunteered to dig. They left the barracks after breakfast and walked to the American cemetery just outside the main camp, about eight hundred yards from the hospital. They were handed their tools, old spades and pieces of metal bent here and there and barely able to scratch up a pound of dirt. An American officer stepped off the boundaries of the next mass grave—six feet wide, twenty feet long, four feet deep. The diggers began their work. There were dozens of them and the work was urgent because the bodies were rotting.

They arrived in blankets strung between bamboo poles, or on litters fashioned from old doors. The burial parties used anything that would haul a hundred-pound skeleton, many of which had begun decomposing in the heat. The rotting corpses emitted a noxious odor that stung when inhaled.

At each grave, a registration officer handled the paperwork and recorded the name and exact location of each man as he was laid to rest. However, some of the dead had no dog tags and were unknown. Each grave held twenty or more men. When one was filled, the gravediggers went about the glum business of covering their comrades.

The cemetery was nicknamed the Boneyard, and how fitting that became. Pete could count the ribs on virtually every corpse he buried, and he never failed to utter a curse at the Japanese as he covered each American soldier.

Day after day, he and Clay volunteered to dig graves. For Pete, it was a way to hang on to his humanity. Someone had to make sure each soldier received a proper burial, or at least the best under the circumstances. If Pete died, he would do so with the assurance that some kind soul had dug a real grave for him.

As the casualties mounted, the digging became more intense. And with lousy tools and straining energy, the work was difficult. The Boneyard expanded as more graves were necessary. The pallbearers arrived in a steady stream.

A grave was filled and an officer ordered it closed. Pete and Clay and four others began the chore of back-filling, of covering the men. As Pete did so he stopped cold. Below him, just a few feet away, was a face he recognized, even with its closed eyes and thick black whiskers. He asked the registration officer for the name. Salvadore Moreno, of the Twenty-Sixth Cavalry.

Pete closed his eyes and stood motionless. "You okay, Pete?" Clay asked. Pete backed away from the grave and stumbled a few feet to a fence post. He sat down, covered his face with his hands, and wept bitterly.

CHAPTER 29

As things developed, the grave digging was not such a good idea after all. The Japanese were watching from a distance. They needed some of the "healthier" Americans to ship back to Japan to work as slave laborers in coal mines. Pete and Clay were chosen in a group of about a thousand. The first hint of change came after breakfast in late June when a guard appeared and ordered five men from their barracks to follow him. At the parade ground, they formed lines and stood at attention. A convoy of trucks arrived, and as each man boarded he was given a rice ball, a banana, and a can of water.

Pete and Clay knew that this was not a normal work detail, and as they rode for more than an hour some excitement crept into the conversations around them. Could it be possible they were leaving O'Donnell for good? The Japanese were constantly moving prisoners around, and wherever they were going had to be an improvement over O'Donnell.

Soon they were entering the busy streets of Manila, and speculation ran wild about their destination. When they stopped at the harbor, the men were confused. Should they be delighted that O'Donnell was behind them, or terrified of being shipped to Japan? Before long, all excitement vanished.

They were herded onto a dock and began waiting. A group of prisoners from another camp arrived and spread the gossip that the Red Cross had negotiated a prisoner exchange and that they were headed to Australia, and freedom. By that time, though, Pete and the men from O'Donnell believed nothing. As they waited, Pete stared at the freighter, an ancient, rusting vessel with no markings whatsoever. No name, no registration, no nationality.

Finally, they queued up in a long line and began to slowly climb the gangway. On board, they passed the forward bulkhead and came to an open hatch with a ladder down to the hold. Guards were nervous and barking commands. As Pete began to step down into the hold, he was hit with a vile odor from below. As he descended farther, he saw the sweaty faces of hundreds of prisoners already on board. As he would learn, about twelve hundred men had been loaded from a prison north of Manila. And they had been informed by the guards that they were headed to Japan to work in the coal mines.

As more prisoners were stuffed into the hold, the men began to suffocate. They were shoulder to shoulder, body to body, with no room to sit, lie, or even move about. They began shouting and cursing and all order broke down. The guards kept stuffing more men below, beating the reluctant ones with rifle butts. The temperature rose to a hundred degrees and men began fainting, but there was no room to fall. Soon, they were dying.

The emperor Hirohito refused to ratify the Geneva Convention, and from the beginning of its war in Asia his imperial army treated its captured prisoners as slaves. With a severe shortage of labor at home, the Japanese devised a grand scheme to ship American POWs to the coal mines on their mainland. To do so, they used every available cargo vessel, regardless of age and seaworthiness. All ships were commissioned and stuffed with soldiers bound for the Philippines and then restuffed with sick and dying American boys bound for the labor camps.

Throughout the war, 125,000 Allied prisoners were shipped to Japan, with 21,000 dying on board or going down with the ships. On August 6, 1945, four hundred American POWs were underground digging for coal in a mine near Omine, only fifty miles from Hiroshima. When the first atomic bomb landed, the ground rolled and shook and they knew it was something far beyond the usual daily bombings. They fervently prayed it was the beginning of the end.

Among their many great miscalculations in the war, the Japanese failed to build enough boats to haul troops and supplies. Added to this was their failure to eliminate the U.S. submarine fleet at Pearl Harbor and elsewhere during the early days of the war. By the summer of 1942, U.S. subs were roaming like lone wolves in the South Pacific and feasting on Japanese merchant ships. To overcompensate, the Japanese simply crammed more of their soldiers onto their ships to go fight, and more of their

POWs to bring home to work. Their freighters were perpetually overloaded, slow, outdated, easily stalked, and unmarked.

They were known as hellships. Between January of 1942 and July of 1945, the Japanese hauled 156 loads of war prisoners to the mainland to work in labor camps, and the voyages were worse than any abuse the Americans had yet to encounter. Locked below deck with no food, water, lights, toilets, or breathable air, the men succumbed to fainting, madness, and death.

And torpedoes. Because the Japanese did not mark their troop carriers, they were fair game for Allied submarines. An estimated five thousand American POWs crammed into the holds of Japanese freighters were killed by American torpedoes.

Pete's ship left Manila Bay six hours after he boarded, and men around him were already suffocating and screaming. The guards mercifully opened the portholes and a whiff of air spread through the hold. A colonel managed to convince a guard that men were dying, and what good was a slave if he arrived dead? The hatches were opened and the prisoners were allowed to climb to the deck, where they could at least breathe and see the moon. Fresh air was plentiful. Food and water were not mentioned. Guards stood gun to gun, waiting to shoot any poor prisoner who tried to vault into the sea. Though suicide was a constant thought, no one had the energy.

Pete and Clay spent the night on the deck with hundreds of others, under a brilliant sky that back home would have been admired. Now, though, it was just another reminder of how far they were from freedom.

Evidently, the guards had been instructed to kill only

when necessary. Slave labor was now deemed valuable, and the fact that men were dying below was unacceptable. At dawn, dead bodies were lifted from the hold and shoved up the ladder and buried unceremoniously at sea. Pete watched them hit the water, then float for a moment before disappearing, and with each one he thought of the mother and father and young wife back home in Oregon or Minnesota or Florida who were at that moment saying their prayers and waiting for a letter. How long would it be before a man in a uniform knocked on the door and shattered their world?

The sun was up and there was no shade on the deck. No shade, no food, no water, and the prisoners complained to the guards more and more with each passing hour. The guards kept their fingers on their triggers and returned the curses in their language. As the day wore on, so did the nerves and tension. Finally, a prisoner ran for the railing, took a flying leap, and dove for the ocean, eighty feet below. He landed with a splash and in a hail of gunfire. The Japs, while proficient with swords and bayonets, were notoriously bad shots, and it was not possible to know if the prisoner was hit. However, the prolonged volley that followed him down was enough to discourage more diving.

Hours passed as the men baked in the sun. To escape it, they went below for brief respites, but the stench was so overwhelming they could not last. Most were still suffering from dysentery, and the guards allowed them to hang by ropes off the stern and bow to discharge their bloody diarrhea. Anything to keep it off board.

Mercifully, some clouds arrived late in the afternoon of the second day and blocked the sun. The prisoners were ordered below and were promised that food would be served before long. They loitered in long lines to avoid the descent into hell, and the guards seemed somewhat sympathetic and didn't push them. Darkness came, with no hint of food. Suddenly there was a panic among the guards. Some were running from the bow, yakking in extreme agitation for no apparent reason.

The first torpedo hit in the rear by the engine room. The second hit perfectly in the middle. Both explosions rocked the ship. Its steel frame echoed and vibrated. It was an old boat that wouldn't last long, and even Pete, a cavalry guy who'd grown up landlocked, knew they would sink fast. He and Clay squatted on the deck and watched as the panicked guards slammed the hatches, sealing over eighteen hundred Americans below. About a hundred remained on deck, and the guards were suddenly unconcerned with them. The ship was going down. It was every man for himself.

A prisoner, one braver than the others, ran forward and attempted to open a hatch. A guard shot him in the back of the head and kicked his body aside. So much for heroism.

A third torpedo knocked the men off their feet and total chaos ensued. The guards frantically unhitched rubber rafts and tossed life vests into the sea. Prisoners vaulted over the sides and into a black ocean with no idea where they might land. As Pete and Clay scurried to a railing, they passed a guard who had laid down his rifle while he struggled with a raft. Pete instinctively grabbed it, shot the son of a bitch in the face, tossed the rifle over the side, then jumped and followed it to the water, laughing as he fell.

The landing was hard but the water was warm. Clay fell nearby and they began dog-paddling and looking for something to hold on to. The sea was pitch-black and everywhere men were crying for help, both in English and in Japanese. The ship began exploding and Pete could hear the anguished cries of those trapped. He swam away from it as fast as his fatigued and depleted limbs could take him. For a second, he lost Clay, and he called for him.

"Over here," Clay called back. "I've got a raft."

They scrambled into what appeared to be a six-man raft, and as soon as they caught their breath Clay said, "You shot that son of a bitch!"

"I did," Pete said proudly. "And with his own gun."

They heard Japanese voices on the water and went silent. Using the small oars they found in a pocket—along with a flare but no food or water—they paddled furiously away while watching the ship list and begin to sink. The distant screams were sickening.

For ten, fifteen, twenty minutes they paddled, and when their escape was certain they stopped and rested. A thousand yards away, the ship tilted abruptly on its stern and sank in a matter of seconds. By locking the hatches, the guards had killed another eighteen hundred sick and starving American boys.

From the blackness of the sea, a voice called out, and it was not in English. Pete and Clay slid down into the raft and waited. Before long they heard a thump against the raft, then a head popped up. They grabbed the guard and pulled him into their raft. Like most Japs, he was tiny, five feet five max, 120 pounds, and without a bayonet or sword or rifle he looked much smaller. He had no can-

teen, no backpack, no food or water, so he was a worthless Jap who only minutes earlier had been tormenting
his prisoners. Clay punched him so hard his jaw cracked.
They took turns punching and strangling him, and when
the Jap stopped breathing they tossed him into the ocean,
where he would rest forever with their brothers he had
just killed.

And they felt good. In spite of their dehydration and
hunger, and in spite of drifting in a raft and having no
idea where they were, they felt an immense satisfaction.
They had finally struck back, drawn blood, killed the
enemy, turned the tide in favor of the Allies. For the first
time in weeks, they were free. There were no brutal
guards with guns or bayonets watching them. They were
not digging burial trenches. There were no dead bodies
stacked around them.

They were adrift under a clear, star-filled sky, with no
idea which direction held the most promise. So they laid
down the paddles and rested on a calm sea. The South
China Sea was a busy place, and tomorrow someone
would find them.

The first boat was a Japanese frigate, and as soon as
Pete recognized the flag he and Clay slid out of the raft
and hid under it. The ship seemed unconcerned with the
empty raft and never slowed down. It appeared to be
going in the direction of the wreck, probably searching
for Japanese survivors. Pete and Clay had vowed to drown
themselves before being captured again.

The second boat was a forty-foot Filipino fishing rig
owned by a man named Amato and manned by him and

his two sons, three of the nicest people on the face of the earth. When they realized that Pete and Clay were Americans, they pulled them aboard, wrapped them in blankets, and handed them water at first, then hot black coffee, a delicacy they had not had in months. As Teofilo partially deflated the raft and hid it, Tomas captained the boat while Amato peppered the Americans with questions. Where were they from? Where were they imprisoned? For how long? He had a cousin in California and loved America. His brother was a Filipino Scout who was hiding in the mountains. Amato hated the Japanese even more than Pete and Clay did.

Where were they headed? Since they had no idea where they were, they certainly had no destination. Amato said they were about twenty miles from land. He said that last week the Americans had torpedoed another ship filled with their own soldiers. Why were they doing this? Pete explained that the troopships were unmarked.

Teofilo served them bowls of hot rice with *pandesal,* a fluffy roll that was the national bread. They had eaten it before the war and thought little of it. Now, though, it was manna from heaven, with a little butter added. While they ate, and Amato cautioned them to eat slowly because it was easy to overwhelm their fragile systems, Teofilo grilled small fillets of mackerel and milkfish in a skillet on a portable gas grill. Pete and Clay knew to eat slowly. Starvation had been a way of life for the past six months and they had learned too much about it. But, they struggled to control their desire to stuff their mouths. With his first bite of the warm fish, Pete hardly chewed, and he smiled as it descended wonderfully to his stomach.

Amato was under contract to the Japanese army to deliver his catch each day, so it was important that they go about their business. They worked their lines, catching yellowfin tuna, salmon, and ruby snapper, while Pete and Clay slept for hours in the cabin. When they awoke, they ate more rice and fish, and drank water by the gallon. At dusk, as Tomas mopped the deck and put away the rods, Amato opened a fruit jar filled with a fermented rice home brew and poured it into their empty coffee cups. It was bitter and tasteless and not something Pete would ever find at the Peabody bar, but it was potent, and the alcohol hit fast and hard.

By the second serving, Pete and Clay were giddy. They were free, well fed for the first time since Christmas, and happily getting buzzed on a home brew that improved with each sip.

Amato's home was the small fishing village of San Narciso on the west coast of the Luzon peninsula. By land, Manila was four hours away, or five or six depending on the roads, mountain paths, and ferries. By sea, it was three hours and the route curved around Bataan, the last place they wanted to see. Amato said Manila was crawling with Japanese and they should stay away. He would not take his boat there.

Late in the day, when San Narciso came into view, Tomas reduced the engine to an idle. It was time for a serious discussion. There would be Japanese at the harbor waiting for their fish, but they were cooks, not soldiers, and they would not inspect the boat. Pete and Clay would be safe to sleep on the boat that night, but tomorrow they must move on. If they were seen or caught,

Amato and his sons would lose their boat and probably their heads.

Their first option was to escape, and Amato had a friend they could talk to. But escape meant a long voyage across open seas in a bad boat, and Amato didn't like the odds. Since the war started, he knew of several Americans who had tried it. No one knew if they were successful. Plus, there was the issue of compensation, and most of the prisoners were penniless. Pete assured him that they were too.

The second option was to fight. Amato had contacts who could take the men into the mountains where the guerrillas were operating. There were a lot of Americans and Filipino Scouts organized in the dense jungles of Luzon. They were hitting the enemy from all directions, at times seriously disrupting the movements of troops and supplies. The imperial army had declared war on the guerrillas and was offering bounties. The situation was beyond dangerous.

"We're not running away," Pete said. "We came here to fight."

"And we have some scores to settle," Clay added.

Amato smiled and nodded his agreement. He was a proud Filipino and sickened by the Japanese invasion. If he could somehow poison his fish to kill enemy soldiers he would gladly do so. He prayed that the Americans would one day prevail and free his country, and he longed for that moment.

With the harbor in sight, Pete and Clay went below deck and hid in the cabin. At the pier, Tomas and Teofilo removed the heavy tin crates filled with their catch and waited for their only customer. A short, fat Japanese man in a bloodied apron approached without a hello or any greeting and inspected their fish. He made an offer, one that Amato laughed at. His counteroffer was rejected outright, and this went on, back and forth, the same ritual every afternoon. The cook was in too much of a hurry to weigh the fish. He made his final offer, one that Amato really could not reject, and the deal was done. Money changed hands, and from the look on Amato's face he had been shortchanged again. Two privates arrived with a wagon, loaded the fish, and left while the cook was bargaining with the captain of the next fishing boat.

When they were gone, Teofilo fired up his grill again and prepared dinner. The menu was the same—boiled rice, hot buttered *pandesal,* and grilled mackerel fillets. It had been ten hours since their breakfast, and neither Pete nor Clay felt sick from overeating. They had consumed a light lunch, been through a couple of cocktail hours with the home brew, and so far their traumatized bodies were holding up well. When they had been starved, all they thought about was food. Now that it was available and the gnawing hunger pains were gone, their thoughts drifted elsewhere.

Amato instructed them to stay in the cabin, regardless of how hot and humid it became. The harbor would be deserted throughout the night, but no one could be trusted. If a deckhand or some kid on a bike saw two Americans on a fishing boat, that information could be sold to the Japanese.

The three packed their rucksacks and said good night. Wisely, Amato took the home brew with him. The Americans had had enough.

It wasn't long before the cabin was suffocating. Pete cracked the door and took a peek. The harbor was pitch-black. The boat next to them was a silhouette. The only sounds were of the water gently splashing against the boats. "It's clear out here," he said, and Clay joined him. They kept low and still on the deck. When they talked, and it wasn't often, they whispered. There were a few lights in the town, but they saw not a single person moving about.

In the cabin there was a small basin. Next to it was a bar of soap that had evidently been shrinking for some time. Pete took it, broke it cleanly in two, and handed Clay his portion. Pete stripped naked, eased over the side of the boat, and without a sound entered the water. He assumed it was polluted and filthy, like all harbors, but he didn't care. He squeezed every possible bubble out of his soap and bathed in luxury. When he finished, Clay tossed down his shirt, pants, and socks, and he washed them for the first time in months. They were rags, but he had nothing else.

At some point, they had no idea of the hour, the heat broke suddenly and a gentle wind brought relief. They retreated to the cabin and locked the door. They were tempted to sleep on the deck, under the stars, but the fear of being seen was too great. So far, they had survived everything a brutal war could throw at them. It would be a tragedy to get caught by a kid on a bike.

The date was around June 20; they weren't sure. There was no calendar in the cabin and they had not seen one in months. After a while, a starving prisoner stops worrying about the date. They had surrendered on April 10. Pete had marched up the Bataan Peninsula for six days. For Clay it had been five. They had spent approximately two months at O'Donnell, and thinking of that miserable hellhole made them cringe. But they had survived it, as they had the death march, the siege of Bataan, the fighting, the surrender, the packed railcars, the hellships, along with starvation and disease and death scenes they could never forget. They marveled at the human body's ability to endure, and the spirit's resourcefulness in the face of deprivation.

They had survived! The war was not over, but certainly they had seen the worst of it. They were no longer captives, and now they would soon be on equal footing with the enemy.

With the issue of food temporarily behind them, they talked about their wives and families. They desperately wanted to write letters and send them home. They would discuss it with Amato in the morning.

A kid on a bike rode down the wooden pier, looking for nothing, expecting nothing. He heard voices from the cabin of a fishing boat and eased closer to listen. Strange voices in another language. English.

He rode away, finally went home, where his mother was looking for him, and told her. She was angry and smacked him about the ears. Such a strange kid, always telling tall tales and exaggerating.

CHAPTER 30

Amato and his sons arrived at dawn as the harbor came to life. Of the three, Teofilo was the tallest, but only slightly, maybe five feet eight. His clothing would fit neither Pete, who was six feet two, nor Clay, who was an inch shorter. Length was the problem, not the waistlines. The Americans were so gaunt that their belts could almost make two loops around.

Last night, after dinner, Amato had visited the home of a friend, a man believed to be "the tallest man in town." He had negotiated the purchase of two pairs of work pants and two khaki work shirts, along with two pairs of socks. The man at first refused to sell his meager clothing, which was practically his entire wardrobe, and would consider doing so only if Amato divulged what was going on. When the tall man realized who needed the clothing, he refused to accept money. He sent his best wishes, along with his clothes. Amato's wife then washed and ironed the outfits, and as he proudly pulled them from his rucksack and laid them on a cot in the cabin, he had tears in his eyes. So did Pete and Clay.

Amato went on to say that he had been unable to secure new boots. American feet are long and narrow. Filipino feet are short and wide. Only one store in town sold footwear and the merchant almost certainly stocked nothing for foreigners. Amato apologized profusely.

Pete finally asked him to stop and said they had an important matter to discuss. They desperately wanted to write letters to their wives. They'd had no contact since before Christmas and they knew their families were worried sick. They considered this a simple request, but Amato didn't like it. He explained that mail service was unreliable and being watched closely by the Japanese. There were thousands of American soldiers on the loose throughout the Philippines, men just like them, and everyone wanted to send a letter home. Very little mail was allowed to leave the islands. The enemy had a noose around everything. The postal clerk in San Narciso owned the grocery store and they suspected he was a sympathizer. If he, Amato, handed him two letters written by Americans, there would be serious trouble.

The mail was too risky. Pete pressed him and asked if it was possible to mail the letters from another town. Amato finally yielded and sent Tomas into the village. He returned with two sheets of flimsy onion paper and two small square envelopes. Amato found a piece of a pencil. Sitting at the small folding table in the cabin, Pete wrote,

Dear Liza: We surrendered on April 10 and I've spent the last three months or so as a POW. I escaped and am now fighting as a guerrilla somewhere on

*Luzon. I have survived a lot and will continue to
survive the rest and I'll be home as soon as we win the
war. I love you and Joel and Stella and think about
you every minute of every day. Please give my love to
them and to Florry. I am with Clay Wampler. His
wife is Helen. Please contact her at 1427 Glenwood
Road, Lamar, Colorado, and pass along this message.
Love, Pete*

He addressed the envelope, gave no return address,
sealed the letter, and handed the pencil to Clay.

They puttered out of the harbor, the old diesel chug-
ging along as if the day might be its last. They left no
wake and were soon on the sea. Straight ahead and due
west was Vietnam, a thousand miles away. To the right
was China, closer at seven hundred miles.

Teofilo brewed a pot of strong coffee, and as they savored it he prepared breakfast of rice, *pandesal,* and more
grilled mackerel. Pete and Clay ate carefully. Amato's
wife had baked ginger cookies and for the first time in
months they tasted real sugar. Though they had not
mentioned cigarettes, Amato produced a fresh pack of
Lucky Strikes, somehow smuggled all the way from Manila, and the tobacco had never tasted better.

After two hours, the boat found a school of tuna. As
Amato and Tomas reeled them in, Teofilo clubbed them
with a mallet until they were still, then gutted and cleaned
them. Through a haze of tobacco smoke, Pete and Clay
watched and marveled at their efficiency.

At midday Tomas turned the boat back toward Luzon.
Its jagged mountain ranges had never been out of sight,
and as they grew nearer Amato gave them the plan. The

boat finally stopped about two hundred yards offshore along a deserted stretch of rocky shoreline. Teofilo inflated the raft that had saved their lives and helped them into it. Amato handed them a rucksack filled with food and water and wished them well. They saluted, offered their humblest thanks again, and cast off. Teofilo turned the boat around and headed back to sea.

When Pete and Clay were out of sight, Amato took the two envelopes, ripped them into tiny pieces, and flung them into the ocean. His boat had been searched twice by the Japanese navy, and he simply could not run the risk.

They came from the cavalry and the infantry and were not competent with a boat of any size. The raft proved hard to navigate and crashed into some rocks. Pete managed to keep the rucksack dry as he and Clay scrambled over the rocks and came close to drowning. Once on dry soil, they waited. Hiding in the bush and watching their arrival was a Filipino named Acevedo. He sneaked into position behind them, whistled, and waved them over.

Acevedo was just a kid in a straw hat, but his hardened face and lean body gave the clear impression that he was a seasoned guerrilla. Most important, he was heavily armed, with a rifle strapped over his shoulder and pistols on both hips. In good English, he explained that they would hike on some dangerous trails into the mountains, and if all went well they should reach the first camp by dark. Japs were everywhere, and it was imperative that they move fast and silently, without a word.

The bush immediately became a dense jungle with trails that only Acevedo could see. And all trails were headed up. After an hour of climbing, they stopped for a rest. Pete and Clay were exhausted. The thinning air didn't help. Pete asked if they could smoke, and Acevedo frowned and shook his head vehemently. He knew something of what they had endured and it was obvious they were not strong. He promised to slacken the pace. He lied. They took off again, even faster. He suddenly raised a hand, stopped cold, and ducked low. As they peeked over a ridge they saw a road in the distance, and it was crammed with Japanese troop carriers on the move. They watched the convoy as they gasped for breath and said nothing. Moving again, they caught a break and descended into a narrow valley. At a creek, they stopped while Acevedo scanned the area for the enemy. Seeing none, they quickly waded across and disappeared into the jungle. The terrain changed and they began climbing again. When his calf muscles were burning and he was out of breath, Pete called for a break. They sat in a thicket and ate rice cakes and coconut cookies.

In a soft voice, Acevedo said that his brother had been a Filipino Scout and had died down on Bataan. His vow was to kill as many Japanese as possible before they killed him. So far, his body count was eleven known dead and there were probably others. The Japs tortured and beheaded every guerrilla they caught, so it was part of the code that you never surrendered. Far better to blow your own brains out than to allow the Japs to do it their way. Clay asked when they might get guns, and he said there would be plenty at the camp. Food and water too. The guerrillas were not well fed but nobody was starving.

The food energized them and they were off again. As the sun began to dip behind the mountains, they came to a narrow trail hugging the side of a steep hill. It was a treacherous walk over loose rocks. The wrong step could send them falling into a bottomless ravine. For about fifty yards they were exposed. Halfway into the clearing, as they ducked low and tried not to stumble, shots rang out from the other side of the ravine. Snipers, just waiting. Acevedo was hit in the head and fell backward. A bullet nicked Pete's right sleeve, barely missing his chest. He and Clay jumped into the ravine as bullets landed around them. They tumbled violently downward, bouncing off saplings and tearing through the bush. Clay managed to snatch a vine and stop his fall, but Pete continued down, head over heels. He crashed into a *dao* tree and almost lost consciousness.

Clay could barely see the back of Pete's shirt and managed to slide down on his rear. When they were together they took stock and counted no broken bones, yet. Their faces and arms were scratched and bleeding, but the cuts were not deep. Pete had taken a blow to the head and was groggy but after a moment was ready to move on. They heard voices, and not in English. The enemy looking for them. As quietly as possible, they continued down, but in doing so knocked stones loose and made a racket. At the bottom, near a creek, they ducked into a thicket of brush and stickers and waited. Something was splashing in the water. Three privates with rifles at the ready were wading their way. They walked within ten feet of Pete and Clay, who lay still and barely breathed. An hour passed, maybe two, and the ravine grew dark.

In whispers, they discussed the insane idea of climbing back up and looking for the rucksack and possibly

Acevedo. They were sure he was dead, but they needed his guns. They knew the Japanese would not simply give up and return to their camp. The trophy of two American heads was too tempting. So Pete and Clay didn't move. Alone, deserted, unarmed, hunted, with no idea where they were or where they might be headed, they spent the sleepless night covered with insects, bugs, lizards, sticker cuts, and prayed the pythons and cobras would stay away. At one point, Pete asked who had had the bright idea of becoming guerrilla fighters. Clay chuckled and swore that he had never had such a ridiculous thought.

At dawn, they had to move. Hunger returned with a vengeance. They drank from the creek and decided to follow it, to where they had no clue. Throughout the day they moved in shadows, never for a second leaving themselves exposed. Twice they heard voices and soon realized that they would have to move at night and rest during the day. Move to where, exactly?

The creek fed into a narrow river, and from the bush they watched a Japanese patrol boat drift by. Six men with rifles, two with binoculars, all scouring the shorelines in search of someone. Late in the afternoon, they stumbled upon a foot trail and decided to follow it after dark. They were not sure where to go but their current location was too dangerous.

The trail was impossible to follow in the blackness of the night. They soon lost it, walked in circles, found it again, then gave up when they lost it again. They bedded down under a formation of rocks and tried to sleep.

When they awoke in the early morning, a thick mist had settled through the jungle. It provided cover and they soon found another footpath that was barely noticeable. After they had climbed for two hours, the sun burned away the mist and the trail widened. They were exhausted and starving when they came to a cliff over a steep and rocky ravine. A hundred feet below was a creek filled with boulders. They rested in the shade, looked down at the creek, and discussed the possibility of simply jumping. Death would be better than the torture they were enduring. At that moment, death would be welcome. Their chances of survival were nonexistent anyway. If they jumped, they would at least die at their own hands.

Gunfire erupted not too far away and they forgot about suicide. Gunfire meant the two sides had found each other. There were guerrillas close by. The gunfight lasted only a minute or so but inspired them to keep walking. The trail turned down and they crept along it, always with their heads low, always looking for a break in the bush that would expose them. They found a creek with clear water and refreshed themselves. They rested for an hour and moved on.

When the sun was directly above them, they came to a clearing. In its center was a small fire that was still smoldering. Sitting against a large boulder was a Japanese soldier, apparently taking a nap. From the bush, they studied him for a long time and noticed blood on both legs. Evidently, he had been wounded and left behind by his unit. Occasionally, his right arm moved, proof that he was alive. Without a sound, Pete moved through the cover of the bush while Clay inched closer behind trees. Pete climbed the boulder, and when he was directly above the target, he lifted a ten-pound rock and lunged.

The rock landed squarely on top of the Jap's head. Clay was on him in an instant. Pete struck him again with the rock while Clay grabbed his rifle and gutted him with the bayonet. They dragged him into the bush and ripped open his backpack. Tins of sardines, salmon, and mackerel, along with a packet of dried beef. They ate quickly, their shirts and hands covered with his blood. They hid his body in a thicket and hustled away from the clearing.

For the first time in months, they were now armed. Clay carried the Arisaka rifle with the bayonet, along with his canteen. Pete wore his holster with a semiautomatic Nambu pistol. In the belt, he stuffed thirty cartridges, two magazines, and a six-inch knife. They ran for an hour before stopping to rest and devouring another tin of sardines. If captured now, they would be tortured and beheaded on the spot. Capture, though, would not happen. With bloody hands, they shook and made a pact that neither would be taken alive. If surrounded, they would shoot themselves with the pistol. Pete first, then Clay.

They pressed on, climbing again. They heard gunfire again, heavy at times, a more prolonged skirmish than before. They could not decide if they should move toward it, or away. So they waited, hiding beside the trail. The gunfire faded, then stopped. An hour passed and the sun began to fade in the west.

At a turn in the trail they came face-to-face with a young Filipino who was sprinting in their direction. He was slight, skinny, sweating from his run, and unarmed. He stopped cold and wasn't sure about the strangers.

Pete said, "Americans."

The teenager stepped closer and looked at their weapons. "Japanese," he said, nodding at the bayonet.

Clay smiled, pointed to the blood on his hands and arms, and said, "No, this is Japanese blood."

The boy smiled and said, "American soldiers?"

They nodded. Pete said, "We need to find the guerrillas. Can you take us to them?"

His smile widened and he proudly drawled, "Aw shit, where y'all from?"

Pete and Clay exploded with laughter. Clay bent double and dropped his new rifle. Pete laughed and shook his head in disbelief. He had the image of this Filipino kid sitting around a campfire with a bunch of Americans having too much fun teaching him their brand of colorful English. Without a doubt, there were some boys from Texas or Alabama in the gang.

When the laughter passed, the kid said, "Follow me. About an hour."

"Let's go," Pete said. "But not so fast."

The kid was called a runner, one of hundreds used for communication by the guerrillas, who had almost no radios. The runners often carried written messages and orders. They knew the trails intimately and were rarely caught, but if that happened they were tortured for information and killed.

They climbed again for a long time as the air continued to thin. The break in the heat was welcome, but Pete and Clay struggled to keep up. As they approached the first bivouac point, the kid whistled three times, waited, heard something that Pete and Clay did not, and continued. They were on guerrilla turf now, and as safe as any American soldier could be in the Philippines. Two heavily armed Filipinos appeared from nowhere and waved them through.

They passed through a tiny barrio where the people barely noticed them. The trail led to the first camp, where more Filipino guerrillas were cooking over a small fire. There were about twenty of them, living in lean-tos and preparing for the night. At the sight of the two Americans, they stood and saluted.

Half an hour later, still climbing, they walked into a small compound hidden under a dense jungle canopy. An American in faded fatigues and fresh combat boots greeted them. Captain Darrell Barney, formerly of the Eleventh Infantry Brigade but now of the unofficial West Luzon Resistance Force. After introductions were made, Barney yelled at a row of bamboo huts and other Americans came forth. There were a lot of smiles, handshakes, backslapping, congratulations, and soon enough Pete and Clay were seated at a split-bamboo table and served rice, potatoes, and grilled pork chops, a delicacy reserved for special occasions.

As they ate, they were peppered with questions from around the table. The biggest talker was Alan DuBose from Slidell, Louisiana, and he proudly admitted that he was indeed teaching the Filipinos all manner of American slang. In all, there were six Americans, in addition to Pete and Clay, and none of the others had been on Bataan. After the surrender, they had fled to the mountains from other parts of the islands. They were far healthier, though malaria was everywhere.

The Americans had heard about the death march and they wanted the stories, all of them. For hours, Pete and Clay talked and talked, and laughed and reveled in the safety of their surroundings. For two soldiers who had seen so much, it was at times difficult to fathom the fact that they were with American soldiers who were still fighting.

Pete savored the moment, but he could not stop the flashbacks to O'Donnell. He thought about the men he knew there, many of whom would not leave alive. They were still starving while he feasted. He thought about the Boneyard, and the hundreds of starved corpses he had buried. He thought about the hellship and heard the screams of the trapped men as they went under. One moment he enjoyed the food and banter and soothing American English with its variety of accents, and the next moment he sat muted, unable to eat as another nightmare flooded his memory.

The flashbacks, nightmares, and horrors would never go away.

Late in the evening, they were led to the showers and given bars of soap. The water was lukewarm and felt marvelous. At first they wanted to shave, but every other American had a heavy beard, so they passed on the opportunity. They were given underwear and clean socks and mismatched army fatigues, though in the bush there were no established uniforms. The doctor, also an American, examined them and noted the obvious problems. He had plenty of medicines and promised them that after a couple of weeks they would be ready to fight. They were shown to a bamboo hut, their new barracks, and given real cots with blankets. In the morning, they would meet their commander and be given more guns than they could carry.

Alone in the darkness, they whispered of home, which seemed closer than ever.

CHAPTER 31

The West Luzon Resistance Force was under the firm command of General Bernard Granger, a British hero from World War I. Granger was about sixty, lean and tough and military to the core. He had lived in the Philippines for the past twenty years and at one time owned a large coffee plantation that the Japanese confiscated, killing two of his sons in the process and forcing him to flee to the mountains with his wife and what was left of his family. They lived in a bunker deeper in the jungle, and from there he commanded his force. His men adored him and referred to him as Lord Granger.

He was at his desk under a canopy of camouflaged netting when Pete and Clay were ushered in and introduced. He sent his aides away, though his bodyguards stayed close. He welcomed the Americans in his high-pitched, very proper British cadence and ordered a round of tea. Pete and Clay sat in bamboo chairs and admired him from the first moment. At times his left eye was partially hidden by a crease in his smart safari hat. When he spoke he removed the stem of a corncob pipe, and when he listened he stuck it between his teeth and chewed it as if digesting every word. "I hear you survived the nastiness down on Bataan," he said in his singsong voice. "Probably worse than we've heard."

They nodded and described it for a few moments. Bataan was brutal, but O'Donnell was worse.

"And the Nips are shipping off boys to the coal mines back home, I hear," Granger said as he poured tea in porcelain cups.

Pete described the hellship and their rescue at sea.

"We'll get the bloody bastards eventually," Granger said. "If they don't get us first. I hope you realize that your odds of survival have improved, but in the end we're all dead men."

"Better to go down fighting," Clay said.

"That's the spirit. Our job is to create enough mischief to hamstring the Nips and prove that these islands are worth saving. We fear that the Allies might try to beat them without bothering with us. The high command thinks it can bypass these islands and hit Japan, and it's entirely possible, you know? But MacArthur promised to return and that's what keeps us going. Our Filipino boys must have something to fight for. It's their property to begin with. Milk and sugar?"

Pete and Clay declined. They would have preferred strong coffee, but they were still thankful for the large breakfast. Granger chatted on, then abruptly stopped and looked at Pete. "So what's the skinny on you?"

Pete went through a short bio. West Point, seven years active in the Twenty-Sixth Cavalry, then sort of a forced retirement for personal reasons. Had to save the family farm. Wife and two kids back in Mississippi. Rank of first lieutenant.

Granger's eyes danced and never blinked as he caught and analyzed every word. "So you can ride a horse?"

"With or without a saddle," Pete said.

"I've heard of the Twenty-Sixth. Expert marksman, I take it."

"Yes, sir."

"We need snipers. Never enough snipers."

"Give me a rifle."

"You were at Fort Stotsenburg?"

"Yes, but only briefly before December."

"Bloody Nips are using the base there for their Zeros and dive-bombers. Heavier stuff they moved out after Corregidor. I'd like to hit some planes on the ground but we haven't put together a plan yet. And you?" he asked, looking at Clay.

Enlisted in 1940, Thirty-First Infantry. Mortar specialist. Rank of sergeant. A cowboy from Colorado who could also ride and shoot.

"Jolly good. I like men who want to fight. Sad to say but we have some Americans here who are simply hiding with us and want to go home. Some are mad. Some are too sick. Some went AWOL from their units and wandered through the jungles, I suspect. They're deadweight, to be honest, but we can't exactly run them off. The first lesson you'll learn is to not ask questions of the others. Everyone has a story, and the cowards never tell the truth."

He sipped his tea and pulled out a map. "A bit about our operations. We're here in the middle of the Zambales

Mountains, really rugged terrain, as I'm sure you've learned. Elevation of nine thousand feet in places. We have about a thousand fighters scattered over a hundred square miles. If we dug in and hid we could last for a long time, but digging in is not in our cards. We are guerrillas and we fight dirty, never in frontal assaults, never in the open. We strike quick and disappear. The Nips raid our camps at the lower elevations and it's very dangerous down there. You'll find out soon enough. We're gaining in numbers as more Filipinos run for the hills, and after a rough start we're finally landing some punches."

"So you don't worry about the Japs coming here?" Pete asked.

"We worry about everything. We pack light, always ready to pull back at the slightest danger. We can't fight them one on one. We have almost no artillery, save for a few mortars and light cannons, goodies we stole from the enemy. We have plenty of rifles, pistols, and machine guns, but no trucks or carriers. We're foot soldiers, with the advantage of the terrain. Our biggest problem is communication. We have a few old radios, nothing portable, and can't use them because the Nips are always listening. So we rely on runners to coordinate things. We have no contact with MacArthur, though he knows we're here and fighting. To answer your question, we are relatively safe here, but always in danger. The Nips would bomb us from the air if they could see us. Come along and I'll show you our goodies."

Granger sprang to his feet, grabbed his walking stick, and took off. He rattled something in Tagalog to his guards and they sprinted in front of him. Others followed as they left the camp and started up a narrow trail. As they walked Granger said, "The Twenty-Sixth, quite an outfit. Don't suppose you know Edwin Ramsey?"

"He was my commander," Pete said proudly.

"You don't say. Bloody good soldier. He refused to surrender and headed for the hills. He's about a hundred miles from here and organizing like mad. Rumor is that he has over five thousand men in Central Luzon and plenty of contacts in Manila."

They turned a corner and two sentries pulled back a wall of vines and roots. They entered a cave. "Get the torches," Granger barked and two guards lit the way. The cave became a cavern, an open room with stalactites dripping water from above. Candles were lit along the walls and the scope of the armory came into focus.

Granger never stopped talking. "Supplies left behind by the Yanks and taken from the Nips. I'd like to think we have a bullet for every one of the bloody bastards."

There were pallets of ammunition. Crates of rifles. Stockpiles of canned food and water. Thick bags of rice. Barrels of gasoline. Stacks of boxes holding supplies that were not identified.

Granger said, "Down the hall in another room we have two tons of dynamite and TNT. Don't suppose you have any experience with explosives."

"No," Pete said. Clay shook his head.

"Too bad. We are in dire need of a good bomb boy. Last one blew himself up. A Filipino, and a damned fine one. But one will come along. Seen enough?"

Before they answered, he whirled around. The tour was over. Pete and Clay were shocked at the stash of supplies, but also greatly comforted by it. They followed Granger out of the cave and began their descent. They stopped at an overlook and took in a stunning vista of waves of mountains that went on forever.

The general said, "The Nips won't get this far, really. They're afraid to. And they know that we are forced to come down for the fight. So we do. Questions?"

Clay asked, "When do we fight?"

Granger laughed and said, "I like that. Sick and malnourished but ready for battle. A week or so. Give the doctors some time to fatten you up and you'll soon see all the blood you want."

For the next two days, Pete and Clay lay about in luxury, napping and eating and drinking all the water they could hold. The doctors plied them with pills and vitamins. When they were finally bored, they were outfitted with rifles and pistols and taken to a firing range for a round of practice. A Filipino veteran named Camacho was assigned to them, and he taught them the ways of the jungle: how to build a small fire to cook, always at night because the smoke could not be seen; how to build a lean-to out of vines and shrub to sleep under in the rain; how to pack a rucksack with only the essentials; how to keep their guns and ammo dry; how to handle an angry cobra, and a hungry python as well; how to do a hundred essentials that might one day save their lives.

On the third day, Pete was summoned to Lord Granger's post for tea and cards. They sat at a game board and chatted, with the general doing the bulk of the talking. "Ever play cribbage?" he asked as he pulled out a deck of cards.

"Sure. I played it at Fort Riley."

"Bloody good. I have a round each afternoon at three with tea. Relaxes the soul." He shuffled as he talked and dealt the cards. "Two nights ago the Nips raided an advance post a good ways down the mountain, one that was well defended. They surprised us with a large unit. There was a nasty fight; we lost. They were looking for Bobby Lippman, a tough major from Brooklyn, and they found him, along with two other Americans. The Filipinos in the unit were either killed in battle or beheaded on the spot. That's a favorite of the Nips, whack off the heads and leave them lying near the bodies to frighten the neighbors. Anyway, Lippman and the other Americans were taken to a prison in Manila to have a chat with some of the Nips' toughest interrogators. I'm told that some of these officers speak the King's English better than most Brits. Lippman's in for a nasty time. They'll whip him and burn him for a few days, they have a variety of methods, and if he talks we could feel it here. If he doesn't, and I doubt he will, then they'll have a little ceremony for him that involves one of those long swords you've seen. It's a war, Banning, and as you've seen there are many ways to kill."

"I thought there were bivouacs and rings of sentries at each post," Pete said. "How did they pull a surprise?"

"We'll never know. Their favorite trick is to bribe a local, some Filipino who needs money or rice and is willing to sell information. As the Nips close the noose, we're starting to see less food. In some villages the peasants are skipping meals. The Nips know how to bribe. We have many posts in these mountains. Sometimes we stay in them, sometimes we don't, but they're our safe houses. If we're in for the night, or perhaps a week, the locals usually find out. It's rather easy to find a Nip and sell the intel. Are you ready for combat?"

"Damned right I am."

"The doctor says you're in reasonably good shape. Hell, we're all underweight and sick with something, but you and Clay look especially gaunt. Suppose you've seen the worst of it."

"We're fine and we're bored. Give us an assignment."

"The two of you will go with DuBose, a squad of about ten. Camacho will always be with you, and he's the best. You'll leave in the middle of the night, hike three or four hours, have a look. It's part recon, part assault. If Lippman is talking under duress we should know it by what the Nips do and where they go. After a couple of days on the trails, you'll hook up with another unit, some of our boys from another mountain. They've borrowed a bomb maker who'll string some wires and such. The target is a convoy. Should be an easy job and you'll get to shoot some Nips. Jolly good fun."

"I can't wait."

"Assuming all goes well, the bomb maker is willing to spend some time with you boys and teach you how to play with TNT. Listen and learn."

As Pete shuffled and dealt, Granger reloaded his pipe with tobacco, and managed to do so without missing a word. "Poor Lippman. All of us vow that we'll not be taken alive. It's a far better thing to put a bullet in one's head than let the Nips have their way. But it's not always that easy. Men are often wounded first and unable to shoot themselves. Sometimes they're asleep and surprised. And often, Banning, I think that we become so adept at survival that we believe we can survive anything, so we drop our guns, raise our hands, and are led away. Usually, I suppose, within hours there is an awful feeling of regret. You ever come close to ending it all?"

"Many times," Pete said. "The thirst and hunger drove us all crazy, along with the constant killing. I thought that if I could only go to sleep, then I would pass on the bit about waking up. But we survived. We're surviving now. I plan to get home, General."

"Attaboy. But don't let the Nips take you alive, hear me?"

"Don't worry."

CHAPTER 32

They left camp shortly after midnight, ten guerrillas in all, following two runners who could find the trails in their sleep. Six Filipinos and four Americans, all heavily armed and loaded with backpacks full of tinned food, canned water, blankets, tarps, and all the ammo they could carry. Mercifully, all movements were downward. The first lesson Pete and Clay learned was to concentrate on the boots of the man in front of them. Looking around was fruitless because there was nothing to see in the blackness. A missed step could cause a stumble and a fall and an uncertain landing.

For the first hour nothing was said. As they approached the first barrio, a lookout greeted them. In an unknown dialect, he informed Camacho that all was well. They had not seen the enemy in days. The squad circled around the huts and kept moving. There was no lookout at the second barrio and not a sound from the settlement. After three hours the ground leveled and they stopped at an advance post, four shelters built into the bush and empty. They rested for half an hour and snacked on sardines and water. DuBose drifted over and asked quietly, "Y'all doin' all right?"

Pete and Clay assured him that they were having fun, though they were already fatigued. The others looked like they were just warming up. Off again, they began to climb, and after an hour stopped again to rest. DuBose knew what his two rookies had been through and wanted to protect them. The squad descended into a ravine, waded across a creek, and came upon a large barrio. From the bush, they watched the area for a few minutes; then Camacho ventured forth and found the lookout. Again, there had been no sign of the enemy. As they waited, DuBose eased beside Pete and drawled, "Folks here are pretty safe. Each little village is run by a boss, and the one here is a solid guy. From here, though, it's no-man's-land."

"Where's the road?" Pete asked.

"Not far."

At daybreak, they were hiding in a ditch beside a dirt highway that was obviously well used. They heard movements on the other side, then silence. Someone said, "DuBose."

He answered, "Over here."

Heads suddenly popped out of the brush, and an American named Carlyle stepped forward. He commanded a dozen men, including three Yanks with mangy beards and the same weatherbeaten look. They hurried to retrieve wooden boxes filled with more TNT, and for an hour they laid the explosives and ran wires to the detonators. The bomb maker was a Filipino veteran who had obviously laid many traps. When the TNT was in place, the men retreated to the bush, with DuBose assigning positions. Pete, the sniper, hid behind some rocks and was instructed to shoot anything that moved. Clay was given a light machine gun and positioned fifty yards away.

Camacho stayed close to Pete and whispered as the sun rose. The Japanese were moving tons of supplies inland on many routes, and their mission was to harass and disrupt the lines. Spies at the port had sent word that a convoy of four or five trucks was on the way. They had no idea of the cargo, but blowing it up would be a thrill. You'll see.

As he waited, Pete's trigger finger itched as his stomach flipped in anticipation. It had been months since he'd been in combat and the waiting was nerve-racking. When he heard the rumble of trucks, Camacho said get ready.

Four of them. The lead and rear trucks were filled with troops to protect the cargo in the middle two. The guerrillas waited and waited and for a long moment Pete thought the explosives would not work. But when they did, the ground shook with such a fury that Pete was thrown against the rocks. The lead truck flipped like a toy, slinging soldiers into the air. The third and fourth trucks were blown onto their sides. Gunfire exploded from the bush as two dozen hidden guerrillas unloaded a brutal barrage. The Japs who had survived the explosions crawled and staggered and most were shot before they could fire a shot. The driver of the second truck crawled through the shattered front window, and Pete picked him off. Clay was in a nest to the rear of the convoy with a direct line of fire into the troop carrier. Using a Japanese Type 99 lightweight machine gun, he mowed down one Jap after another as they tried to crawl out and find their weapons. Several of them took cover behind the trucks but were shot in the back by guerrillas on the other side of the road. There was no place to hide. The gunfire was withering and went on for a good five minutes. One Jap managed to hide between trucks two and three and spray a few rounds into the trees before being hit high and low.

Slowly, the shooting came to a halt. During a lull, they watched and waited, hoping a Jap on the ground would move for a weapon. All was still as the dust began to settle. DuBose and Carlyle crept forward and waved their men back onto the road. Every Jap, dying or already dead, got an extra bullet to the head. Prisoners were nothing but baggage. There was no place to hold them and no extra food to feed them. In this version of the war, neither side took prisoners, unless American officers were captured. Their deaths were delayed.

DuBose and Carlyle barked orders with a sense of urgency. Two Filipinos were sent back down the road to watch for more trucks. Two were sent ahead. The dead bodies—thirty-seven of them—were stripped of weapons and backpacks. Luckily, the second supply truck had not been disabled. It had been packed with boxes of rifles, grenades, machine guns, and, unbelievably, hundreds of pounds of TNT. In every ambush there is a miracle, and the fact that a stray bullet had not hit the explosives was a gift. The first supply truck was on its side and a total wreck. It was filled with boxes of rations. DuBose made the decision to pack as much food as possible in with the armaments and use the second truck for their getaway.

Stepping over dead bodies, and kicking them out of the way, the guerrillas managed to roll the first truck into a ditch. With a Filipino behind the wheel, the second truck limped away. Pete and five others sat on top of it, their butts just inches above tons of explosives. As they turned a corner, the men looked back with great satisfaction at the mayhem they had caused. Three smoldering trucks, piles of dead bodies, and not a single wounded soldier on their side.

Japanese Zeros routinely watched the roads at an altitude that seemed just inches above the trees, and it was only a matter of time before they arrived. DuBose wanted to get off the road before they were spotted and a Zero hit the truck and blew them all to bits. The pilots would see the carnage, know immediately what had happened, and attack with a vengeance.

Their driver turned in to a clearing and gunned the engine. The truck was exposed until it found a parking spot under a canopy of thick trees. It stopped and Du-Bose ordered the men to quickly cover it with vines and brush. When it couldn't be seen from twenty feet away on the ground, the men retreated to the shade and tore into the Japanese backpacks. They feasted on tins of fish and loaves of hard rice bread. One Jap, obviously a guy with a drinking problem, had been carrying four cans of sake, and the break became an impromptu cocktail hour.

While their troops had a drink, DuBose and Carlyle huddled by the truck. Their discussion was interrupted by the unmistakable high-pitched whining of approaching Zeros. Two of them swooped low over the highway, then pulled up fierce vertical ascents. They circled back for another look and disappeared.

There was talk of returning to the road and to the wreckage. The spot had proven perfect for the ambush, and the Japs would undoubtedly send a large search party. The killing had been so easy, the body count so impressive, it was tempting to go back for more. But DuBose thought better of it. Their job was to hit and run, not to plan offensives. Besides, at that moment the contraband was far more important than a few more dead Japs.

The truck could not handle the mountain trails, and DuBose made the decision to unload it and devise a scheme to transfer the goodies back to their base. Since his men certainly couldn't carry it all, he sent a dozen Filipinos into the nearest barrios to barter for oxen and pack mules. They offered plenty of food for the "rentals" of the animals.

The party ended abruptly when DuBose ordered the remaining men to begin the arduous task of unloading. After noon, a few oxen and mules began to appear, not nearly enough, but a good number of local men had agreed to swap their labor for food. The first elements of the convoy had just disappeared into the bush when a runner sprinted from a trail with the news that a large unit of Japanese soldiers was just around the corner. Without hesitation, DuBose ordered the bomb maker to rig the truck and the explosives still on board. He and Carlyle agreed that the wreckage would block the road, giving them some extra time. The guerrillas uncovered the truck so the Japs could find it, then retreated into the bush and waited.

The advance team arrived on motorcycles, saw the

truck, and got excited. Before long, three troop carriers stopped and dozens of soldiers spilled out, all crouching low in anticipation of another ambush. There was none, and they advanced slowly upon the truck. When they realized the enemy was gone, they relaxed and milled around the truck, all yakking with great concern. When their officer strutted forward and stepped into the truck for a quick look, the bomb maker pulled a wire from a hundred feet away. The explosion was magnificent and sent dozens of bodies flying.

DuBose and his men admired it with a quick laugh, then scurried back to their trails. Each man was now laden with as much gear and stolen armaments as possible, and they were climbing again. Pete and Clay were fatigued to the point of collapse, but they trudged on. They had marched under much worse conditions, and they knew their weak bodies could endure the hardship.

Well after dark, they arrived at their first advance post, and everyone collapsed. Runners had reported to Lord Granger and he sent more men to help with the haul. DuBose called it a day and ordered them to set up camp. More runners arrived with the welcome news that they were not being followed.

The men ate until they were full, and even managed another shot of sake. Pete and Clay found a spot on the dirt floor of a hut and relived the glory of the day. Their whispers soon faded, and they fell fast asleep.

For two days, the convoy climbed over the mountains, stopping often to rest and eat. Twice, they were diverted when runners warned them that the enemy was near, searching in full force. Zeros patrolled the skies like angry wasps, itching to strafe something, but seeing nothing. The men took cover in ravines and caves.

When they finally arrived home, Lord Granger was waiting on them with a smile and hug for every man. Splendid work, boys, splendid work. Other than blistered feet and aching muscles, not a single man had been wounded.

They rested for days, until they were bored again.

The rainy season arrived in a fury when a typhoon swept through the northern Philippines. Torrents of rain pounded the mountains and the winds ripped the roofs off the bamboo huts. At its peak, the men retreated to the caves and hunkered down for two days. The trails turned to mud and many were impassable.

But the war raged on and the Japanese had no choice but to continue moving men and supplies. Their convoys were often mired in knee-deep mud and stalled for long periods. They became easy targets for the guerrillas, who moved on foot, though not as quickly. Granger kept his squads busy, hitting targets with brutal strikes, then disappearing into the bush. Japanese reprisals were vicious and the civilians paid the price.

Pete was given his own squad, G Troop, twenty men that included Clay and Camacho, and he was promoted to the rank of major in the West Luzon Resistance Force. Such a position would not be officially recognized by the real army, but then the real army had retreated with MacArthur to Australia. Lord Granger ruled his own force and promoted as he saw fit.

After a successful raid on a convoy, Major Banning

and his men were withdrawing when they approached a barrio. They smelled smoke from the trail and soon came upon a horrible scene. The Japanese had raided and destroyed the village. Every hut was on fire and children were running everywhere, screaming. In the center there were about fifteen dead men, all with their hands tied behind their backs. Their bodies were bloodied and mutilated; their detached heads were a few feet away, lined in a neat row. Several women had been shot and they lay where they fell.

A teenage boy bolted from the bush and ran toward them, crying and screaming. Camacho grabbed him and spoke to him in a dialect. As the boy wailed he shook his fists angrily at the guerrillas.

Camacho said, "He blames us, says we brought the Japanese here." Camacho kept talking to the boy, who was inconsolable.

"He says the Japanese came here a few hours ago and accused the people of helping the Americans. They demanded to know where the Americans were hiding, and since we didn't know and couldn't tell them, they did this. Both his mother and his father were murdered. They took his sister and some of the young women away. They'll rape them and then kill them too."

Pete and his men were speechless. They listened to the exchange and gawked at the carnage.

Camacho went on, "He says his brother went to find the Japanese and tell them that you're here. It's all your fault, all your fault. The Americans are to blame."

Pete said, "Tell him we're fighting the Japanese, we hate them too. We're on the side of the Filipinos."

Camacho jabbered on but the boy was out of his

mind. He was bawling and kept shaking his fist at Pete. He finally tore away and ran to the dead men. He pointed at one and screamed at the corpse.

Camacho said, "That's his father. They were forced to watch as the Japs cut off their heads, one at a time while threatening to kill all of them if they didn't give up the information."

The boy ran to the bush and disappeared. Children were clinging to the bodies of their mothers. The huts were still burning. The guerrillas wanted to help in some way, but the situation was too dangerous. Pete said, "Let's get out of here." They hurried away, sloshing through the mud. They marched until dark as heavy rain began, then set up camp under leaking lean-tos and tarps. The rain was unrelenting and they slept little.

Pete had nightmares about the ghoulish scene.

Back at the base, he reported to Lord Granger and described the raid on the barrio. Granger refused to show emotion, but he knew Major Banning was rattled. He ordered him to rest for a few days.

Around the fire that night, Pete and Clay told the story to the other Americans. They had their own stories and they had grown callous to such tales. The enemy had a limitless capacity for savagery, and it made the guerrillas vow to fight even harder.

CHAPTER 33

In Pete's absence the cotton grew anyway, and by mid-September the picking began. The weather cooperated, the prices held firm on the Memphis exchange, the field hands worked from dawn to dusk, and Buford managed to keep enough itinerant labor in place. The harvest brought a level of normalcy to the land and to a people living under the dark clouds of war. Everyone knew a soldier who was either waiting to be shipped off or already fighting. Pete Banning was the first casualty from Ford County, but then other boys were killed or wounded or missing.

Four months into widowhood, Liza managed to establish some semblance of a routine. Once the kids were off to school, she had coffee with Nineva, who slowly became her sounding board and her strength. Liza puttered in the garden with Amos and Jupe, met each morning with Buford to discuss the crops, and tried to stay away from town. She quickly grew tired of the endless inquiries about how she was doing, how she was holding up, how the kids were handling it all. If spotted in town, she was forced to endure hugs and tears from people she hardly knew. For the sake of her children, she forced the family to go to church, but the three of them grew to dislike the Sunday ritual. They began skipping occasionally to avoid the constant condolences, and instead walked to Florry's cottage for brunches on the patio. No one condemned them for their "chapel cuts."

Most weekday mornings, Dexter Bell drove out to visit Liza. They had coffee, a devotional, and prayer. They sat in Pete's study with the door closed and talked in soft voices. Nineva, as always, hovered nearby.

Pete had been gone for almost a year, and Liza knew he was not coming home. If he were alive he would find a way to send a letter or a message, and as the days and weeks passed without a word she accepted the unspeakable reality. She admitted this to no one, but gamely went about her dark days as if she held out hope. It was important for Joel and Stella, and for Nineva and Amos and everyone else, but in private she wept and sat for hours in her dark bedroom.

Joel was sixteen, a senior in high school, and was talking of enlisting. He would soon turn seventeen, and upon graduation could join the army if his mother agreed. She said she would not and such talk upset her. She had lost her husband and was not about to lose her son. Stella fought with Joel to quell such nonsense, and he reluctantly stopped talking about fighting. His future was in college.

• • •

In early October, the rains stopped and the skies cleared. The soggy terrain bred a fresh wave of mosquitoes, and malaria hit the guerrillas hard. Virtually every man had it to some degree, many for the third or fourth time, and living with it became normal. They carried bottles of quinine and cared for their sicker comrades.

With the roads passable, the Japanese convoys became more frequent, but the guerrillas were often too weak to strike. Pete had gained a few pounds, though he guessed he was still fifty pounds below his fighting weight, when fevers and chills knocked him down for a week. During a lull, when he was wrapped in a blanket and semilucid, he realized it was October 4, one year to the day after he left home. Without a doubt, it had been the most memorable year of his life.

He was sleeping when a runner woke him with orders to report to Lord Granger. He and Clay staggered from their hut and reported to the general's post. Intelligence had reported a large convoy of oil tankers leaving a port and headed inland. Within an hour, G Troop was moving down the mountain in the darkness. It bivouacked with DuBose's D Troop, and forty guerrillas were on the move, most of them weakened with malaria but excited to have a mission. The rains and mosquitoes had not stopped the war.

Engineers from the imperial army had carved a new supply road, one that Granger had heard rumors of. DuBose found it first, and he and Pete hiked it with their men in search of an ambush point. Finding none, they began to backtrack when four Zeros suddenly appeared at treetop level. Majors Banning and DuBose ordered their men to retreat to a hillside and bury themselves in the bush to wait. A recon unit soon appeared, two platoons of Japanese soldiers on foot. They carried machetes and hacked their way through the bush beside the road, looking for guerrillas. It was a new tactic, one that clearly showed the importance of the convoy. Trucks could soon be heard, and lots of them. The first three were open carriers packed with soldiers at the ready. Behind them were six tankers loaded to the brim with gasoline and diesel fuel. Their rear was protected by three more carriers.

The plan was to attack with hand grenades and ignite a massive fireball, but the guerrillas were not close enough. The target was tempting, but Major Banning wisely backed off. He signaled DuBose a hundred yards away. DuBose agreed and the guerrillas withdrew even deeper. The convoy inched along and was soon out of sight.

The hike back to base was dispiriting.

The clear skies brought not only waves of mosquitoes but waves of Zeros and scout planes as well. Granger feared the Japanese knew his location and were closing in, though he still maintained that a ground assault was unlikely. The enemy had shown little interest in a prolonged fight up the mountain into forbidding territory. What worried Granger, though, was a threat from the air. A few well-aimed bombs could do immeasurable damage. He met daily with his commanders and discussed moving the base, but they were not in favor of it. They were heavily camouflaged. Their supplies and armaments were untouchable in the caves. Moving the base would create too much activity that might be noticed from the air. They were at home and felt as though they could defend anything.

An informant had passed along the news that the Japanese were offering a bounty of $50,000 on the head of Lord Granger, but, typically, he took it as an honor. Rewards of up to $5,000 were offered for the capture of any American officer involved with the resistance.

One afternoon, over a game of cribbage and a cup of tea, Granger handed Pete a small green metal box about the size of a brick but much lighter. At one end there was a dial and a switch. Granger explained, "Called a Lewes bomb, a new toy from a bomb maker in Manila. Inside is a pound of plastic explosive, a quarter pound of thermite, a bit of diesel fuel, and a detonator. The back side is magnetized. Stick it to the side of an airplane near the fuel tank, turn the dial, flip the switch, run like hell, and a few minutes later enjoy the fireworks."

Pete admired it and set it on the table. "Brilliant."

"Cooked by a British commando named Jock Lewes in North Africa. Our boys there wiped out entire fleets of Italian and German planes. Bloody good idea if you ask me."

"And so?"

"And so the Nips have a hundred Zeros at Fort Stotsenburg, the bloody buggers that are tormenting us. I'm thinking about a raid. You know the place well, I take it."

"Very well. It was the home of the Twenty-Sixth Cavalry. I spent time there before the hostilities."

"Can it be done, Major? Nips would never see it coming. Dangerous as hell, though."

"Is this an order?"

"Not yet. Think about it. You and DuBose, forty men. Forty more from a base operating above Stotsenburg. The Lewes bombs can be delivered from Manila to a post near the fort. From here it's a three-day hike, grueling. I'm thinking that you go prepared for the raid, and have a look. Security is tight, Nips on the ground everywhere. If it's impossible, back away and don't get hurt."

"I like it," Pete said, still admiring the Lewes bomb.

"We've got maps, the layout and all. Plenty of intelligence on the ground. You'll be in command, it's all yours. And you probably won't come back."

"When do we leave?"

"Are you strong enough, what with the shivers and all?"

"We've all got the fevers, but I'm recovering."

"Are you sure? It's not an order and you can say no. As you know, I don't order suicide missions."

"We'll be back, I promise. Plus, I'm bored."

"Jolly good, Major. Jolly good."

They left at dark, with DuBose and D Troop half an hour behind. They hiked for ten hours and stopped at dawn above a village. They rested throughout the day and noticed several Japanese patrols moving through the area. At dark, they moved on. The mountains turned to hills and vegetation thinned. At dawn of the third day, they topped a rise and Fort Stotsenburg was before them, about a mile away in the center of a sweeping plain.

From his position, Pete took in the vastness of his old fort. Before the war, it had housed not only the Twenty-Sixth Cavalry Regiment but also four artillery regiments, two American and two Filipino, along with the Twelfth

Quartermaster Regiment. The rows of barracks housed eight thousand soldiers. The stately gateposts at the front entrance were visible. Between two long runways were dozens of buildings once used by good guys and now bustling with the enemy. Behind them were the wide parade grounds where Pete had played polo, but the moment did not allow nostalgia. Parked in neat rows along the runways were more Zeros than he could count, along with twenty or so two-seated fighters the Allies called Nicks. There was no wall around the fort, no fencing or barbed-wire barriers. Just thousands of Japs going about their business. Troops drilled on the parade grounds while Zeros took off and landed.

The runners led them to an advance post where they met a squad led by Captain Miller, a baby-faced enlisted man from Minnesota. His squad had ten men, all Filipinos, and they knew the area well. Miller was waiting on another squad that was supposed to have arrived the day before. At the post, the men huddled over maps, and waited. At midnight, when the fort was quiet, Pete, DuBose, and Miller crept closer to it and spent the rest of the night circling the area. They returned at dawn, exhausted but with a plan.

The shipment of Lewes bombs did not arrive as scheduled, and they waited two days for word from Manila. They also waited on the other guerrillas Granger had promised, but they did not materialize. Pete worried that they had been captured and the entire mission had been compromised. In all, he had fifty-five men available for some mischief. By the third day at the post food was running low and the men were becoming irritable. Major Banning scolded them and maintained discipline.

The Lewes bombs finally arrived on the backs of three mules led by teenage boys, skinny kids who would hardly raise suspicions. Again, Pete marveled at Granger's network.

The fort was outside Angeles City, a sprawling town of 100,000, with plenty of bars and brothels to keep the Japanese officers entertained. The raid began at one in the morning with a carjacking when two drunken captains staggered out of a nightclub and headed to their sedan for the ride back to the fort. Three Filipino guerrillas posing as local peasants slit their throats in an alley, stripped off their uniforms, and changed clothes. They fired three shots as a signal, then ten minutes later drove the car past the sentries at the front gate of Fort Stotsenburg. Once inside, they parked the car in front of the commander's residence and disappeared into the darkness. Three Lewes bombs were stuck to the car's undercarriage, and the explosion disrupted the peaceful night. Guerrillas hiding behind the gymnasium began firing into the air, and the guards panicked.

The airplanes were watched closely at night by sentries. At the sound of the explosion and wild gunfire, they broke ranks and began running in the direction of the commotion. Major Banning swept in from the north, DuBose from the east, Miller from the west. They gunned down every sentry in sight, then quickly began sticking the Lewes bombs to the underside of eighty of the hated Zeros. In the darkness, the precious little bombs were not visible.

As they backed away, Don Bowmore, a brawler from Philly, caught a bullet in the head. He was near Pete, who quickly dropped the sentry and grabbed his pal. Camacho helped him drag Bowmore a hundred yards to cover, but he had died instantly. When it was apparent he was dead, and couldn't talk, Pete decided to leave his body. The code of the jungle did not allow the dead to be retrieved. Guerrillas relied too much on speed. Pete took Bowmore's rifle and handed it to Camacho. From his holster he grabbed his Colt .45, one he would use for the rest of the war and carry with him back to Mississippi.

Within minutes, the guerrillas retreated into the darkness as lights and sirens came on and hundreds of spooked Japanese soldiers scurried about in a frenzy. Most gathered in the vicinity of the burning car and waited for orders. The dazed officers barked conflicting commands and pointed here and there. The shooting had stopped. The sentries finally convinced the officers that the planes were targeted, with something. Patrols were organized to search the planes, but the fireworks began.

Five minutes after setting the Lewes bombs, Pete ordered his men to halt. They turned and watched. The explosions were not loud, but quite colorful, and remarkably efficient. In quick succession, the Zeros began popping as the little bombs erupted and ignited the fuel tanks. Each Zero was consumed in its own fireball, and they burned in the neat rows where they sat. In the glorious glow of the fires, the soldiers could be seen backing away, stunned.

Pete savored their handiwork for only a moment, then ordered his men to withdraw, and rapidly. The Japanese would immediately send out search squads, and there was no time to waste gawking. They would not be safe until they were in the bush.

Casualties were astonishingly light, but crucial. Three

guerrillas had slight wounds that did not impede their getaway. In addition to Bowmore, a Filipino had been killed by a sentry, and two had been shot, could not escape, and were captured. They were quickly rounded up and taken to the jail, where the torture began.

At the advance post, a head count revealed fifty-one survivors. They were giddy with their success and still pumped with adrenaline, but when Pete learned of the two wounded left behind he knew it meant trouble. They would be tortured without mercy. It was never safe to assume a man wouldn't talk under duress. Some were able to withstand incredible pain and never break. Others suffered for as long as they could, then gave up information. Sometimes the information was false, sometimes accurate.

Regardless, the men were dead.

Pete ordered his men to pack as lightly as possible and hit the trail. He said good-bye to Miller and his men, and led D and G Troops into the darkness.

The first Filipino prisoner was bleeding heavily from a chest wound. The Japanese assessed it and assumed he was dying. They tied him to a table, cut off his clothing, and attached wires to his genitals. When the first current hit, he screamed and begged. Next door, the second Filipino, also strapped to a table, heard his comrade beg for mercy.

The first one gave no information. When he was unconscious, he was taken outside and decapitated with a sword. His head was retrieved and taken inside, where an officer placed it on the chest of the second one. The officer explained the obvious—don't talk and you'll soon take your secrets to your grave. Wires were tightened around his testicles and penis, and after half an hour he began talking. The severed head was removed from his chest and placed in a corner. The wires were removed from his genitals and the prisoner was allowed to sit and drink water. A doctor looked at his shattered fibula and left without treating it. The prisoner gave the name of General Bernard Granger and a bogus location of his base in the mountains. He gave the names of all of the American officers he knew, and revealed that Major Pete Banning had led the raid. He had no idea who made the small bombs but they came from someone in Manila. To his knowledge, no further raids were being planned.

The doctor was back. He cleaned the wound, wrapped it in a bandage, and gave the prisoner some pills for pain. They helped little. The interrogation lasted through the night. When the prisoner could not answer all the questions, he simply created fiction. The more he talked the friendlier the Japanese became. At dawn, he was given hot coffee and a bread roll and informed that he would be given special treatment because of his cooperation. When he finished eating, he was dragged to a corner of the parade ground where his buddy's nude and headless body hung by the feet from a gallows. Not far away, the burned skeletons of seventy-four Zeros continued to smolder.

The prisoner was strung up by his hands and lashed with a bullwhip as a crowd of soldiers laughed and enjoyed the mauling. When he was unconscious, he was left to bake in the sun as the cleanup began.

CHAPTER 34

When news of the Stotsenburg raid reached Australia, General MacArthur was ecstatic. He immediately cabled President Roosevelt and, characteristically, took full credit for an operation he knew nothing about until a week after it was over. He wrote that "my commandos" executed "my detailed plan" with incredible brazenness and bravery and suffered only minor losses. His guerrilla forces were striking the Japanese in similar raids throughout Luzon, and he was orchestrating all manner of havoc behind enemy lines.

The raid embarrassed and infuriated the Japanese, and by the time the men of D and G Troops staggered home, exhausted and starving, four days after the attack, the skies were buzzing with fresh Zeros. The Japanese had an endless supply, and they intensified their efforts to find Granger. They did not, but their constant strafing at anything that moved in the mountains caused the guerrillas to thicken their camouflage and hunker down even deeper into the jungle. It also hampered their movements.

The Japanese stepped up their patrols around the barrios at the lower elevations and brutalized the locals. Food became scarcer and resentment toward the Americans increased. Never one to sit idly by, Granger began sending squads to ambush Japanese patrols. The highways and convoys were heavily protected and too dangerous to hit. Instead, his men stalked the trails and lay in wait. The attacks were quick and led to fierce gunfights that annihilated the patrols. The Japanese foot soldiers were no match for the well-hidden guerrillas, all of whom were excellent snipers. As the weeks passed and their casualties mounted, the Japanese lost interest in finding Granger and retreated to the valleys where they guarded the highways. Not once did the guerrillas and their intelligence gather information that indicated plans for a full-scale assault on their home base.

Granger and his growing forces were safe in the mountains, but the war was happening elsewhere. By the spring of 1943, Japan was in firm control of the South Pacific and threatening Australia.

The bridge crossed the Zapote River at the bottom of a steep and forbidding valley. From it, cliffs on both sides rose at such steep angles that crossing them on foot was impossible. The river was narrow but deep and fast, and the Japanese engineers had been unable to build suitable pontoons to ford it. So they built a bridge out of *narra* trees, which were plentiful and sturdy. Its construction was treacherous, with dozens of Filipino slaves lost in the process.

When Granger received orders to destroy it, he sent Majors Banning and DuBose with a squad of ten to have a look. They hiked two days through difficult terrain and finally found a safe ridge to observe from. The bridge was in the distance, deep in the valley, at least a mile away. Using binoculars, they watched it for hours, and the convoys never stopped. Occasionally, a single truck or troop carrier went across, and a few sedans with high-ranking officers were spotted. The bridge's importance was evident by the packs of soldiers guarding it. There was a post on each side with dozens of guards milling about, and on top of each hut were mounted machine guns. Below, at the edges of the river, even more Japanese camped around the abutments and killed time. The current was too swift and violent for boats.

After dark, the convoys became scarce. By 8:00 p.m., the bridge was much quieter. The Japanese had learned that their enemy worked best at night, and for this reason kept their supplies off the roads. An occasional truck, presumably empty, crossed going west to reload.

Banning and DuBose agreed that it would be impossible to destroy the bridge with explosives. An assault with men and guns would be suicide. Other than a few grenade launchers, the guerrillas had nothing in the way of artillery.

They returned to camp and briefed Granger, who was not surprised. His runners had reported as much. After resting a day, the commanders met with their general under his canopy, and over tea debated their options, of which there were precious few. A plan emerged and became the only idea with even a remote chance of success.

Most of the convoys were loaded with armaments, food, fuel, and other supplies from several ports along the western shore of Luzon, and from there they fanned out through the mountains over a grid of highways and bridges the Japanese worked hard to maintain. The first stop for most trucks was a sprawling munitions fort outside the city of Camiling. There, in endless warehouses, the enemy stored enough supplies to win the war. Once inventoried and safe, the supplies were later shipped throughout Luzon. Camiling was at the top of every guerrilla wish list, and the Japanese knew it. Even Granger had decided it was unassailable.

Truck traffic in and around Camiling was chaotic. The roads were inadequate, so the Japanese hastily built more. Riffraff always follows the army, and around the city the highways were lined with new truck stops, cafés, bars, flophouses, brothels, and opium dens.

What Major Banning needed was an empty cargo truck with a canvas cover, and there were plenty of them parked almost bumper to bumper outside the busy bars and cafés on the main highway into Camiling. Camacho and Renaldo wore the matching uniforms of officers of the imperial army. Their disguises were detailed down to the round wire-rimmed eyeglasses worn by virtually every Jap and hated by every American. The cargo truck they were watching was empty; thus, headed west to reload. Its fuel tank was full.

After a few beers, the drivers, both privates, left the bar and headed to their truck. They bumped into Camacho and Renaldo, who suddenly began throwing punches. Fights were common outside the bars—hell, they were army boys—and bystanders hardly noticed. The fight ended abruptly when Camacho slit both throats and tossed the bodies into the back of the truck, where Pete was hiding. With no pity whatsoever, he watched them bleed out as Camacho drove away. On the outskirts of a barrio, they bivouacked with G and M Troops and took on a hundred pounds of TNT and twenty gallons of gasoline. The guerrillas packed into the truck, after flinging the two dead soldiers into a ravine. An hour later, as they began the steep descent into the valley, the truck stopped and the guerrillas got off. A runner led them along a treacherous trail that fell to the Zapote.

As the truck approached the bridge and its guard post, Camacho and Renaldo gripped their weapons and held their breath. After hours of observation, they knew the guards never checked their own trucks. And why should they? Hundreds passed each day and night. In the back, Pete crouched with a finger on the trigger of his machine gun. The guards hardly noticed and waved the truck through.

Camacho volunteered because he was fearless, and unafraid of water. Renaldo claimed to be an excellent swimmer. As commander, Pete would never consider sending someone else on such a dangerous mission.

The truck stopped in the middle of the bridge. Camacho and Renaldo shed their weapons, strapped on makeshift life vests, and hustled to the rear of the truck. Pete, who had become proficient with explosives, rigged the detonator, and gave the one-word order "Jump."

They hit the blackness of the cold, raging Zapote and were swept up by the current. In a bend half a mile away,

DuBose perched on a rock and waited. His men were in the water, roped together in a human lifeline, ready to fish their comrades out of the river.

The explosion was beautiful, a violent shock in the otherwise peaceful, moonlit night. A fireball engulfed the truck and the bridge fifty feet in both directions. Panicked guards raced from both sides until they realized they could do nothing. Then they realized a collapse was imminent and retreated to safety.

Pete thrashed about in the current and tried to orient himself. The life vest worked well enough and he stayed afloat. He heard guards yelling and gunshots, but he felt safe in the rushing water. Swimming was impossible and he tried to steady himself. Several times the current swept him under, but he fought to find air. In one split second he looked back and caught a glimpse of the burning truck. Near the bend, the current slammed him into boulders he couldn't see, and his left leg splintered. The pain was instant and almost overwhelming, but he managed to get away from the rocks. He soon heard voices and screamed a reply. The current quelled in the bend, and the voices were closer. Someone grabbed him and he was pulled to the bank. Camacho was already there, but Renaldo was not. As minutes passed, they watched the fire in the distance. A second explosion tore a gaping hole in the bridge, and the flaming skeleton of the truck dropped into the river.

DuBose and Clay linked their arms under Pete's and they hit the trail. The pain was excruciating and radiated from his toes to his hip. The trauma made him dizzy and he almost lost consciousness. After a short hike they stopped and DuBose administered a shot of morphine.

The guerrillas had put together many stretchers in the jungle, and they quickly cut two bamboo poles and looped them with blankets. While they worked, the others watched the river for any sign of Renaldo, but he was never found.

For two days, Major Banning writhed in agony, but never complained. The morphine helped considerably. Runners alerted Granger, and as the men began their final ascent to home a medic arrived with even more of the drug, along with a bona fide field stretcher. Fresh troops carried him into camp for a hero's welcome. Granger strutted around like a peacock, hugging his men and promising medals.

A doctor set the leg in tight splints, and informed Pete that his fighting days were over for a few months. His femur was broken in at least two places. His tibia was snapped in two. His kneecap was cracked. Surgery was needed to reset it all, but that was not possible. Pete was forbidden to move off his cot for two weeks, and thoroughly enjoyed making demands of Clay.

He was instantly bored and began moving about as soon as Clay found a set of crutches. The doctor demanded that he remain stationary, but Pete pulled rank and told him to go to hell. He parked himself each morning under Granger's canopy and became a nuisance. Without being asked, he began advising the general on all aspects of guerrilla warfare and operations, and to shut him up Granger pulled out the cribbage board. Pete was soon beating him almost daily and demanded payment in U.S. dollars. Granger offered only IOUs.

Weeks passed as Pete helped the general plan one raid after another. He watched forlornly as the guerrillas cleaned their weapons, stuffed their backpacks, and set off for their missions. Clay was elevated to the rank of lieutenant and put in command of G Troop.

On a damp, misty morning in early June, a runner sprinted to Granger's canopy with the news that DuBose and D Troop had been ambushed as they slept. The Filipino guerrillas had been shot. DuBose and two Americans had been captured before they could commit suicide. They had been beaten severely, then hauled away.

Pete hobbled back to his hut, sat on his cot, and wept.

By the summer of 1944, American forces were within three hundred miles of the Philippines and close enough to bomb the Japanese with B-29s. Warplanes based on U.S. aircraft carriers were hitting Japanese airfields with strikes and sweeps.

The guerrillas watched the skies with grim satisfaction. An American invasion was imminent, and MacArthur was demanding more and more intelligence from the jungles. The Japanese were amassing troops and constructing garrisons along the west coast of Luzon, and the situation, at least for the guerrillas, was more dangerous than ever. Not only were they expected to continue their raids and ambushes; they were needed to monitor the enemy's troop movements and strengths.

Granger had finally secured a serviceable radio and was in sporadic contact with U.S. headquarters. He was barraged with orders to find the enemy and report daily. Intelligence supplied by the West Luzon Resistance

Force became crucial for the American invasion. Granger was forced to split his men into even smaller groups and send them farther afield.

Pete's G Troop was reduced to himself, Clay, Camacho, three other Filipinos, and three runners. His wounded leg had healed to the point of being somewhat serviceable, but every step was painful. In camp, he limped about on a cane, but on the trails he gritted his teeth and, aided with a light walking stick and a dwindling supply of morphine, led his men. They packed even lighter, moved even faster, and used the runners to keep Granger informed. Their patrols went on for days and they were often without food and sufficient ammunition.

Luzon was being fortified with divisions of Japanese infantry, and they were everywhere. Ambushes were avoided because gunfire only attracted enemy forces that could not be overcome.

On October 20, 1944, the U.S. Sixth Army landed on the shore of Leyte, east of Luzon. Supported by naval and air bombardments, the American and Australian forces overwhelmed the Japanese and continued westward. On January 9, 1945, the Sixth Army landed on Luzon, routed the Japanese, and rapidly pushed inland. Granger again changed tactics and enlarged his squads. Once more, they were let loose to ambush the retreating Japs and attack convoys.

On January 16, after a successful raid on a small munitions camp, Pete and G Troop stumbled into the middle of an entire Japanese battalion. They were immediately taking fire from three directions with little room to escape. The Japs were as weary as they were, but they had

the advantage of men and weapons. Pete ordered his men
to take cover behind some boulders and from there they
fought for their lives. Two of his Filipinos were hit. Mortars began dropping. A hand grenade landed near Camacho and killed him instantly. A shell landed behind Pete
and shrapnel tore into his right leg, the good one. He
went down screaming and dropped his rifle. Clay grabbed
him, lifted him onto his shoulders, and disappeared into
the bush. The others covered them for a moment, then
abandoned the fight and backed away. There was only
one trail and where it led no one knew, but they scrambled on. Evidently, the Japs were too tired to pursue, and
the gunfire stopped.

Pete's leg was bleeding and Clay was soon covered
with blood, but he didn't stop. They came to a creek,
crossed it cautiously, and finally collapsed in a thicket.
Clay took off his shirt, ripped it into pieces, and wrapped
Pete's wounds as tightly as possible. They smoked cigarettes and counted their losses. Four men were gone, including Camacho. Pete would grieve later. He tapped his
Colt .45 and reminded Clay that they would not be taken
alive. Clay promised him they would not be taken at all.
Throughout the afternoon, they took turns shouldering
Pete, who insisted on walking with assistance. At dark,
they slept near a barrio, one they had never seen before.
A local boy pointed one way and then the other. They
were far from Granger's base, but the boy thought some
Americans were close by. Real soldiers, not guerrillas.

At dawn, they hiked again and soon came to a road.
Hiding in the bush, they watched and waited until they
heard trucks. Then they saw them—beautiful trucks,
filled with American soldiers. When Pete saw the Stars

and Stripes waving from the antenna of the lead jeep, he felt like crying. He walked without aid to the center of the road, his torn fatigues covered with blood, and waited for the jeep to stop. A colonel got out and came forward. Pete saluted him and announced, "Lieutenant Pete Banning, of the Twenty-Sixth Cavalry Regiment, U.S. Army. West Point class of 1925."

The colonel looked him over. He studied the bedraggled crew around him. Unshaven, half-starved, some also wounded, armed with a hodgepodge of weapons, most of which were Japanese.

The colonel never saluted. Instead, he stepped forward and bear-hugged Pete.

The remnants of G Troop were taken to the port of Dasol where the Sixth Army was still coming ashore. Dozens of landing craft poured fresh soldiers onto the beaches while naval gunboats roamed the coastline. Thousands of army personnel swamped the port. It was chaos, but one big beautiful mess of it.

The men were rushed to a first aid tent where they were fed and given hot showers, soap, and razors. They were examined by doctors who were accustomed to treating battle wounds inflicted on healthy young men, not disease-ravaged guerrillas from the jungle. Pete was diagnosed with malaria, amoebic dysentery, and malnutrition. He weighed 137 pounds, though skinny as he was he had managed to gain weight during the past two and a half years. He guessed that he had been twenty pounds lighter when he left O'Donnell. He and three others with wounds were examined by doctors in an adjacent hospital. It was quickly determined that Pete needed surgery to remove shrapnel from his leg, and he was given priority. The hospital was filling up with casualties from the front.

Clay and the others were outfitted in crisp, new army fatigues. His new waist size was twenty-eight inches, down six from boot camp. They were shown to a tent with cots, told to rest, and given a pass to the cafeteria, where they ate nonstop.

The following day, Clay visited his commander in a hospital ward and was relieved to hear that the surgery went well. The doctors could treat wounds, but they did not have the tools to reset Pete's broken bones. That would have to wait until he was stateside. Pete and Clay worried about their comrades back at the home base and said a prayer for Camacho, Renaldo, DuBose, and the others they had lost. They thought of those still suffering at O'Donnell and the other camps and prayed they would soon be rescued. They also managed to laugh at themselves and their wild adventures in the jungles.

Clay returned the next day with the news that he was being given the choice of fighting with the Sixth Army or being reassigned to a base in the U.S. Pete insisted he go home, and Clay was inclined to. They had fought enough.

Three days later, Pete said good-bye to his men, most of whom he would never see again. He and Clay embraced and vowed to keep in touch. He and ten other badly wounded men were gently arranged on a medical pontoon and ferried to a large army hospital ship. They waited two days for it to fill, then cast off and headed home. The ship was staffed with pretty nurses who fed him four times a day and treated him like a hero. The sight of their legs and shapely backsides, along with the smell of their perfume, made him long for Liza's embrace.

Four weeks later, the ship sailed into the San Francisco Bay, and Pete remembered the last time he had seen the Golden Gate Bridge. November of 1941, just days before Pearl Harbor.

He was transported to Letterman Army Hospital in the Presidio. Like every other soldier on board, all he wanted was a telephone.

CHAPTER 35

The news that Pete Banning was alive was even more shocking than the news that he was dead. Nineva heard it first because she was in the kitchen when the phone rang. Always reluctant to answer it, because she considered it a toy for the white folks, she finally said, "Banning residence." A ghost spoke to her, the ghost of Mista Banning. When she refused to believe it was Pete, he raised his voice an octave or two and told her to go find his wife, and to hurry.

Liza was standing outside the barn holding the reins of her horse while Amos repaired a stirrup. Both were startled at the scream from the back porch, and ran to see what was wrong with Nineva. She was on the porch, in a fit, jumping up and down, crying, yelling, "It's Mista Pete! It's Mista Pete! He's alive! He's alive!"

Liza was certain Nineva had lost her mind but ran to the phone anyway. When she heard his voice, she nearly fainted but managed to fall into a kitchen chair. With some effort, Pete convinced her he was indeed alive and resting comfortably in a hospital in San Francisco. He had several wounds but all his limbs were intact and he would recover. He wanted her on a train as soon as possible. Liza could hardly say a word at first and tried not to burst into tears. As she regained her senses she remembered that their conversation was probably not private. Someone was always listening on their rural party line. They agreed that she would scoop up Florry, rush into town, and call Pete on a private line. She sent Amos to fetch Florry while she changed clothes.

Agnes Murphy lived a mile up the highway and was known to eavesdrop on every call. The neighbors suspected she had nothing better to do than sit by the phone and snatch it when it rang. Indeed, she had listened to Pete's call, in disbelief, and immediately began calling friends in town.

Florry arrived in a rush and the two women jumped into Liza's Pontiac. Liza hated to drive and was even worse at it than Florry, but at the moment that didn't matter. The two raced toward town, weaving along the drive and slinging gravel. Both were crying and babbling at the same time. Liza said, "He said he was wounded but okay, said he had been captured but escaped, and that he had been fighting as a guerrilla for the past three years."

"Good God Almighty!" Florry kept saying. "What in the world is a guerrilla?"

"I have no idea, I have no idea. I can't believe this."

"Good God Almighty."

They roared to a stop in the street, and raced into the home of Shirley Armstrong, Liza's closest friend. She was puttering around the kitchen when Liza and Florry barged in with the news. After a round of crying and hugging, Liza borrowed her phone, on a private line, and called the hospital in San Francisco. While she waited and waited, she wiped tears and tried to compose herself. Florry made no such effort and sat on the sofa with Shirley, both bawling away.

Liza chatted with Pete for ten minutes, then handed the phone to Florry. She left the house, drove to the school, found Stella in class, pulled her into the hallway, and delivered the unfathomable news. By the time she checked her out of school, the teachers and principal were gathering around the office for another round of hugs and congratulations.

Meanwhile, Florry worked the phone. She called the president's office at Vanderbilt and demanded that Joel be located immediately. She called Dexter Bell at the church. She called Nix Gridley at the jail. As the high sheriff, Nix served as the county's unofficial contact point for crucial news.

Within an hour of Pete's call, every phone in town was ringing.

Liza and Florry returned home and tried to put together a plan. It was late February and the fields were idle. In the backyard, the Negroes were coming on foot to see if it was true. Liza stood on the rear porch and confirmed the news. Dexter and Jackie Bell arrived first to share in the moment, and they were soon followed by a parade of cars as friends flocked to the Banning home.

Two days later, Florry drove Liza to the train station, where they were met by a farewell party. Liza thanked and hugged them all, then boarded for a three-day journey to San Francisco.

. . .

The first surgery lasted for eight hours as doctors went about the complex job of breaking and resetting most of the bones in Pete's left leg. When they finished, it was encased in a thick plaster cast from hip to ankle, with pins and rods running through it. The leg was elevated to a painful angle and held in place with straps, pulleys, and chains. His right leg was wrapped in gauze and was just as painful. The nurses plied the patient with painkillers, and for two days after the surgery Pete was rarely awake.

And that was a blessing. For a month on the hospital ship, he had suffered nightmares and flashbacks and slept little. The horrors of the past three years haunted him day and night. A psychiatrist spent time with him and made him talk, but reliving his ordeal only made things worse. The medications only confused him. One moment brought euphoria so extreme he laughed out loud, and the next moment he crashed into utter depression. He slept fitfully during the day and often screamed at night.

At Letterman, the nurses eased off the painkillers when they learned his wife would soon arrive. He needed to be as alert as possible.

Liza followed a nurse onto the ward and saw two long rows of beds separated by thin curtains. As she walked she couldn't help but look at the patients, most of them just boys not too far removed from high school. When the nurse stopped, Liza took a deep breath and pulled back the curtain. Careful not to touch the chains and pulleys and injured legs, she fell onto his chest for a fierce embrace, one that she had never expected. Pete, though, had been dreaming of it for years.

She was as gorgeous as ever. Dressed to the hilt and smelling of a perfume that he had never forgotten, she kissed him as they whispered and wept and laughed as time stood absolutely still. He rubbed her backside in full view of the nearby patients, and she didn't care. He clutched her to his chest, and all was right in the world.

In voices as low as possible, they talked for a long time. Joel, Stella, Florry, the farm, their friends, all the gossip from home. She carried the bulk of the conversation because he had no desire to describe what he had been through. When the doctors arrived on rounds, they gave her a quick summary of the patient's condition and what was to be expected. They anticipated several more surgeries and a long recovery, but with time he would be as good as new.

An orderly brought her a comfortable chair with a pillow and blanket, and she set up camp. She hauled in books and magazines and read, and talked and talked. She left his side only after dark to return to her hotel.

Before long, Liza knew the names of the other boys and was flirting shamelessly. They perked up when she was around, delighted to have such a lively, beautiful woman showering them with attention. She virtually commandeered the wing. She wrote letters to girlfriends and made phone calls to mothers, always with news that was cheerful and optimistic, regardless of the wounds. She read letters from home, often fighting back tears. She brought in chocolates and candy when she could find them.

Pete was one of the luckier ones. He was not paralyzed or disfigured and all limbs were intact. Some of the boys were pitiful, and they received even more of her attention. Pete was more than happy to share his wife and reveled in her ability to brighten up a hospital ward.

She stayed for two weeks and left only because Stella was at home with Florry and Nineva. When she was gone, the ward returned to its gloominess. Every day the patients yelled at Pete and asked when Liza was coming back.

She returned in mid-March and brought the family with her. Joel and Stella were on spring break and eager to see their father. For three days, they camped around his bed and in general turned the ward upside down. When they were gone, Pete slept for two days, aided by sedatives.

On May 4, he was taken by ambulance to the train station and loaded onto an army hospital ward car for a ride across the country. It stopped many times as men were carried away to other hospitals closer to home. On May 10, it arrived in Jackson, Mississippi, and Liza, Stella, and Florry were waiting. They followed the ambulance across town to the Foster General Hospital, where Pete spent the next three months convalescing.

PART THREE

———•———

THE BETRAYAL

CHAPTER 36

Two weeks after his execution, the last will and testament of Pete Banning was probated in the Chancery Court of Ford County. John Wilbanks had prepared the will not long after the trial. It was straightforward and left the bulk of Pete's assets in a trust for Liza, with Wilbanks serving as the trustee, or controller. Pete's most valuable asset, his land, had already been deeded to Joel and Stella in equal shares, and this included their fine home. Pete had insisted on a stipulation that Liza be allowed to live in the home for the rest of her life, provided she did not remarry, and provided that she was one day released from Whitfield. John had cautioned him that such a clause might be hard to enforce if the children, as owners, for some reason wanted to prevent their mother from living there. The will had other problems, all carefully pointed out by the lawyer and all stubbornly ignored by the client.

At the time of his death Pete owned his farm equipment, vehicles, and bank accounts, from which Liza's name had been removed after her commitment. Before then, the accounts had been held jointly, but Pete did not want her to have access to the money. His personal checking account had a balance of $1,800. His farm account, $5,300. And he had $7,100 in a savings account. A week before his execution he transferred $2,200 to Florry's account to cover the expenses of Joel's and Stella's education. He also gave her a small metal safe containing just over $6,000 in cash and gold coins, money that could never be traced. He had no loans and no debts, save for the usual ongoing expenses of running the farm.

He instructed John Wilbanks to probate his estate as soon as possible and file tax returns. He appointed Florry his executrix, and, in writing, told her to pay the Wilbanks firm whatever was owed, and left her a list of other matters to attend to.

In 1947, good farmland in Ford County was worth approximately $100 an acre. In broad strokes, Pete left to his children real estate worth around $100,000, including the home. To his wife, he left about one-fourth of that amount, all tied up in a trust, and, as John Wilbanks pointed out over and over, all subject to trouble should Liza decide to challenge the will.

Pete was certain that she would not.

Upon opening the estate, Wilbanks followed the statutory requirement of posting a notice in the county newspaper on three consecutive weeks to alert potential creditors that all claims against the estate must be filed within ninety days. No other information about the estate was given, none was required.

Over in Rome, Georgia, Errol McLeish received

through the mail his weekly copy of *The Ford County Times*. He scoured it every week to monitor the news, and he was waiting on the notice to creditors.

Soon after the burial, Joel and Stella left the pink cottage. It had been a pleasant place to come home to from college, with hot food on the stove, a fire in the winter, music on the phonograph, and Florry with all of her eccentricities and animals, but she was such a large presence that the walls closed in quickly.

They settled into their old bedrooms, and went about the impossible task of trying to breathe some life into their home. They opened the doors and windows in an effort to circulate fresh air; it was summer and the heat and humidity suffocated the land. The phone rang constantly as all manner of strangers and friends called with kind words, or ridiculous questions, or meddlesome requests. They finally stopped answering it. There was a flood of mail and they opened and read the letters. Most were from war veterans who said nice things about Pete, though few had known him personally. For a few days, Joel and Stella attempted to answer the letters with short notes, but soon grew weary of the task and realized it was futile. Their father was gone. Why respond to total strangers? The mail piled up in his abandoned study. A few kind souls from town brought out dishes and desserts, the usual ritual after a death, but when Joel and Stella realized that most of the visitors were only curious, they stopped going to the door.

Reporters came and went, all looking for an angle or

a quote, but they received nothing. One from a magazine hung around until Joel shooed him away with a shotgun.

Nineva was of no help. She was crushed by the death of her boss and couldn't stop crying. She busied herself in the mornings with halfhearted efforts at cooking and cleaning, but by noon she was too exhausted to work. Stella usually sent her home midday, happy to have her out of the house.

Each evening, after supper and just before dark, as the heat broke, Joel and Stella walked the dirt trail to Old Sycamore and had a word with their father. They touched his tombstone, had a tear, said a prayer, and walked back toward the house, arm in arm and speaking softly and wondering what in the world had happened to their family. As the long days passed, they accepted the reality that they would never know why their father had killed Dexter Bell, just as they would never know why their mother had had such a devastating mental breakdown.

They told themselves that they did not want to know. They wanted to escape this nightmare and get on with their lives, lives to be lived somewhere far away.

Joel called the director at Whitfield, for the third time, and asked to visit his mother. The director promised to consult with her doctors, and called back the following day with the news that a visit was not permissible. It was the third denial, and as with the first two the reason was that she was not able to receive visitors. Nothing more was said, and the family speculated that Liza had been informed of Pete's death and had slid even deeper into her dark world.

Before he died, Pete made no provision for the appointment of a successor guardian for his wife. Joel met with John Wilbanks and insisted that he ask the judge to appoint either him or Stella, but Wilbanks wanted some time to pass.

This angered Joel and he threatened to hire another lawyer to represent him and the interests of his mother. Under pressure, he proved to be quite an effective advocate, quick with his tongue and smart with his reasons. John Wilbanks was impressed enough to mention to his brother Russell that the kid might have a future in the courtroom. After two days of constant badgering, John relented and walked with Joel across the street to meet with Judge Abbott Rumbold, the ancient dictator of chancery court. For many years, Judge Rumbold had been doing whatever John Wilbanks asked him to do, and within an hour Joel was appointed the new guardian of his mother's care. He obtained a certified copy of the new court order and immediately called Whitfield.

On August 7, four weeks after the death of their father, Joel and Stella drove south to see their mother for the first time in more than a year. Florry was ambivalent about tagging along, and Joel, the new man of the house, suggested that she wait until the next visit. Eventually, that was fine with Florry.

The same guard they had confronted months earlier was waiting with a clipboard at the gate, but the paperwork seemed less cumbersome. Joel drove straight to building 41 and, armed with his court order, marched inside to see Dr. Hilsabeck. The two had spoken by phone the day before and everything was in order. The doctor was somewhat pleasant for a change, and after reviewing the edict from old Rumbold, he clasped his fingers together and asked how he might help.

Stella went first. "We want to know what is wrong with our mother. What is her diagnosis? She's been here for more than a year, so surely you can tell us what's wrong with her."

A tight smile, then, "Of course. Mrs. Banning is suffering from intense mental distress. The term 'nervous breakdown' is not really a medical diagnosis, but it's used quite often to describe patients like your mother. She suffers from depression, anxiety, and acute stress. Her depression leaves her with no hope and thoughts of suicide and self-harm. Her anxiety is evidenced by high blood pressure, tense muscles, dizziness, and trembling. She suffers from insomnia one week and then sleeps for hours and hours the next week. She hallucinates, sees things that are not real, and often yells at night when she has nightmares. Her mood swings are extreme, but almost always on the dark side. If she has a good day, one in which she appears somewhat happy, it is almost always followed by two or three days of darkness. At times she is virtually catatonic. She is paranoid and thinks someone is stalking her, or that someone else is in the room. This often leads to panic attacks in which she is stricken with absolute fear and has trouble breathing. These usually pass within an hour or two. She eats little and refuses to take care of herself. Her hygiene is not good. She is not a cooperative patient, and in group therapy she goes into total isolation. We were seeing a slight improvement before the murder of Dexter Bell, but that event proved to be catastrophic. Months passed and she got better, then your father was executed and Liza regressed considerably."

"Is that all?" Stella asked, wiping her eyes.

"I'm sorry."

"Is she schizophrenic?" Joel asked.

"I don't think so. For the most part, she understands reality and does not engage in false beliefs, with the exception of an occasional bout of paranoia. She does not hear voices. It is difficult to determine how she would act in social settings since she has not been released from here. But, no, I do not diagnose your mother as schizophrenic. Severely depressed, yes."

Stella said, "Eighteen months ago our mother was fine, or at least she certainly appeared to be. Now she's suffering from what sounds like a severe nervous breakdown. What happened, Doctor? What caused this?"

Hilsabeck was shaking his head. "I don't know. But I agree with you in that it was something traumatic. From what I gather, Liza and the family managed to survive the news that your father was missing and presumed dead. His return was a joyous event, one that I'm sure brought great happiness, not severe depression. Something happened. But, as I said, she is not very cooperative and refuses to go into her past. It's quite frustrating, really, and I fear that we may not be able to help her until she is willing to talk."

"So, how is she being treated?" Joel asked.

"Counseling, therapy, a better diet, sunshine. We try and get her outside but she usually refuses. Barring any more bad news, I think she will progress slowly. It's important that she sees you."

"What about medications?" Stella asked.

"In this business, there are always rumors of antipsychotic drugs in development, but they appear to be years away. When she's not sleeping or overly anxious we give her barbiturates. Also, an occasional pill for high blood pressure."

There was a long pause as Joel and Stella absorbed the words they had been desperate to hear for so long. The words were not encouraging, but perhaps they were the beginning. Or, the end of the beginning.

Joel asked, "Can you put her back together, Doctor? Is there a chance she can one day go home?"

"I'm not sure home is a good place for her, Mr. Banning. From what I gather, it's a rather dark and somber place these days."

"You could say that," Stella said.

"I'm not sure your mother can handle more bad news at home."

"Nor can we," Stella mumbled.

Dr. Hilsabeck suddenly stood and said, "Let's go see Liza. Please follow me."

They marched down a long hall and stopped at a window. Below them in the distance was a grove of trees and a series of wide walkways around a small pond. Near a pretty gazebo a lady sat in the shade, in a wheelchair, with a nurse close to her side. They seemed to be chatting. "That's Liza," Hilsabeck said. "She knows you're coming and she's eager to see you. You can exit through that door." He nodded and they backed away.

Liza smiled when she saw them. She reached for Stella first and pulled her close, then did the same with Joel. The nurse smiled politely and disappeared around a corner.

They maneuvered the wheelchair to a park bench and sat facing her. Joel held one hand, Stella the other. They had braced themselves for how terrible she might look, so they tried to appear unsurprised. Pale, extremely thin and gaunt, and with no makeup or lipstick or jewelry, nothing to remind them of the beautiful and vivacious woman they knew and loved. Her sandy-colored hair was graying and pulled back into a bun. She wore a thin white hospital gown and her bare feet were exposed.

"My babies, my babies, my babies," she said over and over as she clutched their hands and tried to smile. Her eyes were so disturbing. Gone was their color and exuberance, replaced by a hollow, unblinking stare that, at first, did not meet their eyes. She cast her eyes down a few inches and seemed to be looking at their chests.

Minutes passed as Liza mumbled about her babies while Joel and Stella patted her gently and tried to think of something to say. Assuming any conversation was good, Joel finally said, "Dr. Hilsabeck says you're doing great, Mom."

She nodded and said softly, "I guess. Some days are good. I just want to go home."

"And we're going to take you home, Mom, but not today. First, you're going to get well, you're going to eat better, get some sun, do whatever the doctors and nurses tell you, and then one day soon we'll take you home."

"Will Pete be there?"

"Well, uh, no, Mom, Dad will not be there. He's gone, Mom. I thought the doctors told you this."

"Yes, but I don't believe them."

"Well, you should believe them because Dad is gone."

Stella rose gently, kissed her mother on the top of her

head, and walked behind the gazebo, where she sat on its steps and buried her face in her hands.

Thanks for nothing, sis, Joel thought to himself. He began a windy narrative about nothing, or at least nothing to do with the obvious fact that they were sitting in the garden of an asylum with their mother, who was mentally ill. He talked about Stella and her upcoming return to Hollins for her junior year, and her plans to land a job in New York. He talked about his own decision to enroll in law school. He was accepted at Vanderbilt and Ole Miss but was thinking of taking a year off, maybe to travel. As he gabbed, Liza heard his words and lifted her eyes as if soothed by his voice. She smiled and began to nod slightly.

He wasn't sure about the law and therefore might take a break from his studies. He and Stella had spent time in D.C. and enjoyed themselves, and he had met a friend there who owned a restaurant and had offered him a job.

After a good cry, Stella returned and joined in the one-way conversation. She went on about her time as a nanny in Georgetown, and her upcoming courses, and her plans for the future. At times, Liza smiled and closed her eyes as if their voices were a pleasant narcotic.

The clouds disappeared and the midday sun beat down with a fury. They pushed her wheelchair to a shaded area under some trees. The nurse watched them but kept her distance. During a lull, Liza whispered, "Keep talking." And they did.

An orderly brought sandwiches and glasses of iced tea. They arranged their lunch on a picnic table and encouraged Liza to eat. She took a few bites of a sandwich but showed little interest. She wanted to listen to their lovely young voices, and so they talked, tag-teaming and always careful to keep their stories far away from Clanton.

Long after lunch, Dr. Hilsabeck appeared and suggested that the patient needed some rest. He was delighted with the visit and asked if Joel and Stella could return the following day for another round. Of course they could.

They kissed their mother good-bye, promised to be back soon, and drove to Jackson, where they found rooms at the stately Hotel Heidelberg in downtown. After checking in, they set out on a walk to the state capitol and back, but the heat and humidity were too much. They retreated to the coffee bar, asked the waiter about alcohol, and were directed to a speakeasy behind the hotel. There they ordered drinks, and tried not to talk about their mother. They were tired of talking.

CHAPTER 37

Because he did not have a license to practice law in Mississippi, Errol McLeish was required to associate local counsel for his carefully laid plans. He never considered hiring anyone from Clanton. All the good lawyers there were kin to the Wilbankses anyway. McLeish wanted a lawyer with an aggressive reputation who was well-known in north Mississippi, but with no close ties to Ford County. He took his time, did his research, asked around, and finally selected a Tupelo lawyer named Burch Dunlap. The two met a month before Pete's execution and began laying the groundwork. Dunlap liked the case because it had the potential for press coverage, and, at least in his opinion, it would be an easy win.

On August 12, Dunlap, on behalf of his client Jackie Bell, filed a wrongful death suit against the estate of Pete Banning. The lawsuit set forth the facts as virtually everyone knew them, and asked for half a million dollars in damages. In an unexpected twist, it was filed in federal court in Oxford, not state court in Clanton. Jackie Bell claimed to now be a resident of Georgia and thus entitled to relief in federal court, where the jurors would be summoned from thirty counties, and where sympathy for a convicted murderer would be difficult to find.

Since Florry was the executrix of the estate, papers had to be served upon her. She was in the backyard tending to her birds when Roy Lester appeared from nowhere with a look of deep concern.

"Bad news, Florry," he said, tipping his hat. He handed over a thick envelope and said, "Looks like more legal trouble."

"What is it?" she asked, knowing full well that he and Nix and probably everybody at the jail had read whatever was in the envelope.

"A lawsuit filed by Jackie Bell, over in federal court."

"Thanks for nothing."

"Would you sign right here?" he asked, holding a sheet of paper and a pen.

"For what?"

"It says that you have been served with the lawsuit and you have it in your possession."

She signed, thanked him, and took the papers inside. An hour later, she barged into John Wilbanks's office and charged up the stairs. She thrust the lawsuit at him and fell onto the sofa in tears. John lit a cigar as he calmly read the three-page pleading.

"No real surprise here," he said as he sat in a chair across from the sofa. "It seems as though we've discussed this as a possibility."

"A half a million dollars?"

"An exaggeration, just part of the business. Lawyers typically demand far more than they expect to receive."

"But you can handle this, right, John? There's nothing to worry about?"

"Oh, I can handle it all right, in the sense that I can defend the lawsuit, but there is much to be concerned with, Florry. First, the facts, and they are fairly well established. Second, Burch Dunlap is a fine lawyer who knows what he's doing. Filing in federal court is a brilliant move, and, frankly, one I didn't expect."

"So you knew this was coming?"

"Florry, we discussed this months ago. Jackie Bell's husband was murdered and the killer had assets, which is unheard of."

"Well, I don't remember what we discussed, John, to be honest. My nerves have been shot to hell this past year and my poor brain can't take much more. What are we supposed to do now?"

"Nothing for you. I'll defend the lawsuit. And we'll wait for more to come."

"More?"

"Wouldn't surprise me."

They waited two days. Burch Dunlap filed his second lawsuit in the Chancery Court of Ford County and named as defendants Joel and Stella Banning. Errol McLeish figured the two would soon be leaving to pursue their studies, and decided to serve them with process before they left town. Roy Lester again drove out to the Banning farm and handed papers to Joel, Stella, and Florry.

Being sued by a good lawyer was uncomfortable enough, but facing two lawsuits with little in the way of defenses was terrifying. The three defendants met with John and Russell Wilbanks, and while it was somewhat comforting to be in the presence of loyal friends who were fine lawyers, there was an unmistakable sense of uncertainty in the air.

Could the Bannings really lose their land? Florry's, of course, was safe, but the deed to Joel and Stella was being attacked by a lawyer who knew what he was doing. It was clear that Pete had planned the murder, and in doing so attempted to transfer his most valuable asset to his children in an effort to avoid the claims of judgment creditors.

The Wilbanks brothers discussed what might happen in the months to come. They agreed that Dunlap would probably press hard for a trial on the wrongful death claim, and, assuming he won, and frankly it was difficult to see how he could lose, then he would bring his judgment to the Chancery Court of Ford County and assault their land. Depending on who won and who lost in which trial, the litigation and appeals could drag on for years. Attorneys' fees could be substantial.

John Wilbanks promised a vigorous defense on all fronts, but his show of confidence was not altogether believable.

They left his office in a depressed state and, on a whim, decided to drive to Memphis, to the Peabody, where they could drown their worries at the elegant bar, eat a fine meal, spend a carefree night, and get out of Ford County. Better burn some cash while they had it.

Joel drove, perched like a chauffeur alone up front with the gals in the rear seat, and for several miles nothing was said until they crossed into Van Buren County.

Stella broke the ice with "I really don't want to go back to Hollins. Classes start in three weeks and I cannot imagine walking into a classroom and trying to listen to a lecture on something as unimportant as Shakespeare when my father has just been executed and my poor mother is in a mental institution. Seriously? How can I be expected to study and learn?"

"So you're quitting college?" Florry asked.

"Not quitting, just taking a break."

"And you, Joel?"

"I'm having the same thoughts. The first year of law school is a boot camp and I'm just not up to it. I was leaning toward Vanderbilt but now with money more of an issue I was thinking about Ole Miss. Truth is, though, I can't see myself sitting in a classroom getting hammered by a bunch of crusty old law professors."

"Interesting," Florry said. "And with no classes and no jobs what will the two of you be doing in the months to come? Sitting around the house and driving Nineva crazy? Or perhaps you could help out in the fields and pick cotton with the Negroes? Buford can always use some extra hands. And if you get bored in the fields, you can always pull weeds and gather vegetables from the garden so we'll have something to eat this winter. Amos will be happy to show you how to milk cows at six every morning. Nineva would love to have you under foot in her kitchen as she cooks and cans. And when you get bored on the farm you can always venture into town, where everyone you bump into will ask how you're doing and pretend to be so sad about your father. Is that what you want?"

Neither Joel nor Stella responded.

Florry continued. "Here's the better plan. In three weeks you're getting the hell out of here because you need to finish school before we lose all the money. Your father put me in charge of your education, so I'm writing the checks. If you don't finish school now, then you never will, so you have no choice but to go. Stella, you're going back to Hollins, and Joel, you're going to law school. I don't care where, just get away from here."

A few miles passed in silence as the finality of the decision sank in.

Stella finally said, "Well, on second thought, Hollins is not a bad place to hide these days."

Joel said, "If I go to law school, I'll probably go to Ole Miss. That way I can visit Mom on the weekends, and I can also hang around Wilbanks's office and help with the lawsuits."

"I'm sure he has things under control," Florry said. "We can afford Vanderbilt if that's what you want."

"No. Four years there is enough. I need to branch out. Besides, there are more girls at Ole Miss."

"When did that become important?"

"Always."

"Well, I think it's time you got serious about a girl. You are, after all, twenty-one and a college graduate."

"Are you giving unsolicited advice on romance, Aunt Florry?"

"No, not really."

"Good. Just keep it to yourself."

Before leaving for the fall, Joel and Stella made three more trips to Whitfield to sit with Liza. Dr. Hilsabeck encouraged this and assured them their visits helped immensely, though they certainly could not see any improvement. Liza's physical appearance remained unchanged. For one visit, she refused to leave her dark little room and said virtually nothing. For the other visits, she allowed them to roll her around the grounds in a wheelchair, looking for shade from the August heat. She smiled occasionally but not often enough, said very little, and never strung together enough words for a complete sentence. So she listened as her children tag-teamed their way through the same long narratives. To break the monotony, Joel read articles from *Time* magazine and Stella read from *The Saturday Evening Post*.

The visits were emotionally exhausting, and they said little driving the long way home. After four trips to Whitfield, they were becoming convinced that their mother would never leave.

Early on September 3, Joel loaded his sister's luggage into the trunk of the family's 1939 Pontiac, and together they drove to the pink cottage for a farewell breakfast with Aunt Florry. Marietta stuffed them with biscuits and omelets and packed a lunch for the road. They left Florry in tears on the porch and hustled away. They stopped for a somber moment at Old Sycamore and said a prayer at their father's tombstone, then sped to the train station, where Stella almost missed the 9:40 to Memphis. They hugged each other, tried not to cry, and promised to keep in touch.

When the train was out of sight, Joel got in the car, drove a lap around the square, then through the side streets past the Methodist church, and finally returned home. He packed his own bags, said good-bye to Nineva and Amos, and drove an hour to Oxford, where law school was waiting. Through a friend of a friend he had a lead on a tiny apartment near the square, above a widow's garage, a cheap place rented only to graduate students. The widow showed him a tiny three-room flat, laid out the rules, which included no alcohol, no parties, no gambling, and of course no women, and said the rent was $100 cash for four months, September through December. Joel agreed to her rules, though he had no plans to follow them, and handed over the money. When she left, he unpacked his bags and boxes and arranged his clothing in a closet.

After dark, he walked along North Lamar toward the courthouse in the distance. He lit a cigarette and smoked it as he strolled past stately old homes on shaded lots. Porches were filled with the post-supper gossip as the families and neighbors waited for the heat and humidity to break for the night. Though the students were back the square was dead, and why wouldn't it be? There were no bars, clubs, lounges, dance halls, or even nice restaurants. Oxford was a small, dry town, and a long way from the bright lights of Nashville.

Joel Banning felt a long way from everywhere.

CHAPTER 38

The lawsuit was over a deadly collision between a sedan filled with a young family and a flat railcar loaded with several tons of pulpwood. It occurred late at night on a main highway between Tupelo and Memphis, at a crossing that for reasons never to be known had been built at the foot of a long hill, so that the traffic coming down the hill at night could not always see the trains until the last moment. To avoid collisions, and there had been several, the railroad installed red flashing lights on both sides, east and west, but did not splurge on gates that descended and actually blocked the highway. The flat car was the eleventh in a long train of sixty, with two engines and an old red caboose.

The lawyers defending the railroad made much of the fact that any driver paying sufficient attention to the road could certainly see something as large as a flat railcar that was eighty feet long and stacked fifteen feet high with timber. They passed around enlarged photos of the flat railcar and seemed confident in their proof.

However, they were no match for the Honorable Burch Dunlap, attorney for the deceased family—both parents and two small children. In two days of trial, Mr. Dunlap attacked the men who designed the crossing, exposed the railroad's lousy safety record, proved that it had been warned that the crossing was dangerous, discredited two other drivers who claimed to be eyewitnesses, and presented the jury with his own set of enlarged photos that clearly revealed a severe lack of maintenance by the railroad.

The jury agreed and awarded the family $60,000, a record verdict for federal court in north Mississippi.

Sitting low in the back row, Joel Banning watched the trial from beginning to end, and felt sick. Burch Dunlap was masterful in the courtroom and owned the jury from start to finish. He was at home, comfortable and relaxed and thoroughly credible. He was meticulously prepared, smooth on his feet, and always two steps ahead of the witnesses and the defense lawyers.

Now he was coming after the Bannings and their land.

Because Joel was watching the court's Oxford docket with a keen eye, he happened to notice the upcoming trial involving the railroad collision. Out of curiosity, he decided to skip classes and watch it. And then he wished he had not been so curious.

After the verdict, Joel thought about calling Stella, but why ruin her day? He thought about calling Florry, but her phone line was not private. And why bother? He needed someone to talk to, but in his first weeks of law school he had remained reclusive and met few other students. He was detached, aloof, almost rude at times, and always on the defensive because at any moment he expected some loudmouth to ask about his father. He could almost hear the whispers behind his back.

Three months after the fact, the wounds from the execution were still open and raw. Joel was certain that he was the only student in the history of Ole Miss whose family had suffered through the shame of such a spectacle.

On October 9, he skipped class and drove to a lake where he sat under a tree and sipped bourbon from a flask. One year ago, his father had murdered Dexter Bell.

Joel studied hard but found the classes boring. On Saturdays, when the talk was of nothing but football, he drove to Whitfield to sit with his mother, or he drove home to check on Florry and look at the crops. Home had become an awful, empty place with only Nineva to talk to. But she, too, was depressed and moped around the kitchen with little to do. Hell, it seemed as if everybody was depressed. On most Friday afternoons, Joel stopped by John Wilbanks's office to discuss the family's legal troubles, or to hand over a brief or a memo he had polished off at law school. Wilbanks was impressed with young Joel and had mentioned more than once that the firm could use some fresh talent in a few years. Joel was polite and said he had no idea where he wanted to live and practice law.

The last place would be Clanton, he thought to himself.

.   .   .

As the holidays approached, Florry began dropping hints about another road trip to New Orleans. However, her plans seemed to collapse almost as soon as she made them. Joel and Stella suspected the reason was money. With the family's finances so uncertain, they had noticed a few cutbacks here and there. The 1947 cotton crop was good but not great, and with Pete gone the picking had lacked some intensity and efficiency.

Stella arrived home on December 21, and that night they decorated a tree while carols played on the phonograph. And they were drinking, a bit more than usual. Bourbon for Joel and Stella, gin for Florry. Nothing for Marietta, who hid in the basement and was convinced they were all cracking up and going to hell.

As gloomy as things were, they tried their best to find the holiday spirit, with small gifts and big meals and lots of music. The two lawsuits facing them and threatening their future were never discussed.

On Christmas Day, they once again loaded into Florry's Lincoln and drove to Whitfield. A year earlier, they had made the trip, only to be denied access to Liza. Those days were over now because Pete was certainly out of the way and Joel was now his mother's legal guardian. They sat with her in one corner of a large activity room, and gave her gifts and chocolates sent by Nineva and Marietta. Liza smiled a lot and talked more and seemed to enjoy the attention.

In every corner there was a quiet little family doting on a loved one, a patient with pale skin and hollow cheeks. Some were ancient and appeared half-dead. Others, like Liza, were much younger, but they seemed to be going nowhere too. Was this really her future? Would she ever be well enough to come home? Were they destined for decades of such pathetic visits?

Though Dr. Hilsabeck maintained that he was pleased with her progress, they had seen little improvement in the past four months. She hadn't gained a pound, and the nurses kept her in a wheelchair so she wouldn't burn calories walking. She often went for long stretches of time without a word. Occasionally, her eyes had a sparkle, but it never lasted.

Driving home, they discussed whether the trips to Whitfield were worth the trouble.

After Christmas, the music stopped and the cold rains began. Making merry became a chore, and even the pink cottage, with its eccentricities, was enveloped in moodiness. Stella suddenly needed to return to Hollins to finish some vague projects. Florry spent more time in her room reading and listening to opera.

To escape the gloom, Joel left a day early and returned to Oxford. When the law school opened, he eagerly checked his grades and was pleased with his first-semester test scores.

At the end of January, he found himself back in federal court as a representative of the family. A magistrate had scheduled a pretrial hearing and all lawyers were present. Florry, as executrix of the estate of Pete Banning, was supposed to attend, but, typically, she called in sick with the flu. Besides, Joel was already in Oxford and he could certainly handle things.

Joel nervously sat at one table between John and Russell Wilbanks, and kept an eye on Burch Dunlap and his associate at the other table. Just being in the same arena with Dunlap was terrifying.

The magistrate covered the list of all potential witnesses at trial and wanted summaries of the testimony of each. The lawyers politely discussed exhibits, jury lists, the usual pretrial details. The magistrate studied his calendar and announced a trial date of February 24, barely a month away. He then asked if there was any chance of settling the case without going to trial. The lawyers looked at each other and it was obvious they had not yet reached that point.

Burch Dunlap stood and said, "Well, Your Honor, I am always ready and willing to settle, on good terms of course. As you are aware, we have another lawsuit pending in the Chancery Court of Ford County in which we are attempting to set aside the conveyance by the deceased of his section of land to his children. This happened three weeks before the murder. We've had the land appraised." He picked up a binder and sort of waved it at the magistrate. "The land is worth $100 an acre, or about $65,000 total, and we firmly believe this land belongs in the estate of Pete Banning, and is therefore subject to the claim of our client, Mrs. Jackie Bell. The home is appraised at $30,000, and there are other assets."

John Wilbanks stood, smiling and shaking his head as if Dunlap were an idiot. "Those figures are much too high, Your Honor, and I'm not prepared to argue over them. But any talk of settlement is premature. We expect to prevail in Ford County and protect the acreage. And who knows what the jury will do in this case? Let's allow the litigation to run its course; then we can have this discussion."

"It might be too late, Mr. Wilbanks," the magistrate said.

Listening to Burch Dunlap so casually discuss land that had been purchased, cleared, and plowed by Joel's great-great-great-grandfather made his blood boil. How dare this gifted shyster toss around values of hard-gained assets and sums of someone else's money as if bidding at an auction or wagering in a card game. Did he really intend to somehow squeeze the Bannings for everything they owned? And how much of the loot would his sticky fingers steal?

The lawyers swapped comments but made no progress. The magistrate called the next item on his docket. Outside the courthouse, Joel and John Wilbanks walked around the square while Russell ducked into a diner.

"We should at least discuss the possibility of settlement," Wilbanks said.

"Okay. I'm listening," Joel said.

"Dunlap is high with his numbers, but not outrageously so. We could offer them $20,000 in cash and see what happens. That's a lot of money, Joel."

"Damned sure is. Where would we find that much?"

"There's about $15,000 in cash in the estate. You and Stella could mortgage the land. My family owns the bank, remember? I'm sure I can arrange a small loan."

"So you want to offer $20,000?"

"Discuss it with Florry. I don't need to remind you that the facts are not with us in this case. Your father did what he did and there's no excuse for it. The jury will be sympathetic to the Bell family, and sympathy is our enemy."

CHAPTER 39

Errol McLeish scoffed at the suggestion that Jackie settle so cheaply. Nor would they consider $25,000. McLeish wanted it all—the land, the house, the livestock, the people who worked there—and he had a plan to get it.

Late in February, he and Jackie drove to Oxford and checked into a hotel on the square. Same room, though they were not yet married.

The trial began on the morning of the twenty-fourth. Jackie, the plaintiff, sat with Dunlap and her lawyers, and was attractive in solid black. Florry, on tranquilizers, sat between John and Russell Wilbanks, with Joel right behind her.

When the opportunity had presented itself, Joel spoke to Jackie, shook her hand, and tried to be polite. She did not. She was the grieving widow, out for justice and revenge. Florry loathed her and never acknowledged her presence.

As Judge Stratton went through the preliminaries with the fifty or so prospective jurors, Joel turned and faced them and the spectators. There were a few reporters in the front row. The doors opened, and much to his dismay a class of third-year law students filed in with their professor. It was a federal procedure class, and since the trial had some notoriety, it needed to be studied. He noticed a few other law students in the crowd, watching intently. At that moment, he wished he had chosen another law school on a campus in another state.

The morning was consumed with jury selection, and by noon six had been selected and seated. A seventh would sit as the alternate. Since it was a civil case, four votes would be needed for a verdict. Three to three would hang and cause a retrial.

After lunch, Burch Dunlap walked to the podium in front of the jury box, straightened his fine silk tie, flashed a big smile, and welcomed the jurors to the center of justice. Joel watched every move, absorbed every word, and in his biased opinion Dunlap was a bit sappy in his gratitude for the jurors' time and service, but he soon got down to business. He explained the facts and said liability was clear. It was a cold-blooded murder that led to a just execution of a man they would not meet. The real defendant was dead; therefore, under the law, the plaintiff was forced to proceed against his estate. Much of the trial would revolve around the value of Dexter Bell's life, a value that could not really be measured. Dunlap suggested no amount; that would certainly come later. But he left no doubt that Reverend Bell was an extraordinary man, superb father, devoted pastor, and so on, and his life was worth a lot of money, even though he earned little as a preacher.

As Dunlap spoke with great eloquence, Joel could almost feel the family's assets slipping away. Several times during his opening statement, Dunlap referred to Pete Banning as a "wealthy farmer" and a "rich landowner." Each time Joel heard it, he flinched and glanced at the jurors. He and Stella had not been raised to believe their family was wealthy, and being described as such by a silver-tongued orator was discomfiting. The jurors, all middle-class at most, seemed to be onboard. Rich farmer murders poor preacher. The theme was established at the very beginning of the trial, and it would stick with the jurors until the end.

John Wilbanks made a brief opening statement in which he asked the jurors if it was really fair to make the family of a man convicted of murder pay the price for his sins. Pete Banning's family had done nothing wrong, absolutely nothing. Through no fault of their own, his children had also lost a father. Why should they be punished? Hadn't the Banning family been punished enough? The lawsuit was nothing but a naked grab for the hard-earned money of a family that had toiled the soil for decades, fine, honest, hardworking people who were not rich and were not wealthy and should not be subjected to such claims. In Joel's biased opinion, John Wilbanks did a splendid job of portraying the plaintiff as opportunistic and money hungry. He was almost indignant when he sat down.

The first witness was Jackie Bell, and just as she had done some thirteen months earlier in Clanton, she took the stand in a very tight dress and was soon crying. As she described finding her dead husband, the jurors, all men, absorbed every word and seemed quite sympathetic. John Wilbanks passed on cross-examination.

Nix Gridley was next. He laid out the crime scene as he'd found it, produced the same enlarged photos of poor Dexter bleeding out, showed the jury the Colt .45 owned by the accused, and stated to a certainty that Pete Banning, a man he had known well, had indeed been executed in the electric chair. Nix witnessed the execution, and had been present when the coroner pronounced Pete dead.

After Nix was excused, Burch Dunlap entered into evidence, without objection, certified copies of the court orders finding Pete guilty of the first-degree murder of Dexter Bell, and the orders from the supreme court affirming his conviction.

After the first long day of trial, it had been clearly established that Pete Banning murdered Dexter Bell and had paid with his life. Finally, thought Joel. While it was the same old dreary news to him, it was riveting to the jurors.

With causation established, the trial moved to the question of damages. At nine Thursday morning, Jackie Bell returned to the witness stand and produced the family's tax returns for the years 1940 through 1945. At the time of his death Dexter was being paid a salary of $2,400 a year by the Methodist church of Clanton, and had not received a raise since 1942. He had no other income, nor did she. The family lived in a parsonage provided at no cost by the church, with utilities included in the package. Obviously, the family lived frugally but that was the life they had chosen and they had been content with it.

She was excused, and Dunlap called as an expert witness an economics professor from Ole Miss, one Dr. Potter. He held several degrees, had written a few books, and it was immediately apparent he knew more about money and finances than anyone else in the courtroom. John Wilbanks prodded with a few questions about his field of expertise, but was careful not to push too hard and get embarrassed.

On direct from Burch Dunlap, Dr. Potter went through the history of Dexter Bell's earnings as a pastor, compared that history to other ministers on similar paths, and crunched all manner of numbers. At the time of his death, at the age of thirty-nine, Dexter's total compensation was, in Potter's opinion, $3,300 per year. Assuming a conservative annual rate of inflation of 2 percent, and assuming Dexter would work until he was seventy years old, which was the norm for ministers in 1948, then his expected future lifetime earnings amounted to $106,000.

Dunlap produced large color graphs and charts as he walked Dr. Potter through the numbers, and managed to convey to the jurors that the money being discussed was real, hard cash that had been taken away from the Bell family because of Dexter's untimely death.

On cross-examination, John Wilbanks hit Dr. Potter hard with some of his assumptions. Was it fair to assume Dexter would work until the age of seventy? Fair to assume he would always be employed? Fair to assume a constant rate of inflation? And unending pay raises? Fair to assume his wife would not remarry a husband who earned far more? Wilbanks cast some doubt and scored some points, but, at least to Joel, he was attacking numbers that were so modest to begin with. Preachers earned little. Why make their meager salaries appear even less valuable?

The next witness was a real estate appraiser from Tupelo. After establishing his qualifications, Dunlap asked him if he had appraised the Banning property. He said that indeed he had and offered a binder. John Wilbanks practically exploded and objected to further testimony. This skirmish was expected and had not been settled before the trial.

Wilbanks argued strongly that the land did not belong to Pete Banning and was not to be included in his estate. Pete had gifted it to his children, in much the same manner as his parents and grandparents and great-grandparents had handed it down. He produced certified copies of the deed to Joel and Stella.

Dunlap roared back that the conveyance by Pete was fraudulent, and this upset Judge Stratton. He lectured Dunlap on using such prejudicial words as "fraudulent" when nothing had been proven. Wilbanks reminded the judge and Dunlap that there was another lawsuit pending in the Chancery Court of Ford County that dealt with the transfer of the land. Judge Stratton agreed and ruled that Dunlap could not attempt to prove that Pete Banning owned the land when he died. That matter had not been settled.

It was a crucial win for the defense, and Dunlap apparently had miscalculated. However, he was an actor onstage and soon collected himself. After the appraiser left, he called Florry to the stand as an adverse witness. Wilbanks anticipated this and had tried to prep her for the ordeal. He assured her she would not be on the stand for long, but she was still a wreck.

After a few preliminary questions, Dunlap asked her if she was the executrix of her brother's estate. Yes. And when was she appointed? Ignoring the stares of the jurors and locking in on the friendly face of her nephew, Florry explained that her brother, Pete, made a new will after he was sentenced to die. Dunlap presented a certified copy of the will and asked her to identify it, which she did.

Dunlap said, "Thank you. Now, pursuant to the law, and to the advice of Mr. Wilbanks here, have you filed an inventory of the assets and liabilities of the estate of Pete Banning?"

"Yes." Wilbanks demanded that she keep her answers short.

Dunlap picked up some more papers and handed them to Florry. He asked, "Do you recognize this as the inventory you filed in his estate in November of last year?"

"Yes."

"Once it's filed it's public record, right?"

"I suppose. You're the lawyer."

"This is true. Now, Miss Banning, if you will, would you please look at the list of assets that you filed in this inventory, paragraph C, second page, and read them to the jury?"

"Why can't they just read it themselves?"

"Please, Miss Banning."

Florry made a fuss out of adjusting her reading glasses, flipping a page, locating paragraph C, all performed in obvious frustration. Finally, she said, "Well, number one is Pete's personal checking account at First State, balance of $1,800. Number two is his farm account, same bank,

$5,300. Number three is his savings account, same bank, $7,100. Is that enough?"

"Please read on, Miss Banning," Dunlap replied patiently.

"A 1946 Ford pickup truck, Pete bought it new when he came home from the war, approximate value of $750. I suppose you want to take that too."

"Please continue, Miss Banning."

"His car, a 1939 Pontiac, value of $600." Joel shifted his weight as he pondered the loss of the car, one he had been driving since last summer.

Florry went on to testify that the estate included two John Deere tractors, some trailers and plows, and other assorted items of farm equipment, all appraised at $9,000. It was indeed a farm, complete with the usual collection of pigs, chickens, cows, goats, mules, and horses, and an auctioneer had placed a value on the animals of $3,000. "Plus or minus a chicken or two," she said like a real smart-ass.

"And that's all," she said. "Unless you want his boots and underwear."

She explained that Pete owed no money when he died and no claims had been registered against his estate.

"And what's the value of the Banning mansion?" Dunlap asked loudly.

John Wilbanks bolted to his feet and growled, "Objection, Your Honor! The house is not separate from the land, and the land was deeded to the children. We just had this argument."

"Indeed we did," Judge Stratton said, obviously annoyed with Dunlap, who mumbled something like "I'll withdraw the question."

Withdrawn or otherwise, the word "mansion" hung in the air. When Florry was excused and stepped down, Joel glanced at the jurors and was not comforted by their faces. The rich guy who lived in the mansion had killed a humble servant of God, and justice was in order.

In the usual course of a wrongful death trial, the defense would contest liability with a parade of witnesses all testifying that the death was not caused by the accused, or that the deceased was at least partially responsible through his own negligence. Not so in *Bell v. Estate of Banning*. John Wilbanks could offer nothing to create even the slightest doubt about the cause of death, and to attempt such a feeble effort would risk losing what little credibility he had.

Instead, he chose to nibble around the edges of the damages and lighten the impact of the verdict. He called his only witness, another economics expert, and one from California, of all places. Wilbanks believed in the old maxim that, at least in litigation, the farther an expert traveled the more valid his testimony.

His name was Dr. Satterfield and he taught at Stanford. He'd written books and testified a lot. The gist of his testimony was that the total sum of Dexter Bell's future earnings, whatever figure the jury accepted, must be reduced significantly to show a fair picture of its present value. Using a large colored chart, he tried to explain to the jury that, for example, $1,000 paid each year for ten straight years equals $10,000. Simple enough. But if ten thousand was given in a lump sum right now, the recipient would be able to turn around and invest that money, and the eventual earnings would be much greater. Therefore, it was only fair to reduce the immediate payment—that is, the verdict—to a present value.

Dr. Satterfield explained that this method had been adopted by courts across the country in similar cases. He implied that perhaps Mississippi was a bit behind the curve, and this did not sit well with the jurors. His bottom line, when a "more likely rate of inflation was applied," was the figure of $41,000 in lost future earnings for the family of Reverend Bell.

John Wilbanks believed that any verdict under $50,000 was survivable. The land could be mortgaged to withstand it. Most farmers were saddled with debt anyway, and with hard work, decent weather, good prices—the daily prayer on every farm—the Bannings could eventually pay off the mortgage. Wilbanks was also counting on the traditional conservatism of rural jurors. People with almost no spare change always found it difficult to award big sums to others.

On cross-examination, Burch Dunlap haggled with Dr. Satterfield over his numbers, and within minutes everyone was confused over present values, discounted values, projected rates of inflation, and structured payouts. The jurors especially seemed baffled, and as Joel watched them drown he realized that Dunlap was intentionally muddying the water.

Late in the afternoon, after the testimony was over and the lawyers had finished their motions and legal posturing, Burch Dunlap rose to address the jury. Without notes and seemingly without forethought, he talked about the gravity of this wrongful death, one not caused by negligence. At times, everyone is negligent, so we can understand why certain accidents happen. We are all human. But this was no accident. This was a well-planned, premeditated, cold-blooded murder. A fatal assault against an unarmed man by a soldier who knew how to kill.

Joel could not take his eyes off the jurors, and they were spellbound by Dunlap.

The damages for such a monstrous deed? Let's forget about the dead people—Reverend Bell and Pete Banning—and let's talk about those left behind. He, Dunlap, wasn't too worried about the Banning family. The two kids were being beautifully educated. Florry, well, she owned her own section of land, free and clear. They've had privileged lives. What about Jackie Bell and her three children?

Here, Dunlap digressed into a side story that was nothing short of brilliant. Near tears, he told the jury of how his own father died when he was only six years old, and of the heartbreaking devastation it brought to his mother and siblings. He went on, and when he began to describe the burial and watching his father's casket disappear into the grave, John Wilbanks finally stood and said, "Please, Your Honor, this has nothing to do with our case."

Judge Stratton shrugged and said, "It's a closing argument, Mr. Wilbanks. I give great leeway."

Dunlap thanked His Honor, then suddenly turned nasty and ridiculed the "wealthy Bannings" for trying to appear broke. They owned "hundreds of acres of rich farmland" while his clients, the Bells, had nothing. Don't be fooled by the Bannings and their lawyers.

He ridiculed Professor Satterfield from Stanford, and

asked the jurors who had a better understanding of life in rural Mississippi—"some bow-tied, pointy-headed liberal professor from California, or Dr. Potter from Ole Miss"?

Dunlap performed beautifully, and when he sat down, Joel felt nauseated.

John Wilbanks never mentioned liability, but chose to argue the numbers. He tried desperately to lowball everything, but the jurors appeared unmoved.

During his rebuttal, Burch Dunlap took off the gloves and demanded punitive damages, damages invoked in only the most offensive cases. Damages fitting here because of Pete Banning's callous disregard for human life and his complete lack of responsibility.

Judge Stratton had presided over many trials, and he had a hunch this jury would not take long. He sent them away at 6:00 p.m. and adjourned court. An hour later, the jury was ready.

In a unanimous verdict, it found Pete Banning and his estate liable for the death of Dexter Bell, and awarded $50,000 in actual damages and $50,000 in punitive damages. For the second time in less than a year, Burch Dunlap set the record for the largest verdict in the Northern District of Mississippi.

CHAPTER 40

As Joel's first year of law school wound down, he became more reclusive, even antisocial. The verdict against his father's estate was well-known in legal circles, not to mention the now infamous execution. The Banning family was in free fall, and Joel suspected there were a lot of whispers behind his back. He envied Stella, a thousand miles away.

He drove to Whitfield to sit with his mother for a long weekend. First, though, Dr. Hilsabeck wanted to chat, and they strolled the grounds on a glorious spring day, with azaleas and dogwoods blooming. Hilsabeck lit a pipe, clasped his hands behind him, and ambled along slowly, as if heavily burdened.

"She's not making a lot of progress," he said gravely. "She's been here for two years and I'm not pleased with her condition."

"Thanks for admitting that," Joel replied. "I've seen little improvement in the past eight months."

"She cooperates to a point; then she shuts down. Something traumatic happened to her, Joel, something she cannot, or will not, confront. From what we know, your mother was a strong woman with an outsized personality with never a hint of mental instability or depression. There were several miscarriages, but they are not uncommon. With each, she withdrew and went through periods of darkness, probably temporary depression, but she always bounced back. The news that your father was missing and presumed dead was horrible, and we've discussed this many times. Me, you, Stella, Florry, we've covered this. That was in May of 1942. Almost three years passed, and, as you've said, the family did the only thing it could do—it survived. But something happened to her, Joel, during that period. Something traumatic, and I simply cannot get it out of her."

"Are you suggesting I try?"

"No. It was something so awful I'm not sure she'll ever discuss it. And, as long as she keeps it buried, improvement will be most difficult."

"Do you think it involved Dexter Bell?"

"Yes. If not, why would your father do what he did?"

"That's the big question. I've always assumed it was Bell, but the mystery is, how did my father learn their secrets? Now he's dead, Bell's dead, and she's not talking. Looks like a dead end, Doc."

"Indeed it does. The people who work for the family, have you quizzed them?"

"Not really. Nineva came with the house and doesn't miss much. She's also loyal to a fault and would never utter a word. She practically raised me and Stella, so we know her well. She never talks."

"Even if she might be able to help us?"

"Help us in what way?"

"Perhaps she knows something, saw something, heard something. If she could confide in you and you to me, it could give me the opportunity to confront Liza. It might shock her, and that might be a good thing. She needs to be confronted. We're in a rut here, Joel, and things need to change."

"I guess it's worth a try. What is there to lose?"

They walked past an old gentleman slouched in a wheelchair in the shade of an elm tree. He eyed them suspiciously but said nothing. Both nodded and smiled and Hilsabeck said, "Hello, Harry." But Harry did not respond because Harry had not spoken in ten years. Joel often said hello to Harry as well. Sadly, Joel knew the names of many of building 41's permanent residents. He prayed fervently that his mother would not become one.

"There's something else," Hilsabeck said. "There's a new medication called Thorazine that's slowly making its way onto the market. It's an antipsychotic drug that's being used to treat schizophrenia, depression, and a few other disorders. I think Liza is a good candidate for it."

"Are you asking for my approval?"

"No, just wanted you to know. We'll start it next week."

"Any side effects?"

"So far, the most common one is weight gain, which in her case would be welcome."

"Then I say we do it."

They walked to the edge of a small lake and found a bench in a shaded, cool spot. They sat down and watched some ducks splatter about. "How often does she talk of going home?" Joel asked.

Hilsabeck thought for a moment, took a puff. "Not every day, but it's certainly on her mind. Liza is too young for us to consider her a permanent resident here, so we treat her as if she'll one day be healthy enough to go home. She doesn't dwell on this, but she assumes, as do we, that the day will come. Why do you ask?"

"Because home might be in trouble. I've told you about the lawsuits brought by the family of Dexter Bell. We just lost the first one. We'll appeal, and appeal again, and we'll fight to the end. Another lawsuit is looming, and we could lose it too. There could be liens, judgments, injunctions, even a bankruptcy. A lot of legal maneuvering yet to come, but there is a real possibility that when the dust settles, we could lose the land and the farm."

"And when might this dust settle?"

"Hard to say. Not this year, probably not next. But within two years all of the lawsuits and appeals could be over."

Hilsabeck tapped his pipe on the edge of the bench and scraped out the burned tobacco. He deftly refilled it with fresh tobacco from a pouch, fired up a match, lit the bowl, and took a long puff. Eventually, he said, "That would be catastrophic for her. She dreams of being home with you and Stella. She talks of working the gardens with Amos, of riding her horses, of putting flowers on your father's grave, of cooking and canning with Nineva." Another long puff. "Where would she go?"

"I have no idea, Doc. We haven't had that discussion yet. I'm just looking far down the road. We have good lawyers, but so does the family of Dexter Bell. And in addition to good lawyers, they have the facts and the law on their side."

"It would be devastating, just devastating. I cannot imagine treating Liza if she knew her home was gone."

"Well, just file it away. Meanwhile, we're brawling in court."

On a Friday morning when he was supposed to be in Oxford, Joel awoke early in his own bed, hustled to the kitchen and put on the coffee, bathed and dressed while it was percolating, and was waiting at the kitchen table with a fresh cup when Nineva arrived on the dot at 7:00. They exchanged "Good mornings" and Joel said, "Let's have some coffee, Nineva. We need to talk."

"Don't you want breakfast?" she asked, pulling on an apron.

"No, I'll get something later in town. I'm not much for breakfast."

"Never was, not even as a little boy. A bite or two of eggs and you'd be off. What's on your mind?"

"Fix your coffee."

She took her time with heavy cream and heavier sugar, and finally sat, apprehensively, across the table from him. "We need to talk about Liza," he said. "Her doctor is not happy with her progress down there at Whitfield. There are a lot of secrets in her world, Nineva, little mysteries that don't add up. Until we know what happened to her, there's a good chance Liza is never coming home."

Nineva was already shaking her head as if she knew nothing.

"Pete's gone, Nineva. Liza might be too. There's a chance her doctor can help her but only if the truth is told. How much time did she spend with Dexter Bell when we thought Dad was dead?"

She held her cup with fingers from both hands and took a small sip. She set it on the saucer, thought for a second, and said, "He was here a lot. It was no secret. I was always around, so was Amos, even Jupe. Sometimes Mrs. Bell came with him. They would meet in Mista Banning's study and read the Bible, say a prayer. He never stayed long."

"Were they alone?"

"Sometimes, I guess, but like I say, I was always right here. Nothin' happened between them, not in this house."

"Are you sure, Nineva?"

"Look, Joel, I don't know ever'thing. I wasn't with 'em. You think she fooled around with the preacher?"

"He's dead, isn't he, Nineva? Give me another good reason for Pete killing him. Did they see each other when you weren't around?"

"If I wasn't around how would I know?"

As always, her logic was pure. "So nothing suspicious? Nothing at all?"

Nineva grimaced and rubbed her temples as if coaxing something painful from her memory. Softly, she said, "There was one time."

"Let's have it, Nineva," Joel said, on the verge of a breakthrough.

"She said she had to go to Memphis, said her mother was in the hospital there and in real bad shape. Said she had cancer. Anyways, she wanted the preacher to go visit with her mother in her last days. Said her mother had drifted away from the church and now that she was at the end she really wanted to talk to a preacher to, you know, get things right with God. And since Liza thought so much of Dexter Bell she wanted him to do the Lord's work with her mother in Memphis. Liza hated to drive, as you know, and so she told me one day that she and the preacher would leave early the next day, after you and Stella got off to school, and go to Memphis. Just the two of them. And they did. And I didn't think anything about it. Reverend Bell came in that morning, by hisself, and I fixed him a cup of coffee, and the three of us sat right here and he even said a little prayer asking God for safe travels up there and back, and for His healin' hand on Liza's mother. It was real touchin', as I remember. I thought nothin' of it. Liza told me not to tell you kids about it because she didn't want you worryin' about your grandmother, so I said nothin'. They took off and they were gone all day and came back at dark. Liza said she was carsick and had an upset stomach and went to bed. She didn't feel good for a few days after that, said she thought she caught somethin' at the hospital in Memphis."

"I don't remember that."

"You was busy with school."

"When was this?"

"When? I don't take down notes, Joel."

"Okay, how long after we got the news about Dad? A month, six months, a year?"

"A long time. We heard about Mista Banning, when?"

"May of 1942."

"Right, okay, then it was cool weather; they was pickin' cotton. At least a year after we got the news."

"So the fall of 1943?"

"I guess. I don't do well with dates and times."

"Well, that's odd because her mother didn't die. Grandmother Sweeney is alive and well in Kansas City. Got a letter from her last week."

"Right. I asked Liza how her mother was doin' and all, and she never really wanted to talk about her. Said later that the visit with Reverend Bell must've been a good one because the Lord reached down and healed her."

"So they spent the day together and Liza came home sick. Did you ever get suspicious about it?"

"I didn't think about it."

"I doubt that, Nineva. You don't miss much around here."

"I tend to my business."

"And everyone else's too. Where was Jackie Bell that day?"

"I don't keep up with Jackie Bell."

"But there was no mention of her?"

"I didn't ask. They didn't say."

"Well, did you ever look back at that day and think something didn't add up?"

"Like what?"

"Like, well, there are a lot of preachers in Memphis and plenty between here and there. Why would Liza's mother need a preacher from Clanton? She belongs to an Episcopal church in Memphis, one that Stella and I visited a few times before they moved away. Why wouldn't Liza tell Stella and me that her mother, our grandmother, was real sick in a Memphis hospital? We used to see her from time to time. No one ever told us she had cancer and she damned sure didn't die from it. This whole story smells bad, Nineva, and you were never suspicious?"

"I suppose."

"Suppose what?"

"Well, I'll just tell you. I never understood why it was such a big secret, their trip to Memphis. I remember thinkin' that if her mother was real sick, then she ought to take you kids and go visit. But no, she didn't want you to know about it. That was strange. It was like she and the preacher just wanted to go away for the day, and they needed some reason to feed to me. Yeah, all right, I got suspicious afterward but who was I gonna tell? Amos? I tell him everythin' anyway and he forgets it all. That man."

"Did you tell Pete?"

"He never asked."

"Did you tell Pete?"

"No. I ain't never told nobody, other'n Amos."

Joel left her at the table and went for a long drive through the back roads of Ford County. His head spun as he tried to put the facts into place. He felt like a private investigator who had just tracked down the first major clue to a mystery that seemed permanently unsolved.

As confused as he was, though, he was also convinced that Nineva had not told him everything.

CHAPTER 41

In addition to studying for final exams, Joel wrote the briefs and perfected the appeal of the jury's verdict in federal court. Since stalling was an integral part of their strategy, he and John Wilbanks waited until the last possible day and filed the final brief with the Fifth Circuit Court of Appeals on June 1, 1948.

Two days later, on June 3, Chancellor Abbott Rumbold finally got around to the second lawsuit filed by Jackie Bell, her petition to set aside the allegedly fraudulent conveyance by Pete Banning of his land to his children.

Burch Dunlap had been demanding a trial for months, and Rumbold's docket was not that crowded. However, the docket was the sole province of the chancellor, and he had been manipulating it for decades. Rumbold routinely did whatever John Wilbanks wanted him to do, plus he had enormous sympathy for the Banning family.

If Wilbanks wanted to delay, then the case was certainly in the right court.

Dunlap expected to get a strong dose of home cooking. He wanted to take his lumps, get it over with, perfect his record, and appeal to the state supreme court, where the law meant much more than old friendships.

There were no juries in chancery court. The chancellors ruled like kings, and, as a general rule, the longer they served the more dogmatic they became. Procedures varied from one district to the next and were often changed on the spot.

Rumbold took the bench in the main courtroom without fanfare and said hello. Walter Willy's screeching call to order was reserved for circuit court only. Rumbold would have none of it.

He noticed the nice crowd and welcomed everyone to the festivities. Present were the usual courthouse regulars—the bored retirees who whittled outside in the shade, the county employees on break, the secretaries from just down the hall, Ernie Dowdle, Hop Purdue, and Penrod up in the balcony with a few other Negroes—along with several dozen spectators.

The news of the $100,000 verdict in federal court three months earlier had not been well received around town, and folks were curious. The legend of Pete Banning continued to grow in Ford County, and most of the people took a dim view of Jackie Bell trying to steal land that had been in one family for over a hundred years.

Since Joel and Stella were named defendants in the case, they were required to attend. They sat at the defense table with a Wilbanks on each side and tried to ignore

Jackie Bell at the other table. They were trying to ignore a lot of things—the crowd behind them, the stares from the clerks and lawyers, the fear of being sued and pursued—but the real horror of the moment was the fact that they were seated at a table that was about twenty feet from where their father had been electrocuted eleven months earlier. The entire courtroom, and courthouse for that matter, was a dark, wretched place that they wished to never see again.

Rumbold frowned at Burch Dunlap and said, "I'll allow some very brief opening remarks. For the plaintiff."

Burch stood and held a notepad. "Yes, thanks, Your Honor. Now, most of the facts have been stipulated, so I don't have a lot of witnesses. On September 16 of 1946, some three weeks before the unfortunate death of the Reverend Dexter Bell, the late husband of my client, Mr. Pete Banning executed a quitclaim deed to his section of land, all 640 acres, to his children, the defendants, Joel and Stella Banning, in equal shares. A copy of that deed has been entered into evidence."

"I've read it," Rumbold growled.

"Yes, sir. And we will prove that this deed is the first deed to be used by the Bannings to transfer their land to the next generation since 1818. The family has always passed down their land through last wills and testaments, never deeds. Pete Banning's purpose in using this deed was clearly to protect his land because he was contemplating the murder of Dexter Bell. Plain and simple."

Dunlap sat down and John Wilbanks was already on his feet. "May it please the court, Your Honor, I'm not sure Mr. Dunlap is smart enough to explain to us what Pete Banning was contemplating when he signed the deed. He's correct, though, this land has been in the family since 1818, back when Pete Banning's great-great-grandfather Jonas Banning started piecing together his farm. The family has always kept the land and added to it whenever possible. Frankly, it's appalling that a nonresident of Mississippi, or anyone else for that matter, now wants to take it from the family. Thank you."

"Call your first witness," Rumbold said to Dunlap. "You have the burden of going forward."

"The Honorable Claude Skinner, attorney-at-law."

Skinner rose from the spectator section, walked through the bar, swore to tell the truth, and took the witness stand.

Dunlap said, "Please state your name and occupation."

"Claude Skinner, attorney. My office is in Tupelo and I do primarily real estate work."

"And when did you meet Pete Banning?"

"He came to my office in September of 1946 and asked me to prepare a property deed for him. He had full title to a section of land here in Ford County, along with the house on it, and he wanted to deed it to his two children."

"Had you met him before that day?"

"No, sir, I had not. He brought with him a plat and a full description of the property and house, and I asked him who did his legal work in this county. He said it was the Wilbanks firm but he preferred not to use them for this matter."

"Did he give a reason for not using the Wilbanks firm?"

"He did not and I did not inquire. I found Mr. Banning to be a man of few words."

"And you prepared the deed as he wished?"

"I did. He returned a week later and signed the deed. My secretary notarized it, then mailed it with the filing fee to the chancery clerk just down the hall. I charged him $15 for my work and he paid me in cash."

"Did you ever ask him why he was deeding the property to his children?"

"Well, sort of. After reviewing the chain of title, I realized that the family had never used deeds before. Their property always passed down through wills. I commented on this, and Mr. Banning said, and I quote, 'I'm just protecting my assets.'"

"Protecting from what?"

"He didn't say. I didn't ask."

"No further questions."

John Wilbanks looked rather perturbed as he stood and frowned at Skinner. "When you realized that my law firm had represented Mr. Banning for many years, did it occur to you that perhaps a phone call to me might be appropriate?"

"No, sir. It was quite evident that Mr. Banning did not want to use your firm or any other lawyer in this county. He drove to Tupelo to hire me for that reason."

"So a professional courtesy by you was not considered."

"It was not needed, in my opinion."

"No further questions."

"You may step down," Rumbold said. "Call your next witness."

Dunlap stood and said, "Your Honor, we would like

to call Mr. Joel Banning to the stand, as an adverse witness."

"Any objections?" Rumbold asked John Wilbanks. The move was expected and Joel was thoroughly prepared for his testimony.

"None," Wilbanks said.

Joel swore to tell the truth and sat in the witness chair. He offered a quick smile to his sister, took in the view from a unique vantage point, nodded at Florry in the front row, then braced himself for questions from one of the state's finest trial lawyers.

Dunlap began with "Mr. Banning, where were you when you heard the news that your father had been arrested for the murder of Dexter Bell?"

Joel instinctively said, "Why is that relevant to the issues in this case?"

"Please answer the question, sir," Dunlap replied, somewhat startled by the question.

"And why don't you answer my question?" Joel shot back like a real smart-ass.

John Wilbanks was on his feet. "Your Honor, the witness has a point. The question asked by Mr. Dunlap is completely irrelevant to the issues in this case. I object to it."

"Sustained," Rumbold said at full volume. "I see no relevance."

"Never mind," Dunlap mumbled. Joel wanted to grin at him as if to say, "Score one for me," but managed to maintain a frown.

Dunlap asked, "Now, before your father deeded this property to you in September of 1946, did he discuss it with you?"

"No."

"Did he discuss it with your sister?"

"You'll have to ask her."

"You don't know?"

"I don't think he did but I'm not completely certain."

"Where were you on that date?"

"At college."

"And where was she?"

"At college."

"And after that date, did your father ever discuss this deed with you?"

"Not until the day before he died."

"And that was when?"

Joel hesitated, cleared his voice, and said slowly and with volume, "My father was executed in this courtroom on July 10 of last year."

After that bit of drama, Dunlap reached for a file and began withdrawing documents. One by one, he handed Joel copies of old wills signed by his ancestors, and asked him to validate each. The entire lot had already been introduced into evidence, but Dunlap needed some live testimony to spruce up his case. His intentions were clear, his points well made: The Banning family had religiously handed down their land to the next generation through well-prepared wills and testaments. Pete took ownership of his 640 acres and the house in 1932, when his mother died. She acquired it three years earlier, when her husband died. Slowly and studiously, Joel laid out the chain of title, along with a fair amount of family history. He knew it by heart and had virtually memorized the old wills. In every generation, the men died first—and at disturbingly young ages—and passed the land to their wives, none of whom remarried.

Dunlap asked, "So your father was the first man in the history of your family to bypass his wife in favor of his children, correct?"

"That's correct."

"Does this strike you as unusual?"

"It's no secret, sir, that my mother is having some problems. I prefer not to go into this."

"I didn't ask you to."

As the hours passed, Dunlap slowly proved his point. Pete's deed was suspicious on many levels. Joel, Stella, Florry, and even John Wilbanks admitted privately that Pete signed the deed to protect his land as he planned to kill Dexter Bell, and this became evident.

By noon, there were no more witnesses. The lawyers made some brief remarks, and Rumbold said he would issue a ruling "in the future."

"When can we expect a ruling, Your Honor?" Dunlap asked.

"I don't have deadlines, Mr. Dunlap," Rumbold snapped, irritated. "I'll review the documents and my notes and I'll issue a ruling in due course."

Dunlap, with an audience, drew a line in the dirt. "Well, certainly, Your Honor, it shouldn't take long. The trial lasted less than four hours. The facts and issues are clear. Why should there be a delay?"

Rumbold's cheeks flushed red and he pointed a crooked finger at Dunlap. "I'm in charge around here, Mr. Dunlap, and I don't need any advice on how to run things. You've said enough."

Dunlap knew what was common knowledge among

local lawyers. Rumbold could sit on a case forever. The rules provided no time frame for chancellors to decide their cases, and the state supreme court, which always comprised several ex-chancellors, had never been willing to implement deadlines.

"Adjourned," Rumbold said, still glaring at Dunlap, and slammed down his gavel.

Jackie Bell and Errol McLeish left the courtroom without a word to anyone and went straight to the car. They drove to a home a few miles from town and lunched with her closest friend from the Clanton days. Myra was her source of gossip and information about who was saying what in church and in the town, and she didn't like the new preacher, Dexter's replacement. Few in the church liked him and she had a list of grievances. The truth was that everyone missed Dexter, even now, almost two years after his death.

Nor did Myra like Errol McLeish either. He had shifty eyes and a soft handshake, and he had a quiet way of manipulating Jackie. Even though he was a lawyer who owned properties and put on airs about money, Myra suspected that his real objective was Jackie and whatever she might get out of the Bannings.

He had far too much influence over Jackie, who, in Myra's opinion, was still fragile from her tragedy. Myra had voiced this concern, confidentially of course, to other ladies in the church. There were already rumors that Jackie had designs on the Banning land and fine home, and that McLeish would be calling the shots.

A source at the Bedford Hotel leaked the gossip that

they signed into one room as Mr. and Mrs. Errol McLeish, though Jackie had assured Myra she had no plans to get married.

Two unmarried adults in the same hotel room in downtown Clanton. And one was the preacher's widow.

CHAPTER 42

The train ride from Memphis to Kansas City took seven and a half hours, with more stops than they could keep up with. But they didn't care. It was summertime. They were out of school, away from the farm, riding in first class, where the porters served chilled wine when beckoned. Stella read the collected short stories of Eudora Welty while Joel struggled through *Absalom, Absalom!* He had seen Mr. Faulkner twice around Oxford, where his presence was hardly noticed. It was no secret that he liked to have supper late at night at a restaurant called the Mansion, just off the square, and Joel had sat close to him once as he ate alone. Before Joel finished law school, he was determined to muster the courage to introduce himself. He dreamed of having a bourbon on the great man's porch and telling the tragic story of his father. Perhaps Mr. Faulkner had heard the story. Perhaps he would use it in a novel.

From the station in Kansas City, they took a cab to a

modest home in the center of town. Papa and Gran Sweeney moved there from Memphis after the war, and neither Joel nor Stella had ever visited. The truth was they had spent little time with Liza's parents because, as they realized as they grew older, Pete didn't care for the Sweeneys and the feelings were mutual.

The Sweeneys had no money but had always tried to rub elbows with the upper classes. That was one reason Liza spent so much time at the Peabody when in high school. Her parents pressured her to. However, instead of snagging a rich Memphis boy for a husband, she'd gotten herself pregnant by a farmer from Mississippi, of all places.

As with most Memphis people, the Sweeneys looked far down their noses at anyone from Mississippi. They had been polite to Pete when Liza first brought him home, secretly hoping he was not the one, regardless of his good looks and West Point credentials. And before they could seriously object, he swept her away in a marriage that left them traumatized. They weren't certain that she was pregnant when she eloped, but little Joel arrived quite soon thereafter. For years they had been forced to assure their friends that he was born a full nine months after the "wedding."

When Pete was presumed dead, the Sweeneys provided little comfort to Liza, at least in her opinion. They seldom visited the farm, and when they did venture into the boondocks they were always eager to leave as soon as they arrived. Privately, they were embarrassed that their daughter had chosen to live in such a backward place. As ignorant city people, they had no appreciation of the land, the cotton, or livestock or fresh eggs and vegetables.

They were appalled that the Bannings used "coloreds" to work in the house and toil in the fields. When Pete returned from the dead, they showed little interest and did not see him for months after he came home.

When the war ended, Mr. Sweeney was transferred to Kansas City, a move that was described as a major promotion, but was in reality a desperate effort to save a job. Their new home was even smaller than the one in Memphis, but both girls were gone and they didn't need a lot of space. Then Liza had her breakdown and was sent to Whitfield. The Sweeneys told no one that their younger daughter had been banished to an insane asylum deeper down into Mississippi. They visited her once and were horrified at her condition and her surroundings.

Then Pete was arrested, tried, and executed, and the Sweeneys were grateful they had moved even farther away from Clanton.

Their only contact had been the occasional letters from Joel and Stella, who were growing up as the years flew by, and perhaps it was time to reach out and have a visit. They welcomed them into their home and seemed genuinely thrilled that they had traveled all the way to Kansas City. Over a long dinner, of impossibly bland food because Gran had never liked to cook, they talked of college and law school and plans for the future. They talked about Liza. Stella and Joel had just spent two days with her and claimed to have noticed improvement. Her doctors were optimistic that some new medications were working. She had gained a few pounds. The Sweeneys wanted to travel south to see her but Papa's work schedule was downright brutal.

There was no mention of the mountain of legal troubles facing the Bannings, not that Papa and Gran would care much anyway. They preferred to talk about themselves and all the wonderful and wealthy friends they had made in Kansas City. It was a vast improvement over Memphis. Surely the kids were not thinking of settling in Mississippi.

Stella slept in the spare bedroom while Joel took the sofa. After a rough night, he awoke to sounds in the kitchen and the smell of coffee. Papa was at the table, eating toast and flipping hurriedly through the morning paper, while Gran mixed pancake batter. After a few minutes of chatting, Papa grabbed his briefcase and hustled away, eager to get to the office to save an important deal.

"He just works all the time," Gran said as soon as he left. "Let's sit and chat."

Stella soon joined them and they enjoyed a long breakfast of pancakes and sausage. About halfway through, Stella broached the subject of an assignment she was working on for a class in the fall. She was required to gather as much information as possible about the health and fitness histories of her immediate relatives. The profiles would be studied in class with the goal of projecting the longevity of each student. On the Banning side, things looked rather grim. Pete's father had died of a heart attack at forty-nine; his mother of pneumonia at fifty. Aunt Florry was fifty and seemed to be in reasonably good health, but not a single Banning, male or female, in the past century had lived to see seventy.

Joel claimed to be helping with the project and took notes. They discussed Gran's parents, both dead, as well as Mr. Sweeney's.

Mrs. Sweeney was sixty-six and claimed to be in excellent health. She was suffering from no maladies and taking no medications. She had never had cancer, heart disease, or any other serious illness. She had been hospitalized twice in Memphis for the births of her daughters, nothing else. She hated hospitals and tried to avoid them. Joel and Stella claimed to be relieved to learn that they had inherited more promising genes from the Sweeney side.

If Nineva told the truth, as she almost always did, why would Liza and Dexter Bell lie and create the ruse of visiting her mother, who was dying of cancer in a Memphis hospital? And hide it from the kids and everyone else?

Which led to the next question: What did they really do that day?

Two nights in Kansas City were enough. Gran drove them to the station and everybody had a hug. Promises were made to see each other soon and keep in touch. Back in the dining car, Joel and Stella took deep breaths and asked for some wine.

They stopped in St. Louis and checked into a downtown hotel. Joel wanted to watch a Cardinals game at Sportsman's Park and insisted that his sister go with him. She had no interest in baseball but really had no choice. The team was in second place. Stan Musial was on a rampage and leading the league in hitting and homers, and this meant a great deal to her brother. Both enjoyed the game.

From St. Louis, they continued east, switched trains in Louisville and Pittsburgh, and finally arrived at Union Station in D.C. on the evening of June 17. Stella's two-month internship with a textbook publisher began the following Monday and she needed to find a cheap room.

Joel's hit-or-miss unpaid summer clerkship with the Wilbanks firm would resume when he returned to Clanton. He was not looking forward to it. He was fed up with the law and law school and was thinking of skipping a year, maybe two. He wanted to get away, to go search for adventure out west, where he could hide from all the crap he was dealing with. Why couldn't he spend a few months fishing for trout in shallow mountain streams instead of sitting through dull classes, or driving to Whitfield for another depressing visit, or worrying about which legal hijinks Burch Dunlap might be cooking up next, or stopping by the pink cottage to hold Florry's hand as opera wailed in the background?

He was low on cash, so he passed on first class and bought a regular ticket to Memphis. He was sitting on a bar stool drinking a beer in Union Station when she walked by. Short black hair, dark eyes, perfect features. Maybe twenty years old, a real stunner, and he wasn't the only man in the bar to take notice. Tall, thin, nicely proportioned. When she was out of sight he returned to his beer, and his troubles, and found it hard to believe that he had passed on a first-class ticket because he was worried about money.

He drained his glass, walked toward departures, and there she was again. He maneuvered close and hoped she was going his way. She was, and he noticed a couple of other men measuring her up and down. He boarded behind her and managed to snag the seat next to her. He got himself situated, ignored her, opened a magazine, and stuck his nose in it. With their elbows almost touching, he managed to sneak another glance as the train jolted and began to move. There was some exotic ethnic stuff in play, and the result was stunning. Joel had never seen a face as beautiful. She read a paperback and acted as if she were alone on an empty train. Must be a defensive mechanism, he thought. She probably gets hounded every time she leaves home.

Outside D.C., as the temperature rose, he stood and removed his jacket. She glanced up. He smiled; she did not. He sat down and asked, "Where you headed?"

A smile that weakened his knees. "Jackson."

There were several Jacksons down south and fortunately they were all at least a thousand miles away. If he got lucky, he would be at her elbow for hours. "Mississippi?"

"Yes."

"I know it well. That your home?"

"No, I'm from Biloxi, but I'll stay a night or two in Jackson."

Soft, sultry voice, a trace of Gulf Coast accent. To the rest of Mississippi, the coast was another world. Heavily Catholic, influenced by the French, Spanish, Creoles, Indians, and Africans, it had become a melting pot with lots of Italians, Yugoslavs, Lebanese, Chinese, and, as always, Irish.

"I like Jackson," he said, which was only partially true, but it was his turn to say something.

"It's okay," she said. She had lowered her paperback, a clear sign to him that she wanted to chat. "Where do you hang out in Jackson?" she asked.

Whitfield, because my mother is locked away in the nuthouse. He would offer his first name but not his last. That was his defensive mechanism. "There's a little speakeasy behind the Heidelberg that I'm quite fond of. I'm Joel."

"I'm Mary Ann. Malouf."

"Where does Malouf come from?"

"My father is Lebanese; my mother is Irish."

"And the dominant genes win. You are quite beautiful." He couldn't believe he had just said that. What an idiot!

She smiled and again his heart skipped a beat.

"Where are you going?" she asked.

"I'll get off at Memphis." Or, I'll ride this train to Mars and back if you'll stay right there. "I go to school at Ole Miss. Law school." One reason to stay in law school was that young ladies liked to chat with young men who were about to become lawyers. During his first year at Ole Miss, he had quickly learned this clever trick and used it whenever appropriate.

"How long have you been at Ole Miss?" she asked.

"This will be my second year."

"I haven't seen you around."

"Around? Around where?"

"Around campus. I'll be a sophomore at Ole Miss this fall."

The school had four thousand students and only 15 percent were female. How had he missed her? He smiled and said, "Small world, I guess. The law students tend to stay in one place." He marveled at his good fortune. Not only did he have her to himself for the next ten hours, but they would be on the same campus in a couple of months. For a rare moment, he had reason to smile.

"What brought you to D.C.?" she asked.

"I was helping my sister get moved in, a summer job. We're from a small town not far from Oxford. And you?"

"Visiting my fiancé. He works for a Senate committee."

And just like that, the party ended. He hoped he didn't frown or grimace or look as though he might weep. He hoped he managed to keep the same pleasant look and seem somewhat understanding, which he doubted in the face of such a calamity.

"That's nice," he managed to say. "When is the big day?"

"We're not sure. After I graduate. We're in no hurry."

With romance and a future together no longer a possibility, they talked about their plans for the rest of the summer, and college and law school and what they hoped to do after graduation. As gorgeous as she was, Joel eventually lost interest and fell asleep.

CHAPTER 43

After Rumbold had sat on the case for three months without a word, Burch Dunlap took action, though his maneuver was ineffective and designed only to embarrass the chancellor. In early September, he petitioned the state supreme court for an order demanding a ruling from Rumbold within thirty days. Nowhere in the rule book was such a petition allowed, or even mentioned, and Dunlap knew it. In his petition he claimed bias on the part of Rumbold and made much of the fact that the chancellor should have recused himself. He summarized the testimony and proof during the trial that lasted only hours. He covered the law nicely, said it was straightforward and uncomplicated, and summed up everything by saying, "The docket for the Twenty-Second Chancery District is rather light. Even a cursory review of it reveals the chancellor's workload is not demanding. It is inconceivable that such a wise, respected, and experienced jurist as the Honorable Abbott Rumbold could not have decided this case and issued a ruling within a matter of days. A delay of three months, and counting, is unfair to the parties. Justice delayed is justice denied."

John Wilbanks admired the gall of Dunlap and thought his ploy was brilliant. The supreme court would dismiss it without comment, but the court was also being forewarned in an unconventional manner that an important case was coming its way and perhaps it involved some home cooking up in Ford County. Wilbanks filed a one-page response in which he reminded the court that the rules of procedure did not allow such petitions, nor did they allow lawyers to attempt to create new rules of their own volition.

The supreme court ignored the petition and refused to dignify it with a response.

One month later, and without a peep from old Rumbold, Dunlap filed another, identical petition. John Wilbanks's response included a reminder that Dunlap's frivolous petitions were causing the litigants to incur unnecessary legal fees. Dunlap fired back. Wilbanks responded. The supreme court was not amused. Rumbold continued napping.

Joel's last class each Wednesday ended at noon, and he fell into the habit of driving home for lunch. Marietta cooked something delicious each Wednesday, and he and Aunt Florry ate on her back porch with the birds cawing in the distance. Beyond her aviary the acres were laden with cotton and the picking would start as soon as the weather cooled. They had the same conversations about Stella and Liza and law school, but they did not dwell on the lawsuits and legal troubles. Losing the land was never discussed.

After a long lunch, Joel stopped by his home to check on Nineva and Amos and make sure nothing had changed. It had not. He usually met with Buford to discuss the cotton. And he eventually made it to town, where he parked on the square and walked into the Wilbanks firm for a few hours of work. John and Russell assigned him briefs to research and write in his spare time at Ole Miss. Late in the day they would have a quick bourbon on the terrace; then Joel would load up his files and head back to Oxford.

After a couple of attempts, he realized he could not spend the night in his home. The place was too quiet, lonely, and depressing. There were too many photographs of the family in happier times, too many reminders. In his father's study, on the wall next to his desk, there was a large photo of Pete taken the day he graduated from West Point. Joel had admired it his entire life. Now it was so heartbreaking he couldn't make himself look at it.

He and Stella had discussed removing all of the photos and books and medals, and boxing them all up for storage, but couldn't muster the energy. Besides, Liza might return one day and attempt to renew her life, and such memories would be important to her.

So their fine home sat gloomy, dark, and deserted, with only Nineva easing through it each day, dusting here and there and doing as little as possible.

With each visit to the farm, Joel found himself eager to leave it. His life there would never be the same. His father was dead. His mother's future was uncertain. Stella was headed for the bright lights up north and a life far removed from Ford County. The Wilbanks brothers were dropping serious hints about Joel joining their firm after graduation, but that would not happen. In Clanton, he would always be "Pete Banning's boy," the son of the guy they fried in the electric chair right up there in the main courtroom.

Seriously? Did they really expect Joel to practice law in a courtroom where they killed his father? Did they really expect him to live a normal, successful life in a town where half the people viewed his father as a murderer and the other half suspected his mother was fooling around with the preacher?

Clanton was the last place he would live.

Biloxi, on the other hand, looked promising. He wasn't stalking Mary Ann Malouf, but he knew her dormitory and her class schedule. Armed with this intelligence, he managed to bump into her a couple of times on campus. She seemed to enjoy the encounters. Occasionally, he watched her from a distance, and was irritated at the number of other boys doing the same. When Kentucky rolled into town for a football game on October 1, Joel asked her for a date. She declined and reminded him that she was engaged. Her fiancé had also attended Ole Miss and still had friends on campus. She couldn't be seen with someone else.

She did not say that she didn't want to date someone else, only that she couldn't be seen dating someone else. Joel noted the important distinction. He replied that, at least in his opinion, it wasn't fair for such a beautiful coed to have her social life so restricted while her fiancé was off no doubt having a grand time in D.C. He asked her why she wasn't wearing an engagement ring. She didn't have one.

He persisted and she finally agreed to a late dinner. Not a date, just a meal. He met her outside the Lyceum after dark, and they drove downtown to the square, parked in front of Neilson's department store, and walked a block along South Lamar to the Mansion, the only restaurant open late. As they entered, Joel saw William Faulkner at his customary table, alone, eating, and reading a magazine.

He had just published *Intruder in the Dust,* his fourteenth novel. A critic writing for the *Memphis Press-Scimitar* gave it a mixed review, but more important, another story in the same newspaper revealed that Faulkner had sold the film rights to MGM. Joel bought the book at a small store in Jackson when he was visiting his mother. At that time, there was no bookstore in Oxford and the locals cared little about what their most famous son happened to be writing and publishing. As a general rule, he ignored them and they ignored him.

In a paper sack, Joel had two hardbacks: *Intruder in the Dust,* which was brand-new and yet to be read, and his father's well-worn edition of *As I Lay Dying*.

The restaurant was empty at that hour, and Joel and Mary Ann sat as close to Mr. Faulkner as was reasonable without violating his privacy. Joel was hopeful that Faulkner would notice the stunning coed and wish to flirt, something he was prone to do, but he was too absorbed with his reading. He was oblivious to everything around him.

They ordered iced tea and vegetable plates and spoke quietly while waiting for an opening. Joel was at once thrilled to be staring into the lovely face of the girl he was dreaming of and to be so close to Faulkner, with the determination to say hello.

When Faulkner was half-finished with his barbecued chicken, he shoved it aside, took one bite of peach cobbler, then pulled out his pipe. He glanced around, finally, and noticed Mary Ann. Joel was amused at his double take and obvious interest. Faulkner stared her up and down as he fiddled with his pipe. Joel was on his feet. He stepped over, apologized for the intrusion, and asked the great man if he would be so kind as to autograph his father's copy of *As I Lay Dying,* a book that Joel loved, and also his own edition of *Intruder in the Dust.*

"Of course," Mr. Faulkner said politely in a high-pitched voice. He removed a pen from his coat pocket and took both books.

"I'm Joel Banning, a law student here."

"A pleasure to meet you, son. And your friend?" Faulkner asked, smiling at her.

"Mary Ann Malouf, also a student."

"They look younger every year." He opened the first book, wrote nothing but his name in small print, closed it, smiled, handed it back, then signed the second one.

Joel said, "Thanks, Mr. Faulkner." And when he could think of nothing else, and it was obvious Faulkner was finished with his end of the conversation, Joel backed away and returned to his seat. He had not managed to shake hands, and he was certain Faulkner would never remember his name.

Nevertheless, Joel had had his encounter, one that he would talk about for the rest of his life.

· · ·

In November, Burch filed his third petition, and in December his fourth. After sitting on the case for six months, Chancellor Rumbold decided it was time to rule. In a two-page decision, he found that the conveyance by Pete Banning of his land to his two children was proper and in no way fraudulent. He denied any relief to Jackie Bell.

Expecting as much, Burch Dunlap perfected his appeal almost overnight, filed his brief, and hurried the case to Jackson, to a supreme court that was already quite familiar with the facts.

Over the Christmas holidays, Joel stayed with Florry and spent his days at the Wilbanks firm writing the reply brief in opposition to Dunlap's appeal. His research, much of which had already been done, was exhaustive and thorough and troubling. As a general rule, when looking at all jurisdictions, the case law tended to favor the orderly transfer of land among generations of family members. However, the law also took a dim view of those involved in criminal activity transferring assets to avoid the claims of their victims. There was little doubt Pete tried to get rid of his land before he killed Dexter Bell.

As Joel labored for hours over his research and writing, he often felt as though generations of his ancestors were present in the room with him. They had cleared the land, clawed it from the wilderness, tilled the soil with oxen and mules, lost crops to floods and pests, added acreage when they could afford to, borrowed money, endured lean years, and paid off their loans after bumper harvests. They had been born on the land and buried there, and now, after more than a century, it all came down to young Joel and his legal skills.

In Old Sycamore, they were resting under neat rows of tombstones. Were their ghosts watching Joel and praying for a win?

Such questions were heavy burdens, and Joel went about his day with a thick knot in his stomach. The family was humiliated enough. Losing the land would haunt them forever.

He was also burdened by the obvious reality that he and Stella were counting on the income for many years. They would pursue careers and find success, but they had been raised to believe that the family farm would always provide some level of support. Raised on the soil, they knew that there were good years and bad, bumper crops and floods, ups and downs in the market, and that nothing was guaranteed. But their land was free and clear, and thus able to withstand the lean harvests. Losing it would be hard to accept.

Then there was Liza. She talked more and more of coming home, of getting back into her life on the farm. She claimed to miss Nineva, which Joel doubted. But she missed her rituals, her gardening, her horses, her friends. If it all vanished, the damage could be catastrophic. At every visit, Dr. Hilsabeck inquired about the lawsuits and appeals and all that legal mess that to him was indecipherable.

So Joel researched and wrote. John Wilbanks reviewed his drafts, edited, and offered comments. He filed his brief on January 18, and the waiting game began. The supreme court could hear the case in three months, or twelve.

That afternoon Joel packed his papers, cleaned his desk, and tidied the little office where he had spent so many hours. He had already said good-bye to Florry and planned to drive to Oxford that night to begin his fourth semester of law school. He joined John Wilbanks on the terrace for a drink. The weather was unseasonably warm and springlike.

John lit a cigar and offered one to Joel, who declined. They sipped Jack Daniel's sour mash and commented on the weather. Wilbanks said, "We hate to see you go, Joel. It's nice having you around the office."

"I enjoy it," Joel said, though it was a stretch.

"We'd like to have you back this summer for another clerkship."

"Thanks. I appreciate that." He had no plans to return for the summer, or next year or the one after that, but it was too soon to inform John Wilbanks. "I may stay in school this summer," he said. "Finish next December."

"What's the rush? You'd better enjoy the college days, son."

"I'm tired of those days. I want to get out and start a career."

"Well, I hope you'll consider our offer of an associate's position."

Why beat around the bush? His father never minced words and was admired for his bluntness. Joel took a long pull on the whiskey and said, "Mr. Wilbanks, I'm not sure I can practice law in this town. When I see that courthouse, and it's rather hard to miss, I think of my father's last moments. I think of him walking bravely down the street, crowds on both sides, all the veterans here to honor him, to support him, and I can just see him walking into the building and up the stairs to his death. His long walk to the grave. And when I enter that courtroom, I can think of only one image. My father getting strapped in."

"I understand, Joel."

"I'm convinced I'll never be able to erase that image. How can I represent clients in that courtroom?"

"I understand."

CHAPTER 44

On March 28, thirteen months after the trial in Oxford, the Fifth Circuit Court of Appeals in New Orleans affirmed the $100,000 wrongful death verdict. The opinion was short and unanimous. While the justices were alarmed at the size of the verdict, they were thoroughly unsympathetic to the interests of a man of means who so brazenly murdered his own pastor. The crime was calculated. The victim's family suffered greatly. The jurors heard the case, listened to the witnesses, reviewed the documents, and deliberated thoughtfully. The justices would not substitute their opinions for those of the jurors. Affirmed on all counts.

For the Bannings, the decision was devastating. The Wilbanks brothers and Joel had convinced themselves that the verdict would indeed stand on appeal, but would certainly be reduced. Fifty thousand dollars in punitive damages was unheard of. Given the value of Pete's land and his other assets, it was conceivable that his estate could withstand a lesser award, perhaps something in the neighborhood of $50,000. The eventual owners of the land, whether Joel and Stella, or Pete's estate, could borrow that much with a mortgage and satisfy the judgment. But, an enforceable lien of $100,000 looked insurmountable.

The future of the land now rested solely with the Mississippi Supreme Court. If it upheld Rumbold's ruling that the conveyance was proper, then Joel and Stella would keep the land. Burch Dunlap and his now permanent sidekick, Errol McLeish, would be forced to attack Pete's other assets—bank accounts, farm equipment, livestock, automobiles—in order to squeeze whatever money they could find. But, if the court reversed Rumbold, the land reverted to Pete's estate and would become subject to the jury's verdict. Everything, including the home and furnishings, would be lost.

With Joel's assistance, John Wilbanks appealed the Fifth Circuit's decision to the U.S. Supreme Court, a complete waste of time. However, the appeal would keep Dunlap busy and buy a few months. Dunlap enrolled the $100,000 judgment, now with interest clicking away, with the circuit clerk in Ford County. Wilbanks ran to chancery court, woke up old Rumbold, and petitioned for an injunction to prevent Dunlap from trying to grab assets pending the appeal. After a brief and contentious hearing, Rumbold once again ruled in favor of the Bannings. Dunlap petitioned the Mississippi Supreme Court for an expedited hearing. Wilbanks opposed it.

Joel monitored the assaults and counterattacks from the safety of his garage apartment in Oxford. For $10 a month, he leased the ground floor of the garage and, using his father's Ford truck, began quietly moving furniture and furnishings from their home to the safety of the garage. Nineva didn't like it, but she had no say in the matter.

In mid-May, Joel and Florry loaded into her 1939 Lincoln and commenced a long road trip to Virginia. They checked into the Hotel Roanoke, where they hosted a cocktail party for Stella and her friends at Hollins. On a glorious spring day, they sat with a crowd of other proud parents and family members and watched Stella accept her degree in English literature. The following day, while the ladies sipped tea in the shade, Joel hauled boxes and bags from her dorm room to the car. When it was stuffed and he was exhausted, Stella said good-bye to college, to a school she loved, and to her friends. Joel had never seen so many tears, not even at a good funeral.

With the women in the rear seat barking instructions, and with the view in every mirror blocked by luggage and boxes, they roared away from Hollins and headed north. Three hours later, they were lost in Richmond, but stopped anyway at a barbecue place in a lesser part of the city. A local pointed this way and that, and after a quick lunch they were off again, headed for D.C.

Stella's grand plan was still to live in New York, work for a magazine, and write serious fiction on the side. Getting there, though, would take more time than she realized. Jobs in publishing were scarce, but every school needed young teachers. St. Agnes in Alexandria was an Episcopal girls' day and boarding school, and it offered her a contract to teach English to ninth graders and serve as a dorm parent. While she and Florry enjoyed even more tea with the headmistress, Joel schlepped her bags and boxes into a suffocating dorm room even smaller than the last.

The school allowed him to park the car in a safe place. For $10, a janitor agreed to keep air in the tires and crank the engine once a day. They called a cab and crossed the Potomac into D.C. At Union Station, they caught their train to New York.

Before Burch Dunlap and his greedy clients could seize their money, they had decided to spend some of what was left of it. Stella's tuitions were now in the past and she had a job. Joel had only one more year of law school and he would start working. Florry's land was safe from the vultures, and she had some money buried. Nineteen forty-nine could be their last summer together, so why not do it in style?

At the port in lower Manhattan, they boarded an ocean liner bound for London, and for two weeks had a delightful time resting and reading and trying to forget all the troubles back home. On deck, Joel and Stella noticed for the first time how slow Florry was getting about. She was carrying too much weight, as usual, but she had always been vigorous and busy. Now, though, she was missing a step and seemed winded after even a short walk. She was only fifty, but aging and looking tired.

In London, they spent a week at the St. Regis Hotel and saw the sights, then traveled to Edinburgh, where they boarded the Royal Scotsman for a week in the Highlands. When they were tired of visiting castles, manor homes, historic sites, and distilleries, they returned to London for a two-day rest before pushing on to Paris.

Stella and Joel were having coffee in the lobby of the Hôtel Lutetia when they got the news. Florry was not feeling well and had decided to rest through the morning and not walk the city at full throttle. A porter approached and handed Joel a cablegram. It was from John Wilbanks. The Mississippi Supreme Court had voted 7–2 to reverse Rumbold. The conveyance of the land to Joel and Stella was null and void. The property would remain in their father's estate; thus, subject to all claims and liens.

"Reversed and rendered," Joel said in disbelief.

"What does that mean?" Stella asked.

"It means the case is over. It means the supreme court felt strongly that Rumbold was wrong and decided to end the matter without further hearings."

"What about an appeal?"

"Yes, we'll file another appeal to the U.S. Supreme Court and try to buy some time. Wilbanks and I will discuss bankruptcy."

They sipped coffee and watched the foot traffic pass through the luxurious lobby. Stella said, "I have a question, and I want an honest answer. Does this mean that Jackie Bell and her children could one day be living in our home?"

"It's possible but I still don't believe it. At some point, Wilbanks will sit down with her lawyer and push hard to settle everything."

"And how does that work?"

"We offer them cash."

"I thought we tried that once."

"We did, and they turned down $25,000. It'll cost more now."

"How much?"

"I don't know. It'll be a question of how much money is left in the bank accounts and how much money we can borrow against the land."

"Do you really want to mortgage the land, Joel? You know how much Dad hated banks."

"We may not have a choice."

In its ruling, the state supreme court found that Pete's conduct amounted to fraud in several ways. First, he retained an interest in his land by living on it and farming it and profiting from it. Second, he received nothing in return for the deed to his children. Third, the transfer of ownership was to family members, which is always suspicious. And, fourth, at the time he signed the deed he had reason to believe that he would one day be pursued by creditors because of his actions.

John Wilbanks read the opinion a dozen times and found the court's logic sound. He went through the useless routine of appealing the decision to the only court left, the U.S. Supreme Court, but knew there was no chance the case would be accepted for argument. He consulted with a close friend in Memphis who was a bankruptcy specialist, and was not encouraged by the conversation. Putting Pete's estate into bankruptcy would be a smart delaying tactic, but a successful outcome would be difficult.

Wilbanks went back to chancery court for another injunction to prevent a foreclosure pending appeals, and, of course, Rumbold gave it to him. Dunlap took another lump and appealed. Soon enough, though, not even a highly biased judge like Rumbold could forestall the inevitable.

After the hearing, a composed and quite confident Dunlap chatted with Wilbanks and offered a proposal. It was time to stop running up legal bills and face the obvious. The appeals would not work, nor would a bankruptcy. Why not simply deed the land, all 640 acres, plus the house and furnishings, over to Jackie Bell? If the Bannings would agree to it, then Jackie would forgo all claims to the bank accounts.

Wilbanks bristled at the proposal and said, as he walked away, "The Bannings will burn the house and the crops before they sign over a deed."

Dunlap shot back, "Great, but please remind your clients that arson is still a crime, punishable by a long prison sentence."

When Joel and Florry crossed the state line into Mississippi in late July, they began to notice, as always, the cotton, and it was not encouraging. Heavy rains in the spring had delayed the planting, and in the two months they had been living it up in England and Europe the weather had obviously not cooperated. In a good year the cotton bloomed by July 4, and by Labor Day it was chest high.

This was the worst-looking crop in recent memory, and as they crossed through the farmlands of north Mississippi the cotton looked worse. There were no blooms.

The stalks were hardly knee high. In low spots entire acres had been washed out.

Nineva made a pot of coffee and asked about their trip. They asked about the weather and got an earful. While they were gone it rained every day, it seemed, and even when it wasn't raining the skies were cloudy. Cotton needed days and days of dry weather and hot sun, and, well, it was obvious the weather was killing the crops. Amos was fighting it in the garden but the yield was far below normal.

As if life on the Banning farm wasn't depressing enough.

Joel drove his aunt to the pink cottage and unloaded her luggage. They had a drink on the porch, stared at the pathetic crops, and wished they were back in Scotland.

John Wilbanks wanted to see him, and as badly as Joel wanted to avoid the law office and the courthouse and everything else about downtown Clanton, he had no choice. They met in the large conference room on the ground floor, a sign that the meeting was of extra importance. Russell also joined them, another sure signal.

The brothers promptly fired up their smokes, the standard short black cigar for John and a cigarette for Russell. Joel declined and said he would join them just by breathing the air.

John recapped the litigation. They had two frivolous appeals filed with the U.S. Supreme Court and they could expect both to be rejected within a couple of months, as soon as a clerk there got around to the paperwork. There was no reason whatsoever for the Court to

show any interest in either case. Burch Dunlap had enrolled the $100,000 judgment across the street, and would
wait patiently for the Bannings and their lawyers to tire
themselves with useless legal maneuverings and throw in
the towel.

"What about bankruptcy?" Joel asked.

"It won't work, because the estate is not bankrupt.
We could do it and stall, but Dunlap would waste no
time getting a hearing before the bankruptcy judge. And
remember, if we put the estate into bankruptcy, the
trustee then assumes control of the estate. We don't name
the trustee. The court does."

Russell let loose a cloud of smoke and said, "There's
an excellent chance the trustee could order the executrix, Florry, to hand over all assets to the judgment cred-
itor, Jackie Bell."

"None of this is surprising," Joel said.

"And there's something else," Russell said. "We need
to get paid. Our bill is now over $7,000 and I'm not sure
there's enough in the estate to pay us. We've been shot-
gunning petitions and motions right and left, hoping for
a miracle, and it's taken a lot of time. Using a bankruptcy
as a stall tactic just eats more clock."

"I understand."

John said, "We're at the end of the road, Joel. There's
nothing left except a good-faith effort to settle with these
people. We have one idea left, and it's the only one that
might save the land. It requires a mortgage on both pieces
of property—Pete's and Florry's. All twelve hundred
acres. You borrow as much as you can, and offer it to
Dunlap to settle everything."

Cautiously, Joel asked, "How much?"

"The house is valued at thirty thousand. The land is worth about a hundred bucks an acre, on the high side, but you'd have a hard time getting that much in this market. As you know, only about a thousand acres are planted. No bank is going to lend the full value because of the risk. Think about it. Pete managed to either break even or show a profit most years because he owned the land free and clear, plus he worked himself to the bone, pushed his workers, and watched every dime. Burden the land with a mortgage and suddenly you're in business with a bank. A couple of bad crops, like this one, and you fall behind. Before you know it, the bank starts talking about foreclosure. Happens every year around here, even in good years."

Russell took the handoff and said, "We've talked to our brother over at the bank and he's not too keen on the deal. If Pete were alive and cracking the whip, the farm would be more attractive. But he's gone, you're not a farmer, Florry's crazy as hell. I can see the banks running from this one."

Joel asked, "How much would your brother lend?"

"Seventy-five thousand at the most," John said.

Russell added, "And I'm not sure about that. There's another problem that's rather obvious. We represent your family, and we represent the bank. What if there's a default? The law firm suddenly has a huge conflict of interest, one that could land us in serious trouble."

John said, "And we haven't discussed this with the other bank in town. As you know, there's a good bit of rivalry involved between the families. I doubt they would touch it, but we could possibly take it to a larger bank in Tupelo."

Joel stood and walked around the room. "I can't ask Florry to mortgage her land. That's simply too much. It's all she's got and if she lost it I don't know where she'd go. I can't do it. I'm not going to ask her."

John flicked ashes into a dish and said, "Here's a plan. Tell me what you think. I'll sit down with Dunlap and negotiate. He probably took this case on a contingency and hasn't been paid a dime yet, so he might have an interest in a cash settlement. I'll start at fifty thousand and we'll see what he's thinking. You can handle fifty, right?"

"I suppose," Joel said. "But the thought of owing that much makes me sick."

"It should, but you and Stella can keep your land and your home."

"What if they want too much?"

"We'll see. Let's have the first round of negotiations. I'll act as poor as possible."

CHAPTER 45

In the stifling heat of August, Liza's little room was unbearable. There was no window to catch a breeze, nothing to break the suffocating humidity but a flimsy box fan Joel had brought her the summer before. After a few minutes, they were both sweating and decided to go hunt for shade. She was walking well these days; her condition had improved, at least physically. She had gained a few pounds, though still ate little. At times the Thorazine gave her an appetite. It certainly calmed her and she didn't fidget nonstop and pull at her hair as before. She cut her hair short and washed it more often, and she had ditched the pale and permanently stained hospital gowns for the simple cotton dresses Stella sent. A milestone had been reached a month earlier when Stella brought in three tubes of lipstick, and Liza was thrilled. Now each visitor was greeted with a bright red smile.

Dr. Hilsabeck continued to say that he was pleased with her progress, but Joel had lost hope that his mother would ever recover enough to leave. After three years in the institution, it had become her home. Yes, she had improved, but then she'd had so far to climb.

They left the building and walked to the pond, where they sat on a picnic table under the shade of an oak. The heat was brutal and the air was too thick to stir, so it hung in one place with no hint of a breeze. Unlike most visits, Joel looked forward to this one because he had so much to talk about. In vivid detail, he recounted their travels to New York, London, Scotland, and Paris.

Liza listened with a pretty smile, one that broke his heart because it was the best she could ever hope for. His mother was not coming home, and home was a subject he could not discuss.

He found a dirty room in a cheap tourist motel near the beach in Biloxi and went looking for Mary Ann Malouf, who was no longer engaged to the guy in Washington. In the past year she had seen a lot of Joel, primarily because he simply would not go away. At Ole Miss, they had sneaked around for late dinners. They had taken two road trips to Memphis, where they would not be seen. He had pressed her to ditch the guy in D.C. and hook up with a real man.

During the summer she was working a few hours a week in a dress store on Main Street, and when he walked through the door she was pleasantly surprised. He hung around long enough to get harsh looks from her boss, then left. They met for a soda after hours and discussed meeting her family. He insisted on it. She was hesitant.

Her parents approved of her fiancé and would not understand a new suitor hanging around.

Feeling a bit stiff-armed, Joel bummed around the coast for a few days, trying to avoid both the return home and anything resembling meaningful employment. He knocked on the doors of several law firms, landed two quick interviews but no job offer. The longer he stayed the more he liked Biloxi, with its ethnic blend, cafés offering all manner of fresh seafood, lounges that somehow served alcohol without getting busted, boats rocking in the harbors, and the laid-back atmosphere usually found along the ocean. And the longer he chased Mary Ann Malouf, the more determined he was to catch her.

Burch Dunlap spent the month of August in Montana away from the heat. Evidently, the vacation served him well. He returned to the office after Labor Day filled with energy and determined to make more money. His nearest target was the Banning case.

In chancery court, still and always the unquestioned domain of Chancellor Abbott Rumbold, he filed a lawsuit seeking a judicial foreclosure of the Banning land. He had no choice but to file in Ford County. The law was clear. Indeed, the law was so clear Burch was curious to see how the old judge could manipulate it to favor the Bannings.

A week later he sat down in his conference room to welcome his friend John Wilbanks, who was coming to Tupelo to open settlement negotiations. Or, as Dunlap had confided to his ever-present confidant, Errol McLeish, to beg for mercy.

And there would be none.

John was served coffee and offered a seat on one side of the handsome table. Across from him sat Dunlap, and to his right was McLeish, a man John had quickly learned to despise.

Dunlap lit a cigar and after some small talk said, "You have the money, John. Why don't you tell us what you have in mind?"

"Of course. Obviously, my clients would like to keep the family land. They are also tired of payin' me."

"You've done a lot of work that wasn't necessary," Dunlap said almost rudely. "We've been worried about your fees, frankly. That money comes out of the estate."

"Look, Burch, why don't you worry about your fees and I'll worry about mine. Fair enough?"

Reprimanded, Burch laughed loudly as if his pal had really nailed a great punch line. "Fair enough. Go on."

"There's not a lot of cash in the estate, so whatever we offer you to settle has to come from money that will be borrowed against the house and land."

"How much, John?"

"It's a question of how much income the farm can produce each year in order to service the mortgage. This year is a disaster. As you know, it's a risky business. My family has been farming cotton for decades, and I often wonder if it's really worth it."

"Your family's done well, John."

"In some endeavors, yes. The Bannings think they can borrow fifty thousand against their property and survive the mortgage. That's the best they can do."

Dunlap offered a sappy smile as if he'd really enjoyed round one, and said, "Come on, John, they own twelve hundred acres free and clear and a thousand of it is rich farmland. Their home is one of the finest in the county. They have half a dozen outbuildings, fine structures all, plus the farm equipment, and livestock, and how many Negroes?"

"Please, Burch, they don't own those people."

"For all practical purposes they do. Fifty is really low-ball, John. I thought we agreed to meet for a serious discussion."

"Well, you can't be serious if you include the land owned by Florry Banning. That's half of it, and she's not involved in the litigation. She's completely unaffected by all of this."

"Not so fast, John. Pete Banning farmed his sister's property just like he farmed his and gave her half the profits. Both sections came from the same source—their parents, and their grandparents, and so on."

"This is absurd, Burch. Florry had nothing to do with the killing of Dexter Bell and you know it. To imply that her land is in play is ridiculous. If you think otherwise, then try and foreclose on it."

"We can't foreclose on anything as long as you keep old Rumbold in your hip pocket."

John smiled and said, "He's a brilliant jurist. One of the best."

"Maybe, but down in Jackson the Supremes are not so impressed. Fifty thousand ain't flyin', John."

"I've put a figure on the table. Now it's your turn."

McLeish said coldly, "At least a hundred thousand. Frankly, Jackie deserves more because we need to pay Mr. Dunlap."

Mr. Dunlap said, "One twenty, John. I have this case

on a contingency, and I've won it fair and square. I've done a heck of a job for my client, and I don't want my fees to come out of her settlement."

"You've done a superb job, Burch, no question about it. But your numbers are far above anything we can afford. No bank will lend more than $75,000 for Pete's land and the house. Florry's land is off-limits."

"Are you offering $75,000?" Dunlap asked.

"Not yet, but would you take $75,000 if it were on the table?"

McLeish shook his head and said, "No."

Both lawyers were good negotiators, and it was obvious who held the upper hand. When swimming against the tide, John knew it was often beneficial to muddy the waters. He said, "Look, Burch, the kids would really like to save the house, the only home they've ever known. You know about their mother and her troubles. There's the chance that Liza may come home one day, and it's crucial that she has her place. Can we discuss separating it and the buildings from the farmland? I'm working on a plat that would carve out only four acres that includes the house, the gardens and barns and such, and your client would take the rest."

"The deed for the farm, minus the four acres?" Dunlap asked.

"Something like that. I'm just exploring alternatives here."

"How much are they willing to pay for the four acres?"

"The house is appraised at thirty thousand, which is definitely on the high side. These are two fine kids who are trying to hang on to something."

"How are they going to service a mortgage on the home?"

"Good question. We'll figure it out. Florry might help them."

The biggest obstacle to this proposal was one that would not be mentioned. Jackie Bell wanted the house. In fact, she wanted the house far more than she wanted the land. Her boyfriend fancied himself a gentleman farmer and was already counting his money, but Jackie just wanted a beautiful home.

McLeish shook his head and said, "No way. Those four acres are worth almost as much as the farmland. We can't do it." He spoke with the air of a man who was entitled to his rewards, in this case the treasured soil of some of the finest people John Wilbanks had ever known. He despised McLeish for his arrogance and his sense of entitlement.

John said, "Well, it looks as though we have nothing left to discuss."

In late September, on back-to-back days, the U.S. Supreme Court laid waste to a batch of frivolous requests for hearings. On one day it hammered home the final nail in the coffin in the Banning appeal of the verdict in federal court, and on the very next day it brushed aside the Banning appeal from the Mississippi reversal of Rumbold's ruling.

The path was now clear for a hearing on the petition by Dunlap for a judicial foreclosure; rather, the path should have been unobstructed. Standing in the way was His Honor himself, and old Rumbold was getting creakier by the month. Dunlap bellowed and screamed and demanded a timely day in court. Rumbold, almost deaf, heard nothing.

And then he died. On October 9, 1949, Abbott Rumbold succumbed to old age and passed at eighty-one. He died peacefully in his sleep, or as the colored folks preferred to say, he "woke up dead." With thirty-seven years of service, he was the ranking chancellor in the state. Joel drove from Ole Miss and attended his funeral at First Baptist with John and Russell Wilbanks.

The service was a tribute to a man who lived a long, happy, and productive life. There were few tears, a lot of humor, and the warm feeling that one of God's saints had simply gone home.

Joel's next burial would be far different.

CHAPTER 46

To escape the monotony, and to ease some of the healthier patients into normalcy, the doctors and administrators at Whitfield arranged weekly visits to the Paramount Theatre on East Capitol Street in downtown Jackson. For each matinee, an unmarked bus stopped on a side street a block from the theater and twenty or so patients got off. They were accompanied by orderlies and nurses, and once off the bus they worked hard to appear as if they had simply arrived like everyone else. They wore street clothes and blended in with the crowd. An untrained eye would never suspect that they were being treated for all manner of serious mental illnesses.

Liza loved the movies and volunteered at every opportunity. She worked on her hair, put on makeup, layered on the lipstick, and wore one of the dresses Stella had sent.

The Paramount was showing *Adam's Rib,* a comedy with Spencer Tracy and Katharine Hepburn, and the lobby was busy by 1:00 p.m. The head nurse bought their tickets and guided them to two rows of seats. On Liza's left was an older lady named Beverly, an acquaintance who'd been institutionalized for years, and to her right was Karen, a sad young woman who usually slept during the shows.

Fifteen minutes into the movie, Liza whispered to Beverly that she needed to visit the ladies' room. She eased to the aisle, whispered the same thing to a nurse, and left the auditorium. Then she left the theater.

She walked two blocks along East Capitol to Mill Street and entered the Illinois Central Station, where she purchased a second-class ticket for the 1:50 train to Memphis. Her hand was shaking as she took the ticket, and she needed to sit down. The station was practically empty and she found an empty seat far away from anyone else. She breathed deeply, composed herself, and from a small pocket pulled out a folded sheet of paper. It was a list of "What To Do Next," one she had been putting together for weeks. She feared she would easily become overwhelmed and need guidance. She read it, refolded it, and returned it to her pocket. She left the station, walked one block along Mill Street to a department store, and purchased a cheap handbag, an even cheaper straw hat, and a magazine. She stuffed her remaining cash, a small bottle of pills, and one tube of lipstick into the purse, and hurried back to the station. As she waited there she reviewed her list again, smiled at herself for the success so far, and watched the entrance in case anyone from the hospital appeared. They did not.

The nurse enjoyed the comedy so much she forgot about Liza and her trip to the ladies' room. When she finally remembered, she immediately left to go look. Finding nothing, she corralled two orderlies and they began searching the theater, which was almost full. In the lobby, no one remembered seeing a slim lady in a yellow dress leave after the movie started. They continued searching but soon ran out of places to look. The two orderlies began roaming the streets of downtown Jackson, and one finally strolled through the train station. By then, Liza was an hour north of town, sitting alone by a window, clutching her list, staring blankly at the passing countryside, and struggling with the rush of sights and sounds from the real world. She had been locked up for three and a half years.

The police were called and Dr. Hilsabeck was notified. Everyone was alarmed, but not panicked. Liza was not deemed a threat to anyone else, and she was stable enough to take care of herself, for a few hours anyway. Dr. Hilsabeck did not want to alarm the family, nor did he want his staff to appear incompetent, so he delayed calling either Joel, Florry, or Sheriff Nix Gridley.

Liza had purchased her ticket with cash and there was no record of who the passengers were. However, a ticket clerk remembered a lady who fit Liza's description and said she was headed north, to Memphis. This was around 3:00 p.m. The movie was over and the bus had to return to Whitfield.

When the train arrived in Batesville, its sixth stop, at 4:15, Liza decided to get off. She assumed someone was looking for her, and she suspected they might be watching the trains and buses. Outside the station were two taxis, both old prewar sedans that appeared even more unreliable than the two drivers who were leaning on a bumper. She asked the first one if he would take her to Clanton, an hour and a half away. She offered $10, but he was worried about his tires. The second one said he would do it for $15. His tires looked even worse, but she didn't have many options.

As she got into the rear seat, her driver said, "No luggage?"

"No. I'm traveling light."

He got behind the wheel and they drove away from the station. He glanced into the mirror and said, "Mighty pretty dress you got on."

Liza lifted her purse and said, "I carry a Colt pistol whenever I travel, and I know how to use it. Anything funny, and you'll be sorry."

"Sorry, ma'am." Outside town, he found the nerve to speak again. "Anything on the radio, ma'am?"

"Sure, whatever you like."

He turned on the radio, fiddled with the dial, and found a country station out of Memphis.

It was after dark when Hilsabeck finally made contact with Joel. He explained what had happened and admitted they were searching in vain. Joel was stunned to think that his mother was loose and doing something that she had obviously planned. He was petrified by fear and uncertain where to go. Should he drive to Jackson and help with the search? Or Memphis, where she was believed to be going? Or Clanton? Or just sit and wait? He called Stella and assured her things would be fine. He needed to call Florry, but decided to wait. Her phone was still on a rural party line with a dozen others, and the eavesdroppers would go berserk with the news that Liza Banning had escaped from Whitfield.

For an hour, Joel paced around his apartment, uncertain, waiting for the call that his mother had been found and was fine. He called the sheriff's department in Clanton but no one answered. He figured old Tick Poley was in a deep sleep. A total jailbreak could be under way and Tick wouldn't know it.

He finally reached Nix Gridley at home, on his private line, and told him about Liza's latest. Nix offered his sympathies and said he would drive out and tell Florry.

When the taxi left the highway and pulled onto the long drive to the Banning estate, Liza told the driver to stop. She paid him $15, thanked him, and got out. When he disappeared down the dark and deserted road, she began walking slowly in the pitch blackness, barely able to see the gravel drive in front of her. There was not a single light on in the house, the barns, any of the outbuildings. In the distance, a dim glow emanated from a window in the small house where Nineva and Amos had lived forever. As she felt her way along the gravel, the outline of the house settled into view. She crossed the front lawn, then the porch, and rattled the doorknob. It was locked, which was unusual in the country. No one locked their doors.

She wanted to inspect the flower beds and shrubs, to see how much had changed in three and a half years, but there was no light, no moon on a cloudy night. She walked to the side and saw Pete's truck parked exactly where he'd left it. She knew that Joel had assumed ownership of the Pontiac. In the backyard, she inched her way through the dead grass. A breeze kicked in from the west and she shivered and rubbed her arms. The rear door to the kitchen was unlocked. She entered her home and stood in the kitchen, stopped cold by an aroma that was so thick and familiar it overwhelmed her: a mix of cigarette smoke and coffee, bacon grease, fruity pies and cakes, thick beef and venison stews that Nineva simmered on the stove for days, steam from the canning of stewed tomatoes and a dozen vegetables, wet leather from Pete's boots in a corner, the sweet soapy smell of Nineva herself. Liza was staggered by the dense fragrances and leaned on a counter.

In the darkness, she could hear the voices of her children as they giggled over breakfast and got themselves shooed away from the stove by Nineva. She could see Pete sitting there at the kitchen table with his coffee and cigarettes reading the Tupelo daily. A cloud moved somewhere and a ray of moonlight entered through a window. She focused and her kitchen came into view. She breathed as slowly as possible, sucking in the sweet smells of her former life.

Liza wiped some tears and decided to keep things dark. No one knew she was there and lights would only attract attention. At the same time she wanted to give the house the full, white-gloved inspection to see what Nineva had been up to. Were the dishes all washed and stacked neatly where they belonged? Was there a layer of dust on the coffee tables? What had been done to Pete's things—the clothes in his closet, the books and papers in his study? She could vaguely recall a conversation with Joel about this but the details were gone.

She eased into the den and fell into the soft leather sofa, which felt and smelled just the way she remembered. Her first memory of the sofa was perhaps the worst. Joel to her right, Stella to her left, all three staring in utter fear at the army captain as he delivered the news that Pete was missing and presumed dead. May 19, 1942. Another lifetime.

Headlights swept through the windows and startled her. She peeked through the curtains and watched as a Ford County patrol car crept along her drive, then turned onto the side road that led to Florry's. It disappeared, and she knew they were looking for her. She waited, and twenty minutes later the car came into view, passed the house again, and headed to the highway.

She reminded herself that she was sitting in her own home and she had committed no crime. If they found her, the worst they could do was send her back to Whitfield. They would not get the chance.

She began rocking, her shoulders jerking back and forth, a tedious habit that often afflicted her and she couldn't control. When she worried or was afraid she began rocking, and humming, and twitching her hair. A lot of the crazy people at Whitfield engaged in all manner of rocking and twitching and groaning as they sat alone in the cafeteria or by the pond, but she always knew she would not be like them. She would get fixed, and soon, and pull her life back together.

After an hour or so—she had lost all concept of time—she realized that she was no longer rocking, and the crying had stopped too. There were so many burdens to unload.

She walked to the kitchen, to the only phone, and

called Florry. To confound the eavesdroppers, she said, "Florry, I'm here."

"Who? What?" Florry was startled, and rightfully so.

"I'm at the house," Liza said and hung up. She walked to the back porch and waited. Only a few minutes passed before she saw headlights bouncing across the landscape. Florry parked beside the house.

"Over here, Florry," Liza said. "On the porch."

Florry walked to the rear, almost stumbling in the dark, and said, "Why don't you turn on some damn lights around here?" She stopped at the steps, looked up at Liza, and asked, "What the hell are you doin', Liza?"

"Come give me a hug, Florry."

Well, she must be crazy if she wants a hug from me, Florry thought but certainly didn't say. She climbed the steps and they embraced. Florry said, "Again, I'll ask what are you doing here?"

"Just wanted to come home. The doctor said it was fine."

"That's a lie and you know it. The doctors are worried. The kids are beside themselves. The police are looking for you. Why'd you pull a stunt like this?"

"Got tired of Whitfield. Let's go inside."

They entered the kitchen and Florry said, "Hit the lights. I can't see a damned thing."

"I like it dark, Florry. Besides, I don't want Nineva to know I'm here."

Florry found a switch and turned on the kitchen lights. She had visited Liza at Whitfield and, like Stella and Joel, had always been troubled by her appearance. She had improved a little, but she was still painfully thin, gaunt, hollow. "You look good, Liza. It's nice to see you."

"Nice to be home."

"Now we need to call Joel and let him know you're safe, okay?"

"I just talked to him. He'll be here in an hour."

Florry relaxed and said, "Good. Have you eaten? You look hungry."

"I don't eat much, Florry. Let's go sit in the den and talk."

Whatever you want, dear. She would pacify her until Joel arrived, and then they would decide what to do.

"Shouldn't we call your doctors?" Florry asked. "They need to know you're okay."

"I told Joel to call them. He'll take care of it. Everything is fine, Florry."

They walked into the den and Liza turned the switch on a small lamp. A faint light gave the room an eerie, shadowy feel. Florry wanted more light but said nothing. She took one end of the sofa. Liza propped pillows on the other and reclined on them. They faced each other in the semidarkness.

"Would you like some coffee?" Liza asked.

"Not really."

"Me neither. I've almost stopped drinking it. The caffeine doesn't sit well with all the pills I take and it gives me headaches. You wouldn't believe the drugs they try to stuff into me. Sometimes I take them; sometimes I don't swallow and spit them out. Why haven't you been to see me more often, Florry?"

"I don't know. It's a long trip down there and it's not exactly an uplifting place to visit."

"Uplifting? You expect to be uplifted when you visit the nuthouse? It's not about you, Florry, it's about me, the patient. The crazy woman. I'm the sick one and you're supposed to visit me and show some support."

The two had never been close, and Florry remembered why. However, at the moment she was willing to take some shots if that would help. Hopefully, they'd come get her tomorrow and take her back.

"Are we going to bicker, Liza?"

"Haven't we always?"

"No. We did at first, and then we realized that the best way to get along was to give each other plenty of room. That's what I remember, Liza. We've always been cautiously friendly, for the sake of the family."

"If you say so. I want you to tell me a story, Florry, one that I've never heard."

"Maybe."

"I want to hear your version of what happened the day Pete killed Dexter Bell. I know you probably don't want to talk about it, but everyone knows it all, everyone but me. For a long time they wouldn't tell me anything down there. I guess they figured it would just make bad matters worse, and they were right because when they finally told me I went into a coma for a week and almost died. But, anyway, I'd like to hear your version."

"Why, Liza? It's not a good story."

"Why? Because it's a pretty damned important part of my life, don't you think, Florry? My husband kills our preacher and gets executed for it, and I don't know the details. Come on, Florry, I have a right to know. Tell me the story."

Florry shrugged, and the story flowed.

.   .   .

One led to the next. Life at the jail; the hearings in court; the reactions around town; the reports in the newspapers; the trial; the execution; the burial; the veterans who still stopped by the grave.

At times Liza cried and wiped her face with the back of her hands. At times she listened with her eyes closed, as if absorbing the horrors. She moaned occasionally and rocked a little. She asked a few questions, made only a couple of comments.

"You know he came to see me the day before they killed him?"

"Yes, I remember that."

"He said he still loved me but that he could never forgive me. How about that, Florry? A lot of love but not enough for forgiveness. Facing a certain death, he still could not forgive me."

"Forgive what?" And with that, Florry managed to ask the great question.

Liza closed her eyes and leaned her head on a pillow. Her lips were moving as if she were mumbling something only she could understand. Then she was completely still and silent.

Softly, Florry repeated, "Forgive what, Liza?"

"We have so much to talk about, Florry, and I want to do it now because I'm not going to live much longer. Something is wrong with me, Florry, and not just the crazy stuff. There's a disease deep in my body and it's getting worse. Might be cancer, might be something else, but I know it's there and it's growing. The doctors can't find it but I know it's there. They can give me drugs that soothe the nervous breakdown, but they have nothing for my disease."

"I don't know what to say, Liza."

"Say nothing. Just listen."

Hours had passed, hours with no sign of Joel. Liza seemed to forget about him, but Florry was well aware that he should have been there.

Liza stood and said, "I think I'll change clothes, Florry. I've been thinking about a certain pair of linen pajamas and a silk bathrobe that Pete always loved." She walked to their bedroom door as Florry stood and stretched her legs.

Florry went to the kitchen and poured a glass of water. A wall clock gave the time as 11:40. She took the phone to call Joel, and then she saw the problem. The wire running from the baseboard to the phone had been cut, snipped cleanly in two as if by scissors. The phone was useless, and it had probably not been used that night to call Joel.

She returned to the den and waited. Liza was in her bedroom with the door open, and she was crying, louder and louder. She was lying on the bed she had shared with Pete, wearing the white linen pajamas under a cream silk bathrobe. Her feet were bare.

Florry leaned over her and said, "It's okay, Liza. I'm here with you. What's wrong, honey?"

Liza pointed to a chair and said, "Please." She wiped her face with a tissue and struggled to get control. Florry took a seat and waited. Liza had not called Joel. Joel had not called the doctors, nor Stella. They were all waiting frantically for news from somewhere, and here was Liza on her bed, in her home.

Florry wanted to ask why she had cut the phone line, but that conversation would go nowhere. Liza was on the verge of talking and perhaps revealing secrets that they thought would never be revealed. Best not to distract her. She didn't want Joel around at this moment.

Liza finally asked, "Did Pete talk to you before he died?"

"Of course. We discussed a lot of things—the kids, the farm, the usual things you might expect a dying person to cover."

"Did he talk about us and our troubles?"

Indeed he did, but Florry wasn't taking the bait. She wanted to hear it all from the closest source. "Of course not. You know how private he was. What kinds of troubles?"

"Oh, Florry, there are so many secrets, so many sins. I really can't blame Pete for not forgiving me." She began crying again, then sobbing. The outbursts became something of a wail, a loud, aching, agonized groan that startled Florry. She had never heard such painful mourning. Liza's body retched as if she might vomit violently, then she heaved and convulsed as she sobbed uncontrollably. It went on and on, and finally Florry could watch no longer. She went to the bed, lay down beside her, and clutched her tightly.

"It's okay, Liza. It's okay, honey. You're okay."

Florry hugged and whispered and cooed and promised and patted her softly, and she rocked her and whispered some more and Liza began to relax. She breathed easier, seemed to withdraw into her own little emaciated body, and cried gently. In a whisper, she said, "There are some things you should know."

"I'm listening, Liza. I'm here."

· · ·

She awoke in a dark room, under the covers, the door open. The house was dark, the only light from the small lamp in the den. Liza quietly shoved back the covers, got to her feet, and walked out of her bedroom. Florry was on the sofa, under a quilt, dead to the world. Without a sound, Liza walked by her and into the kitchen, through the door, across the porch, down the steps. The air was cold; her feet were bare and soon wet. She glided through the grass and onto the footpath that led to the barns, her silk bathrobe flowing behind her.

The moon came and went between the clouds, with its bluish light washing over the outbuildings and the fields before disappearing again. She knew where she was going and didn't need the light. When she passed the last barn she saw the silhouettes of her horses in a paddock. She had never passed by without speaking to them, but she had nothing to say.

Her feet were wet, muddy, and frozen, but she did not care. Pain was of little consequence now. She shivered in the cold and walked with a purpose. Up the slight rise to Old Sycamore, and she was soon among the dead—all those dead Bannings she had heard so much about. The moon was hidden and she could not read the names on the tombstones, but she knew where he was buried because she knew where the other ones were. She pressed her fingers to the limestone and traced his name.

She had found her husband.

Though overwhelmed with grief, guilt, and shame, she was tired of crying. She was frozen and praying for the end.

They say people are at peace when they reach this point. They lie. She felt no peace, no sense of comfort, no belief that what she was doing would ever be considered anything other than the desperate act of a crazy woman.

She eased down and sat with her back against his headstone, as close as she could possibly get. His body was just a few feet below hers. She told him she loved him and would see him soon, and prayed that when they were together again, he could finally forgive her.

From a pocket in her bathrobe, she removed a small bottle of pills.

CHAPTER 47

Amos found her at daybreak, and when he got close enough to the tombstones to make sure he saw what he thought he saw, he broke and ran back to the house, yelling and running faster than he had in decades. When Florry heard that she was dead, she fainted on the back porch. When she came to, Nineva helped her to the sofa and tried to console her.

Nix Gridley and Roy Lester arrived to help with the search, and when Amos described what he'd found in the cemetery, they left him behind and drove to it. The empty pill bottle was sufficient evidence. There was no crime scene to bother with. A misty rain was falling and Nix decided that she should not get wet. He and Lester loaded Liza into the rear seat and returned to the house. Nix went inside to deal with the family while Lester drove her to the funeral home.

Around 5:00 a.m., Florry had awakened and realized Liza was gone. She panicked and ran to Nineva's house, where Amos had just started breakfast. He and Nineva searched frantically around the house and barns while Florry drove to the pink cottage to use the phone. She called Joel and Dr. Hilsabeck and briefly described the situation.

Joel was en route from Oxford when he passed the sheriff's car leaving his home. Once inside, he heard the rest of the story. Florry was a mess, blaming herself relentlessly and gasping for breath. After Joel finally talked to Stella by phone, he insisted his aunt ride with him to the hospital. She was admitted with chest pains and subdued with tranquilizers. He left her there and went to the sheriff's office to use Nix's phone on a private line. He talked to Dr. Hilsabeck, who was distraught. He forced himself to call Gran and Papa Sweeney in Kansas City with the news that their daughter was dead. He called Stella again and they tried to think through the next few days.

He left the sheriff's office and drove to Magargel's Funeral Home. In a cold, dark room somewhere in the rear of the building, he looked at his mother's beautiful face for the last time. And selected a casket.

He made it back to his car before he broke down. Sitting in the parking lot, staring at nothing as the wipers clicked back and forth, Joel was thoroughly overwhelmed by grief and cried for a long time.

The service was at the Methodist church, the one built by Pete's grandfather, the one in which Joel and Stella were baptized as children. The minister was new and freshly rotated into town by the Methodist hierarchy.

He knew the history but had not lived through it, and he was determined to reunite the factions and heal his congregation.

At first, Joel and Stella planned a private burial, one similar to the quick send-off Pete had planned for himself at Old Sycamore, but friends convinced them that their mother deserved a proper funeral. They relented and met with the minister.

The crowd was huge, twice the size of all available seating, and people sat in their cars in the parking lot and waited for a glimpse of the casket. The friends and acquaintances who had been denied the chance to say good-bye to Pete made sure they arrived early for Liza's farewell.

Mr. and Mrs. Sweeney sat between Joel and Stella and stared at the closed casket five feet away. Mrs. Sweeney was inconsolable and never stopped wiping her face. Mr. Sweeney was stoic, almost angry, as if he blamed the entire backward state for his daughter's demise. Joel and Stella were tired of crying and sat stunned, disbelieving, desperately waiting for the hour to pass. The occasion was too somber for any effort at levity. There were no warm eulogies of good and funny times with the deceased. No mention of Pete, not in that church. The Bannings' nightmare was continuing, and those watching it were helpless to intervene.

A few hymns, a brief sermon, some scripture, and it was over in less than an hour, as promised by the minister. As Miss Emma Faye Riddle began her last mournful number, the congregation rose, and the closed casket was pushed down the center aisle, followed by Joel and Stella, arm in arm. Behind them Mr. and Mrs. Sweeney held each other and tried to keep themselves together. Behind them were other members of the Sweeney family, but no Bannings. Florry was at home in bed. The rest of the small family was rapidly dying off. Of course, none of the coloreds were allowed inside the church.

As Joel trailed the casket, and the organ played, and the ladies cried, he was aware of the many stares. Near the rear, he glanced to his right, and in the back row was the prettiest face he had ever seen. Mary Ann Malouf had made the trip from Oxford with a sorority sister to pay her respects. Seeing her was the only pleasant moment of the day. Stepping into the vestibule, he told himself that one day he would marry that girl.

An hour later, a small crowd gathered at Old Sycamore for the interment. Just the family, a few friends, Amos and Nineva, Marietta, and a dozen other Negroes who lived on the land. Florry insisted on being there, but Joel insisted that she remain in the pink cottage. Joel was very much in charge now, making decisions that he had no desire to make. After a prayer, some scripture, and the same haunting rendition of "Amazing Grace" by Marietta, four men lowered Liza's casket into the ground, less than a foot from the one holding the remains of her husband. Side by side, they could now rest together for eternity.

She was as responsible for his death as he was for hers. Above them, they left behind two fine children who didn't deserve to be punished for the sins of their parents.

The week after the funeral was Thanksgiving. Joel sorely needed to return to law school and start cramming for finals, though as a third-year student he was coasting with a much easier schedule. On Monday, he and Stella drove to Oxford. He met with the dean and laid it all on the table. Some rather complicated family matters had to be dealt with, and he needed to be excused for a few more days. The dean knew what was happening, was sympathetic, and promised arrangements could be made. Joel was in the top 10 percent of his class and would graduate the following May.

While in Oxford, Joel invited Mary Ann to lunch at the Mansion to meet his sister. Driving over, he had admitted to Stella his feelings for the girl, and Stella was delighted her brother was finally involved in a serious romance. Since their mother's breakdown and the death of their father, the two had talked more, and more openly. They leaned on each other and held back little. As Bannings, they had been raised to say almost nothing, but those days were gone. There had always been too many secrets in the family.

The two young ladies were immediate friends. In fact, they bonded so quickly and talked and laughed so much that Joel was astonished. He said little during lunch because he hardly got the chance. Driving home, Stella told him he'd better get a ring on her finger before someone else did. Joel said he wasn't worried. The lunch lifted their somber spirits, but by the time they crossed into Ford County they were thinking about their mother again, and the conversation died. When Joel turned in to the drive, he inched along the gravel and stopped halfway to the house. He turned off the motor and they looked at their home.

Stella finally spoke. "I never thought I would say this,

but I really don't like this place now. The happy memories are all gone, shattered by what's happened. I never want to set foot in that house again."

"I think we should burn it," Joel said.

"Don't be stupid. Are you serious?"

"Sort of. I can't stomach the idea of Jackie Bell and her kids and that creep McLeish living here. He'll become the gentleman farmer, a real big shot. That's hard to swallow."

"But you're never going to live here again, right, Joel?"

"Right."

"Nor am I. So what difference does it make? We'll come back when we have to and visit Florry, but after she's gone I'll never come back."

"What about the cemetery?"

"What about it? How are we supposed to benefit from staring at old tombstones and wiping tears? They're dead, and it's painful because they shouldn't be dead, but they're gone, Joel. I'm trying to forget how they died and remember how they lived. Let's remember the good times, if that's possible."

"It seems impossible now."

"Yes, it does."

"It's all moot, Stella. We're losing the place anyway."

"I know. Just sign the deed and get it over with. I'm going back to the big city."

The headmistress at St. Agnes was sympathetic too, and told Stella she would be excused for the week. She was expected back the Sunday after Thanksgiving.

They stayed in the pink cottage and away from their house. Marietta roasted a turkey and prepared all the side dishes and pies, and they worked hard to get through the day in a grateful spirit. Florry was rallying and trying to enjoy the time with them.

Early Friday morning, Joel loaded Stella's bags into the Pontiac, and they hugged their aunt good-bye. They stopped at Old Sycamore and had a tear. At their house, Stella hurried inside for a hug with Nineva; then they were off.

She had insisted on taking the train to D.C., but Joel would have none of it. She was quite fragile—weren't they all?—and he did not want her sitting alone on a train for hour after hour. They needed the time together, so a road trip was in order. As they left the farm and turned onto the highway, Stella looked at her home and the fields around them. She hoped to never return.

And she never would.

Dead judges were replaced by the governor, who appointed interims until the next round of elections. Governor Fielding Wright, who had witnessed Pete's execution two and a half years earlier, was flooded with the usual requests for patronage after the death of Chancellor Rumbold. One of Wright's biggest supporters in north Mississippi was none other than Burch Dunlap, who was lobbying hard for a Tupelo sidekick named Jack Shenault. Dunlap had a plan to collect a quick, lucrative fee from the Banning case, and he needed Shenault on the bench.

In early December, while Joel was sweating through

final exams at Ole Miss, Governor Wright appointed Shenault the interim chancellor to succeed Rumbold. John Wilbanks and most of the other lawyers disliked the choice, primarily because Shenault did not live in the district. He said he planned to move.

Wilbanks was pushing another candidate, but Wilbanks and Governor Wright had never been on the same team.

Out of respect for the family, Dunlap waited a month after Liza's burial before swinging into action. He convinced Shenault to convene a meeting in Clanton with John Wilbanks and Joel Banning, who was home for the holiday break and had been appointed substitute trustee for his father's estate. They met in the judge's chamber behind the courtroom, a place Joel would always detest.

On the docket was Dunlap's lawsuit seeking a judicial foreclosure of the land now held by Pete Banning's estate, the last remaining salvo in the lengthy war over the property, and it was readily apparent that the new chancellor planned to move with haste.

By reputation, Shenault was an office practitioner and not a trial lawyer, and was generally well thought of. He was certainly prepared for the meeting, and John Wilbanks suspected he had been well rehearsed by Burch Dunlap.

According to His Honor, and Shenault even wore a black robe for the occasion, the scenario was straightforward. The hearing on the foreclosure would last only an hour or so, with both sides submitting documents and court orders, and perhaps a witness or two, but there was almost nothing disputed. He, Shenault, would most likely order a judicial sale of the property, which entailed an auction on the front steps of the courthouse. The highest bidder would take title, with the winning bid going straight to Jackie Bell, who held the judgment of $100,000. No one expected a bid that high, and any deficit would remain on the books as a lien against the property.

However, according to Mr. Dunlap, the plaintiff, Jackie Bell, was willing to accept a deed from the estate for the acreage, the house, and other assets in lieu of her claim.

Also, if Shenault ruled in favor of Jackie Bell, as he obviously planned to do, the Banning estate could appeal to the Mississippi Supreme Court, a delaying tactic that had been used before. Such an appeal would be fruitless, in his opinion.

Joel knew it too, as did John Wilbanks. They were at the end of the road. Additional delaying strategies would only postpone the inevitable, and drive up the attorneys' fees.

With everyone in general agreement, Shenault allowed the lawyers thirty days to work out the details, and scheduled the next meeting on January 26, 1950.

In the spirit of the season, and with the promise of a brighter future, Jackie Bell and Errol McLeish were married in a small ceremony two days before Christmas. Her three children were dressed up and proud, and a few friends joined them in the small chapel behind an Episcopal church.

Her parents were not invited. They did not approve of the marriage, because they did not trust Errol McLeish and his motives. Her father had insisted that she consult with a lawyer before the marriage, but she refused. McLeish was far too involved with her lawsuits and her money and she was certainly being set up for financial disaster, according to her father.

And she was not attending church, which greatly disturbed her parents. She had tried to explain her crisis of faith, but they would not listen. One was either in church or not, and those on the outside faced damnation.

Jackie was thrilled with the plan to leave Rome and return to Clanton. She needed space from her parents, and more important, she was eager to assume ownership of the Banning home. She had been there many times and never dreamed it would one day belong to her. After a life in cramped parsonages and rentals, a life where every house was too small and too temporary, she, Jackie Bell, was about to own one of the finest homes in Ford County.

CHAPTER 48

On a freezing morning two days after Christmas, Joel was walking through the fields after a visit to Old Sycamore. Pellets began landing around him. It was sleeting and there was a good chance of snow by late afternoon. He hustled to the house and was about to suggest a road trip somewhere to the south when Aunt Florry announced that she had decided to spend a couple of months in New Orleans as the houseguest of Miss Twyla. She'd been hinting about leaving. She was depressed about everything—Liza's death and her involvement in it, the cold weather, the dreary fields and landscapes, and, of course, the handing over of Pete's land, which she had to cross to get to hers. There were dark clouds everywhere, and she just wanted to get away.

They left within an hour, as road conditions deteriorated, and barely made it south through Polk County before the sleet slacked off. By Jackson, the weather and roads were better.

Along the way, they covered many important topics. Joel planned to propose to Mary Ann later in the spring. He had bought an engagement ring in Memphis and was excited about giving it to her. He was determined to live in Biloxi and thought he had a job with a small law firm there. Nothing definite, but he was optimistic. They worried about Stella and her nagging depression. She was spending the holidays with friends in D.C. and could not force herself to come home. Wasn't the whole family depressed? The most urgent matter was what to do with Florry's land in the upcoming spring. Neither had the stomach to approach McLeish about a deal. Indeed, Florry wanted to be absent for the next few months to avoid the man. They finally decided that Joel would negotiate a lease with Doug Wilbanks, John's cousin. He farmed thousands of acres in several counties and would not be intimidated by McLeish. They were not sure what would happen to the Negroes on the property, but those poor folks had always managed to survive. McLeish would need them as field hands. No one would starve.

And they couldn't worry about everybody, could they? Their lives had changed dramatically since the killing, and there was no way to recapture the past. They had to take care of themselves. Florry admitted that for the past two years she had been talking about living for a spell in New Orleans with Miss Twyla, a dear old friend from the Memphis years. Twyla was older and getting lonelier, and her rambling town house in the Quarter had plenty of room.

They talked for hours, always about the present or the future, and not about the past. But south of Jackson, some four hours into the journey, Joel said, "Stella and I believe you know a lot more than you've ever told us."

"About what?"

"About Pete and Dexter, about Mom. About what happened. You know something, don't you, Aunt Florry?"

"Why is this important now? Everybody's dead."

"The night Dad died, you went to see him at the jail. What did you talk about?"

"Must we rehash this? That was one of the worst nights of my life."

"Typical Banning response, Aunt Florry. Take the question, duck it, and try to wiggle away without a response. Where did you and Pete learn to be so evasive?"

"Don't be insulting, Joel."

"I'm not. Just answer the question."

"What do you want to know?"

"Why did Dad kill Dexter?"

"He never gave me a reason, and, believe me, I pressed him hard. He was a very stubborn man."

"No kidding. I figure Mom had an affair with Dexter Bell and somehow Dad found out about it when he got home from the war. He confronted her and she was overwhelmed with guilt and shame. She cracked up or whatever, and he wanted her out of the house. Wilbanks convinced Judge Rumbold she needed some time away, and Dad drove her to Whitfield. After that, Dad could never accept the fact that his wife had been unfaithful, especially given the nightmare he survived in the war. Think about it, Aunt Florry, he was over there starved nearly to death, wiped out with malaria and dysentery, getting tortured and abused, then fighting in the jungles, and she's home sleeping with the preacher. It drove him crazy, and that's why he killed Dexter Bell. Something snapped in Pete's mind. Your response, Aunt Florry?"

"You think your father cracked up?"

"Yes, and you don't?"

"No, I think Pete knew exactly what he was doing. He was not crazy. I'll buy the rest of your story, but Pete was thinking clearly."

"And he never told you this story?"

She took a deep breath and glanced out her window. The pause gave the real answer, but she did not. "No, not a word."

Joel knew she was lying.

There was no chance of snow in New Orleans. The temperature was in the fifties, the air clear and crisp. Miss Twyla greeted them with a flurry of fierce hugs and loud hellos, and served them drinks as her maid unloaded the car. Florry brought enough luggage, all hastily packed, to stay for a year. Joel mentioned possibly getting a room at the Hotel Monteleone on Royal Street, but Twyla would have none of it. Her elegant town house had plenty of bedrooms and she needed some company. They sat in the courtyard next to an old fountain with water dripping from a cement tiger, and talked about this and that. As soon as Florry excused herself for a moment, Twyla whispered to Joel, "She looks awful."

"It's been a rough time. She's blaming herself for my mom's death."

"I'm so sorry about that, Joel. Florry was hospitalized, right?"

"Yes, for a few days. Chest pains. I worry about her."

"She looks pale and thinner."

"Well, I guess she needs some gumbo and jambalaya and fried oysters. I've hauled her down here; now you feed her."

"I can do that. And we have better doctors down here. I'll get one to look at her. The family genes are, how shall I say it, not too promising."

"Thank you. Yes, we tend to die young."

"And how is the lovely Stella?"

"Okay. She didn't want to come back so soon, so she stayed in D.C. It's been a rough time."

"I'll say. What you folks need is some good luck."

Florry was back, shuffling along as her large tent of a dress flowed behind her. She was already happier being with Twyla in the big city. On an old wooden table that supposedly came from a farmhouse somewhere in France, a maid arranged a platter of raw oysters and poured cold wine.

They ate and drank and laughed deep into the night. Once again, Ford County was in another world.

Late the following morning, Joel stumbled from his bedroom with an aching head and dry mouth. He found water, quenched his thirst, and badly needed coffee. A maid quietly showed him the front door, and he stepped into the bright sunshine of another perfect day in the Vieux Carré. He steadied himself, found his footing, and ambled down Chartres to Jackson Square and his favorite little café, where the coffee was strong and half chicory. He drank one cup, paid for another to go, and walked across Decatur, through the French Market, and up the steps to the levee walk, where he sat on a bench. It was his favorite spot in the city, and he loved to loaf there for hours and watch the river traffic.

At home in his late father's library, there was a picture book of New Orleans. In one photo from the 1870s, dozens of steamboats were docked side by side at the port, all laden with bales of cotton from the farms and plantations in Arkansas, Mississippi, and Louisiana. As a kid who daydreamed a lot, Joel had convinced himself that the cotton from the Banning farm was on one of those boats and had been shipped to New Orleans for export. Their cotton was important and needed by the world. The people who worked on the boats and docks made their livelihoods because of their cotton.

Back then the docks were rowdy and chaotic, as steamboats swarmed in from upriver and hundreds of stevedores scurried to unload them. That was all gone now. The great river was still busy, but the steamboats had been replaced by low, flat barges carrying grain and coal. In the distance were battleships resting from the war.

Joel was captivated by the river and wondered where each vessel was headed. Some were going farther south, to the Gulf; others were returning. He had no desire to go home. Home meant the last boring semester of law school. Home meant meetings with lawyers and judges and the winding-up of his father's wretched affairs. Home meant saying farewell to the land, the house, to Nineva and Amos, and the others he had known his entire life.

He puttered around New Orleans for three days, and when he was finally bored he hugged Florry good-bye and left town. She had settled in nicely and seemed to be quite at home.

He drove to Biloxi and managed to surprise Mary Ann's father at his office. Joel apologized for the intrusion, but did not want her to know he was in town, and there was no other way to do it. He asked Mr. Malouf for his daughter's hand. Ambushed, the gentleman really had no choice but to say yes.

That night, Joel had dinner with his soon-to-be fiancée, and slept on the family's sofa.

CHAPTER 49

The year 1950 began with as much dreariness as was expected. On January 26, in John Wilbanks's splendid conference room, he and Joel assumed one side of the table while Burch Dunlap and Errol McLeish took the other. Chancellor Shenault, without a robe, sat at the end and refereed the negotiations.

Joel, as substitute executor, signed a deed that conveyed title to the 640 acres, with home, to Jackie Bell, now officially Jackie Bell McLeish. To avoid any misunderstandings with Florry, the land had been surveyed and platted so that the parties involved knew precisely where the property lines ran. All buildings had been identified, and a separate deed listed them: stables, chicken sheds, tractor barns, cow barns, pigpens, the shotgun home of Nineva and Amos, the foreman's house used by Buford Provine, and fourteen shacks in the woods that were currently inhabited by the field hands. A bill of sale listed the personal property: Pete's 1946 Ford truck, the John

Deere tractors, trailers, plows, planters, every piece of farm equipment down to rakes and shovels, along with the horses and livestock. McLeish would get it all. He had allowed Joel to purchase the 1939 Pontiac for $300.

Another document listed the furnishings in the house, what was left of them anyway. Joel had managed to take the books, keepsakes, guns, clothing, jewelry, memorabilia, bed linens, and better pieces of furniture.

As far as cash, McLeish didn't push too hard. He figured, rightfully so, that most of it had been either spent or hidden. Using the inventory Wilbanks had filed after probate in the fall of 1947, he agreed to accept the sum of $2,500, on behalf of his wife, of course.

Joel had loathed the man for so long and so hard it was difficult to conjure up another round of proper loathing. McLeish was at once pompous and pathetic as he considered sums of money and lists of assets earned and built by the sweat of others. He acted as though he truly believed that he and his new wife deserved the Bannings' land.

The meeting was a nightmare, and at times Joel felt nauseated. As soon as possible, he left without a word, slammed the door behind him, and fled from the office. He drove to the farm, and had tears in his eyes as he parked his car.

Nineva and Amos were sitting on the back porch, never the front, and they had the bewildered looks of people who might lose everything. They had been born on the Banning land and never left. When they saw the tears in Joel's eyes they began crying too. Somehow the three managed to wade through the emotions and farewells and separate themselves. When Joel left them on the porch, Nineva had collapsed into tears and Amos was holding her. Joel walked to the barn, where Buford was waiting in the cold. Joel passed along the message from the new owner that he, McLeish, would like to speak with Buford that afternoon. He would probably keep his job. Joel had said many fine things about their foreman and it would be a mistake to replace him. Buford thanked him, shook his hand, wiped a tear of his own.

Facing a raw wind, Joel walked half a mile over frozen soil to Old Sycamore and said good-bye to his parents. By a stroke of luck, the family cemetery was on Florry's section and thus accessible forever, or at least the near future. What did forever mean anymore? He was born to own his land forever.

For a long time he stared at both tombstones and asked himself for the thousandth time how their lives had become so complicated and so tragic. They were far too young to die and leave behind mysteries and burdens that would haunt those they loved. He looked at the other tombstones and wondered how many dark secrets the Bannings had taken all the way to their graves.

He walked the field roads and pig trails and footpaths of the land for the last time, and when he returned to his car his fingers were numb. He was chilled deep to the bone, and he ached to his core. Driving away, he refused to look at the house, and he wished he'd burned it.

Later in the afternoon, Errol McLeish appeared at his new home and introduced himself to Nineva. Neither tried to be polite. He didn't trust her, because she had worked forever for the Bannings, and she thought of him as nothing more than a thieving trespasser.

"Would you like to keep your job?" he asked.

"Not really. I'm too old, sir. Too old for housework anymore. Ain't you got a buncha kids?"

"There are three."

"See there. I'm too old to do all the washin' and cleanin' and cookin' and ironin' for three kids, plus a wife. Me and Amos just need to retire. We're too old."

"Retire where?"

"Can't we stay here? It's just a little house, but it's all we got. Been here for over fifty years. Ain't worth nothin' to nobody else."

"We'll see. I'm told Amos milks the cows and tends the vegetable garden."

"That's right, but he gettin' old too."

"How old is he?"

"'Bout sixty, I guess."

"And you?"

"'Bout the same."

"You got kids?"

"Bunch of 'em but they all gone, up north. Just me and Amos in our little house."

"Where's Mr. Provine?"

"Buford? He down by the tractor barn, waitin'."

McLeish walked through the kitchen and across the porch. He tightened the scarf around his neck, lit a cigar, and strutted across the backyard, passing the barns and sheds, counting the livestock, savoring his good fortune. Jackie and the kids would arrive next week, and they would begin the wonderful challenge of establishing themselves as people to reckon with in Ford County.

With his aunt tucked away safely in the warmth of New Orleans, and with his father's estate closed and his ancestral home now occupied by others, Joel had no reason to return to Ford County. Indeed, he wanted to stay away. Most of the cash left in the estate went to the Wilbanks firm, for its faithful and loyal representation. His weekly telephone chats with John Wilbanks came to a halt, but not before the lawyer passed along the news that McLeish had fired Nineva and Amos and evicted them from their home. They had been given forty-eight hours to move, and were currently living with relatives in Clanton. According to Buford Provine, who was gossiping with the Wilbankses' foreman on Florry's land, McLeish was planning to charge the field hands rent on their shacks while at the same time cutting their wages.

Joel was shocked and furious over the eviction. He could not imagine Nineva and Amos living anywhere else, or being forced to find a new home at their ages. He vowed to drive to Clanton, find them, and give them some money. And the other field hands were being abused for doing nothing wrong. They were accustomed to being treated fairly by his father and grandfather, but now an idiot was taking charge. Meanness does not inspire loyalty. The thought of it made him sick, and it was another reason to forget about the farm.

If not for the magic of Mary Ann, he would have been a brooding, depressed twenty-four-year-old law student facing a bleak future. She had said yes to his marriage proposal, and they were planning a small wedding in New Orleans after graduation in May. When spring arrived with all its promise and splendor, Joel shook off the doldrums and tried to savor his final days as a student. He and Mary Ann were inseparable. For spring break, they took the train to D.C. and spent a week with Stella.

Along the way to D.C. and back, they spent hours talking of finding a better life far away from Mississippi. Joel wanted to run, like his sister, and bolt for the big cities up north where the opportunities seemed boundless, and the memories more distant. Mary Ann was not quite as desperate to get away, but as the grandchild of immigrants she was not opposed to the idea of starting over. They were just kids, madly in love, about to be married, so why not explore the world?

On April 19, Florry awoke in the early morning with aching chest pains. She was faint, could barely breathe, and managed to wake Twyla before collapsing in a chair. An ambulance took her to Mercy Hospital, where she was stabilized. Her doctors diagnosed it as a mild heart attack and were concerned about her overall condition. The next day, Twyla called Joel at Ole Miss, and the following day, a Friday, he skipped his last class of the day and drove nonstop to New Orleans. Mary Ann was worried about exams and could not make the drive.

At Mercy, Florry was delighted to see him—it had been three and a half months—and worked hard to appear aggravated by all the attention. She claimed to be fine, bored with the routine, and ready to go home to start writing a new short story. Joel was surprised at her appearance. She had aged dramatically and looked at least ten years older with gray hair and pasty skin. Always heavy, she had thinned considerably. Her breathing was labored and she often seemed to gasp for breath.

In the hallway, Joel expressed his concerns to Miss Twyla. "She looks awful," he whispered.

"She has degenerative heart disease, Joel, and she is not going to get better."

The thought of Florry dying had never crossed his mind. After losing so many, Joel had blinded himself to the possibility of losing her. "They can't treat it?"

"They're trying, lots of meds and such, but it cannot be reversed, nor can it be stopped."

"But she's only fifty-two years old."

"That's old for a Banning."

Thanks for nothing. "I'm stunned by how much she aged."

"She's very weak, very frail, eats little, though she would like to eat more. I think her heart gets weaker every day. She can go home tomorrow and it would be nice if you stayed the weekend."

"Sure, no problem. I was planning on it."

"And you need to have an honest conversation with Stella."

"Believe me, Miss Twyla, Stella and I are the only ones in our family who have honest conversations."

An ambulance took Florry home Saturday morning, and she rallied considerably. A fine lunch was prepared in the courtyard. It was a perfect spring day with the temperature inching toward eighty, and Florry was delighted to be alive again. Against her doctors' orders, she chugged wine and had a full plate of red beans and rice. The more she talked and ate and drank the stronger she became. Her mind sharpened, as did her tongue, and her voice returned to full volume. It was an amazing comeback, and Joel stopped thinking about another funeral.

After a long Saturday afternoon nap, he hit the streets and roamed the French Quarter, which he always enjoyed, though he felt lost without Mary Ann. Jackson Square was swarming with tourists, and the street musicians had every corner. He had a drink at his favorite sidewalk café, posed for a bad caricature that cost him a dollar, bought a cheap bracelet for Mary Ann, listened to a jazz band outside the market, and eventually drifted to the levee, where he found a seat on a cast-iron bench and watched the boats come and go.

In their weekly letters, Joel and Florry had been arguing about whether she would attend his law school graduation in late May. Three years earlier, when his father was about to be executed and the entire family was in disarray, Joel had skipped his commencement service at Vanderbilt. He planned to skip the one at Ole Miss as well, but Florry thought otherwise. The three of them had enjoyed a glorious time at Hollins when Stella graduated, and they would do the same at Ole Miss, at least in Florry's plans.

The argument resumed Sunday morning over breakfast in the courtyard. Florry insisted that she would travel to Oxford for the ceremony, and Joel said it would be a waste of time because he wouldn't be there. The bantering was good-natured. Twyla rolled her eyes a few times. Florry wasn't going anywhere, except perhaps back to Mercy.

Florry had slept little during the night and was soon weakened. Twyla had hired a nurse who led her back to her room.

Twyla whispered, "She won't be here long, Joel. Do you understand this?"

"No."

"You need to brace yourself."

"How long? A month? A year?"

"It's a guessing game. When do you finish classes?"

"May 12. Graduation is the following week, but I'm skipping it."

"What about Stella?"

"She finishes about the same time."

"I suggest the two of you get here promptly and spend as much time as you can with Florry. You're welcome to stay here."

"Thanks."

"In fact, you can stay here all summer, before and after the wedding. She talks of nothing but you and Stella. Having you here is important."

"That's very generous, Twyla. Thank you. She'll never go home, will she?"

Twyla shrugged and looked away. "I doubt it. I doubt her doctors would agree to it. Frankly, Joel, she doesn't want to go home, not anytime soon."

"I understand that."

CHAPTER 50

The Crescent Limited ran twice daily from New York to New Orleans, a journey of fourteen hundred miles and thirty hours. At 2:00 p.m. on May 4, a Thursday, Stella boarded the train at Union Station in D.C. and settled into a comfortable seat in coach for a ride that would be anything but comfortable. To help pass the time, she removed her wristwatch, tried to nap, read magazines and a novel, ate nothing but snacks she brought with her, and tried to justify the trip. The headmistress at St. Agnes had not been happy with her request to take off. Because of her complicated family issues, she had missed too many days already, and, well, classes would be over in a week. Couldn't she wait?

No, according to Miss Twyla, there was no time to wait. Florry was at the end. For Stella, being there with her aunt was far more important than any job. The headmistress was slightly sympathetic, and decided they would discuss a new contract later. Stella had become a popular teacher and St. Agnes did not want to lose her.

According to Twyla, Florry had been rushed to Mercy Hospital for the second time, then the third, and her doctors were doing little more than medicating her and frowning a lot. Now she was back home, bedridden, fading, and wanting to see the kids. Joel was already there. He was missing exams but unconcerned.

Because of delays, the train arrived in New Orleans late Friday afternoon. Joel was waiting at the station and they took a cab to Miss Twyla's town house on Chartres Street. She met them at the door and ushered them into the courtyard, where cheese, olives, bread, and wine were waiting. As they nibbled and sipped, she said that Florry was resting but should wake up soon.

Twyla shooed away a maid and lowered her voice. "She wants to talk to you before it's too late. She has some important matters to discuss, some secrets that she wants to tell. I've convinced Florry that now is the time to talk. Tomorrow might be too late."

Joel took a deep breath and shot Stella a look of fear.

"Has she told you?" Stella asked.

"Yes, she's told me everything."

"And these stories are about our parents, right?" Joel asked.

Twyla took a deep breath, then a sip of wine. "The night your father died, just hours before his execution, Florry spent an hour with him at the jail, and for the first time he talked about his motives. He made her swear on a Bible that she would never tell anyone, especially the two of you. Six months ago, the night your mother died, she and Florry were alone in the house, in the bedroom, and your mother was off her pills and out of her mind. But she told another story, one your father never knew. She made Florry promise to never tell. And she didn't, until a few weeks ago when she was in the hospital. We thought she was gone. The doctors said it was over. She finally wanted to talk, said she could not take the truth to her grave."

"Hearing the truth is like grabbing smoke in our family," Joel said.

"Well, you're about to hear it, and it will not be easy for you. I've convinced her that she must tell you. It will disappoint you. It will shock you. But only the truth can allow you to fully understand, and move on. Without it, you'll carry burdens and doubts and suspicions forever. But with it, you can finally put away the past, pick up the pieces, and face the future. You must be strong."

Stella said, "I'm so tired of being strong."

Joel said, "Why am I suddenly nervous?" He gulped some wine.

"We cut back on the pills a little so she will be more coherent, but she tires so easily."

"Is she in pain?" Stella asked.

"Not much. Her heart is just slowly giving up. It's so sad."

Across the courtyard, a nurse came out of Florry's room and nodded at Twyla, who said, "She's awake now. You can go in."

Florry was sitting in her bed, propped up by pillows and smiling when they entered and started hugging. She was wearing one of her many brightly colored robes, probably to mask the fact that she had lost so much weight. Her legs were under a blanket. For a few minutes she was a chatterbox, prattling on about Joel's upcoming wedding and what she planned to wear. She seemed to have forgotten about his law school graduation in a couple of weeks.

A wave of fatigue hit hard, and she closed her eyes. Stella sat on the end of the bed and patted her feet. Joel eased into a chair close by the bed.

When she opened her eyes, she said, "There are some things you should know."

"When Pete came back from the war, he was all banged up, casts on both legs, you remember. He spent three months at the hospital in Jackson, gaining strength. When he got to the farm he was walking with a cane, doing all sorts of exercises, and moving around more and more each day. It was early fall of 1945. The war was over and the country was trying to get things back to normal. He went through hell over there but never said a word about it. Evidently, your parents engaged in an active marital relationship, shall we say. Nineva once told Marietta, long before the war, that if she turned her back they were trying to sneak away to the bedroom."

Joel said, "They had to get married, Florry. We know this. I've seen my birth certificate and I've seen their marriage license. We're not stupid."

"Didn't imply that you are. I was suspicious but never knew for sure."

"Dad pulled strings and got shipped to Germany before I was born. They were far away from home and the gossips never knew for sure."

"Then that's settled." She closed her eyes and breathed

deeply, as if fatigued. Joel and Stella exchanged nervous looks.

Florry opened her eyes, blinked and smiled, and asked, "Now where were we?"

"In Germany, a long time ago. Our parents had a rather lusty relationship."

"You could say that. They enjoyed each other, and as soon as Pete was back home and able he was ready to go. But there was a problem. Liza had no interest. At first Pete thought it was because his body was scarred and ravaged by war, and not what it once was. But she wouldn't respond. Finally, they had a big fight and she told a tale, the first of several. She concocted a story about having a miscarriage not long after he left home in 1941. She had three of them, you know."

"Four," Stella said.

"Okay, four, and by the time Pete left for war, they were convinced she could never have more children. Well, supposedly, she was pregnant when he left but they didn't know it. When she realized it, she told no one because she was afraid of losing another baby and didn't want to worry him. He was at Fort Riley, waiting to be shipped out. Then she miscarried, or so she said, and because of the miscarriage she had some lingering female problems. She had discharges that were unpleasant. She had seen doctors. She was taking medicines. Her body was doing things she couldn't control, and she had lost the desire for sex. It embarrasses me to say that word in front of you two."

"Come on, Aunt Florry. We know all about sex," Joel said.

"Both of you?" she asked, looking at Stella.

"Yes, both of us."

"Oh, dear."

"Come on, Florry. We're all adults here."

"Okay. Sex, sex, sex. There, I've said it. So when she was never in the mood, he was upset. Think about it. Poor guy spent three years in the jungle half-dead dreaming of food and water, and also thinking a lot about his beautiful wife back home. Then Pete got suspicious. According to her story, they got pregnant right before he left for Fort Riley, early in October of 1941. But in late August of that year, Pete wrenched his back pulling a stump and was in terrible pain. Sex was out of the question."

"I remember that," Stella said. "When he left for Fort Riley he could hardly walk."

"In fact, his back was so bad the doctors at Fort Riley almost discharged him for medical reasons. He was certain that there had been no sex in September because he thought about it a million times when he was a prisoner. Her story was that she got pregnant around early October, kept it quiet for a couple of months, and planned to tell Pete in a letter if she made it to three months. She didn't. She miscarried in early December, two months in, and never told anyone. Pete knew that wasn't true. If she indeed got pregnant, then it was in late August. His point was that she was more than three months along when she claimed to have miscarried. He studied the calendars and pieced together a timeline. Then he ambushed Nineva one day and asked her about the miscarriage. She knew nothing, which, as you know, was virtually impossible. She knew nothing about a miscarriage, nothing about a pregnancy. Pete knew that if Liza was three months along, then Nineva would know it. She delivered a hundred babies, including me and Pete. Once he was convinced Liza was lying about the miscarriage, thus the discharges, thus the total lack of interest in sex, he became really suspicious. She was fanatical about cleaning her own undergarments, and Nineva confirmed this. With time, he waited for the right chance and was able to confirm the discharges. There were small stains on her delicates. And she was taking a lot of pills that she was trying to hide. He wanted to talk to her doctors, but she flatly refused. Anyway, the clues were piling up, the lies were breaking down. Something was physically wrong with his wife and it wasn't caused by a miscarriage. He'd been through three of them, remember?"

"Four," Stella said.

"Right. Nineva had said some things about Dexter Bell and how much time he spent with Liza after the news that Pete was missing and presumed dead. We all remember how horrible that was, and Dexter was at the house a lot. Turns out that Pete had never really trusted Dexter, thought he had a roving eye. There was a rumor at church, one I never heard, about Dexter being too friendly with a young woman, I think she was twenty. Just a rumor, but Pete was suspicious."

Florry exhaled and asked for a glass of water. She wiped her mouth with the back of her hand and breathed heavily for a moment or so. She closed her eyes and continued. "Anyway, Pete got very suspicious. He went to Memphis and hired a private detective, paid him a lot of money, gave him photos of Liza and Dexter Bell. At the time there were three doctors, if you call them doctors,

I'm not sure really what they were, and they're probably still in business, but, they, well, they, uh, did abortions."

Stella nodded stoically. Joel took a deep breath. Florry kept her eyes closed and plowed on. "Sure enough, the private detective found a doctor who recognized them from the photos, but he wanted a big bribe. Pete had no choice. Paid the guy $2,000 in cash, and he confirmed that on September 29, 1943, he did the deed for Liza."

Joel grunted, "Good God."

Stella said, "Well, that explains Nineva's story about the day Mom and Dexter spent in Memphis."

"Yep."

"I'm sorry, I don't know that one," Florry said.

"There are so many," Stella said. "Keep going and we might circle back to it."

"Okay. So, needless to say, Pete was devastated. He had the proof of her betrayal, and not just a little fooling around, but a full-blown pregnancy that got aborted in the back room of some low-end clinic in Memphis. He was furious, devastated, and felt thoroughly betrayed by the woman he had always adored."

She paused and wiped a tear. "This is so awful. I never wanted to tell this story, never."

"You're doing the right thing, Aunt Florry," Stella said. "We can deal with the truth."

"So he confronted her?" Joel asked.

"He did. He picked the right moment, and ambushed her with the proof. The result was a complete and total breakdown. Nervous breakdown, emotional breakdown, call it whatever the doctors want to call it. She admitted everything: the affair, the abortion, the infection that wouldn't go away. She begged for forgiveness, again and again. In fact, she never stopped begging for forgiveness, and he never offered it. He never got over it. He'd come so close to death so many times, but he kept going because of her, and you. And to think that she was having fun with Dexter Bell was more than he could stand. He saw John Wilbanks. They went to the judge. She was committed to Whitfield, and she did not resist. She knew she needed help, and she had to get away from him. Once she was gone, he tried to go about his business, but he reached a point where that was not possible."

"So he killed Dexter," Stella said.

"Not a bad motive," Joel said.

There was a long heavy silence in which all three tried to focus. Joel stood, opened the door, walked to the courtyard, poured a glass of wine, and brought the bottle back with him. "Anyone?" he asked. Stella shook her head no. Florry appeared to be sleeping.

He sat down and took a sip, then another. Finally, he said, "And I guess there's more to the story."

"A lot more," Florry whispered with her eyes closed. She coughed and cleared her throat, propped herself up again. "We all knew Jupe, Nineva's grandson. He worked around the house and the gardens."

"We grew up together, Florry, and played together," Joel said.

"Right, he left home young, went to Chicago, came back. Pete taught him how to drive, let him run errands in his truck, treated him special. Pete was very fond of Jupe."

She swallowed hard, took another deep breath. "And so was your mother."

"No," Joel grunted, too stunned to say anything else.

"It can't be," Stella said.

"It was so. When your father confronted your mother with the proof of the abortion, he demanded to know if it was Dexter Bell. At that awful moment, she had to make a decision. A choice. The truth or a lie. And your mother lied. She could not bring herself to admit she had carried on with Jupe. It was unthinkable, unimaginable."

"How did it happen?" Joel asked.

"Did he force himself?" Stella asked.

"He did not. The night your mom died, she obviously knew what she was about to do. I did not. I was with her and she was at the end. She talked and talked and told me everything. At times she seemed lucid, at times out of it, but she never stopped talking. She said that Nineva got sick with something and stayed at home for a week. Jupe was working around the house. One day he was in the house, alone with Liza, and it just happened. It was a year after the news of Pete, and something just came over her. It wasn't planned. There was no seduction, no forcing, all consensual. It just happened. And it happened again."

Joel closed his eyes and exhaled mightily. Stella stared at the floor, mouth open, stunned.

Florry plowed ahead. "Your mother has always hated driving, so Jupe became her driver, and to get away from Nineva they would go to town. They had some hiding places along the way, around the county. It became a game and Liza frankly admitted to enjoying herself. It's not unheard of, kids, the races have been mixing from day one. Again, she considered herself a widow, she was single, she was just having a little harmless fun, or so she thought."

"Impossible," Joel grunted.

"It doesn't seem harmless," Stella said.

"It happened; we can't change any of it. I'm just telling you what your mother told me. Sure, she was out of her mind that last night, but what could she gain by fabricating such a tale? She wanted someone to know before she went to the grave. That's why she told me."

"You were there and you were never suspicious?" Joel asked.

"Never, not for a minute. I never suspected Dexter Bell, never suspected anyone. All of us were trying to get on with our lives after Pete. It never crossed my mind that Liza was carrying on with anybody."

"Can we get through the rest of this god-awful story?" Stella asked.

"You've always wanted the truth," Florry said.

"Now I'm not so sure," Joel said.

"Please continue."

"Okay, I'm trying, kids. This is not easy. Anyway, the frolicking came to an end when Liza realized she was pregnant. For a month or so she was in denial, but then she started to show and realized Nineva or someone else would get suspicious. She was in a panic, as you might guess. Her first idea was to do what white women have always done when they get caught—scream rape. That puts the blame somewhere else and makes it easier to take care of the pregnancy. She was at her wit's end when she decided to confide in Dexter Bell, a man she could trust. He never touched her in a bad way. He was always the kind, compassionate pastor who provided comfort. Dexter convinced her not to go through with the rape story, and in doing so saved Jupe's life. They would've strung the boy up in a heartbeat. At about the same time, word got to Nineva and Amos about the grandson and the boss lady carrying on. They were terrified and got him out of town."

Joel and Stella were speechless. The door opened a few inches and Twyla looked in. "How are we doing?"

"We're fine," Florry whispered, and the door closed. They were anything but fine.

Joel eventually stood with his glass of wine and walked to the small window overlooking the courtyard. He asked, "Did Nineva know she was pregnant?"

"Liza was convinced that she did not. No one knew, not even Jupe. They got him out of town about the time she realized she was pregnant."

"How did Nineva know they were doing it?"

Florry closed her eyes again and breathed as if waiting for a surge of energy. Without opening them, she coughed and continued. "A colored boy was fishing down by the creek and saw something. He ran home to his momma and told her. Word eventually got to Nineva and Amos, and they were horrified and appreciated the danger. Jupe was on the next bus to Chicago. I think he's still there."

A long, heavy pause settled over the room. Minutes passed and nothing was said. Florry opened her eyes but avoided eye contact. Joel returned to his seat, put his wineglass on the table, and ran his fingers through his thick hair. Finally, he said, "So, I guess Pete killed the wrong man, right, Florry?"

She did not answer his question. Instead, she said, "I've often thought about Liza in that awful moment when she was confronted with her abortion. She had to make a choice, one that she had not had time to prepare for. Pete assumed it was Dexter Bell, and it was much easier for her to say yes than to stop and think for a moment. One choice, made under extreme duress and confusion, and look at the consequences."

Stella said, "True, but if she'd had the time, she would never have admitted to the truth. No white woman in her position could do that."

Florry said, "Don't make your mother a whore. If she had believed that there was even the slimmest chance your father was alive, she would never have carried on so. She was a fine woman who loved your father endlessly. I was with her the night she died, and she ached and ached and ached for her sins. She begged forgiveness. She longed for her old life back with her family. She was so broken, so pathetic. You must remember her as a good, kind, loving mother."

Joel stood and left the room without a word. He crossed the courtyard, said nothing to Miss Twyla in her wicker rocker, and left the town house. He drifted down Chartres Street to Jackson Square where he sat on the steps of the cathedral and watched the circus of street performers, musicians, hucksters, con men, artists, pickpockets, pimps, and tourists. Every black man was Jupe up to no good. Every painted white woman was his mother with desire. Everything was a blur; nothing made sense. His breathing was labored, his eyes out of focus.

And then he was on the levee, though he didn't remember walking over. The barges were passing by and he was staring at them, staring at nothing. Damn the truth. He'd been much happier without it. Every day for the past three and a half years he had tortured himself with questions about why his father did what he did, and countless times he had conceded that he would never know. Well, now he knew, and he missed all those blissfully ignorant days.

For a long time, Joel sat lost in his own world, hardly moving, occasionally shaking his head slightly in disbelief. Then he realized his breathing had slowed, his senses were normal. He convinced himself that no one would ever know, other than himself, Stella, and Miss Twyla. Florry would soon be dead, and like all good Bannings she would take her secrets to her grave. He and Stella would eventually follow suit. A broken and disgraced family would not suffer further humiliation.

And what did it really matter? Neither he nor Stella, nor Florry, for that matter, would ever again live among those people in Ford County. Let the truth be buried there, at Old Sycamore. He wasn't going back.

A hand touched his shoulder and Stella sat next to him, close. He put his arm around her shoulders and pulled her tight. There was no emotion. They were too stunned for any of that.

"How is she?" he asked.

"It won't be long."

"She's all we have left."

"No, Joel, we have each other, so please don't die young."

"I'll try not to."

"A question, Counselor," she said. "If Mom had told the truth, what would Dad have done?"

"I've been thinking of nothing else. I'm sure he would have divorced her and run her out of the county. He would have sworn revenge against Jupe, but then he's safe in Chicago. Different laws up north."

"But she would be alive, wouldn't she?"

"I guess. Who knows?"

"But Dad would certainly be alive."

"Yes, along with Dexter Bell. And we would have our land."

She shook her head and mumbled, "What a lie."

"Did she really have a choice?"

"I can't say. I just feel so sorry for her. And for Dad. And for Dexter. For all of us, I guess. How did we get here?"

She was shaking and he hugged her tighter. He kissed the top of her head as she began crying.

"What a family," he said softly.

AUTHOR'S NOTE

Many years ago I served two terms as a state representative in the Mississippi Legislature. I didn't particularly enjoy public service, and you'd have to dust the capitol in Jackson for fingerprints to find proof I was there. I left no record; indeed, I left in a hurry. The job involved vast stretches of wasted time, and to fill those hours we gathered around various coffeepots and water fountains and listened to long and colorful and often hilarious stories told by our colleagues, all of whom were veteran politicians from around the state and accustomed to spinning tall yarns. I doubt if the truth really mattered that much.

At some point during my little career there, I heard the story of two prominent men living in a small town in Mississippi in the 1930s. One killed the other for no discernible reason, and he never offered a clue as to his motive. Once convicted and facing death by hanging, he turned down an offer from the governor to have his death sentence commuted if only he would divulge a motive. He refused and was hanged the next day on the courthouse lawn while the governor, who'd never witnessed a hanging, watched from the front row.

And so, I stole this story. I believe it to be true but cannot remember who told it, or where it happened, or when. There is an excellent chance it was all fiction to begin with, and after heaping on an abundance of my own embellishments, I have no qualms about publishing it as a novel.

However, if any reader out there recognizes this story, please let me know. I would love to have it verified.

As always, I relied upon the generosity of friends for their help in chasing down facts. Many thanks to Bill Henry, Linda and Tim Pepper, Richard Howorth, Louisa Barrett, and The Bus Boys—Dan Jordan, Robert Khayat, Charles Overby, and Robert Weems. And a special thanks to John Pitts for the title.

Dozens if not hundreds of books have been written about the Bataan Death March. The ones I found and read are all fascinating. The suffering and heroism of those soldiers is difficult to imagine, then or now, some seventy-five years later.

I gleaned facts from the following:

Shadows in the Jungle, by Larry Alexander; *Bataan Death March,* by Lt. Col. William E. Dyess; *American Guerrilla: The Forgotten Heroics of Russell W. Volckmann,* by Mike Guardia; *Lapham's Raiders,* by Robert Lapham and Bernard Norling; *Some Survived,* by Manny Lawton; *Escape from Davao,* by John D. Lukacs; *Lieutenant Ramsey's War,* by Edwin Price Ramsey and Stephen J. Rivele; *My Hitch in Hell,* by Lester I. Tenney; *Escape from Corregidor,* by Edgar D. Whitcomb.

Tears in the Darkness, by Michael Norman and Elizabeth M. Norman, is a thorough and engaging history of the Bataan Death March as seen from both American and Japanese perspectives. *The Doomed Horse Soldiers of Bataan,* by Raymond G. Woolfe, Jr., is a compelling account of the famous Twenty-Sixth Cavalry and its final charge. I highly recommend both books.

Read on for a sneak peek at

THE ROOSTER BAR

We hope you have enjoyed *The Reckoning*.
We're pleased to present you with
a sneak peek of John Grisham's novel,
The Rooster Bar, available now. Enjoy!

1

The end of the year brought the usual holiday festivities, though around the Frazier house there was little to cheer. Mrs. Frazier went through the motions of decorating a small tree and wrapping a few cheap gifts and baking cookies no one really wanted, and, as always, she kept *The Nutcracker* running nonstop on the stereo as she gamely hummed along in the kitchen as though the season *was* merry.

Things were anything but merry. Mr. Frazier had moved out three years earlier, and he wasn't missed as much as he was despised. In no time, he had moved in with his young secretary, who, as things developed, was already pregnant. Mrs. Frazier, jilted, humiliated, broke, and depressed, was still struggling.

Louie, her younger son, was under house arrest, sort of free on bail, and facing a rough year ahead with the drug charges and all. He made no effort to buy his mom anything in the way of a gift. His excuse was that he couldn't leave the house because of the court-ordered monitor attached to his ankle. But even without it, no one expected Louie to go to the trouble of buying gifts. The year before and the year before that both of his ankles had been unburdened and he hadn't bothered to shop.

Mark, the older son, was home from the horrors of law school, and, though even poorer than his brother, had managed to buy his mother some perfume. He was scheduled to graduate in May, sit for the bar exam in July, and begin working with a D.C. firm in September, which, as it so happened, was the same month Louie's trial was on the docket. But Louie's case would not go to trial for two very good reasons. First, the undercover boys had caught him in the act of selling ten bags of crack—there was even a video—and, second, neither Louie nor his mother could afford a decent lawyer to handle the mess. Throughout the holidays, both Louie and Mrs. Frazier dropped hints that Mark should rush in and volunteer to defend his brother. Wouldn't it be easy to stall matters until later in the year when Mark was properly admitted to the bar—he was practically there anyway—and once he had his license wouldn't it be a simple matter of finding one of those technicalities you read about to get the charges dismissed?

This little fantasy of theirs had some rather large holes in it, but Mark refused to discuss it. When it became apparent that Louie planned to hog the sofa for at least ten hours on New Year's Day and watch seven straight bowl games, Mark made a quiet exit and went to a friend's house. Returning home that night, while driving under the influence, he made the decision to flee. He would return to D.C. and kill some time puttering around the law firm where he would soon be employed. Classes didn't start for almost two weeks, but after ten days of listening to Louie bitch and moan about his problems, not to mention the nonstop *Nutcracker,* Mark was fed up and looking forward to his last semester of law school.

He set his alarm for eight the following morning, and over coffee with his mom explained that he was needed back in D.C. Sorry to leave a bit earlier than expected, Mom, and sorry to leave you here all alone with your bad boy, Mom, but I'm outta here. He's not mine to raise. I got my own problems.

The first problem was his vehicle, a Ford Bronco he'd been driving since high school. The odometer had frozen at 187,000 miles, and that had happened midway through college. It desperately needed a new fuel pump, one of many replacement parts on the Urgent List. Using tape and paper clips, Mark had been able to wire and jerry-rig the engine, transmission, and brakes for the past two years, but he'd had no luck with the fuel pump. It worked but at a lower capacity than normal, so that the Bronco's max speed was forty-nine on level ground. To avoid being clobbered by 18-wheelers on the expressways, Mark stuck to the back roads of rural Delaware and the Eastern Shore. The two-hour drive from Dover to central D.C. took twice as long.

This gave him even more time to consider his other problems. Number two was his suffocating student debt. He'd finished college with $60,000 in loans, and no job. His father, who seemed happily married at the time but was also in debt, had warned him against further studies. He'd said, "Hell, boy, four years of education and you're sixty grand in the hole. Quit before it gets any worse." But Mark thought taking any financial advice from his father was foolish, so he worked a couple of years here and there, bartending and delivering pizza, while he haggled with his lenders. Now, looking back, he wasn't sure where the idea of law school had originated, but he did remember overhearing a conversation between two frat brothers who were pondering weighty matters while drinking heavily. Mark was the bartender, the lounge was not crowded, and after the fourth round of vodka and cranberry juice they talked loud enough for all to hear. Among many interesting things they had said, Mark had always remembered two: "The big D.C. law firms are hiring like crazy." And, "Starting salaries are one-fifty a year."

Not long after that, he bumped into a college friend who was a first-year student at the Foggy Bottom Law School in D.C., and the guy gushed on about his plans to blitz through his studies, finish in two and a half years, and sign on with a big firm for a fat salary. The Feds were throwing loans at students, anybody could qualify, and, well sure, he would graduate with a mountain of debt but nothing he couldn't wipe out in five years. To his friend, at least, it made perfect sense to "invest in himself" with the debt because it would guarantee all that future earning power.

Mark took the bait and began studying for the Law School Admission Test. His score was an unimpressive 146, but this did not bother the admissions folks at the Foggy Bottom Law School. Nor did his rather thin undergraduate résumé with an anemic grade point average of 2.8. FBLS accepted him with open arms. His loan applications were quickly approved. Sixty-five thousand bucks were simply transferred from the Department of Education each year to Foggy Bottom. And now, with one semester to go, Mark was staring miserably at the reality of graduating with a combined total, undergrad and law school, principal and interest, of $266,000 in debt.

Another problem was his job. As it happened, the market wasn't quite as strong as rumored. Nor was it as vibrant as FBLS had advertised in its slick brochures and near-fraudulent website. Graduates from top-tier law schools were still finding work at enviable salaries. FBLS, though, was not quite in the top tier. Mark had managed to worm his way into a midsized law firm that specialized in "governmental relations," which meant nothing more than lobbying. His starting salary had not been established, because the firm's management committee would meet in early January to review profits from the previous year and supposedly jiggle the pay structure. In a few months, Mark would be expected to have an important talk with his "loan counselor" about restructuring his student debt and somehow repaying the entire mess. This counselor had already expressed concern that Mark did not know how much he would be earning. This concerned Mark too, especially when added to the fact that he didn't trust a single person he'd met at the law firm. As much as he tried to fool himself, he knew deep in his gut that his position was not secure.

Another problem was the bar exam. Because of demand, the D.C. version of the test was one of the more challenging in the nation, and FBLS grads had been bombing it at an alarming rate. Again, the top schools in town did well. The year before, Georgetown had a 91 percent pass rate. For George Washington it was 89 percent. For FBLS, the pass rate was a pathetic 56 percent. To succeed, Mark needed to start studying now, in early January, and hit the books nonstop for six months.

But the energy simply wasn't there, especially in the cold, dreary, depressing days of winter. At times the debt felt like cinder blocks strapped to his back. Walking was a chore. Smiling was difficult. He was living in poverty and his future, even with the job, was bleak. And he was one of the fortunate ones. Most of his classmates had the loans but not the jobs. Looking back, he'd heard the grumbling even in his first year, and with each semester the mood at school grew darker, the suspicions heavier. The job market worsened. The bar exam results embarrassed everyone at FBLS. The loans piled up. Now, in his third and last year, it was not unusual to hear students verbally spar with professors in class. The dean wouldn't come out of his office. Bloggers blistered the school and screamed harsh questions: "Is this a hoax?" "Have we been had?" "Where did all the money go?"

To varying degrees, almost everyone Mark knew believed that (1) FBLS was a subpar law school that (2) made too many promises, and (3) charged too much money, and (4) encouraged too much debt while (5) admitting a lot of mediocre students who really had no business in law school, and (6) were either not properly prepared for the bar exam or (7) too dumb to pass it.

There were rumors that applications to FBLS had fallen by 50 percent. With no state support, and no endowment, such a decline would lead to all manner of painful cost cutting, and a bad law school would only get worse. This was fine with Mark Frazier and his friends. They would endure the next four months and happily leave the place, never to return.

Mark lived in a five-story apartment building that was eighty years old and visibly deteriorating, but the rent was low and this attracted students from George Washington and FBLS. In its earlier days it had been known as the Cooper House, but after three decades of frat-like wear and tear it had earned its nickname as the Coop. Because its elevators seldom worked, Mark took the stairs to the third floor and entered his cramped and sparsely furnished flat, for which he paid $800 a month for five hundred square feet. For some reason he'd cleaned the place after his last exam before the holidays, and as he flipped on lights he was pleased to see that everything was in order. And why shouldn't it be? The slumlord who owned the place never came around. He unloaded his bags and was struck by the silence. Normally, with a bunch of students, and with thin walls, there was always a racket. Stereos, televisions, arguments, pranks, poker games, fights, guitar playing, even a trombone played by a nerd on the fourth floor that could rattle the entire building. But not today. Everyone was still at home, enjoying the break, and the halls were eerily quiet.

After half an hour, Mark was bored and left the building. Walking along New Hampshire Avenue, with the wind cutting through his thin fleece and old khakis, he decided, for some reason, to turn onto Twenty-First and stop by the law school to see if it was open. In a city with no shortage of hideous modern buildings, FBLS managed to stand out in its unsightliness. It was a postwar edifice covered with bland yellow bricks on eight levels slung together in asymmetrical wings, some failed architect's effort at making a statement. Supposedly, it once was an office building, but walls had been knocked out with abandon to create cramped lecture halls on the four lower floors. On the fifth was the library, a rabbits' warren of large, retrofitted rooms packed with seldom-touched books and some replicated portraits of unknown judges and legal scholars. The faculty had offices on the sixth and seventh floors, and on the eighth, and as far away from the students as possible, the administration carried on, with the dean solidly hidden in a corner office from which he seldom ventured.

The front door was unlocked and Mark entered the empty lobby. While he appreciated its warmth, he found the area, as always, utterly depressing. A huge bulletin board covered one wall with all manner of notices and announcements and enticements. There were a few slick posters advertising opportunities to study abroad, and the usual assortment of handmade ads offering stuff for sale— books, bikes, tickets, course outlines, tutors by the hour—and apartments for rent. The bar exam loomed over the entire school like a dark cloud and there were posters extolling the excellence of some review courses. If he searched hard enough he could possibly find a few employment opportunities, but at FBLS those had become scarcer by the year. In one corner he saw the same old brochures hawking even more student loans. At the far end of the lobby there were vending machines and a small coffee bar, but nothing was being brewed during the break.

He fell into a battered leather chair and soaked in the gloominess of his school. Was it really a school or was it just another diploma mill? The answer was becoming clear. For the thousandth time he wished he had never walked through the front doors as an unsuspecting first-year student. Now, almost three years later, he was burdened by loans he couldn't imagine paying off. If there was a light at the end of the tunnel, he couldn't see it.

And why would anyone name a school Foggy Bottom? As if the law school experience itself wasn't dreary enough, some bright soul had, some twenty years earlier, tagged it with a name that conveyed even more cheerlessness. That guy, now dead, had sold the school to some Wall Street investors who owned a string of law schools that were reportedly producing handsome profits while cranking out little in the way of legal talent.

How do you buy and sell law schools? It was still a mystery.

Mark heard voices and hurriedly left the building. He hiked down New Hampshire to Dupont Circle, where he ducked into Kramer Books for a coffee and a quick thaw. He walked everywhere. His Bronco lurched and stalled too much in city traffic, and he kept it tucked away in a lot behind the Coop, always with the key in the ignition. Unfortunately, so far no one had been tempted to steal it.

Warm again, he hustled six blocks north along Connecticut Avenue. The law firm of Ness Skelton occupied a few floors in a modern building near the Hinckley Hilton. The previous summer Mark had managed to weasel his way inside when he accepted an internship that paid less than minimum wage. At major law firms, the summer programs were used to entice top students to the big life. Little work was expected. The interns were given ridiculously easy schedules, along with tickets to ball games and invitations to fine parties in the splendid backyards of the wealthy partners. Once seduced, they signed on, and upon graduation were soon thrown into the meat grinder of hundred-hour weeks.

Not so at Ness Skelton. With only fifty lawyers, it was far from a top-ten firm. Its clients were trade associations—Soybean Forum, Retired Postal Workers, Beef and Lamb Council, National Asphalt Contractors, Disabled Railroad Engineers—and several defense contractors desperate for their share of the pork. The firm's expertise, if it had any, was maintaining relationships with Congress. Its summer intern program was designed more to exploit cheap labor than to attract top students. Mark had worked hard and suffered through the stultifying work. At the end of the summer, when he had received an offer that somewhat resembled a position upon passing the bar exam, he couldn't decide if he should celebrate or cry. Nonetheless, he jumped at what was being offered—there was nothing else on the table—and proudly became one of the few FBLS students with a future. Throughout the fall, he had gently pressed his supervisor about the terms of his upcoming employment but got nowhere. There might be a merger in the works. There might be a split. There might be a lot of things, but an employment contract was not one of them.

So he hung around. Afternoons, Saturdays, holidays, anytime he was bored he would stop by the firm, always with a big fake smile and an eagerness to pitch in and help with the grunt work. It was not clear if this was beneficial, but he figured it couldn't hurt.

His supervisor was named Randall, a ten-year guy on the verge of making partner, and thus under a lot of pressure. A Ness Skelton associate who didn't make partner after ten years was quietly shown the door. Randall was a George Washington law grad, which, in the city's pecking order, was a step down from Georgetown but several notches above Foggy Bottom. The hierarchy was clear and rigid, and its worst perpetrators were the GW lawyers. They detested being looked down upon by the Georgetown gang; thus they were eager to look down with even more disdain on anyone from FBLS. The entire firm reeked of cliques and snobbery, and Mark often wondered how in hell he wound up there. Two associates were from FBLS, but they were so busy trying to distance themselves from their school they had no time to lend Mark a hand. Indeed, they seemed to ignore him more than anyone else. Mark had often mumbled, "What a way to run a law firm." But then he figured that every profession had its levels of status. He was far too worried about his own skin to fret over where the other cutthroats had studied law. He had his own problems.

He had e-mailed Randall and said he would be dropping by to do whatever grunt work was available. Randall greeted him with a curt "Back so soon?"

Sure, Randall, and how were your holidays? Great to see you. "Yeah, got bored with all the holiday crap. What's up?"

"Two of the secretaries are out with the flu," Randall said. He pointed to a stack of documents a foot thick. "I need that copied fourteen times, all collated and stapled."

Okay, back to the copy room, Mark thought. "Sure," he said as if he couldn't wait to jump in. He hauled the documents down to the basement, to a dungeon filled with copiers. He spent the next three hours doing mindless work for which he would be paid nothing.

He almost missed Louie and his ankle monitor.

2

Like Mark, Todd Lucero was inspired to become a lawyer by booze-tinted conversations he'd overheard in a bar. For the past three years, he had been mixing drinks at the Old Red Cat, a pub-style watering hole favored by students from GW and Foggy Bottom. After college at Frostburg State, he'd left Baltimore and drifted into D.C. in search of a career. Finding none, he hired on at the Old Red Cat as a part-timer and soon realized he had a fondness for pulling pints and mixing strong drinks. He'd come to love the pub life and had a gift for schmoozing with the serious drinkers while placating the rowdies. Todd was everybody's favorite bartender and was on a first-name basis with hundreds of his regulars.

Many times over the past two and a half years he had thought of quitting law school to pursue his dream of owning his own bar. His father, though, had strong opinions to the contrary. Mr. Lucero was a cop in Baltimore and had always pushed his son to obtain a professional degree. Pushing was one thing, but paying for it was something else. And so Todd had fallen into the same trap of borrowing easy money and handing it over to the greedy folks at FBLS.

He and Mark Frazier had met the first day, during orientation, back when they were both starry-eyed and envisioning big law careers with fat salaries, back when they, along with 350 others, were horribly naive. He vowed to quit after his first year, but his father yelled at him. Because of his commitment to the bar, he had never found the time to knock on doors around D.C. and hustle for summer internships. He vowed to quit after his second year and cut off the flow of debt, but his loan counselor strongly advised against it. As long as he was in school he did not have to confront some brutal repayment schedule, so it made perfect sense to keep borrowing in order to graduate and find one of those lucrative jobs that, in theory, would eventually take care of the debts. Now, though, with only one semester to go, he knew only too well such jobs did not exist.

If only he'd borrowed $195,000 from a bank and opened his bar. He could be printing money and enjoying life.

Mark entered the Old Red Cat just after dark and took his favorite place at the end of the bar. He fist-bumped Todd and said, "Good to see you, man."

"You too," Todd said as he slid over a frosty mug of light beer. With his seniority, Todd could comp anyone he damn well pleased, and Mark had not paid in years.

With the students away, the place was quiet. Todd leaned on his elbows and asked, "So what are you up to?"

"Well, I've spent the afternoon at dear old Ness Skelton, in the copy room sorting papers that no one will ever read. More stupid work. Even the paralegals look down their noses at me. I hate the place and I haven't even been hired yet."

"Still no contract?"

"None, and the picture gets fuzzier every day."

Todd took a quick sip from his mug stashed under the counter. Even with his seniority, he wasn't supposed to drink on the job, but his boss wasn't in. He asked, "So how was Christmas around the Frazier house?"

"Ho, ho, ho. I lasted ten miserable days and got the hell out. You?"

"Three days, then duty called and I came back to work. How's Louie?"

"Still seriously indicted, still looking at real jail time. I should feel sorry for him but compassion runs thin for a guy who sleeps half the day and spends the other half on the sofa watching *Judge Judy* and bitching about his ankle monitor. My poor mom."

"You're pretty hard on him."

"Not hard enough. That's his problem. No one's ever been hard on Louie. He got caught with pot when he was thirteen, blamed it on a friend, and of course my parents rushed to his defense. He's never been held accountable. Until now."

"Bummer, man. I can't imagine having a brother in prison."

"Yeah, it sucks. I just wish I could help him but there's no way."

"I won't even ask about your dad."

"Didn't see him and didn't hear from him. Not even a card. He's fifty years old and the proud papa of a three-year-old, so I guess he played Santa Claus. Laid out a bunch of toys under the tree, smiled like an idiot when the kid came down the stairs squealing. What a rat."

Two coeds walked to the bar and Todd left to serve them. Mark pulled out his phone and checked his messages.

When Todd returned, he asked, "Have you seen any grades yet?"

"No. Who cares? We're all top students." Grades at Foggy Bottom were a joke. It was imperative that the school's graduates finish with sparkling résumés, and to that end the professors passed out As and Bs like cheap candy. No one flunked out of FBLS. So, of course, this had created a culture of rather listless studying, which, of course, killed any chance of competitive learning. A bunch of mediocre students became even more mediocre. No wonder the bar exam was such a challenge. Mark added, "And you really can't expect a bunch of overpaid professors to grade exams during the holidays, can you?"

Todd took another sip, leaned even closer, and said, "We have a bigger problem."

"Gordy?"

"Gordy."

"I was afraid of that. I've texted and tried to call but his phone's turned off. What's going on?"

"It's bad," Todd said. "Evidently, he went home for Christmas and spent his time fighting with Brenda. She wants a big church wedding with a thousand people. Gordy doesn't want to get married. Her mother has a lot to say. His mother is not speaking to her mother and the whole thing is blowing up."

"They're getting married May 15, Todd. As I recall, you and I signed on as groomsmen."

"Well, don't bet on it. He's already back in town and off his meds. Zola stopped by this afternoon and gave me the heads-up."

"What meds?"

"It's a long story."

"What meds?"

"He's bipolar, Mark. Diagnosed a few years back."

"You're kidding, right?"

"Why would I kid about this? He's bipolar and Zola says he's off his medication."

"Why wouldn't he tell us?"

"I can't answer that."

Mark took a long drink of beer and shook his head. He asked, "Zola's back already?"

"Yes, evidently she and Gordy hurried back for a few days of fun and games, though I'm not sure they're having much fun. She thinks he quit his meds about a month ago when we were studying for finals. One day he's manic and bouncing off the walls; then he's in a stupor after sipping tequila and smoking weed. He's talking crazy, says he wants to quit school and run off to Jamaica, with Zola of course. She thinks he might do something stupid and hurt himself."

"Gordy is stupid. He's engaged to his high school sweetheart, a real cutie who happens to have money, and now he's shacking up with an African girl whose parents and brothers are in this country without the benefit of those immigration papers everyone is talking about. Yes, the boy is stupid."

"Gordy's in trouble, Mark. He's been sliding for several weeks and he needs our help."

Mark pushed his beer away, but only a few inches, and clasped his hands behind his head. "As if we don't have enough to worry about. How, exactly, are we supposed to help?"

"You tell me. She's trying to keep an eye on him and she wants us to come over tonight."

Mark started laughing and took another sip.

"What's so funny?" Todd asked.

"Nothing, but can you imagine the scandal in Martinsburg, West Virginia, if word got out that Gordon Tanner, whose father is a church deacon and whose fiancée is the daughter of a prominent doctor, lost his mind and quit law school to run off to Jamaica with an African Muslim?"

"I can almost see the humor."

"Well, try harder. It's a scream." But the laughter had stopped. "Look, Todd, we can't make him take his meds. If we tried to he'd kick both our asses."

"He needs our help, Mark. I get off at nine tonight and we're going over."

A man in a nice suit sat at the bar and Todd walked over to take his order. Mark sipped his beer and sank into an even deeper funk.